Joanna Wayne began her professional writing career in 1994. Now, more than fifty published books later, Joanna has gained a worldwide following with her cutting-edge romantic suspense and Texas family series, such as Sons of Troy Ledger and Big "D" Dads. Joanna currently lives in a small community north of Houston, Texas, with her husband. You may write to Joanna at PO Box , Montgomery, TX 77356, or connect with her at annawayne.com

Ever since **Lisa Childs** read her first romance novel (a Mills & Boon story, of course) at age eleven, all she wanted was to be a romance writer. With over forty novels published with Mills & Boon, Lisa is living her dream. She is an award-winning, bestselling romance author. Lisa loves to hear from readers, who can contact her on Facebook, through her website, lisachilds.com, or her snail-mail address, PO Box 139, Marne, MI 49435.

Also by Joanna Wayne

Riding Shotgun
Quick-Draw Cowboy
Fearless Gunfighter
Dropping the Hammer
Trumped Up Charges
Unrepentant Cowboy
Hard Ride to Dry Gulch
Midnight Rider
Showdown at Shadow Junction
Ambush at Dry Gulch

Also by Lisa Childs

His Christmas Assignment
Bodyguard Daddy
Bodyguard's Baby Surprise
Beauty and the Bodyguard
Nanny Bodyguard
Single Mom's Bodyguard
In the Bodyguard's Arms
Soldier Bodyguard
Guarding His Witness
Colton's Cinderella Bride

Discover more at millsandboon.co.uk

NEW ORLEANS NOIR

JOANNA WAYNE

COLTON 911: BABY'S BODYGUARD

LISA CHILDS

MIX
Paper from
responsible sources
FSC
www.fsc.org
FSC C007454

This book is produced from independently certified FSC™
paper to ensure responsible forest management.

For more information visit: www.harpercollins.co.uk/green

Printed and bound in Spain
by CPI, Barcelona

MILLS & BOON

First Published in Great Britain 2019
by Mills & Boon, an imprint of HarperCollins*Publishers*
1 London Bridge Street, London, SE1 9GF

New Orleans Noir © 2019 Jo Ann Vest
Colton 911: Baby's Bodyguard © 2019 Harlequin Books S.A.

Special thanks and acknowledgement are given to Lisa Childs for her contribution to the *Colton 911* series.

ISBN: 978-0-263-27433-2

0819

NEW ORLEANS NOIR

JOANNA WAYNE

To everyone who loves a south Louisiana mystery.
To my great friends who live there and to everyone
who has ever longed to visit New Orleans.

Prologue

Elizabeth Grayson jerked forward as the car skidded to a slippery stop. The deserted dirt road that had been barely passable before had suddenly disappeared, replaced by clumps of tall grass, deeper pockets of brown water and what appeared to be a wide stretch of swampland.

Her nerves grew edgy. "Where are we?"

"Somewhere we can finally be totally alone." He flicked off the headlights.

"It's pitch-black out here," she murmured.

"Are you afraid of the dark or of being alone with me?" he teased, his voice deep and sexy, *almost* melting her anxious vibes.

"I'm never afraid when I'm with you."

"That's what I like to hear, baby. You always know how to please me."

She loved the way he talked to her, as if she were his equal though he was older and much more mature than the high school boys she'd dated back home. The sloppy kisses of teenage boys never thrilled her the way his did. She'd never melted at their touch.

He killed the motor, then stretched his arm across

the back of the seat and slipped it around her shoulders. "This is a favorite place of mine when I need to get away," he said.

"Really? It seems so isolated."

"I see it as private and a little forbidden," he said, "but if it makes you nervous, I can drive back into town."

"No. I don't want to go back," she answered quickly.

All she'd been able to think about for the past two days was seeing him again. She craved his touch and the way her body came alive when he slid his hands beneath her blouse or when he slipped his tongue inside her mouth.

Unfortunately, their making out had been limited to what they could manage in the back seat of his sports car parked behind a sleazy bar in a part of town she hadn't known existed until a few nights ago. Even then she'd wanted more, but he'd held back. He'd wanted to wait until everything was right.

They'd met last Saturday night when Elizabeth had been out with a girlfriend who lived in Metairie. Her friend Melinda had managed to snare fake IDs for both of them before Elizabeth had flown to New Orleans to visit her great-aunt for spring break.

Melinda had already been tipsy by the time Elizabeth noticed the hunk of a man staring at her. He nodded when they made eye contact but didn't approach them. When he smiled and left the bar, she followed him outside.

One hello in his deep, sexy voice and she was certain he was the most gorgeous and exciting man she'd ever met. She'd whispered her phone number into his ear as he opened the door to his black sports car.

He'd called the very next day. She'd thought of nothing but him since then.

He wasn't driving the sports car tonight, but a mud-encrusted pickup truck more suitable for the terrain. He pulled a flashlight from the truck's console and flicked it on as he climbed from behind the wheel. He reached behind the driver's seat and picked up what appeared to be a blanket.

Her pulse went crazy. Spring break was almost over. She'd be flying back to Tulsa on Sunday and might never see him again. Her heart would surely break but how much worse would it be if she didn't have this time with him tonight to treasure?

Complete privacy. And a blanket. They were surely going to make love. It would be the first time for her to go all the way. He would be experienced. He'd teach her all she needed to know.

He walked around the truck, opened her door and took her hand. She quivered in anticipation, ready for this in every way.

Aunt Ella still thought of Elizabeth as a kid and constantly warned her to be careful. As much as Elizabeth had hated lying to her tonight, she'd had no choice.

If her great-aunt could see her now, she'd be horrified. She would tell Elizabeth she was tempting disaster. The thought intensified Helena's anxiety.

"Okay. I can tell you're not ready," he said, dropping her hand. "I obviously misread the signs."

"You didn't," she assured him. "There's nowhere I'd rather be than here with you." That much was true.

Taking a deep, steadying breath, she stepped out of the truck. The earth was damp, sucking like quicksand. The grass was almost to her knees, hiding anything that might be crawling beneath it. Like snakes. Or tarantulas.

He put a thumb beneath her chin and nudged until she faced him. He leaned over and his lips met hers. Desire pummeled her as heated juices seeped into the silky red panties she'd worn just for him.

She'd be a fool to do anything to spoil this moment. He wasn't the man of her dreams. She'd never had dreams this good.

They walked for ten minutes or more, dodging spreading palmetto fronds, clumps of reeds and the exposed roots of cypress trees until they reached the slippery bank of a murky bayou.

The moon finally peeked from behind the clouds, providing enough illumination that he turned off the flashlight. A few yards farther and he took a different path, not stopping until they reached a slightly higher and dryer area. He dropped her hand and her insides quaked as he spread the blanket.

He kicked out of his shoes and lay down on his side, his right elbow supporting him so that he could meet her gaze. He opened his arms for her to join him.

She hesitated and scanned the area one last time. "Are you sure there are no snakes or alligators around here?" she asked.

"I guarantee you that before this night is over, you won't be worried at all about snakes, alligators or any other creatures of the swamp. Now undress slowly so I can watch," he said, an authoritative bent to his voice that hadn't been there before. By the time she was totally naked, passion enflamed her.

She lay down beside him, anticipating heaven.

Instead she fell into the depths of hell.

Chapter One

Helena Cosworth gathered her luggage from the taxi and walked the short distance to an intricately designed seven-foot-high metal gate. She stood there for a moment, letting the familiarity seep into her tired bones until grief-crinkled memories invaded and dampened her spirit.

The historic French Quarter carriage house just beyond the gate had been her second home for as long as she could remember. Her mother had died when she was only five.

Her dad had been an oil and gas executive who went wherever he was needed. If the location wasn't right for raising a daughter, she went to boarding schools in the States. Even when she lived with him, she spent most summers and many holidays in New Orleans with her energetic, fun-loving grandmother Mia.

During those visits, Mia had made her the center of her life and the adventure-laden Crescent City was their playground. The zoo, Audubon Park, the bustling Mississippi River, theater, trips down St. Charles Avenue on the cable car, parades galore. And the many hours spent in museums nurturing Helena's passion for art.

The lifestyle wasn't ideal by everyone's standards, but it worked for them. When her father had died from a sudden heart attack a week before her high school graduation, she moved in with Mia and began her college career the following fall at Tulane University.

Helena reached to the keypad and punched in the code for the security system Mia had installed a few years back. A twist of the handle and a firm shove and the gate squeaked open.

Heat and humidity hit like a wave of steam as she stepped inside the courtyard where the day's fetid air seemed trapped by the surrounding walls. She was quickly revived by the fragrance of night jasmine that overflowed from a huge pot and the cooling mist from the impressive angel fountain in the middle of the spacious area.

She didn't even glance toward the four apartments surrounding the rest of the courtyard as she made her way to the bright red door that served as the main entrance to the carriage house. The original, barn-style doors on the front of the house that had once swung open for horses and carriages had been replaced with brick walls and fake, shuttered windows years ago.

A shudder of emptiness shook Helena's resolve not to fall into a state of teary-eyed depression. It had been just over five weeks since she'd received the heartbreaking news of Mia's tragic accident, and although she'd been here for the funeral, the wound of grief felt fresh.

She opened the door and stepped into the marble foyer. The air conditioner was blasting away. Thankfully, she'd let Ella Grayson know when she was arriving. Ella had been one of Mia's tenants for years and she and Mia had been fast friends. They'd become closer than ever after Ella's great-niece, Elizabeth, had been brutally murdered last spring.

Helena parked her luggage by the door and dropped her handbag onto the antique cherrywood table before flicking on the delicate Tiffany lamp. Illumination climbed the foyer walls in enchanting patterns. Everything looked the same as it had when Mia was alive. Even the citrusy fragrance of the candles she'd burned nightly lingered in the air.

The property now belonged to Helena—at least until she found a buyer. Giving up the old carriage house would be like giving away a chunk of her soul, but her career was in Boston. She would start her new job with one of the most successful individually owned art galleries in the city on November 1. A few of her paintings already hung in the gallery.

Helena traipsed across the cozy sitting room with its worn Persian rug, comfortable furniture and shelves filled with books and framed photographs.

When she stepped into the kitchen, memories attacked full force. She'd had morning coffee at the small, round mahogany table with Mia for as long as she could remember, though when she was young, Helena's cup was filled mostly with cold milk and a shot of honey.

They'd sipped the chicory-laden brew from dainty flowered cups while Mia filled Helena's young head with simple answers to life's mysteries.

Like why king cakes had plastic babies hidden inside them and why people riding floats at Mardi Gras always wore masks. And why even rich people ate po'boy sandwiches that needed to be dressed.

Heart aching, Helena finally walked to the foot of the elegant, curved staircase. The staircase where her grandmother had slipped and fallen to her death.

According to the medical examiner, a severe brain trauma caused by the fall had likely killed her within minutes. Minutes that she'd been totally alone.

Helena forced herself to go on, climbing the stairs slowly, stopping only a few seconds at the landing before making it to the second floor and the bedroom she'd always thought of as her own.

A pale orchid coverlet and countless pillows covered the four-poster bed. Beyond that, tall French doors opened onto a balcony that overlooked Dumaine Street.

Helena unlatched the doors, swung them open and stepped onto the balcony.

Spicy odors of fried seafood wafted through the air and suddenly Helena was starved. She hadn't eaten since breakfast and that was only her usual yogurt and granola. It was nearly seven now.

There would be time for memories and unpacking later. A beer and a po'boy were calling her name.

Chapter Two

Alyssa Orillon rinsed her empty teacup and placed it on the countertop to be carried upstairs to her main living quarters later. The small downstairs kitchen was barely big enough for the mini-fridge, a microwave, a card table and two padded wooden chairs she'd picked up for next to nothing in a used furniture store on Magazine Street.

The remaining five hundred square feet of the home's ground floor was dedicated to her cozy waiting room and a private counseling area. Located only two blocks from Jackson Square, she was right in the thick of the tourist pedestrian traffic, though business was slow tonight.

Not untypical for a Tuesday night. Last weekend's convention goers had gone home. This week's hadn't arrived yet.

She glanced at her watch. Half past eight. Too early to call it a night—especially since she didn't open her doors until early afternoon on weekdays.

Inconveniently, the beginning of a headache was tapping at her right temple. An uneasy feeling had been messing with her nerves all afternoon, the kind of vague sense of anxiety one might expect from a psychic—unless said psychic was a complete and total fraud—like Alyssa.

Fake, but not a rip-off artist, as some of her competitors were. Alyssa was an expert at giving customers what they wanted. Most people were fairly easy to read if you honed your skills as well as Alyssa had.

The professionally printed sign painted on her door lured in the type of customers she handled best.

Alyssa Orillon—Psychic.
Is true love in your future?
Is the man in your life right for you?
Is something wonderful about to bless your life?
The answers you desire are waiting inside.

The sparkling, crystal ball rotating in the large front window provided an additional enticement for the curious or extrasensory believer. The crimson velvet drape behind the ball blocked the view of the studio's dimly lit interior, making it even more mysterious.

Unlike Alyssa, her grandmother Brigitte had the gift in spades. At least she had until she claimed old age weakened her powers. Before moving into an assisted living center in Covington, Brigitte had frequently told Alyssa how lucky she was not to be constantly haunted by other people's nightmares.

Alyssa walked to the window, notched back the heavy drape and peeked out. Things were getting livelier on the street. A few more drinks and hopefully someone would knock on her door, enter her chambers and cross her palms with cash.

The only person she recognized was Andy, the scruffy young man at the curb playing his sax for tips. A nice guy, but bad luck found him at every turn. Good tippers didn't.

Just as she started to let go of the curtain's edge, she

spotted another familiar figure. Hunter Bergeron. Tall, ruggedly handsome, with dark brown hair that always looked mussed. Alyssa suspected there were plenty of young women who'd love to run their hands through it and straighten it for him.

Had she been a decade or so younger, she might have been one of those women.

Hunter was low-key for a hard-nosed homicide detective. He could push when he had to, though. He'd proved that when questioning half the people in the French Quarter after Elizabeth Grayson's murder.

She walked over, opened her door and tried to get his attention, just to say hello and perhaps pick his brain for a minute about the serial killer investigation. He didn't look up, his attention focused on a stunning young woman in a bright yellow sundress, who didn't appear to see him watching.

The young woman leaned over and dropped a bill into the musician's open sax case. When she straightened, she turned Alyssa's way.

Oh my God. That is Mia Cosworth's granddaughter. She had no idea Helena was back in town.

Alyssa stepped outside, waving frantically until she got Helena's attention. Helena smiled and began to maneuver her way around a cluster of tourists.

Seconds later, Helena stepped through the open door and threw her arms around Alyssa in the same enthusiastic way she had when Helena had been a kid and her grandmother would bring her to visit.

Good memories until...

Alyssa trembled. She pulled away from Helena and reached for the back of one of the waiting room chairs for balance.

"What's wrong?" Helena asked.

"It's this dreaded headache," Alyssa lied. "I've been fighting it all day. I just need to sit down."

Helena helped her into the chair. "Can I get you something for it?"

"If you don't mind. There's a bottle of aspirin on the table in the small kitchen and a pitcher of cold water in the fridge." This was far more than a headache, but she needed time alone to regain her equilibrium.

She leaned back and closed her eyes. It didn't help. Instead weird images popped into her head as if she were hallucinating. She'd experienced this before but not in years and not often.

The harder she tried to force the images from her mind, the more vivid they became. It was Helena being chased by a man who was too blurry to identify. And blood. Lots of blood, covering Helena's clothes and her hair and part of her face.

This isn't real. I'm not an authentic medium. This is some nightmarish trick my mind is playing on me.

But why now?

The images faded as fast as they'd come. Alyssa shuddered, determined to ignore the cold horror that rode her spine, and pulled herself together. She could not plant her groundless, horrifying hallucinations into Helena's mind.

Chapter Three

Helena shook two aspirin from the bottle into Alyssa's palm and then handed her a glass of cold water. Alyssa was no longer shaking the way she had been, but she didn't look well.

"Should I call 911?" Helena asked. "Just in case you're coming down with something." Or was having a stroke—or worse.

"No. No doctors. No ambulance. I was dizzy for a minute, but I'm fine now."

"You don't look fine. You look as if you saw a ghost."

"No chance of that. I couldn't conjure one up if I tried. Believe me, I know."

Her attempt at humor fell flat. "You should at least get checked out at the emergency clinic," Helena said. "I'll be glad to go with you."

"That's totally not necessary, but thanks. What I could really use is some conversation with someone who doesn't expect me to read their mind."

To emphasize her point, Alyssa stood, walked to the door and flipped the rectangular plaque from Open to Closed.

"Have a seat," Alyssa insisted, "and fill me in on all you've been doing since I saw you last. You cut out so soon after your grandmother's memorial service that I didn't get a chance to properly say goodbye."

"I was in a state of shock," Helena admitted. "Her death was so sudden, so unexpected. I'm not sure what I said to anyone."

"I understand that," Alyssa said. "Her death was a shock to all of us. She was a dynamo those last few months, as driven as I'd ever seen her."

"I know she was busy trying to raise money to offer an award to anyone who helped identify Elizabeth's killer."

"She raised over a hundred thousand dollars. Everyone was amazed."

"Mia could always do anything she set her mind to." Helena settled in the nearest chair. "I didn't realize she raised that much, though."

Alyssa dropped into the facing chair and kicked out of her beaded sandals. She pulled her bare feet into the chair with her, tucking them beneath her long, flowing skirt.

There was no overhead lighting in the reception area, but red silk squares were draped over the shades of a pair of brass, dragon-shaped lamps. Flames flickered from a cluster of fragrant candles that dominated a round table in the center of the space, bathing the room in a warm, sensual glow.

As a small child, Helena had thought Alyssa's home was as magical as the Greek and Roman gods in Mia's colorfully illustrated books.

By the time she understood what powers a psychic supposedly possessed, she'd outgrown her belief in magic.

"What's going on in the neighborhood?" Helena asked. "Any gossip I should know about?"

"I'll start with the bad and get it out of the way. Fancy died."

"Fancy, the portrait painter?"

"That's the one. She'd set up her paints and easel in that same spot outside Jackson Square every day for as long as I've lived here—and that's more years than I care to admit."

"I credit much of my interest in art to her," Helena said. "When I was five all I wanted for Christmas was an easel and some paints so I could make pictures like Miss Fancy."

"She would have loved that story," Alyssa said.

"I wish I had shared it with her."

"The locals threw her a real New Orleans funeral with a jazz parade and lots of dancing in the streets, similar to what we all did for Mia, except less organization and fewer musicians."

"You guys definitely sent Mia off in style," Helena agreed. They'd left very little of the organization up to her.

Most tourists saw the French Quarter as a hodge-podge of bars, restaurants and souvenir shops. They didn't realize what a diverse group of locals resided beyond the historically correct exteriors.

Mia had fit right in the community and couldn't walk down the street without stopping to talk to half a dozen people and waving to more.

"Any other happenings I should know about?" Helena asked.

"You can order groceries locally now and have them delivered. That's the most exciting new thing we've got going for us. The second most popular topic is the French Kiss Killer and I really don't want to talk about him tonight."

"I'm with you, but I admit facts of the brutal murder still haunt me, perhaps because I'd met Elizabeth several times over the years and was always impressed by her vibrant personality. Or maybe it was just the senselessness of it all."

"Me and my big mouth," Alyssa said. "I said I wasn't going to talk about the murder and then I just throw it right out there."

"It was bound to come up, sooner or later. Elephants in the room never stay unnoticed for long."

"I'm convinced they'll find the killer," Alyssa said. "Hunter Bergeron is heading up the task force and he's not the type of cop to give up until he arrests his man."

Hunter Bergeron. Helena's nerves went edgy. She swallowed hard, angry with herself that she was having any kind of reaction to merely hearing his name. She couldn't keep that up.

It had been six years since he'd broken her heart. She'd moved on. So had he, even doing a tour of duty with the Marines or so Mia had told her.

The memories were still there, but they were buried so deep they no longer had the power to rip her apart.

"I'm so glad we had this visit," Helena said, "but if you're sure you're okay now, I really should go." She stood before Alyssa could drag her into a conversation about Hunter. "We should have lunch together soon."

"I'd like that." Alyssa followed Helena and switched her sign back to Open before she unlatched the door.

"Are you sure you feel like seeing more customers tonight?" Helena asked.

"I'm sure. Besides, the later it gets the drunker they tend to be and the easier it is for them to part with their bucks and believe whatever I tell them."

"No doubt." Helena smiled as she took both Alyssa's hands in hers.

"Be careful," Alyssa murmured. Her words took on an ominous tone.

"I will."

"I don't mean just tonight. I mean all the time. You never know who you can trust these days."

"You're right." Hunter Bergeron had taught her that. She gave Alyssa a quick parting hug and then hit the busy street again.

The music, laughter and smiling faces didn't have their usual uplifting effect. Helena found it hard to shake the talk of the serial killer and the fearful timbre of Alyssa's parting warning.

Could it be that Alyssa was more psychic than she'd ever admitted to Mia?

Helena tried to ignore the plunge in her own spirits as she reached the tall metal gate and punched in Mia's private code.

Once inside the courtyard, the anxiety eased. She was home.

Only Mia was gone forever, and home wasn't home anymore.

HUNTER BERGERON HAD followed Helena at a distance, mesmerized by the sway of her narrow hips. He wasn't the only one noticing her. Almost every man she passed gave her at least a futile glance.

The first time he'd laid eyes on her, he'd thought her the most beautiful girl in the world. She'd changed in the six years since then, wore her hair longer, developed the curves of a woman instead of a young coed.

Tonight, she was so damned stunning she boggled his mind. She was out of his league and had always been. Any hope of rekindling the fire that had once raged between them would end in heartbreak. He didn't need that now.

He leaned against the front of a building across the street from the carriage house, staying deep in the shadows beneath an iron balcony. Several minutes later, the light in the upstairs bedroom flicked on.

He knew that bedroom intimately. His legs felt like rubber as he finally turned and walked away.

But he'd be back. He had no choice. Unknowingly, she might be his only link to the French Kiss Killer.

And that could get her killed.

Chapter Four

Helena jerked awake to the sound of clanking metal garbage cans and the grinding of compactors. She'd closed the airy privacy curtains last night but had failed to close the heavy, noise reducing drapes.

She stretched beneath the crisp, cotton sheet and punched her pillow over her ears. A couple more hours of sleep would provide a much better start to a very busy day. Unfortunately, her mind was already splintering into a dozen different directions.

By the time the streets had become relatively quiet again, she'd given up on sleep. She threw her legs over the side of the bed, tugged her cotton nightshirt down midthigh and shoved her bare feet into a pair of fuzzy flip-flops.

The first thing on her agenda was coffee. The difficult part would be that this morning she'd have it alone.

The antique Swiss grandfather clock on the wide landing struck the hour. The six melodic chimes echoed in the quiet house.

If Mia were still alive, her sweet soprano voice would have wrapped itself around an old hymn or maybe she'd be in a twangy country mood. Her musical tastes ran the gamut.

Cherishing the memories while trying not to let them

slide into overpowering grief, Helena forced herself to continue down the stairs and into the kitchen. She flicked on the overhead light and started a pot of coffee.

When it was ready, Helena filled one of the colorful cups she and Mia had purchased in the French Market the last time they'd gone shopping for spring's first Creole tomatoes. So many great yet simple times they'd spent together.

All never to be again. She wondered if the sorrow at being back here would be less intense if Mia's death hadn't come so suddenly—not that she could change that.

Helena took her coffee and walked to what had been Mia's bedroom suite. As always, a pile of books was messily stacked on her bedside table.

Helena padded across the lush crème-colored carpet and picked up the top book. She expected one of the historical romances that her grandmother loved or a nonfiction book dealing with the history of New Orleans.

Instead, it was a study of profiling serial killers in America. Helena scanned the titles of the next three books. All dealt with some aspect of serial killers.

Helena shuddered at the thought of Mia delving into such gore for bedtime reading.

She'd called her grandmother at least once a week between Elizabeth Grayson's murder and Mia's fatal accident. Mia had assured Helena every time that she was too busy with her fund-raising campaign and attempting to cheer up Ella that there was no time left for her to wallow in gloom and doom.

Her reading material suggested differently.

Helena dropped to the side of the bed and picked up a thick gray hardback book with no dust jacket. Several bookmarks were scattered among the pages.

She opened the tome to the first marked page and her eyes went immediately to a paragraph highlighted in neon yellow.

Serial killers may be physically attractive to the opposite sex and function somewhat successfully in society for long periods of time in between their crimes.

A few paragraphs down on that same page:

It is often difficult to predict the future targets of the killers as they may not understand the involved dynamics themselves.

Below that passage, in her meticulous script, Mia had written one name in the margin.

Hunter Bergeron.

Had Mia been questioning Hunter about what she was reading? If so, when had they become friends?

Helena closed the book but took it with her when she left the room. She'd read more later, but she needed to finish unpacking and then shower and dress before her real estate agent, Randi Lester, arrived.

Be careful whom you trust.

Unexpectedly, Alyssa's warning came back to haunt her as she left the bedroom.

She'd heed the warning, especially when it came to Hunter Bergeron. With any luck she wouldn't run into him at all.

HELENA BUZZED RANDI through the gate at exactly 8:28 for their 8:30 appointment. Nice to know the woman who'd hopefully be listing the carriage house and the four apartments surrounding the rest of the courtyard was prompt.

Helena unlocked the door, stepped outside and watched as Randi crossed the courtyard. The Realtor paused near the fountain and turned a full 360 degrees, taking in the view.

The picture on the business card Randi had mailed her didn't do her justice. She appeared to be approximately the same height as Helena's five feet six, or would have been if her stiletto heels hadn't given her at least a four-inch boost.

In her midthirties, Helena judged, with an athletic build and sun-streaked hair cut into a layered bob. Silver bangles dangled from her ears. A frilly white blouse topped a pair of black-and-white checked ankle pants.

"Impressive," Randi pronounced once she met Helena at the door. "One of the biggest and nicest courtyards I've seen in this part of the French Quarter. It will grab any potential buyer's attention immediately. And nothing beats a great first impression in the real estate business."

"Glad to hear that," Helena said as she extended a hand. "I'm Helena Cosworth."

"I know. I recognized you from your picture on Facebook."

"I sometimes forget I have that public image floating around in digital space. I should probably update it."

"I wouldn't," Randi said. "It's a great likeness even if you do look even younger in person."

"Thanks, but flattery will only get you a cup of coffee or a glass of iced tea," Helena said.

"Iced tea sounds terrific." Randi stepped inside and followed Helena to the kitchen. "It's nice to finally meet you in person, although our many phone conversations and the enthusiastic manner in which Beverly Ingram has described you make me feel as if we've old friends."

"I'd hoped Bev might be with you," Helena said. "I

know she's familiar with the rental history of each of the four units as well as the needed repairs and upgrades."

"She'd planned to join us, but she's in Little Rock this morning waiting for the arrival of her first grandbaby. A boy. She left me a spreadsheet showing the rental history for the past five years, so we're good."

"No problem. A new grandson tops a meeting any day."

Helena poured two glasses of iced tea and wrapped them in a cloth napkin to catch the condensation.

She'd met Bev on several occasions while visiting Mia. She owned and operated the French Quarter rental management agency that had handled Mia's four apartments for at least the last decade. Bev had recommended Randi when Helena mentioned selling the house.

"Would you like a tour of the carriage house proper?" Helena asked.

"Absolutely."

The tour took about thirty minutes and Randi seemed more enthralled with each room they visited, raving not only about the architecture but even the choice of colors, furnishings and artwork.

When they returned to the kitchen, Randi removed her laptop from her briefcase and sat it on the table. "Bev told me this place was a stunner, but this is much grander than I was expecting. From all indications, it's in excellent condition for a house almost a hundred years old."

"Mia did a terrific job of keeping it in good repair."

"That's important, but as we all know, you can never be certain what kind of structural problems you'll find when you start checking out these historic houses."

"A truth we've all learned from watching cable house remodeling shows," Helena admitted. Not that she was too worried about that. Mia's estate had left Helena more than enough assets to make any needed repairs to the property.

"Who was your grandmother's decorator?" Randi asked. "I have several clients who could use their advice."

"Mia was her own decorator, right down to the smallest details. Well, I did give her a few suggestions in the artwork department, but that's it."

"Then you both have excellent taste. I love the painting of the young couple running through the rain beneath beautiful French Quarter balconies."

"Thank you. That's actually my first prize-winning painting from a high school art contest."

"You painted that in high school?"

"Eleventh grade."

"Wow. Such talent. I know you said you were starting a new job at a Boston gallery, but I didn't know you'd be exhibiting your own work."

"Hopefully. If not, I'll just be selling others' creations and searching for new talent, but even that is exciting."

"I'm sure you'll be successful. You obviously had a very talented grandmother, as well. She perfectly captured the historic nature of the home without giving up comfort or convenience. That's a hard combo to come by."

"Then you don't think I'll have any trouble selling the property for a decent price?"

The awkward silence and the pained expression on Randi's face said more than words could have.

Helena cringed. "Is the real estate market that bad?"

"It's not actually the market that's the problem."

"Then what is it?"

"It's this particular property, or more to the point

it's that Elizabeth Grayson was staying here with her great-aunt when she was murdered."

"People still need a place to live," Helena said, trying to make sense of Randi's concerns.

"I know, but the media hype isn't making this any easier. Elizabeth was killed six months ago. The three previous victims of the alleged serial killer were murdered at six-month intervals almost to the day."

"We've passed that date," Helena said.

"But only by a few days. People who are familiar with the facts are on edge. It's as if they're all holding their collective breaths waiting for the killer to strike again."

Helena's frustration swelled. "Elizabeth was abducted off the streets. There's no evidence the killer ever set foot on this property."

"I'm not saying it's reasonable," Randi said, "but I have to level with you. Normally, this house would sell in days, might even set off a bidding war. In this climate of fear, all bets of a quick, lucrative sale are off."

"In other words, my property has a curse on it until the killer is arrested and there's nothing I can do about it?"

"Not necessarily. I just want you to be aware that you may be in for some lowball offers if you list the property immediately. If the killer doesn't strike again, this should blow over in a few months."

"Renters don't seem to be afraid of moving in," Helene said, clutching at the only positive thing she could see. "Bev said there's a waiting list of prospective renters."

Randi stared at the well-manicured nails on her left hand for a few seconds before lifting her gaze. "More bad news. The waiting list fell through, according to

Bev. Your recently vacated apartment has not been rented. And Connor Harrington in 4-C gave a thirty-day notice yesterday."

Helena threw up her hands in exasperation. "Connor is single and muscular. I can't believe he's afraid of being the serial killer's next victim."

"I don't know what reason he gave, but I'm sure Bev will get back with you in a day or two on that," Randi explained.

It had taken weeks of soul-searching for Helena to make up her mind to sell her grandmother's beloved home and now that decision might have to be delayed.

One thing was for certain. She wasn't going to give Mia's beautiful home away at below what it was worth just because of the timing.

"I didn't mean to rain on your parade like this," Randi said. "We don't have to decide or sign anything today, but we can talk about how to proceed if you do decide to list with us."

"I suppose that's complicated, too."

"Not at all."

Helena felt a nagging pain starting at the back of her skull. "I'm a novice at selling real estate, so I have no idea where to start. I suppose I should alert the remaining tenants that I'm putting the house on the market."

"Let's don't jump the gun on that," Randi cautioned. "Unless the prospective owner plans to use the entire property for himself and his family, having the units already under lease will be an asset."

They spent the next hour talking about the advantages of working on upgrades and repairs before having the house appraised. Randi clearly knew her stuff and she patiently answered all of Helena's questions while basically alleviating none of her fears.

By the time they'd finished and gone over the selling contract, Helena felt as if she were drowning in details.

She stood and walked to the window that overlooked the courtyard. "I suppose I should run this new information by Pierre Benoit."

"Is that the man that Bev listed as one of your tenants?"

"Yes. He's a divorce attorney with an office in the downtown area. I hired a probate attorney to settle Mia's estate, but Pierre walked me though some of the legal hurdles."

She owed him a dinner for that since he'd refused to accept cash.

"I think I've given you enough to think about for one day," Randi said. "I don't want you to feel pressured, but if you're going to have two vacant units, it might be a good time to do any needed repairs or updates on those first."

"Good point. I hadn't expected so many complexities, but I'll sign the real estate agreement now," Helena said. "I've made the decision to sell. The hard part is already done."

"Are you sure?"

"I am." If she didn't change her mind in the time it took to pick up the pen and sign her name on several dotted lines.

Randi delayed her departure to take her through the agreement again over a second glass of tea. Signing was more stressful than Helena had expected. She did so love this house.

But the life she knew here was gone forever and she would love her life in Boston, too. She had to keep reminding herself of that.

They made small talk as they walked across the

courtyard when they were finished. Randi paused near
the fountain just long enough to catch a few drops from
the cool spray in her outstretched right hand.

"Whoever gets this house and courtyard is going to
be a very lucky buyer," Randi said as she was leaving.

Helena stood by the gate for a few minutes after she
locked it behind Randi. A blue jay darted past her on its
way to the nearest bird feeder. Graceful monarch but-
terflies fluttered among the blooms of a potted verbena.

She was mere steps away from French Quarter rev-
elry, music and great food, yet this space had always
been a peaceful haven. Perhaps her tenants no longer
thought of it as safe.

If that bothered Connor Harrington, it must be a million times worse for Ella. Helena needed to find time
to visit with her today.

She glanced up and then she saw *him*.

Hunter Bergeron—still, quiet, alone, standing on the
edge of Ella's balcony. Old longings vibrated along her
nerve endings as she met his gaze. Her insides melted.

It had been six years, but she would have recognized
him anywhere. Tall and muscular. Same unruly brown
hair. Same cocky way of standing, his thumbs hooked
into his jeans pockets.

Her stomach knotted and she felt the burn of acid
creeping up into her throat.

She'd tried to prepare herself for running into him
while she was back in New Orleans. Just not in this
courtyard. Not where it had all begun—and ended.

Traitorous recollections pounded her relentlessly.

Then, without even a wave of acknowledgment, he
turned and disappeared back inside Ella's apartment.
Helena wrapped her arms around her chest and bit her
bottom lip so hard she tasted blood.

Had he even recognized her? Had she become no more than a distant memory of an infatuation gone bad? Or maybe he looked at it as a commitment he'd escaped just in time.

It didn't matter. There was nothing left of their relationship but regrets.

She should turn and go back inside before he left Ella's.

But she was still standing there as if in a paralyzing trance when Hunter stepped out of Ella's door and into the courtyard. Her insides quaked as he approached, but she managed to keep her head up and her breathing somewhat steady.

"Hello, Helena."

Hello. That was it, as if it hadn't been six years since the goodbye that almost destroyed her. Her resolve not to let him intimidate her strengthened.

"What are you doing here, Hunter?"

"Looking for you, for one thing. Police business. We need to talk."

Chapter Five

Helena stared him down like he was a coiled snake about to strike, waiting so long to respond he felt sweat pooling on his brow. She clearly had the temperature advantage in her white shorts and lacy, summery top.

He was wearing his usual plainclothes detective attire—jeans and a sports shirt with the neck unbuttoned and the sleeves rolled up to his elbows.

Nonetheless, he was starting to feel guilty as hell that he was ruining her homecoming by insisting she have anything to do with him.

He stepped closer. "This won't take long."

"Then start talking."

"I talk faster when I'm not sweltering."

"Does this have anything to do with Elizabeth Grayson's killer?"

He nodded. "Afraid so."

"In that case, we can talk inside."

He followed her into the carriage house. In minutes he'd settled into the same comfortable chair in Mia Cosworth's cozy sitting room as he had dozens of times before over the last few months. Surprisingly, he'd developed a close bond with Mia during this investigation though she'd clearly never forgiven him for running out on Helena. Made sense. He'd never forgiven himself.

Not only had Mia's death hit Hunter hard personally, it had blown a huge hole in his best lead toward catching the French Kiss Killer.

Helena sat across from him. She leaned back and crossed her long shapely legs.

She was as stunning as ever, but she'd changed in ways that hurt deep in his soul. He felt it as much as saw it, though her expression was stony, her eyes a cold fire that froze and burned at the same time.

"Why were you at Ella Grayson's this morning?" Helena asked.

Hunter crossed a foot over his knee. "I'd picked up some beignets at Café du Monde, and we shared them over coffee. She loves them heavy on powdered sugar— same as me—and she makes the best cup of coffee in town."

"I suppose I'm to believe delivering morning pastries to the elderly is a new service of the police department?"

Helena was clearly not going to make this easy.

"No official policy," he said, "but we're allowed to be decent."

Helena ran her fingers through her shoulder-length copper-colored hair, pushing it back from her bewitching face. "In that case, I apologize for doubting your motives."

"No problem. I'm not above playing good cop to get information if I need to, but this time it was all about the donuts and coffee. And the fact that she's having a tough go of it."

He recognized the signs of depression. He'd grown up with them.

"I plan to see her as soon as you leave," Helena said.

"We've kept in touch by phone since my grandmother died."

"She's mentioned that."

"I don't know why," Helena said, "but she seems to feel at least partly responsible for the tragedy, though there was nothing she could have done to save Elizabeth. I keep reminding her that Elizabeth was a random victim of a demented serial killer."

Hunter leaned in closer. This was likely as good a segue as he would get. Might as well take advantage of it.

"We're not sure about the random element."

Helena's brows arched. "Wasn't she abducted while on her way to meet friends?"

"Perhaps not. She'd told Ella that she was meeting friends, but her friends said the night out was planned for the following night. Elizabeth either confused the plans or lied to Ella."

"Do you think she deliberately met with the monster?"

"A definite possibility."

Helena clasped her hands in her lap. "Why would she do such a thing? How could he persuade her to go with him?"

"If we had the answer to those questions, we'd have a lot better chance of stopping him before he strikes again."

"Then you think he will strike again?"

"I believe it's possible."

"I can't believe Elizabeth could be taken in by a murderous lunatic. She was so smart and sweet. She had plans and dreams. Mia said she talked about her future all the time."

Helena's voice shook and her eyes grew moist with tears as the new reality sank in.

Desire racked Hunter's body. Not sexual urges, but just a need to touch her, to wrap an arm around her shoulders, to hold her close.

But she made no move to indicate she wanted his comfort and he wasn't about to risk being tossed out at this point.

"Is there more I should know?" Helena asked.

"Yeah," he said. "None of it good."

"Tell me everything and start with the worst," she urged. "Don't spoon-feed me."

"You got it. Elizabeth's killer or a person claiming to be him was in touch with Mia by phone in the days preceding Mia's fall."

"The killer was contacting Mia? Why didn't I know about that? Why didn't someone tell me?" She straightened, her hands on her knees.

"She didn't want to upset you or disrupt your life when there was nothing you could do."

"I could have done something. I could have been here. She could have come and stayed with me. You should have told me." She leaned forward, and he saw fire in her eyes.

"She didn't want you to know. I had no authority to go against her will." Plus, she'd threatened Hunter eight ways to Sunday if he ignored her wishes and told Helena himself.

"How many times did he call her?"

"Three, over a three-week period."

"What did he talk about? Did he threaten her? Didn't you wiretap her phone?"

"How about one question at a time?" Hunter asked. "He admitted he'd killed Elizabeth." He wasn't about to go into the graphic way he described it to Mia in his first call. He hoped to hell Helena never had to hear those words and was relieved they hadn't been recorded, which would risk her hearing them.

"Did he threaten Mia?"

"No, but he was clearly upset that she was raising award money for his capture and assured her that he would kill again and that he wouldn't get caught."

"You must have traced the calls and found out who he was and where he was calling from. You can do that in minutes."

"You've been watching too many detective shows on TV. Real cops don't work miracles. We did wiretap her phone—after she reported the first call. When she answered the next two, the calls went straight to the precinct where they were monitored."

"Then why couldn't you track him?"

"The calls were from different numbers. The wiretapped calls lasted less than a minute. By the time we could get to the location of origination, the caller and the phones were long gone."

"And Mia didn't recognize the caller's voice?"

"No. Three different voices were used—two appeared to be male, one was female."

"Then three different people were in on this?"

"Very unlikely. We believe a professional grade voice changer was used."

"Where is my grandmother's phone now?"

"In police custody. It hasn't rung since her death."

"Then he must have known her well enough to know when she died," Helena said.

"Maybe, but it made the local news. Your grandmother was pretty much a legend in this area what with all her charitable and historic preservation work."

Helena massaged her arms as if she were cold, the facts no doubt chilling her to the bone.

"I know this is not what you wanted to hear, Helena, but rest assured we'll apprehend this guy sooner or later. He'll make a mistake. Serial killers always do. And when he does, we'll get him."

"But how many other teens or young women will he kill before he makes that mistake?" Helena asked.

"I can't answer that." And that was what kept him up at night, what haunted his mind every hour of the day. That kind of evil had to come from devils residing deep in a person's psyche. Even the killer might not know when he'd succumb to the darkness and strike again.

"Had Mia not died the untimely way she did, she might have led us to Elizabeth's killer," Hunter said.

"Poor Mia. So much to deal with. How horrible to spend the last few weeks of her life being intimidated by a madman who must have wanted her dead. Wanted it bad enough…"

"I know what you're thinking," Hunter interrupted. The haunted look in her eyes and the angst in her expression made it clear. "Mia wasn't murdered by the serial killer or anyone else, Helena. That possibility was thoroughly investigated. There was absolutely no evidence of foul play. Absolutely none."

"Thank God for that."

"If it was the killer's intent to intimidate her, he failed miserably," Hunter said. "Your grandmother considered herself part of the investigative team and she was good at it."

"She was always a fighter," Helena said.

Hunter planted both feet on the floor and leaned forward. "I have one very important request. I don't want you to discuss the phone calls with anyone. Not your best friend. Not Ella. Definitely not a reporter."

"Why?"

He hesitated, choosing his words carefully. He didn't want to frighten her, but he had to warn her. "There's an outside chance the killer may try to contact you now that you've returned to the carriage house."

"What makes you think he even knows I exist?"

"He mentioned you in the last call."

"What did he say about me?"

"Just that she had a beautiful granddaughter. He hoped you'd be visiting soon."

"And obviously, I did. For Mia's funeral, almost as if he knew Mia was going to die."

"There's no way he could have predicted the fatal fall. The important thing is that I need you to call me immediately if you get a suspicious phone call or if anything happens that makes you uneasy," Hunter warned. "Even if you think it's probably nothing—even if the person who makes you uneasy is someone you know."

"Right now, you're making me extremely uneasy."

"Don't be. I'll keep you safe. I promise, but you have to trust me and never hesitate to call me."

"What great timing I have, as if I'm part of the killer's welcoming committee."

"If I'd known you were coming this week, I would have suggested you put the trip off."

"It never dawned on me to check a serial killer calendar."

"Understandable." Hunter walked over, took her hand and pressed his card into her palm. Even that slight touch stirred the old vibes. He struggled to keep them under control.

"Put my cell phone number in your phone on speed

dial. Call anytime, day or night. I'll always answer. Count on it."

She took the card, but quickly moved her hand away from his. "If that's all, you should go now. I'm sure you have more important work to do."

"Okay. Just remember, if you need me, I'm a phone call away and I can have a police officer here in seconds."

She walked him to the door and opened it.

"You always were a good cop, Hunter, even if you didn't know it. I'm glad you took it up again. You must have missed it."

"I missed a lot of things." Nothing as much as he'd missed her.

For a second, her gaze softened to velvet and he could almost swear he sensed a tinge of desire. But the moment passed, and she closed the door behind him.

She didn't want him around. He got that, but he had only two goals right now. To find the French Kiss Killer before he killed again and to keep Helena safe.

He planned to do both.

LEANING AGAINST THE closed door, Helena struggled to make sense of the disturbing emotions churning inside her. She felt like a cannonball had smashed into the house and ran over her, leaving her flattened and unable to react in any appropriate way.

Her first impulse had been to lash out at Hunter and blame him for Mia's having to deal repeatedly with a killer. He was the detective. He should have done more to find the killer or at least kept him from talking to Mia.

If nothing else, he should have at least called Helena and let her know about the phone calls.

Only her grandmother wasn't one to be ordered around by anyone—never had been. Instead of quivering in fear, she'd likely dived in just like Hunter said, knowing full well what she was doing and any risks she might be taking.

She was sixty-eight years old, but Mia had known no limits, accepted no boundaries. Helena would be lucky if she had half Mia's spunk at that same age.

Helena looked at the card Hunter had given her and realized she'd wadded it up in a clutched fist. She took it to the kitchen counter, laid it out flat and used her fingertips to iron out the wrinkles.

Call him if she needed him. She quaked at the thought.

Retrieving his last words from six years ago out of the depths of her memory, she used them like a suit of armor.

I'm sorrier than you'll ever know, but I can't go through with this.

And then he'd left her standing at the flower-bedecked altar like the fool she'd been. The fool she would never let herself be again.

Her phone rang. A quick surge of apprehension rocked through her.

"Hello."

"Helena, it's me, Ella. I hope I'm not disturbing you."

"Absolutely not. It's so good to hear from you. In fact, I was hoping to pay you a visit about eleven if that works for you."

"That would be great. We have so much to talk about now that you're moving back to New Orleans."

There was that bothersome misconception again. She'd clear that up when she saw Ella. The way things were going now, she couldn't get out of here fast enough. She slipped Hunter's card into her pocket.

ELLA MET HELENA at the door, greeting her with a bear hug that wouldn't quit. The clinging was an unnecessary but potent reminder of the angst Ella had been through over the last six months. When Ella finally pulled away, Helena took a good look at her and was shocked to see how much thinner and frail she'd become over the five weeks since Mia's death. The downward plunge in her health had begun months prior to that. Losing her best friend had only made it worse.

Before Elizabeth's murder, Ella had been so plump that her apron ties were barely long enough to make a bow in the back. Her cheeks had been fat and rosy, her hair smooth with a fair amount of brown.

Now, her flowered top practically fell off her shoulders and her blue, flour-stained apron was tied in a big bow. New wrinkles tugged at her mouth and puffy, dark flesh circled her eyes. Her hair was almost totally gray with frayed ends that barely reached the middle of her ears.

Selling the house and property might turn out to be a wash on this trip, but at least Helena could spend some quality time with Ella before she left for Boston.

Helena breathed in the odor of spices wafting from the kitchen. "What is that I smell?"

"Peach cobbler."

"My favorite," Helena said. "You remembered."

"How could I forget? Mia and I spent one whole day a few summers ago gathering peaches at a local pick-your-own orchard. Day was hotter than Lucifer's spa, but she refused to quit until she had enough of the juicy fruit to fill her freezer."

"I take it you did not handpick these peaches."

"Sure I did. Picked them right from the baskets at the French Market when they were at their peak. Then I sliced and froze them."

They both laughed, and it was amazing how much that softened the hard lines in Ella's face. She probably didn't laugh nearly enough.

"I didn't just make cobbler," Ella said. "I made some homemade shrimp salad. And I have fresh French baguettes to spread it on."

"You shouldn't have gone to all that trouble."

"Wasn't that much trouble. Besides I figured we'd have a lot more time and privacy for talking if we ate here. You know how noisy some of the lunch spots can be."

"Especially the ones worth going to where the seafood gumbo is hot and spicy and the po'boys drip all down your shirt."

"Well, when you put it that way, maybe we should have gone out," Ella said.

"Another day," Helena said. "Shrimp salad sandwiches, peach cobbler and being here with you in your comfy, air-conditioned apartment can't be beat."

Ella led the way to her second-floor kitchen.

All of the units were more or less what Helena considered upside down. Kitchen and dining areas and a spare room with floor to ceiling windows were on the second floor. Ella used her extra room for a guest room.

A large family area with a fireplace was on the first floor of every apartment as was a very spacious bedroom suite. All the apartments were entered through the courtyard. All had second-floor balconies and an ambiance that reeked of history and comfort.

Ella pointed to a bottle of white wine on the counter.

"Would you mind opening the wine? I splurged on a bottle of Mia's favorite chardonnay and I've been saving it to celebrate your homecoming."

"Sounds great."

"I chilled it before you got here. Wineglasses are on the table."

They stuck to small talk until they'd settled at the dining nook that overlooked the myriad of greenery and blossoms trailing over the iron balcony.

They devoured the sandwiches and were halfway through bowls of warm cobbler topped with ice cream before the conversation took a nosedive.

"I saw you talking to Hunter Bergeron in the courtyard when he left here this morning," Ella said. "I'm glad to see the two of you are cordial again. Mia would be, too. I'm not sure she ever quite forgave him for backing out of the wedding, but she was convinced he was going to be the one to apprehend Elizabeth's killer."

First Alyssa and now Ella. It was as if Hunter had his own cheering squad. She had no intention of becoming one of his groupies.

"I hope he's successful in getting the killer off the streets," Helena said, "but I don't see the two of us becoming friends."

"Sorry. It was probably thoughtless of me to bring him up. I don't blame you for the bad feelings. It's just that you've both done a lot of growing up since then. I think you'd like him if you'd give him a chance."

"From what I hear, Hunter has plenty of friends."

"Mostly other detectives. He's asked about you several times," Ella added before letting the subject drop.

Helena was not about to get drawn into talk of what Hunter said or thought about her. Seeing him again had shaken loose a few old memories, but she would make certain things between them went no further.

They talked for at least an hour about the neighborhood and the other tenants and all the plans that were in the works for fall festivals.

Fortunately, they managed to avoid any further mention of Hunter and any talk about Elizabeth's murder, keeping things on the lighter edge of the spectrum.

Things had gone so well, Helena was stunned when she saw tears welling in Ella's eyes as she walked Helena down the stairs and to the door.

"I'm thrilled you're back, Helena. I promise not to be a burden, but you can't imagine how much your being close by means to me. I miss your grandmother so much. She held me together when I literally didn't think I could go on. She's the only one who understood how much I was hurting."

Ella's words felt like a jagged cord circling Helena's heart. "I know how close the two of you were, but you must have other friends you can talk to about your grief. It can't be good for you to keep it all bottled up inside you."

"I have lots of friends. They all try to help. Even Hunter comes by at least once a week. They say they understand, but they can't. It's not their pain. It's mine. Most of them had never even met Elizabeth."

"Your niece was beautiful in looks and spirit," Helena said. "I know how much you loved her."

"I still do, and I can't begin to heal as long as the monster who killed her is out there just waiting to take someone else's life."

"They'll find him and make him pay," Helena said, though she wasn't convinced of that herself. "Have you tried talking about your pain with Alyssa Orillon? Mia always said Alyssa had an uncanny talent for connecting with people."

"We talked a few times. I begged her to try to reach Elizabeth across the gulf of death. All she did was tell me to think about happy times Elizabeth and I had together. It didn't help. I'm just glad to have you back."

Helena couldn't leave it like this. A lie of omission even for a good reason was still a lie. "I hate disappointing you, Ella, more than you can know, but I'm not moving back to New Orleans."

"But Mia left all the property to you. It's yours free and clear."

"It is. But my life isn't in New Orleans. I've taken a new job in Boston that starts November 1. I'll be moving there permanently then or sooner if this property sells."

Ella stepped away. "But you loved this place. Mia had always counted on your moving here one day. You can't just put it in the hands of strangers."

It was useless to try to explain her own reasoning when at times she doubted the decision herself.

She took both of Ella's hands in hers. "Let's just take it a day at a time. Who knows? I may never find a buyer."

Ella sighed and shrugged. "You will. It just won't be a Cosworth."

Helena felt like she was deserting Ella as she walked away, but at least Ella would have Hunter around to pay her visits.

And for some crazy, inexplicable reason, that thought made Helena feel worse.

Chapter Six

Determined not to dwell all afternoon on a lunatic killer who had trolled her grandmother, Helena began the task of cleaning out Mia's closets. She'd been far too upset to tackle that when she'd been here for the funeral, although she had picked up numerous large plastic containers to simplify the process.

One pile for throwaway. One for items to keep. And one to be given away to local charities. She even had a fourth pile for items she though Ella might like.

Unfortunately, the task was much more difficult than she'd anticipated. There was basically nothing to throw away out of the linen closet. Mia had always been a neatnik, another of her admirable traits that hadn't been passed on to Helena. Everything was in excellent condition, many items unused.

Unfortunately, there was a fifth pile Helena hadn't counted on—the items Helena had no real use for but couldn't bear to part with.

The tablecloths Mia had used for the various holidays. The Easter one with a Peter Rabbit illustration had been Helena's favorite as a child. And then there were the lace table runners and doilies that they'd purchased the first time Mia had taken Helena to Scotland. And there were the cashmere throws Mia wrapped herself in to read or watch TV in front of the fireplace on cold winter nights.

That barely scratched the surface of the possessions Helena would love to keep, but as nostalgic as they might make her feel, they weren't Helena's style. She'd likely only be moving them from a closet in New Orleans to one in Boston to sit until they dry-rotted.

So, armed with the plastic containers and a will to keep only what was necessary while she lived in the carriage house, Helena began to put everything away and label accordingly.

It was nearly five o'clock when she finished. She stood and stretched, unkinking her tight muscles. When she walked into the kitchen to refill her water bottle, she noticed that the sun's hot rays were no longer beating against the windows.

A layer of dark clouds had moved in, threatening one of the late afternoon showers that were so common in this part of the South. No one complained much since the rain cooled things down a bit.

If she hurried, she might get in a walk and a chance to check on Alyssa before the storm hit. The more she thought about Alyssa's dizzy spell last night, the more it worried her.

Helena ran upstairs for her rain jacket, tossed her handbag over her shoulder and hurried out the door.

With her head lowered to block the breeze that had kicked up, she practically ran into Pierre Benoit at the gate.

"Where are you off to in such a rush?" he asked. "Hot date?"

"No such luck. Only a walk around the neighborhood, hopefully before the thunderstorm breaks loose.

If not, I'll duck into a shop and wait it out—or get wet. Water won't kill me."

"So, you're a walk in the rain kind of gal. Interesting."

"Warm rain. Not the icy downpours we get up North."

"Another good reason you should forget Boston and stay here."

Pierre was a fairly new tenant. He'd moved in shortly after Elizabeth's death and she'd only spent any time with him when she'd come home for Mia's funeral.

He'd been extremely thoughtful, offering to help in any way he could and then following up on that offer by phone when Helena had returned to her job.

He was far more handsome than she remembered. Dark eyes and a dimple in his chin. Expensively dressed in a black, pin-striped suit, every bit as professional looking as she'd expect of a successful attorney.

He smiled. "I saw your light on last night. I started to call and invite myself over for a nightcap, but I figured I'd best give you time to settle in."

"Thanks. I was exhausted but I'm fine today."

"Then how about dinner? There's a new French restaurant in the Garden District. Haven't tried it myself yet but the reviews all claim the food is *délicieux*."

"Now you're going to show off by going French on me."

"Obviously it will take more than that to impress you."

"I do owe you a dinner," she said.

"I ask a pretty woman to dinner, I pay."

"No way. Not after you gave me all that free professional advice. But I'm not hungry enough to do justice to an expensive restaurant or even a dive tonight. I over-loaded on Ella's peach cobbler at lunch."

"Now I'm envious. What about tomorrow night?"

She could hardly say no since he'd been so helpful when she needed it. Besides, she might even enjoy his company. It would beat the chance of facing Hunter again with all the disturbing reactions he ignited.

"Seven?" he verified.

"Works for me."

She turned to leave, but not quickly enough.

"I suppose Hunter Bergeron has already stopped by to welcome you in his inimitable style," Pierre said.

"You don't make that sound like a compliment."

"Hardly. The detective's almost as enjoyable as a bonfire in August."

Hunter had his faults. Being likeable had never been one of them and from the way Mia and Ella talked about him that hadn't changed.

"What did he do to tick you off?" she asked.

"His general modus operandi."

"Which is?"

"Asking the same questions over and over in dozens of different ways like he thinks if he harasses you long enough, you'll confess to something. Or maybe you'll suddenly remember seeing an abduction that had just slipped your mind before."

Hunter had always been persistent, except where she was concerned. It hadn't taken much to make him cut and run then.

"I'm surprised he hasn't driven off all your tenants by now," Pierre continued. "Only reason I'm still here is that I signed a year's lease."

"If Hunter is still asking questions, I'm sure he has a

reason for it," Helena said, for some reason feeling she had to defend him. "He's a good detective."

Pierre shrugged. "If you say so."

"Mia trusted him," she said, by way of explanation. "Now I better get going if I'm going to beat the rain."

"Good luck with that."

"I'm prepared for the worst." She pulled her rain jacket tighter to make her point.

"Be careful," he called as she walked away.

"Be careful" had obviously become the new "See ya." A bit foreboding for her taste, as if disaster might be lurking around every corner. Or maybe it was just talking about Hunter that upset her.

She slid her hand into the front pocket of her crop pants as she reached the gate. Her fingertips brushed the edge of Hunter's business card. Call him anytime.

She wouldn't. She couldn't let herself fall under his spell again.

There was a metal trash receptacle near the curb. She considered dropping Hunter's card in it. She'd punch in 911 before calling him to the rescue.

But the card remained in her pocket as she started on her walk.

ALTHOUGH NOT THE ideal day, it was pleasant enough for Helena to quickly relax among the familiar streets of the French Quarter. She walked to Jackson Square. The artists had taken their easels and left before the rain, but a young man in clown makeup risked the storm to make a few more dollars with his antics and balloon animals. The families standing around him seemed dismissive of the distant thunder, as well.

Helena turned and strolled to the city's famous Moon Walk, a promenade along the busy Mississippi River. A cruise ship was docked nearby and a steamboat paddled past it, the familiar music from its calliope making her feel even more at home.

As excited as she was about her new job in Boston, this area was the setting for her best memories. And her worst, thanks to Hunter. And here she was letting him take up space in her thoughts again.

Helena doubled back so that she'd pass Alyssa's. Following the printed instructions on the placard, she rang the bell. She was about to walk away when Alyssa finally came to the door.

"Did I come at a bad time?" Helena asked.

"I'm with a customer. I won't be but five minutes longer. Can you wait?"

"Sure, or I can come back tomorrow. I just wanted to make sure you're not having any more of those dizzy spells."

"There's a story there," Alyssa said, "but I think I have it all figured out."

"That sounds a bit mysterious." The good news was Alyssa's face was no longer ashen and her smile much more natural.

Her long, colorful skirt made whispery sounds, background for her jangling bracelets and dangling earrings as she ushered Helena into the waiting room.

"There's water, wine, coffee or soft drinks in the fridge. Help yourself."

The odor of fresh brewed coffee lured Helena to the small room Alyssa used as a convenient living area near her workspace. By the time she'd poured herself a cup and taken a few sips, Alyssa was seeing her customer to the door.

She turned her sign to Closed.

"Don't lose paying customers on my account," Helena insisted.

"Believe me, I need a rest after Annabelle. She's in here every week with a new problem she wants me to solve. This time she thinks her husband is having an affair because he doesn't talk to her at bedtime. My bet is he can't get a word in edgewise."

"Well, you should know. You're the psychic."

"I'm not, but I'm starting to feel like one and that's downright scary."

"Tell me more."

Alyssa took the other chair. "I think it's all related to the French Kiss Killer, though I hate that something as sexy as a French kiss is tied to something so depraved."

"How did he get that nickname?"

"No one seems to know, or if they do they're not admitting it. At any rate, I have the feeling that he is just about ready to strike again. Not psychic, more like how my arthritis lets me know the weather is changing."

"A lot of people seem to have that same intuition these days."

Helena didn't believe in psychics, but she didn't necessarily not believe in them, either. Some people might have a sixth sense, sort of the way she saw visions in her head before she painted them.

"There's more," Alyssa said. "I'm starting to feel like I'm caught up in a horror movie."

"How's that?"

"Two very attractive young women were in here earlier and one of them reminded me of Elizabeth. Not just her looks, though I swear they could pass as twins—both as beautiful as supermodels. It was also her personality. You know, lively and charismatic."

"Some people think everyone has a double," Helena

said, doubting they were exactly alike. "I can see how seeing Elizabeth's double might shake you up, but Elizabeth was an only child, so no mysterious twin sister."

"But what if the serial killer is still in this area? If Elizabeth was his type, then this lady must be, too."

"You have a point there. Do you have the young woman's name or know how to get in touch with her?"

"All I know is that her friend called her Lacy and they're staying at the new boutique hotel on Decatur."

"The Aquarelle?"

"That's it. Not a name that sticks to the tip of your tongue."

"I've never been in that hotel," Helena admitted. "You really think this young tourist could be in danger, don't you?"

"It's this niggling fear that won't go away."

"You should call Hunter. If nothing else, you'll feel better if you share your concerns with him."

"He'll think I'm crazy."

"At least you'll know you did what you could. Now I should get out of here before we get a downpour and I have to swim back to the carriage house."

"Okay. Thanks for stopping by, and I think I will give Hunter a call."

"It can't hurt," Helena agreed. She stood to leave. "One other thing," Helena said as she reached the door. "If seeing someone who reminded you of Elizabeth set off your concerns today, what had you so rattled last night? Was that another specific intuitive moment or just general serial killer-induced fear?"

Alyssa hesitated. "Last night I..." She shook her head. "I don't know. It could have been that I was just excited about seeing you."

That made no sense, but Helena let it go. Alyssa seemed to have enough to deal with for now.

HELENA MADE A sudden detour that would take her right past the Aquarelle Hotel. Not that she expected to run into the two tourists Alyssa had described, but it was possible. Her curiosity was definitely piqued.

The serial killer scenario was playing weird tricks on her mind as well, especially knowing that he'd actually talked to Mia by phone.

A streak of lightning split the dark clouds followed by a loud clap of thunder. She instantly regretted making the turn onto Decatur. The first drops of rain pelted her when she was a few feet from the hotel's canopied door.

Instead of raising her umbrella, she made a run for it, making it to cover just in time not to get soaked.

The reception area was empty except for a couple who appeared to be checking in and a bellboy manhandling a cart overflowing with luggage.

As expected, there was no sign of the young woman who'd thrown Alyssa into a tumultuous tizzy.

A quick stop at the ladies' room to finger brush her slightly damp hair away from her face and then Helena followed the carpeted walkway to the bar area.

It was not only busy but ringing with loud voices and laughter as you'd expect from revelers visiting the French Quarter on a stormy late afternoon.

If anyone here was panicking over a serial killer on the loose, they were doing a good job of hiding it. Helena scanned the room and found the perfect spot for people-watching, a table near the end of the bar with a view of everyone who came or went.

Truth be told, she felt a bit like a spy, searching for

the type of young woman the killer might be looking for. That was also a little sick. She needed a martini and a jolt of reality. She was neither a spy nor a detective and wouldn't know a clue if it sat down beside her.

Within minutes she was sipping a lemon drop martini from a sugar-frosted glass. Rain continued to splatter the windows. An attractive, middle-aged woman trilled the keyboard at a grand piano near the front of the bar.

Within minutes the music paired with alcohol soothed Helena's troubled mind. She sipped slowly.

The lights lowered after a half hour or so. More customers wandered in and happy hour began to morph into the dinner hour. The waitress stopped by to see if Helena wanted another drink before the happy hour prices disappeared.

The offer was tempting, but she resisted. She wanted her mind clear if she decided to check out more of Mia's highlighted material or handwritten notations in her research sources.

She jerked to attention when a tall man stopped at her elbow.

"Hello, Helena."

It took her a second to recognize her soon-to-be moving tenant.

"Hi, Connor. I was hoping to run into you. I just didn't expect it to be so soon."

"I saw a light on in the carriage house last night and figured you were home," he said. "We've all been wondering when you'd move back and take over. Are you having dinner with us tonight?"

"With *us*?"

"Yes, here at the hotel. I'm the food and beverage manager at the Aquarelle Hotel now."

"I didn't know. You must be doing a lot of things right. The place is hopping, and my lemon drop martini was superb."

"Nice to hear. Would you like another drink?"

"Thanks, but I'll pass on that this time. How is the position working out for you?"

"I'm loving the job so far. The work is challenging but rewarding and the pay is much better than I was making managing that bar on Bourbon Street."

"Moving on up. Is that why you're giving up your lease on your apartment?"

"You heard? Sorry about that. I'd have told you in person if I'd known you were coming back here so soon. I hate to leave. Three years, that's the longest time I've ever lived anywhere since I left home to go to LSU."

"I hate to see you go. Why are you leaving?"

"I've got a new girlfriend."

"Sounds serious."

Connor nodded. "I think this may be the one, and I figure it's time I settle down with one woman. I'll be thirty-two next week."

"When's the wedding?"

He shoved his hands into his front trouser pockets and grinned. "Not quite that serious yet. We've decided to cohabit for a few months first. You know, make sure our clothes can stand tossing around in the wash together."

"So, you'll be moving in with her?"

"No way. Her bathroom is barely big enough for two toothbrushes and I'd never fit my clothes into her one tiny closet."

"Then why move?" Helena asked. "The apartment you're in has quite a bit of storage and a roomy bathroom if I remember correctly."

"Yeah. The size is great, but my lease specifies one occupant."

"That's probably because you were single when you signed it. We could update that."

He pulled out a chair. "Mind if I join you for a few minutes?"

"Of course not."

"There is another issue," he said, keeping his voice low, obviously not wanting to be overheard by his hotel guests. "Hannah's all hung up with this serial killer hype. Says she'd be afraid to ever stay by herself in my apartment."

"Did you explain that there's no evidence that Elizabeth's killer was ever on the carriage house property?"

"A dozen times. The only way my staying in the apartment is going to work is if the French Kiss Killer gets arrested—which I keep thinking is bound to happen soon. Detective Bergeron is a cop on a mission. No doubt about it."

And now they'd circled back to Hunter. Was every discussion in this town destined to do that?

"Do you see a lot of Hunter Bergeron?" she asked.

"Not lately, but I ran into him fairly often when your grandmother was alive. She raised a lot of money to help the police catch the killer. So far it hasn't helped."

"Did you ever feel like Hunter was interrogating you more than necessary?"

"No way. Where did you get that idea? He asked some questions. That's his job. I only wish I'd had some answers for him. Nice teenager like Elizabeth. She deserves justice."

"How well did you know Elizabeth?"

"I'd only seen her to say hello when she was visiting Ella until her last trip down here. Then we sat around the fountain a couple of nights and talked about her graduating high school and heading off to college."

Connor pushed back in his chair. "I wish we'd talked more. Then I might have been able to tell Hunter something useful to the investigation."

"We all wish that."

"I better get back to work now." Connor stood, adjusted his tie and smoothed his well-fitting sport coat. "Welcome back to New Orleans," he said. "Your drink's on the house. I'll let your waiter know."

"Thanks."

"Yeah. Sorry about moving. I really like living there. Not much chance we'll find another courtyard as beautiful as yours."

The rain had slowed to a gentle mist when she left the hotel and started home. There was still no sign of Lacy and her friend.

HELENA SLOWED AS she approached home. Her heart jumped to her throat when she spotted Hunter leaning against the gate, his right foot propped against the metal scrolls behind him, his thick hair mussed as usual. No one should look that good.

"Are you looking for me," she asked, "or is this more of your good-cop routine?"

"A little of both. We need to talk."

"We just did that a few hours ago."

"Something new has come up since then."

"Something that has to do with Alyssa Orillon?"

"Ahh. Another psychic in our midst."

Hardly. If she were, she would have seen her breakup with Hunter coming in time to pull out with some of her dignity intact. When she ignored the question, he punched in the code, pushed the gate open and stepped back to let her enter first.

"Who gave you the code?" she asked as he followed her into the courtyard."

"Your grandmother. She considered me one of the good guys. This would probably work easier if you did, too."

"I knew you better than she did."

"Touché. Now that the rain's stopped, how about we walk over to Maspero's and grab a sandwich and coffee? I could use some grub. Lunch lost out to a new lead and a request for a warrant."

"Anything to do with the serial killer?" she asked.

"A drug deal gone bad. A machete attack among the crypts in an Algiers cemetery. On second thought, omit that last sentence. Not an appetizing addition to a dinner invitation."

Not appetizing at all, but Maspero's was. Thinking of their infamous muffulettas made her mouth water. Unfortunately, having dinner with Hunter, even in a restaurant as casual and noisy as Café Maspero, would be playing with fire.

"Thanks, but no thanks, on the dinner invitation. Let's keep this strictly business."

"It was always going to be business, but people have to eat."

"I'd rather get this over with as quickly as possible," she said. "We can talk inside."

"Making me the enemy is not going to keep you safe or help me stop a killer."

She nodded, knowing she was more afraid of her reactions than his. She could pretend that her heart had healed completely, but her body wasn't convinced.

They went inside, but this time settled at the small table in the kitchen. "I can offer you coffee."

"Love some."

She could have probably rustled up something more filling, but the more personal this became, the more risk to her emotions.

Hunter took two cups from the cupboard and the carton of half-and-half from the fridge while she started a pot of coffee. He'd obviously spent enough time with Mia that he felt right at home.

"How well do you know Alyssa Orillon?" he asked.

"We're not close, but I've known her since I was a kid. She and Mia were friends, so I guess I kind of inherited her as a friend."

"Do you think she's credible?"

"As a psychic?"

"In general."

"She's honest about her mystic abilities—or lack thereof—unless you go by the sign on her door. Advertisements usually contain a bit of hyperbole. So, yeah, I don't see why she'd lie about her intuitions or about her customers."

"Specifically, one named Lacy," he verified.

"Right."

"Then we're on the same page."

Hunter waited until Helena served the coffee before saying more. "I've never given any credibility to the sixth sense sort of predictions. I like solid facts and concrete evidence.

"On the other hand, I frequently rely on hunches and some of the older guys on the force swear there were times Alyssa's grandmother provided them with information that defied reason."

"Then you think Alyssa's fears are legitimate."

Hunter sipped his coffee. "Legitimate enough that we should check them out. All four of his victims fit the same general description, which means Lacy fits it, too."

"Is that typical with serial killers?"

"There are no hard-and-fast rules, but sometimes appearance seems to be part of the motivation for the next crime. And if Lacy looks that much like Elizabeth, she could be a trigger. That is assuming the killer is anywhere near the French Quarter.

"In a space the size of New Orleans and the surrounding area, the chances they'd cross paths are slim to none."

Helena ran her finger over the top of her cup while her mind played with possibilities. "What will you tell Lacy that won't frighten her and her friend to death?"

"I'll talk it over with the rest of the task force. The best option may be having an undercover female detective befriend them and warn them about hooking up with strangers even if they seem perfectly safe. She can also chat with them enough to find out if they've already been hit on. If so, we'll follow up on that."

"I can't imagine Lacy and her friend would just instantly bond with an undercover cop."

"That's where the competence of our undercover officers pays off."

"Wouldn't it be something if Alyssa earned the reward money Mia helped collect?"

"We're talking long shot here," Hunter reminded her. "The killer's been quiet for over six months. He could have moved out of this area completely. He may have been killed in a car crash or died of some cruel disease, though that's likely too much to ask for."

Helena was relieved to hear Hunter hadn't just

brushed off the info from Alyssa, but she didn't see how she fit into this.

"Why rush over here to talk to me before even stopping to grab a bite or get down to the business of checking out Lacy?"

Hunter finished his coffee before answering, visibly avoiding what should be a simple response as to why he was here. Finally, he stretched one hand across the table as if he were reaching for her hand.

Instinctively, she pulled her hand away and placed it in her lap. One touch and the wall of heartache and regret separating them might disintegrate.

Hunter pulled back his hand and propped his elbows on the table. "Lacy and her friend were not the only women who caused Alyssa to see frightening images."

"There were others? Who? When?"

"Only one. You. Last night."

"Alyssa didn't mention disturbing visions to me. She was dizzy but said it was nothing to worry about."

"She didn't want to frighten you," Hunter explained.

"And you do?"

"No. I want to keep you safe."

This made no sense. Alyssa had to be mistaken. "What kind of vision did she see?"

"She saw you, covered in blood, being chased by a man with a knife."

"Who was the man?"

"His face was too blurry to tell."

This was growing more bizarre by the second. "Alyssa must be hallucinating. She's so scared by all this talk of the French Kiss Killer, she's seeing danger everywhere—just like everyone else in this town."

"Probably, but I thought you should know, especially since you went looking for trouble today instead of avoiding it."

"I don't know what you mean."

"You headed straight for the Aquarelle Hotel when you left Alyssa's this afternoon."

"How do you know that? Are you having me followed?"

"Not yet. I dropped by the hotel after talking to Alyssa. You were in the bar talking to Connor Harrington, about what I don't know. But we both know you were there because of what Alyssa told you."

"There's no law against having a drink in a hotel lounge," she quipped.

"No, but there is a law against interfering in an investigation. It's also dangerous."

He finished off his coffee and pushed his cup away from him. "I need to see your phone."

This was going too far. Helena stood and backed away from the table. "I wasn't interfering with anything and I don't need your protection. I'm not afraid."

"Of course you're not. You're Mia Cosworth's granddaughter. Now hand me your phone and I'll program my number into it and put it on speed dial."

She couldn't argue anything he said, so she laid her phone down on the table in front of him. "I don't expect the killer to contact me."

"Good. Neither do I."

"And I'm not planning to go looking for trouble."

"Also good because I'd hate to put you under house arrest."

"On what grounds?"

"I'll think of something."

He was surely bluffing. When he finished with the phone, she walked him to the door.

Instead of leaving, he held the door open and looked down at her, his gaze burning into hers. He leaned closer until his lips were only inches away from her mouth.

Old urges erupted inside her, a hunger that she'd thought was lost forever.

"Play this smart. Stay safe, Helena," he murmured. And then he turned and was gone.

UNWILLING TO SUCCUMB to unbidden memories starring Hunter Bergeron, Helena spent the next two hours buried in one of Mia's nonfictional horror tales. The book on the twisted and horrifying backgrounds of famous criminals made her blood run icy; she upped the temperature control to eighty and still shivered beneath a light blanket.

Mia had made dozens of notations in the book, but none that made a lot of sense to Helena. The only obvious deduction from them was that Mia was trying to figure out how to use the book's contents to help her understand the man who had killed Elizabeth— a madman who in the last few weeks of her life insinuated himself into more than her mind. He'd literally tormented her with his phone calls.

When Helena had all she could stomach for one night, she kicked off the blanket and walked onto her balcony. There were no crowds this late on a Wednesday night, but she could hear music coming from somewhere and laughter and loud talk coming from a group of young adults hanging out on a balcony down the block.

Normal people going on with their lives. She had to get back to that. She had faith that eventually law enforcement would win. The infamous French Kiss Killer would be apprehended and either be killed or face a lifetime in prison.

But when and how many more innocent young women would he kill first? That was the question Hunter personally faced every day. Yet, even with that no doubt haunting his every breath, he'd found time to see her twice today.

Was that all typical police business or perhaps from an allegiance he felt toward Mia? Or was he looking for more from her?

Did he still have romantic feelings for her? Did he think they had a chance to recapture the love they'd once shared?

If so, he was wrong. It had been six years. Her physical and emotional reactions were betraying her. Hunter had destroyed the love and trust she'd felt for him on her wedding day.

The wedding that had never happened.

She walked back inside, showered, brushed her teeth and put on a pair of cotton pj's. Once she'd climbed into bed, she switched off her reading lamp and snuggled beneath the covers.

Hopefully she'd sleep without dreams. In the present situation they'd inevitably become nightmares.

In the foggy sphere between wakefulness and sleep, she heard her phone ring.

Chapter Seven

Helena jerked to an upright position, her heart pounding. Late-night phone calls were always alarming, but this was far worse than the usual trace of dread.

This was her cell phone, not Mia's home phone. That had been disconnected a few days after the funeral. There was no reason to think this could be Elizabeth's killer, but still she hesitated to answer the call.

She checked the ID. There was none. She checked the time. It was a few minutes before two a.m.

Reluctantly, she took a deep breath and pressed the answer button. "Hello."

There was no response, but she could hear heavy breathing through the connection.

"Hello," she said again.

Still no response.

Resolve attacked her fear. "You have ten seconds to answer before I hang up."

Je ne le ferais pas si j'étais toi.

French. The French Kiss Killer. It had to be him, except that he sounded like a young, mischievous boy. Hunter had warned her the caller used a machine to create a robotic voice disguised like either gender. She hadn't expected it to sound like a kid voice.

She knew some French, enough that she knew he was warning her not to hang up.

"What do you want?"

"To welcome you home. *Bienvenue à la maison.*"

"Did you kill Elizabeth Grayson?"

"You are curious like your grandmother and to the point. I like that. Yes, Elizabeth's death was one of my great achievements."

"How could you commit such a sick crime? How could you kill a woman with her whole life in front of her?"

"Lots of people die before their time."

"She didn't just die. She was murdered—by you. The police are closing in on you. You're going to rot in jail."

He laughed. The disguise did not hide his madness. "I'm much too smart for the police. They are a joke."

"What do you want from me?"

"I'm not sure yet, but torture is more satisfying when you share it. Give Hunter my regards. Good night and sweet dreams."

The connection went dead, yet the voice felt as if it were vibrating through every vein in her body.

Helena no longer had a choice. She punched in Hunter's number.

HUNTER REACHED OUT the front car window to retrieve his food with one hand and for his ringing phone with the other. Damn these full moons that seemed to bring out all the crazies. It was two a.m. He should have been off duty hours ago. He needed food and sleep before he collapsed.

He thanked the worker and pulled away from the serving window before checking his caller ID. Helena.

His heart slammed into his chest. Something big had to have happened for her to call him.

"What's wrong?" he asked in lieu of a greeting.

"I think the French Kiss Killer just called."

Adrenaline struck like a tidal wave. "What did he say?"

"That he called to welcome me home. Only he did it with a young boy's voice. That made it all the more chilling."

"No doubt. What else did he say?"

She repeated every word of their conversation, if not verbatim, then close, she assured him.

"Okay. I'm five minutes away, tops."

"You don't need to rush over here. Seriously, I'm not panicking now, though I may have been on the verge at first. I just thought you should know."

"You think? We're talking a killer here."

"I'm not suggesting he's not dangerous, but he was on the phone, not on the premises. The gate is locked. The dead bolts to the house are locked. Besides, from what you said earlier, his method is only to intimidate with phone calls."

His method up to this point. Who knew when that might change? They were dealing with a murderous madman.

"Keep the doors locked until I arrive. I have the courtyard code and an emergency key to the house, both given to me by your grandmother. So don't take me for the lunatic and shoot me when I reach the door."

"I don't have a gun."

"We'll remedy that."

"I don't know how to shoot."

"We'll remedy that, too."

He attached the portable flashing lights to the roof

of his unmarked sedan and revved up the sirens as he maneuvered the narrow streets of the French Quarter.

He needed this tie to the killer. Needed any link that might lead to a decent clue and his capture. But why the hell did it have to come via Helena?

Six years of regret bucked inside him like a wild bull. He blocked it the way he had in Afghanistan when his buddies' lives were at stake.

When push came to shove, a real man did what he had to do.

ONCE THE CALL to Hunter had been made, the sense of terror began to ease. The killer had called Mia for weeks with no physical confrontation.

It might not even be the real killer. For all she knew it was just some crazy person making crank calls. A way to boost his own self-importance with little risk— until he got caught. Maybe he only called when he was on a drug high.

There was no time to dress or put on makeup before Hunter arrived, and even if there were, Helena refused to go to any trouble to look attractive for him. She pulled on her short robe and shoved her feet into her slippers. A quick brush of her disheveled hair and she headed down the stairs and took up guard position at the door.

Concentrating on calming her nerves, she took deep breaths, exhaling slowly. He had the code to the gate. He wouldn't need to be buzzed into the courtyard or let into the house for that matter.

At this moment that was more comforting than disconcerting. The doorbell rang minutes before she expected him to arrive. She put her eye to the peephole to verify it was him before she opened the door.

He burst inside carrying a large paper bag that reeked of peppers and onions.

"You couldn't have stopped for food and gotten here this quickly without a jet engine," she said.

"I had the burgers and fries, just not time to eat them. Sorry for bringing it in with me, but I'm famished. Still getting by on the coffee you gave me earlier."

"You haven't been to bed yet?"

"No, but I was about to head that way when I got your call."

"Then we'll talk in the kitchen while you indulge in your unhealthy feast."

He followed her, dropping his bag to the table. "Are you okay?"

"Yes. I told you that on the phone. You didn't have to rush over here tonight. This could have waited until daylight."

His brows arched. "Now you're going to tell me how to do my job?"

"Of course not, but if my grandmother could handle talking on the phone with the monster without having hysterics, I'm sure I can, too."

"Point made."

He dropped into a kitchen chair. She took the one opposite his.

Here they were, sitting in the cozy kitchen again. He was here as a police officer, but they were connecting on a far more personal level and that's where the real risk came in.

They'd bonded the first time they'd met when she was only nineteen, gone straight from strangers to lovers in less than a week, skipping over all the steps in between. She had no idea where this step would have fallen in their failed relationship, but she knew where it couldn't go.

"Tell me everything," he said.

"I did. Even with the heavy breathing at the beginning, the call probably lasted less than a minute. How many times did you say he called Mia?"

"Three times over a three-week period. All extremely brief. By the end, she was convinced he was reaching out for help, trying to keep himself from killing again."

"What do you believe?"

"That there's a good chance he was just playing her."

He took a huge bite of his hamburger, then wiped his mouth on a paper napkin from his bag.

"Let me get you a plate," Helena offered.

"This is fine. Eating at a table instead of on the run is luxury enough for me. Some milk would be good if you have it, though."

She poured him a glass of milk and set it in front of him. "Did the killer speak French to Mia, too? Is that how you came up with the name of French Kiss Killer?" she asked.

"Actually, it was because one of the crime scenes was on swampland previously owned by a well-known Cajun criminal. No one outside the task force knows about the phone calls."

"Are you sure the caller is the killer and not some crazy fake trying to get attention?"

"I'm ninety-nine percent sure he's the killer."

"Why?"

"He said a couple of things to Mia that only the killer would know."

"What kind of things?"

"Details about the murder itself that were never released to the public."

"So information only cops would have."

"Only a very limited number of cops and a couple of FBI agents working as advisers on the task force."

"Then maybe he was reaching out for help," Helena said. "And now that Mia's dead, he came to me, perhaps hoping I'd take over where she left off."

"He's a brutal serial killer who's already taken four innocent lives," Hunter stressed yet again. "I'm not saying this to frighten you. Well, maybe I am, but just enough to make sure you don't fancy yourself his therapist and do something foolish."

"I'm an artist, not a therapist. What do we do next?"

"For starters, someone will be over here probably around nine o'clock in the morning to put special software on your cell phone that will let us monitor and hopefully trace the origin of his calls."

"*All* my calls will be monitored by the police? That severely limits my privacy."

"All calls that come to your present cell phone. Be aware of that when you answer. The department will provide you with a phone to use for personal calls. You are to give that number only to people you fully trust. Like me."

"I can still use the internet, can't I?"

"Yes, but no social sites. Just to be safe, you should change your email address and all your passwords."

"You think Elizabeth's killer is also a hacker?"

"Isn't everybody?"

"Now you're being facetious."

"Sorry. I tend toward sarcasm after a day like this." He took another bite of his burger, catching a sliced jalapeño with his tongue as it slid from the bun.

"Do I still answer the suspect's calls?" she asked.

"Right. Just like you did tonight. We can assume that he has your private cell phone number and already knows you're back and living in Mia's carriage house."

She'd already figured out that much on her own.

Hunter finished off the first burger and unwrapped a second. "Are you sure you don't want half of this?"

"No, but thanks. Is there anything else I should know?"

He swallowed and wiped his mouth on one of the paper napkins from the food bag.

"A few rules," he said. "The most important is that I need to know where you are every second of the day and who you're with."

"Why? I know the risks. I'm not going to walk into a dangerous situation."

"Standard protocol and the fact that the man making the calls might also be stalking you."

"Did he stalk Mia?"

"No, but we can't take any chances with this man. You may be tailed when you leave the house, but you'll never see the undercover cop. On the other hand, if you notice someone who appears to be following you or if you seem to be running into the same person at different spots, call me at once."

It finally hit her. "This is about more than phone calls. Do you think he's targeting me as his next victim?"

"I'm just covering all the bases."

"Elizabeth was eighteen. I'm twenty-five. She was a blonde. My hair's auburn. I can't possibly fit his victim profile."

"Like I said, we're just covering all the bases. There is another option," Hunter said. "You should consider leaving the city and going back to where you've been living."

"That would get me out of your hair, but it wouldn't guarantee the monster wouldn't track me down. Besides, if I leave, you lose your best chance of contact with the killer. You have to admit that's true."

"You're not in law enforcement. Catching killers is not your responsibility." He pushed his carton of French fries toward her.

She reached for one and popped it in her mouth. Next to chocolate, grease and salt had to be the best food therapy there was.

She did have options. Her new job didn't start until November 1. Thanks to the estate settlement, she had enough cash to travel. Spend a month in Italy or Greece, jet set around Europe and hope the police apprehended the killer before he struck again.

Or she could stay here and be neck deep in an investigation she had no control over—unless she forced a few issues.

This time she dipped her fry into ketchup before eating it. "I'm staying here," she said. "I'll follow your orders but first I want to hear all of the phone conversations between Mia and the killer that you have recorded."

"I'm not at liberty to share those with you."

"Then I'm not playing by your rules. I'll deal with the killer my way. Who knows? I may be the one who'll save him and the next victim."

She was bluffing. He probably guessed that since she wasn't nuts, but they both knew he could share those calls with her if it helped his case.

He stuffed the last bite of burger in his mouth, wadded his trash and shoved it into the bag. He chewed and swallowed and then stared at her for a few long minutes before agreeing to her terms.

"You drive a hard bargain, one that you may be sorry

for. But I'll arrange for you to hear the recordings, probably later today, after we both get some sleep."

That was much easier than she'd imagined.

He took his vibrating phone from his pocket. "I have to take this call."

"Sure. You're welcome to use the sitting room if you need privacy."

"Thanks."

She straightened the kitchen and disposed of the trash. He was still on the phone, so she went upstairs to make notes on her computer about all the things they'd discussed.

It was a good half hour before she came back downstairs. He had a key. He'd likely let himself out the door and locked it behind him.

Still, she checked the sitting room. He was on the sofa, his head half on a throw pillow, his shoes still on his feet, hanging off the end of the plaid couch.

He was fast asleep.

She trembled, suddenly rocked by a longing that left her weak and dizzy. She ached to lie down beside him and spoon her body with his.

And if he pulled her closer... If he burrowed his face in her hair... If she felt his warm breath on her neck...

The past would come back and devour her.

She pulled one of Mia's crocheted afghans from the large basket at the foot of the sofa and laid it across him.

She made it back to her own bed, but it was dawn before she fell asleep.

IT WAS DAYLIGHT when Helena opened her eyes again. Seven o'clock. She stretched, her left foot poking out from between the cool sheets. The AC was already whirring softly. It would probably be another scorcher today.

It was only Thursday, Helena's third day back in New Orleans. Already, Alyssa Orillon had envisioned Helena covered in blood and being chased by a mystery man yielding a knife. She'd learned her grandmother had a secret, dangerous life before her death. A man known as the French Kiss Killer had called Helena for no apparent reason.

And Hunter Bergeron had slept in her house for part of the night.

The reality of all of that sank in slowly as a surge of perplexing emotions rode the ragged endings of her nerves.

She punched her pillow a couple of times as if that could release her frustration before bracing herself to go downstairs and see if Hunter was still here. More likely, he'd dozed an hour or two and then gotten up and let himself out.

Her mouth tasted gritty. She brushed her teeth, washed her face and hit her hair with a few brushstrokes before piling it on top her head and fastening it down with a pair of large clips.

Even with all that was going on in her life, she hesitated on the stair's landing. Her beautiful grandmother who'd given so much of her time to making life brighter for others had spent the last days of her life in a mental war with a murderous monster.

That was reason enough for Helena to stay here and take over where Mia had been forced to leave off.

The house was silent when Helena reached the bottom of the stairs. No rhythmic breathing. No sounds of movement. Hunter was gone. She knew it from the sense of emptiness that stuck in her throat even before she reached the sitting room.

The afghan she'd thrown over him last night was neatly folded and resting on the arm of the sofa. The indentation of Hunter's head was still visible in the throw pillow.

She picked up the pillow to fluff it. Instead she put it to her face. It smelled of musk and soap and burgers. It smelled of Hunter and a new rush of old memories came crashing down on her.

She fought the onslaught by hurrying out of the room before she dropped to the couch and pushed against the cushions that had held his body a few hours ago.

Think of the past, she reminded herself. *The two of you made love like there was no tomorrow and then he walked away with no explanation.*

He'd had problems. She'd known that. He was under investigation for a mistake he'd made while doing his job. A mistake that had cost a life.

But instead of seeing it through, he'd just walked away. Whatever he'd needed to get past his problem, it hadn't been her. No reason to think he was a different man today. No reason to believe he wouldn't break her heart again if she gave him half a chance.

HUNTER HAD OVERSTEPPED all the boundaries last night. He should never have gone to sleep at Helena's place, but a full stomach and sheer exhaustion had called the shots. He'd closed his eyes for a second. When he'd opened them, it was five in the morning.

Fortunately he'd managed to let himself out of the carriage house without waking her.

Mess up this investigation and it could cost lives. Lose Helena's trust and she might not let him stick

around to protect her. She was a lot like her grandmother—both too independent to take orders they didn't
respect.

He paced her kitchen now while his partner, Cory
Barker, showed her how the new phone app worked.
She'd been distant with Hunter when he'd arrived first,
but she appeared to be bonding with Barker just great.

"That's it," Barker said. "It's simple on your part,
Ms. Cosworth. Answer the phone when it rings and try
to keep our alligator goon talking as long as you can.
Time is the major factor here if we're going to find and
apprehend him before he dumps or destroys the phone
and disappears."

"What should I say to keep him talking?" Helena
asked.

"We're looking for anything that might give us a clue
to his identity. Where he had dinner. How he knew Elizabeth and the other girls he killed. Pretend you know
who he is. Urge him to give himself in. And the list
goes on."

"Is that how Mia handled it?"

"She tried. He didn't talk much after the first call.
He obviously knew we'd be listening in then and trying to track him."

"Were all his calls to my grandmother at night?"
Helena asked.

"The first two were. The last one was on a rainy
Sunday morning."

Barker turned to Hunter. "Anything else I should go
over with Helena before I go?"

"Think you covered almost everything. I can take
over from here."

Helena walked Barker to the door. Hunter took the

opportunity to return a phone call to Natalie Martin, an extremely talented profiler on loan from the FBI.

As usual, Natalie wasted no time with small talk. "I've been thinking about our French Kiss guy's call to Helena Cosworth last night. I keep trying to fit him into a recognizable pattern based on his first three murders, but this whole phone call routine throws a monkey wrench into my efforts. Things just aren't adding up."

"Have you talked to anyone else on the team about that?"

"Not yet. I'm working on a new graph that I'd like to run by the whole task force later today. Can you set that up?"

"I'm not sure what everybody else has on their plate, but I'll see what I can do."

"Thanks. Keep me posted."

While he'd been on the phone with Natalie, he'd heard the doorbell and the deep, commanding voice of the team's unofficial, volunteer profiler.

Hunter assumed Barker had let him in before he left since Helena was not supposed to be opening her door to a stranger. No doubt Antoine Robicheaux was already charming Helena's socks off. Hopefully, just her socks.

HELENA STARED AT the latest investigator to arrive—a hunk of a guy who Cory had briefly introduced as one of the team. Late thirties, raven-black hair with wavy locks that fell mischievously across his brow. Chocolate-colored eyes a girl could drown in.

"I suppose you're here to see Detective Bergeron," she said, ushering him through the door.

"If you're Helena Cosworth, I'm here to see you."

Hunter joined them in the foyer. "About damn time

you showed up." His tone clearly indicated the anger wasn't real.

"If you'd told me an angel was waiting, I would have made it a lot sooner."

"Cool it, Romeo. Did Barker take care of introductions?"

"Only the basic," Helena said. "I'm not sure why Detective Robicheaux is here."

"To clear that up, Robicheaux isn't a detective," Hunter explained. "He's former FBI with the best success rate in the country for apprehending serial killers."

"All true," Robicheaux said.

"I forgot to mention modesty," Hunter joked.

"And you must be Mia Cosworth's beautiful and talented granddaughter," Robicheaux said. "Your grandmother raved about you constantly."

"She was a bit biased in my favor. How did you know Mia?"

"I did all her security work for her. Set up the gate system a few years back. Planned a new and more secure system that my company was about to install for her when she had her fall. I wish there would have been something I could have installed to prevent that."

"So do I. Exactly what were you planning to install?"

"Mia wanted improved digital control pads with security cameras at the gate and she wanted personal pass codes for every apartment. That way, she could change a tenant's apartment code when they moved out instead of changing to a new code for everyone."

"I guess that makes sense," Helena agreed. "I'm not sure that now is the best time to tackle that. I just put the property up for sale."

"It'll increase the value of the property significantly

in the current fear crisis. And it will keep you and your tenants safer. But, up to you."

"I'll think about it."

"While we're at it, you should consider replacing the courtyard lighting system with motion sensors that include hidden cameras."

"I suppose you do all of that, as well."

"My security company, Guardian Safe, does all that and more and we do it better than anyone else. We've provided bodyguard services for many sports and entertainment stars as well as foreign dignitaries. Never a screwup."

"That's impressive."

"I'd recommend you put a few hidden cameras in the house, as well."

She wasn't ready to go that far. "No hidden cameras inside my house. No spy equipment of any kind. In fact, I need to think about all of this and go over it with my Realtor before I agree to your recommendations."

One of her phones was already being wiretapped. She wasn't about to trust someone nicknamed Romeo or anyone else to hide cameras inside her house. Next thing she knew, instead of her artwork being on the internet, it would be her boobs and bottom.

"The woman has spoken," Robicheaux said. "The original workups for security improvements are in my car along with a list of recommendations and price estimates. I'll leave them with you."

"I'll walk out with you to get them," Hunter said.

Helena said her goodbyes and went back into the kitchen. She'd been back in New Orleans only three days and she felt as if she were losing total control of her life.

She wondered if Mia had felt the same helplessness

when she started receiving the killer's phone calls and Hunter had taken control of her life. Regardless, she must have fully trusted Hunter to give him the gate code and a key.

Hunter returned a few minutes later, rolled-up blueprints and a large brown envelope in hand. He sat them on the kitchen counter.

"If there's anything here you don't understand, you can give Robicheaux a call. I'm sure he'll stop back by and go over the security additions in more detail."

"I just need time," Helena said. "Everything seems to be coming at me at once. This is a far cry from the ordered, peaceful life I'm used to."

"A life I'm sure you miss and can't wait to get back to."

She couldn't deny that, but she'd never let Hunter know that a huge part of what was making this so difficult was being with him.

Time to change the subject. "Did you bring the recording of Mia's calls with the monster?"

"No. We'll need to go down to the precinct for me to play them for you. That is police policy when dealing with this type of homicide."

And then she'd need a drink. She was a train wreck now. She might freak out completely when she heard those calls.

Chapter Eight

This was Helena's first visit to a police precinct. Dozens of people were crowded into tight quarters, most working in individual cubicles or small private offices. The rest were in groups, engaged in conversation in the open space or clustered around one of the cubicles.

She noted that over half of the offices and cubicles were empty. That made sense. The real police work was undoubtedly done on the streets.

Hunter led her through a maze, acknowledging a few people with a nod or a small wave. He stopped at one office with an open door and introduced her to Lane Crosby, a lanky man with heavy facial hair who looked to be in his midforties, and Natalie Martin, an attractive brunette woman about the same age.

"Do they know why I'm here today?" Helena asked as the continued down the maze of small offices.

"They do and neither of them think it's a good idea, though Natalie Martin does have some ideas for discussion that center around the phone calls you're getting. That's one reason I wanted Barker and Natalie to at least meet you."

"Do you think saying hello changed their mind about my listening to the calls to Mia?"

"No, and I didn't expect it to. But it's a start. They're

concerned about any information leaking out at this crucial stage in the investigation. The more people who know the facts we've kept under wraps, the more likely the press will pick up a leak and run with the info. It's their job, of course, but sometimes it makes it harder for us to do ours."

Hunter stopped at a door near the end of the hall and opened it with a key.

She stepped inside. The room was barely big enough for a rectangular conference table and the eight folding chairs huddled around it. A small, professional grade player was already set up at the end of the table.

"Are others joining us?" she asked.

"No, it will be just the two of us, but we're short on private meeting space." He pulled out a chair for her. "Take a seat and we'll get started."

"Will we be listening to a tape or a digital recording?"

"Digital. We'll start when you're ready, but we can stop at any point to talk about what you've heard or to give yourself a break to recoup."

"If it's that bad, the most difficult part may be knowing that Mia had to listen to it."

"She was always cool. It was almost as if she enjoyed her part in going after this monster."

"I wouldn't know since I was kept out of the loop, but I never knew her to back down from a challenge."

"She would have made a terrific law enforcement officer," Hunter said. "Missed her calling. She'd probably be running the whole FBI now."

"Don't expect the same from me," Helena assured him. "Dealing with killers is positively not my calling."

"You're hanging in there pretty well so far." Hunter

took the seat catty-corner from hers at the end of the table.

"Just as a reminder, we don't have a record of their first conversation since no one saw that one coming. All we have is the report from her as to what she remembered. I don't have that with me, but I've read it enough times, I almost have it memorized."

"Can you brief me on that before we get started?" Helena said. "That will give me a better sense of how the conversations flowed."

"Basically, the first contact was a meet and greet moment."

"Which means?"

"He called her by name and noted that she'd been very busy and successful in raising funds to help get him arrested. He insisted that he wasn't the monster she described him as. Told her he had no more control over his murders then she did over her breathing. And then he threw in a few gory details, some in French."

"He sounds insane."

"He did on the subsequent calls, too."

"What else did he say on the first call?"

"He hoped they could become friends and that she shouldn't go to the cops. Then he stressed he wasn't afraid of the cops because we were too stupid to see what was right in front of our faces. That's pretty much the opinion of criminals in general—that is until they get arrested."

"Did he threaten her?"

"Not other than an implied threat that if she talked to anyone in law enforcement, she would pay dearly for that mistake."

"So, I'm guessing Mia immediately called 911?"

"No. She immediately called me."

Hunter Bergeron to the rescue. Mia's calling him almost felt like a betrayal to Helena except that it had likely been the smartest thing to do.

"I think we've covered call one," Hunter said. "The other two will be much shorter since he was no doubt avoiding our tracking the call and showing up to arrest him."

"He seems to be well versed in how these investigations work."

"He got better at it as he went along. Are you ready to start the machine?"

"As ready as I'll ever be."

She sat up straight in her chair but clasped her hands in her lap. Hunter punched the play button.

"Call two."

"Hello."

A chill struck bone deep when she heard Mia's voice. It was almost as if Mia was speaking to them from the grave.

"*Bonjour, madam.* Have you missed me?" The voice sounded male.

"A little. Why did you wait so long to call?"

Mia was definitely playing along with him. Obviously, she'd been coached on how to handle the calls. She sounded amazingly calm.

"I know you hate me, but you don't know the real me. You think I like killing?"

"Don't you?"

"It's more like an obsession. But there were memorable moments, like when I helped her out of her red silky panties."

"I don't want to hear about panties. I think you want to turn yourself in."

The phone clicked, the connection broken.

The machine kept running.

The third call was in a female voice. "What was your father like, Mia?"

"He was a good and loving man. Was yours?"

"He was a cowardly wimp, let my stepmother walk all over him. I hate wimps."

"You need help. I can get it for you."

"No, but I'd love to meet your granddaughter. I hear she's beautiful. Will she be visiting soon?"

"Don't ever mention her again."

"I won't. It's time to move on. *Aide de Dieu*."

Helena shuddered as the connection broke. *Aide de Dieu*. God help. "What did he mean by that?"

"We're not sure. Mia fell four days later. We investigated thoroughly. Like I said before, no sign of foul play."

"How close did you come to actually tracking his location through the phone calls?"

"Not close enough nor fast enough to ever see him or talk to anyone who had. We can verify that the calls were from somewhere within a sixty-mile radius of the French Quarter."

"And he never contacted anyone about the other murders?"

"If he has, none of them have shared it with the police."

"There must be a reason he contacted Mia and no one else. Maybe Mia was right and it was a cry for help."

"I think it was far more likely he was just running scared because she had everyone talking about him and searching for him, all looking to collect the sizable reward money. She's not here now, so he's taking it out on you."

"All that reward money and yet he still hasn't been

apprehended," Helena said. "So, he might actually be criminally insane and yet brilliant."

"He's smart, but we'll get him eventually," Hunter said. "The challenge is arresting him before he kills his next victim. That's why we've got so many men working this full-time."

"And why you don't get to eat or sleep on a regular basis?"

"Yeah. I didn't mean to crash on your couch in the wee hours of the morning. I just closed my eyes and that was it."

"No problem," she said, though it had been. It had set off a chain of desire and arousal that threatened her shaky control.

"If that's all you have, let's get out of here," she said, suddenly eager to be out in the sunshine and with enough people that hopefully an incidental touch or a sympathetic word wouldn't set her off again.

Hunter unplugged the listening device and wrapped the cord. "What do you have planned for the rest of the day?"

"I thought I'd give Alyssa a call and see if she's free for lunch."

"Good idea. Both of you need a break from this garbage. I can drop you off at her place or drop both of you off at the restaurant of your choice."

"Sounds good."

She placed the call while Hunter waited. Alyssa seemed pleased at Helena's invite, and suggested they have lunch at the Napoleon House, a favorite French Quarter spot of almost everybody who spent any time there. Plus, it was within walking distance.

After getting off the phone Helena saw no reason

not to mention her plans for the evening since Hunter insisted on knowing every move she made.

"I'm having dinner tonight with Pierre Benoit."

He frowned. "Why?"

"He invited me, and I owe him a dinner."

"I ask again. Why?"

"He kind of walked me through some of the legal entanglements in settling Mia's estate. He seems like a nice guy. What is it you have against him?"

"Other than that he's arrogant and rude?"

"I haven't found him to be either of those things. For the record, he doesn't seem to be any fonder of you than you are of him."

"What's he complaining about?"

"He says you harassed him and went overboard with your interrogation. Not in those exact words, but that was the drift."

"I did my job."

"Did you consider him a suspect?"

"I considered everybody a suspect until I could prove they weren't."

"Then he's no longer a suspect in your eyes?"

"He had opportunity and the ability, but no motive. And he has an ironclad alibi, though I never fully trust those, either."

"What about Connor Harrington?" she asked, not sure why he popped into her mind so quickly.

"He checked out, along with everybody else who I could link in any way with Elizabeth. I thought for a while we might have a credible online suspect. Turned out the supposedly college freshman she was hot and heavy with on a chat site was eighty-five and lives half-way around the world." He opened the door and they started down the hallway. "Where are you and Mr. Personality going to dinner?"

There was no way to miss the satire. Could it possibly be that Hunter was jealous of her going out with Pierre? If he was, the emotion was six years too late.

"Pierre mentioned a new French restaurant in the Garden District he wants to try."

"Nice. Somewhere you can swallow slimy snails."

"Says a man who sucks the heads on crawfish. Besides, I like escargot."

"Touché. I'll still need the name of the restaurant."

"I'll be with Pierre. I'm sure I won't need a bodyguard."

"Never trust a Frenchman."

"Your last name is Bergeron. You're French Creole."

"Exactly."

She shook her head at him and struggled to keep from smiling. He could always make her laugh—until the day he'd left her drowning in tears.

She quickened her pace and didn't slow down until they were back in Hunter's car.

Hunter picked Alyssa up on the way and let them out near the front door of the restaurant.

They requested a table in the back corner, so it would be quiet enough to talk.

"You can't imagine how glad I was to hear from you," Alyssa said as soon as the hostess walked away.

"Is anything wrong?" Helena asked.

"Possibly, and it concerns you."

Chapter Nine

The look on Alyssa's face emphasized her dismay. Helena had no idea what was coming next.

"Do you remember that tourist I told you about, the one whose resemblance to Elizabeth Grayson is absolutely uncanny?"

"Lacy?"

"Right. I had a dream about her last night."

"I'm not surprised, considering how upset you got when you met her."

"She wasn't by herself in the dream," Alyssa said. "You were with her."

"Definitely a nightmare," Helena said. "I haven't even met her."

"I'm sure it was you," Alyssa explained. "You and Lacy were running through a swampy area, tripping on underbrush and ducking tree branches."

"Why were we running?"

"To get away from the man who was chasing you."

"The same unidentifiable man with a knife?" Helena asked.

"Yes. The bloody hunting knife was identifiable. I'm not a medium," Alyssa insisted again. "But it sure seems like the universe is trying to tell me something."

Helena reached across the table and laid her hands on top of Alyssa's. They were icy cold.

"I can understand why you're upset, Alyssa, but this is likely your subconscious reacting to all the talk of the serial killer and seeing someone who reminded you of Elizabeth."

"I know that, but the nightmare seemed so real."

"Have you ever correctly predicted a dangerous event?"

"No. Except…"

"Except what?

"Twenty years ago when my six-year-old sister drowned in a neighbor's pool. I saw her floating under the water one night in a dream. She was smiling up at me peacefully. Six days later she was dead."

Chills ran up Helena's spine. She understood Alyssa's fear of dreams and her own imagination a lot better now. "Is that the only time you had a dangerous premonition that came true?"

"Pretty much. I mean I can frequently tell when a woman is cruising for trouble with a lover or job, but that has more to do with what she tells me and how she says it. That comes from years of practicing."

"I know you're worried about me and Lacy, but you've got to leave this in the hands of the police. I'm not in danger. Neither is Lacy. Hunter Bergeron and the NOPD are making certain of that."

"Intellectually, I know that," Alyssa agreed. "There are cops everywhere in the French Quarter. Uniformed and plainclothes. Walking. Driving cars. Some even on horseback. But…"

The waitress came to take their drink order.

"I'd like a glass of chardonnay," Helena said "How

about you, Alyssa? A little alcohol might calm those ragged nerves."

"Can't hurt," she said. "I'll have the same."

Alyssa didn't exactly relax, but after two glasses of wine, a large bowl of seafood gumbo with toasted baguette slices and an hour of avoiding any talk of the French Kiss Killer, they managed to find a few things to laugh about before they said their goodbyes.

In spite of her assurances to Alyssa, Helena found herself turning back more than once on the walk home to make sure she wasn't being stalked.

BY 6:30 THAT EVENING, Helena had showered, glossed her lips, applied a light coat of mascara and did what she could to tame her hair—which wasn't much in this kind of humidity.

She pulled her favorite, slightly revealing little black dress from the closet and slipped into it while her mind replayed her last two phone calls of the afternoon.

Thankfully, both were on her new, private phone and not from the phantom caller.

The first call had been from Beth Macon, the owner of the Boston gallery where Helena would start work in November. Beth had sold one of Helena's favorite paintings for seven thousand dollars.

The amount was dizzying to Helena and several thousand more than she'd ever made on one oil painting.

She'd celebrate with a glass of good champagne tonight with Pierre Benoit. At least they'd have something pleasant to discuss.

She was truly starting to dread their evening though it had little to do with Pierre and all to do with her. It would be hard to be congenial with a guy she barely knew when her life was trapped in a tangled, murderous web.

The second call had been from Beverly Ingram. She still had no inquiries about the vacant apartment. That was a first since the apartments had always been in such demand.

Location. Location. Location. In the heart of the French Quarter. A beautiful courtyard and tons of atmosphere. The shadow of a serial killer hanging over it like a shroud.

Helena unzipped the travel jewelry bag she'd brought with her and chose a favorite pair of silver hoop earrings. She slipped out of her comfortable flats and into a pair of red, strappy sandals with nosebleed heels.

A quick turn in front of the mirror and she decided she looked nice enough for an expensive French restaurant. Or for dinner at the Aquarelle Hotel. Considering that option immediately improved her level of enthusiasm.

She'd have a much better chance of running into Lacy and her friend there and get to see for herself this remarkable likeness that Alyssa kept talking about.

This was what her life had been reduced to. Rather than enjoying a nice dinner with a handsome attorney who might even be fun, she was more excited about a murder investigation and chasing someone else's nightmares.

She picked up her phone and made a quick call to Hunter. He answered on the first ring.

"What's up?"

"Change of plans."

"Dumping Pierre? Smart move."

"I'm not dumping Pierre. Change of restaurants.

We're going to the Aquarelle Hotel if I can get reservations at this late date."

"Ask for Connor Harrington. He'll get you in."

"I'll try that, and I'm telling you this because you asked, but I don't need or want someone to follow me around town. I promise we'll stay on the safe, beaten path."

"Got it. You're on your own. Have fun. Seriously, do have fun. You deserve a break."

He didn't sound a bit jealous this time. She should be happier about that.

PIERRE SEEMED TO resent her discarding his suggestion for a restaurant without checking with him first. She refused to feel too bad about it. After all, it was going to be her treat, though she expected him to protest that, at least half-heartedly.

He wouldn't win. This was a payback for a favor, not a date. Dates required more emotional capital than she could afford right now.

She glanced around the room as the hostess showed them to their table but didn't see anyone she recognized. Unlike the bar last night, the dinner bunch was a reserved group, mostly middle-aged or older.

A very attractive waitress stopped by their table. "Can I get you a cocktail?"

"I'll take a Glenlivet over ice," Pierre said.

Nice and pricey. He probably figured he earned it with his free legal advice. Perhaps he had.

"And for you?" the waitress addressed Helena.

"A glass of celebratory champagne," she said. "What do you have that's nice but reasonable?"

"We have a very good Moët & Chandon."

"Sounds perfect."

Pierre didn't ask what she was celebrating, and she'd just started to tell him about it when he started reading her the menu. When he got to the lobster and filet mignon, he paused.

"That sounds really good if they know how to grill a decent steak," he said.

"You can always send it back if it doesn't meet your expectations."

"Believe me, I've had to do that many times in other restaurants," he assured her. "What are you thinking about? The stuffed trout and the blackened redfish both look like good choices if you're not up for lobster."

"I'm thinking about the avocado and crab salad."

"A salad. That's it? You're celebrating inheriting a fortune in the city with the best food on the planet. You should spring for the most expensive item on the menu."

As he had.

"I inherited an estate but lost a beloved grandmother," Helena said. "That's not something I can celebrate."

"I never knew my grandparents, but I can see why you might feel that way," Pierre said. "How's the new job in Boston working out?" he asked, smartly changing the subject.

"Quite well, though I don't start until the first of November. With luck, I'll have sold the carriage house property by then."

"Then you'll be not only wealthy but beautiful and talented. Men will be falling at your feet. I can't imagine why some lucky guy hasn't grabbed you up before now."

"I'm not partial to men who grab."

He smiled. "I put that badly, but you know what I mean. Come to think of it, I'm good friends with Kelly Abby who owns a gallery in the Warehouse District.

She's recently divorced and thinking about moving to California. She might be putting her shop on the market. You could buy it and immerse yourself in the art world without leaving the New Orleans area. I'm sure you could sell a few paintings if you owned your own gallery. There's probably a lot less competition here."

As if she wasn't talented enough to compete with the best. Okay, maybe Hunter had a point after all. Pierre was a bit arrogant.

Conversation came easier after they finished their drinks. They were halfway through dinner when three stunning women, all who appeared to be in their early- to mid-twenties, walked into the restaurant. Few eyes didn't follow them as the hostess led them to a table near the back of the restaurant.

Helena saw the woman who must be Lacy and felt a tightening in her chest. Same hair color and style as Elizabeth. The same thin, willowy build. The shape of the nose was slightly different and Lacy's lips were not quite as full. Those were the types of minor details few except an artist would notice.

Not identical, but close. No wonder she'd thrown Alyssa for such a loop.

"That looks like three women out for trouble tonight," Pierre noted.

"They just look like young women out to have a good time on their vacation to me."

"What makes you think they're on vacation?"

"Just a hunch."

Only one of the three might be the undercover policewoman that Hunter had mentioned. If so, she was indisputably good at her job. Helena assumed she was the one who looked slightly older than the others, but she couldn't be sure. Only Lacy stood out.

She noticed Pierre staring at the women and kept expecting him to say something about the likeness. He didn't, though he had to notice. Perhaps he didn't want to upset Helena. Not mentioning it was upsetting her more.

Helena moved her salad around with her fork while Pierre finished chewing his last bite of steak. Finally, she gave in to temptation. "Does the blonde in the group you said were looking for trouble remind you of anyone?"

He wiped his mouth on the white linen napkin while he studied the young women. "Seems like I may have seen her before. Is she a movie star or one of those supermodels who pop up on all the magazine covers?"

"She's not famous that I know of. I just think she looks a lot like Elizabeth Grayson."

He shook his head. "Don't tell me you've already contracted the bug."

"What bug is that?"

"Serial killer addiction. It's been a little over six months since Elizabeth's murder and that's all anybody is talking about these days. As if we don't have shootings on a regular basis like every big city."

"It's different," she said, without explaining how.

"Sorry," Pierre said. "It's just getting to the point you can't have a conversation in this town that isn't saturated with fear and gore. Frankly, the girl in the sundress that barely covers her buns could be Elizabeth's body double and I wouldn't know it. I don't think I ever met Ella's great-niece but once."

But he had noticed the slightly daring length of Lacy's attire.

Helena was only half finished with her huge salad, but she'd lost her appetite. Pierre changed the subject to brag about a divorce case he was working on where he was destroying the philandering husband and his well-known attorney.

A few minutes later, Connor walked in. She watched him as he scanned the dining area, looking extremely pleased by the number of customers. He crossed the room and went straight to the table occupied by Lacy's party.

She could tell from the familiar way they greeted each other that they'd met before—only natural since he was an important member of the hotel management team.

The restaurant was almost full now. It was a safe guess that many of the people in the restaurant had witnessed the entrance of three women who were young, beautiful and sexy.

The elusive serial killer could be one of that number. He could be any man in this restaurant, or perhaps even a woman.

Sitting unnoticed. Following his victim and plotting her death or searching for his next victim.

Not murdering by choice but ordered to by some inner demon that ruled him.

Her insides quaked, and she couldn't wait to get out of there, even if all she had to look forward to was a possible phone call from a demented killer.

HELENA HAD JUST slipped out of her shoes and dress when her phone jingled. She reached for the phone. The text was from Hunter. Unwelcome but pleasurable anticipation zinged through her senses followed by a quick burst of dread that it might be bad news.

Target practice tomorrow morning. Pick you up at ten.

Wear something comfortable and shoes you can walk in. Slather on the sunscreen. I'll bring the mosquito spray.

Before she could answer or even digest that message, another text came through.

Doing this as a friend and not a cop, so you can turn me down if you want. I'd rather you didn't.

The thought of holding a gun made her nervous. The idea of pulling a trigger tightened knots in her stomach. Yet deep inside, she knew if it came to saving her life or someone else's she could do it.

There was a time when Hunter hadn't found even killing in self-defense palatable. Her thoughts traveled back to the night their relationship took its first nose-dive. The first time Hunter had killed someone in the line of duty.

He'd rung the doorbell here at the carriage house in the wee hours of the morning. She'd rushed to the door in her pajamas. One peek through the door's peephole and she'd known that something terrible had happened. She'd unlocked the door and swung it open.

Sweat had pooled at his armpits, staining the shirt of his uniform. The muscles in his jaw and neck were stretched thin, the lines in his face pulled tight, blue-corded veins seemed to stitch his face together. His eyes had a wild fire in them that she had never seen before.

Her initial fear had been that he'd been shot, but there was no blood. By that time, Mia had reached the door and had the composure to pull him inside.

It had taken several minutes for him to get the story out. He and his partner had taken a domestic abuse call at a small house near the edge of the Quarter. By the time they arrived, the argument appeared to be over. He was short on details as were the news reports the following day.

The bottom line was that two people ended up dead in an investigation he and his partner didn't take seriously enough. The woman was shot by her husband. The husband lost his life to a bullet from Hunter's gun.

That was the first night Hunter had spent the night on the same couch he'd slept on last night, once again leaving without waking her.

The next morning, he was suspended without pay pending further investigation of the incident. The day after he turned in his resignation and stopped by her house briefly to tell her that he was no longer with the police force.

She'd pleaded with him to talk things over with her, to let her help him get through this. She'd be there for him always. She loved and believed in him with all her heart.

He'd told her how much he loved her. She had faith things would all work out. Their wedding was two days away. The wedding that never happened.

Somehow, he must have gotten his act together over the following six years. He'd done it without her help.

She changed into a flowing lounging gown and stepped out on the balcony. There was no breeze, just layers of thick, stifling humidity.

The area was deserted except for three young men walking down the opposite side of the street, to-go cups in hand. She was about to step back inside when a car pulled up and stopped. A woman jumped out and slammed the door. She staggered away, obviously drunk or maybe drugged. The car followed at the same speed.

Panic hit as thoughts of the serial killer pounded inside Helena's head. "I'm calling 911," she screamed.

The woman stopped and looked up at Helena. "Stay out of this, bitch." Her voice was so slurred the words were barely distinguishable.

Helena got the message. The thanks for being a Good Samaritan. Still, Helena ducked back inside and retrieved her phone. When she got back to the balcony, the car was parked, and the young man was holding the woman's head as she threw up on the street.

When she finished, he pulled a handkerchief from his pocket and wiped her mouth. They stood there in the moonlight, his arms around her protectively, her head resting against his chest.

When she'd steadied, he led her back to the car and helped her inside. Before he climbed behind the wheel, he looked up at Helena and waved.

"Sorry about the noise," he called, in a voice that showed no sign of drunkenness. "Her twenty-first birthday. One too many hurricanes. I've got her. She'll be okay."

False alarm but the fear lingered. There was a killer out there somewhere. Someone who knew both her and Mia. Likely someone who lived in the French Quarter. Possibly someone they knew well and who had known Elizabeth Grayson well.

Someone the young victim would have trusted and gone with willingly. At least that seemed to be the most credible theory. Someone who had killed four times and gotten away with it.

Helena got ready for bed, but with little hope of falling asleep quickly. Counting sheep had never worked for her, so she looked up at the ceiling, watching the dancing shadows of the fan's whirling blades.

Eventually, her traitorous thoughts crept back to Hunter and the way he'd looked sleeping on her sofa last night. Impulsively, her hands slid down her abdomen and touched the hairy triangle between her legs.

She imagined they were Hunter's hands, exploring, finding all the right places to drive her crazy. Lost in desire, she brought herself to pleasure but knew that would never be enough.

She wasn't over him. That couldn't be clearer. She needed closure or she would never be able to move on and love again.

Even if it sent her into another spiral of heartbreak, they had to talk about the past.

Chapter Ten

Helena slipped a pair of worn sneakers into the bottom of her flowered tote bag. Hunter had specified comfortable shoes, so she'd be prepared if she needed them. In the meantime, her cute flat-heel sandals with ties at the ankles did great things for her ankles and thighs.

Her white shorts, off-the-shoulder teal-colored top and reliable silver hoop earrings finished the look.

What was she thinking? The last thing she wanted was to incite a seduction scene.

She checked her closet and pulled out a pair of loose-fitting cargo pants and an olive green cotton T-shirt that looked far more appropriate for shooting pistols or shotguns or whatever type of weapon Hunter had in mind.

The gate buzzer sounded as she finished dressing. She glanced at the clock. Only 9:30. Too early for Hunter. Besides, he knew the code. This is where cameras at the gate would come in handy.

"Can I help you?"

"Hi. It's Robicheaux here. Did I catch you at a bad time?"

"Not exactly, but I'm expecting Hunter any minute."

"We can make this quick. All I need is about ten minutes of your time to go over some modifications my tech team suggested. Not that I'm pushing, but I want you to have all the options before you make a final decision."

"Okay. I'll buzz you in."

He was at her door in minutes.

She opened it and welcomed him inside. Once again, there was no escaping his incredible good looks and masculinity. Odd that she was entirely aware of that and yet felt none of the heated, heart-stopping attraction she felt when Hunter stepped into a room.

"Is that coffee I smell?" Romeo asked.

"It is. Would you like a cup?"

"Wouldn't turn it down."

He followed her back to the kitchen. While she filled his cup, he spread the revised notes and blueprints on the table.

"I hear you and Hunter are going down to bayou country today."

"He only mentioned shooting lessons to me. I'm pretty sure it's a losing cause. I've never even held a gun and I'm not enthused about starting now."

"You may change your mind once you get the hang of it. It can be addictive. Even if you don't like shooting, you are in for a real treat. You'll love Eulalie."

"Is that a person?"

"Barker's mama. When her husband died, she moved back to her old family home on a bayou southwest of town. She runs a B and B and gives swamp tours."

"She does sound fascinating," Helena agreed. "At least the day won't be a total loss."

"If you get tired of paper plate targets or tin cans, you can shoot a water moccasin or two."

"Now I'm excited. *Not.*"

"You should get Hunter to take you exploring in one

of Eulalie's pirogues. Elizabeth Grayson's crime scene is just a short ride down the bayou from the B and B."

This whole shooting idea sounded more bizarre by the minute. Why would Hunter take her anywhere near the murder scene? Surely there were shooting ranges right here in town.

"Speaking of Elizabeth, did her killer contact you again last night?" Robicheaux asked.

"How do you know about the first call? I thought that was highly confidential."

"I'm in the official loop. After the French Kiss Killer's third victim was found, Hunter got permission to call me in as a volunteer adviser to the task force."

"I didn't realize that."

"Yep. So far, I've been very little help. The killer seems to be dealing the cards and we're trying to figure out how to play them. The guy's smart. No one's denying that."

Robicheaux went over the modifications with her while he finished his coffee.

"Any questions?" he asked.

"Not at the moment."

"In that case I've probably taken up enough of your time this morning. Enjoy the rest of your day with Hunter. Who knows when he'll get another day off? I got a hunch the infamous serial killer is puckering up for his next kiss of death."

HUNTER ARRIVED SHORTLY after Robicheaux left. She still thought it strange they were driving out of the city for target practice when he didn't even have time to eat or sleep on a regular basis.

The good news was that Hunter seemed more relaxed on the ride down to Eulalie's than he had since she met him. This might turn into the perfect time and place to seek closure, although any serious reckoning about their past would complicate working with him on the killer's phone calls.

They crossed the Crescent City Connection, the wide cantilever bridge that separated New Orleans from the area known as the Westbank. Forty minutes later, they turned onto a gravel road and she spotted a wooden sign that read Eulalie's Swamp Tours and B and B with an arrow that pointed to the left.

Hunter took the first quick left next to three wooden mailboxes perched atop rusting metal posts.

"It's difficult to believe anyone lives in an area this isolated, much less runs a business."

"Out-of-state tourists love this kind of atmosphere for a swamp tour. But don't fret. The house is comfortable and once you taste Eulalie's cooking, you'll never want to leave."

"It sounds as if you come out here often."

"Every chance I get, which hasn't been much lately. The only reason I can make it today is that my supervisor ordered me to take a day off. Claims I'm going to collapse in the middle of a shoot-out if I don't get some sleep."

"Which you're not getting."

"Actually, the sun got up before I did this morning. Haven't slept that late in weeks."

"Are your long hours tied to the serial killer investigation?"

"Not entirely. I still have to take my share of the department's homicide cases. But dealing with a serial killer who seems to schedule his strikes by the calendar has upped the urgency."

Which meant the odds were good that the killer

might contact Helena again soon. For as long as the call lasted, discovering a clue to the killer's identity would depend solely on Helena's ability to guide the conversation. She'd never backed away from a pressure situation, but neither had she ever felt this unqualified to make the right decisions.

She tried to ease the enormity of that responsibility by studying the passing landscape. There was a scattering of trees, mostly cypress, and huge clumps of tall grasses in various shades of green. Bluebird and purple martin houses were plentiful. Large blackbirds sat on telephone wires. Several buzzards circled an area about fifty yards to the west.

They stopped at a fork in the hard dirt road. Signs indicated one way for the swamp tour and another for the B and B check-in. Hunter stayed left following the arrow to the B and B. Helena's mind slipped into artistic mode and began to frame a painting in her mind. A young woman walking through the tall grass. The woman would be small, the focus on the isolation. Deep shadows. Dark clouds.

A house came into view, breaking her concentration.

It was a small clapboard structure, set on stilts, with a railed veranda that circled the building. A set of wooden steps led to the covered porch.

"This doesn't look big enough to be a B and B."

"That's just the house," Hunter explained. "There are five small fishing cabins on the back of her property."

"Then the house is just where Euralie lives?"

"Only in part of it. She rents the two bedrooms and a shared bath on the back of the house. Her living quarters are the front half of the house. She claims she likes a cozy space."

Hunter followed the road to a graveled parking area

to the left of the house. A big yellow mutt and a smaller black retriever came running to meet them from the far side of the porch. Hunter hunched over to greet and pet them. They responded with excessive licks and tail wagging.

"This is Captain," Hunter said, giving the yellow mutt a good ear scratching. "And the black beauty here is Bailey."

Helena took to the dogs instantly but quickly realized that she'd never seen Hunter interact with any kind of pet before. Another heartwarming side of him she didn't need to discover right now.

When their fingers accidentally tangled in Captain's long hair, a heated zing vibrated through her.

She pulled away and hurried to the steps that led to the veranda. Hunter followed. The dogs went running off again. By the time they reached the porch, Eulalie was waiting for them.

She fell into Hunter's arms for a warm bear hug before she even bothered to look at Helena.

She looked younger than Helena had expected, around midfifties she'd guess. That made sense. Cory Barker was likely only a few years older than Helena.

Eulalie had an athletic build and long brown hair that she wore pulled back in a ponytail. She was dressed in a lightweight denim shirt over khaki trousers and sneakers, as if ready to take off on one of her swamp tours at a minute's notice.

No makeup but a nice tan and a great smile. She turned and flashed it in Helena's direction.

"Who's the *jolie femme*?" Eulalie asked.

"This is Helena Cosworth," Hunter said.

"Are you kin to Mia Cosworth?" Eulalie asked, switching easily from the Cajun expression for "pretty lady" back to English. Helena imagined the Cajun French that seemed to come so naturally to Eulalie was a hit with the tourists.

"Yes. Mia was my grandmother. Did you know her?"

"I never met her, but I saw her on TV when she was raising money to help catch that French Kiss maniac. I was so impressed with what she was doing to help, I made a small donation myself."

"I don't know what you're cooking," Hunter said, "but if it's half as good as it smells, it'll be wonderful."

Helena knew he was trying to change the subject for her benefit. He wouldn't have known that Robicheaux had already told him how close they were to the crime scene. His effort to control the conversation didn't faze their hostess.

"Bad enough he killed that pretty young teenager, but he did it on my stomping grounds. Tell you one thing," Eulalie said, continuing her rant. "If I ever get my hands on that scum, he'll rue the day he ever came my way. I wouldn't feed him to the gators, though. They're too good for him."

"I agree," Helena said. And she had zero affinity for alligators.

"I was sure sorry to hear about your grandmother's fall," Eulalie said. "She looked in perfect health on TV and too young to be your grandmother."

"Thank you. I still miss her very much, but she had a good life, full of passion and joy. She'd be the first to tell you that."

"Sounds like you inherited her good spirit." Eulalie opened the screen door and motioned them inside. "Now how are you two connected? Cory said Hunter was bringing someone out to use the driving range today, but he didn't mention it was a female."

"We're old friends," Hunter said, as he followed Helena and Eulalie inside.

Old friends was definitely not how Helena would have described them.

"Lunch won't be ready until about twelve, but I got a mess of greens cooking on the stovetop and a pineapple-coconut cake baking in the oven. You should see the way Hunter can attack one of my cakes."

"I'm sure he can and will," Helena said, "but I hope you didn't go to all that trouble for us."

"Of course she did," Hunter teased. "And a good thing, too. If I showed up to an empty table, I'd swear I was no longer Eulalie's best beau."

"Listen at you go on. You know I don't play favorites with my guys. Spoil every one of you the same."

"How many do you have to spoil?" Helena asked.

"Well, it's mostly Romeo and Hunter here who Barker brings around, but he sometimes brings other buddies out here to shoot or fish. Now you two just make yourself at home while I stir up a fresh skillet of corn bread. Can't have greens without corn bread."

"Take your time," Hunter said. "In fact, I was thinking Helena and I could get in a little target practice before we stuff ourselves on your home cooking."

"You go right ahead. You know where everything is. Grab yourself a soft drink to take with you. You know where I keep them. It will get hot fast in the sun. I'll be tickled pink when that cool front they keep promising finally gets here."

Helena nodded. "I can't wait for that even if it does mean thundershowers."

"She's talking Louisiana cool, not Boston cool," Hunter said. "Don't get too excited or bother to put your shorts away." He walked to the door and called back to Eulalie. "Be back in about an hour."

Helena followed him down the outside steps. They retrieved their soft drinks from a large black refrigerator just behind the red Jeep that was parked beneath the stilted house. The covered area seemed as much a catchall as a place to park.

There was also a pile of bricks, several large covered containers and a tire swing—rope attached—just waiting for a tree and a kid.

Hunter looked at her feet. "I hope you have some other shoes in that tote bag you brought with you."

"I have a pair of well-worn sneakers." She reached into her tote and pulled them out.

Hunter looked dubious. "I doubt those will keep your feet totally dry. Why not grab a pair of boots—or swamp stompers as they're known around here—from that large basket by the fridge. They're loaners for tourists who show up unprepared."

"Whatever you say, marksman."

"But shake them out first to make sure there's no spiders or scorpions waiting inside."

"On second thought, I'll just go barefoot." She didn't, of course. She could be walking through worse—if there was worse.

Helena checked out Hunter's footwear, hiking boots that could likely handle the worst of the swamp. She retrieved her sunglasses from the car while Hunter picked up his backpack and tossed it over his shoulders.

She walked beside him down a worn path that cut around the side of the house and off to the right. A few yards farther and the damp earth became even more soggy. She was thankful for the boots when the mire grew ankle deep in some spots. A fifteen-minute walk and they reached Cory Barker's famous shooting range. It exceeded her expectations.

"This actually is a gun range," she said.

"What did you think it would be?"

"Beer cans lining a row of fence posts."

"We started with not much more than that," Hunter admitted. "A couple of years ago, we pooled our monetary resources to upgrade a notch or two. Robicheaux put up most of the cash. He's making a killing in the security business."

"Yet he still volunteers to work with your task force?"

"Police work gets in your blood and he made a name for himself while with the FBI. He's even written a very successful book on getting into the mind of a serial killer. He's tried several times to get me to leave the force and go into business with him."

"Did you consider it?"

Hunter placed his backpack on a long cement table. His expression was strangely brooding, the depths of his gaze seeming to swallow her.

"It took years too long, but I'm finally in a place where I feel comfortable in my own skin," Hunter said. "I like where I am. I fit into this world. I feel like what I do makes a difference."

Hunter turned away quickly as if he'd said more than he meant to.

He lifted a petite, solid black pistol from his bag. It had to be for her, but she couldn't leave things this way. She might not like the answer to her question, but she had to ask it.

"Was needing to find yourself the reason you ran out on me, Hunter?"

Chapter Eleven

Hunter turned away and cursed silently. He'd said too much. He'd been afraid he'd have a weak moment like this if he spent too much time alone with Helena.

"This isn't the best time to talk about that."

"Why not? There's certainly no one around to hear it."

"The investigation is consuming me and delving into old emotions could put it and you in danger." That was neither an exaggeration nor a lie. But it was an evasion and he doubted she'd settle for that.

"I can take the truth, Hunter. I'm not looking for another chance with you or even an apology for the way you left. I just need to know why. Really why. Not the pathetic excuse that you gave about not being able to go through with the wedding."

He leaned against the shooting rest and searched his mind for the right words.

"I wasn't lying to you back then, Helena. Walking out was the hardest thing I've ever done, but I had too many inner demons I needed to deal with before I could be a decent husband. Marrying you then wouldn't have been fair to you."

"Do you think giving up on us without discussing

those demons was fair to me? Was making me feel like our whole relationship was fake fair to me?"

He could hear the building anger in her voice, but it was tinged with sadness. He deserved the anger, but he couldn't let her turn on him now. Her safety was at stake.

"The decisions I made had left an innocent woman dead and a young boy an orphan. I had to find a way to live with that before I could face myself much less have anything worthwhile to offer you."

"It was self-defense, Hunter. The police cleared you of everything, only by then you'd resigned and left the area. Just one more question, Hunter."

He nodded, anxiety riding him hard as he dreaded whatever was coming next.

"Why did you bring me here today? That can't be a typical detective responsibility. Why did you go to the trouble to hook me up with Robicheaux and his security firm? We both know what we had died years ago, so why pretend like there's something special between us now?"

A relationship that died six years ago. That made it damn clear how she felt.

He reached for her hands and was shocked when she didn't pull away. "I care about you, Helena. I care a lot. I never stopped caring, but right now the most important thing is keeping you safe."

"You never called," Helena said. "In six years, you never once called. That doesn't sound like caring to me."

"I called Mia several times to ask about you. She said I'd hurt you enough. You'd moved on and the best thing I could do for you was to stay out of your life."

"And you just took her word for that?"

"It made sense. I was stationed in Afghanistan. I watched friends die and worse. I wasn't sure I would get out of there alive. I had nothing to offer you. By the time I moved back to New Orleans, Mia assured me that you were a success and the last thing you needed was me raking up the past. I did what I believed was best for you."

When Helena looked up, her eyes were moist. "You and Mia were probably right. You broke my heart. I'm not sure there's enough of it left to try again even if we dared risk a second chance."

She wiped a tear from her cheek with the back of her hand. "I won't lie. There's still some chemistry between us but I don't know if I can ever love and trust you the way I did back then."

"And that's why all I'm asking now is that you let me keep you safe," he assured her. "Now, are you ready to learn how to use that pistol?"

"No, and I probably never will be, but since we're here, I'll give it a try."

He ached to take her in his arms, but she was right. They'd both gone through a lot in the past six years. They lived in two different worlds now and he couldn't see himself fitting into hers. One thing he knew for certain. He never wanted to fail her again.

HELENA FELT AS if she were caught in a whirlwind of emotions, so disoriented that she had no idea where she was going or why. She'd been searching for closure. Instead she'd been sucked inside an altered reality that bounced wildly in every direction.

She had no doubts about the strength of her sexual attraction to Hunter. Any lingering uncertainty disappeared the night he'd fallen asleep on her sofa. Her reactions to his smile, his touch, the sound of his voice made her dizzy with desire.

That had been true from the first time she'd ever laid eyes on him. True for her, but apparently not for him. Did she dare open her heart to him again?

If killing a man in self-defense made him run from his commitment to her, how could she trust that wouldn't happen again? He was still a cop. Was serving in the Marines enough to desensitize him to killing? If so, was that a good development?

If she let things go too far, if she made love to him, would she lose all ability to make anything close to a rational decision about their relationship? About their future?

Did she want to give up a new life in Boston to stay here with him? She definitely couldn't see him moving to Boston with her. He'd made it clear, he fit right here.

She shouldn't even be thinking about that. It was premature. They'd only just reconnected. But if she sold the house and moved to Boston, would she be giving up any chance of finding out if they could overcome the past and find real love again?

She struggled to push those questions aside and focus on learning to handle the pistol that felt so foreign in her hand.

Her shooting skills showed no marked improvement over the following hour. She was more than relieved when Hunter suggested they'd had enough practice for one day.

Eulalie welcomed them back with her contagious smile and questions about their target practice. "If a ten-foot target is two feet away, I can probably hit it," Helena said.

"She was better than that. She was even opening her

eyes when she pulled the trigger by the time we finished," Hunter teased.

"It takes a while to get comfortable with any kind of weapon," Eulalie assured her. "You'll get the hang of it. Having respect for a weapon is smart."

"Actually, she did exceptionally well for someone who'd never held a weapon before," Hunter bragged.

"And someone who hopes to never shoot one again." Helena walked over to where Eulalie was lifting catfish fillets from the skillet of hot grease.

"That looks and smells great," she said, eager to change the conversation from guns to food. "What can I do to help?"

"You can put some ice in the glasses for tea if you want?"

"I'd love to."

"Hunter, would you check that corn bread? It should be done."

"I'll be happy to." He opened the oven. "If it's black on top, does that mean it's ready?"

Eulalie looked over his shoulder and checked for herself. "That's golden brown and perfect. You mess with me, I'll take this spatula to your bottom and you know it."

"You can't talk that way to law enforcement."

"You just try me."

They were all laughing by the time the food was on the table. Eulalie had them bow for grace and then Hunter wasted no time digging in.

There wasn't much talking until they were all stuffed. They finished the meal off with cake that was as moist and delicious as any Helena had ever tasted. If she ate like this every day instead of her usual lunch salad she'd have to get longer brushes to reach her easel.

"You women have had a busy morning," Hunter said. "I'll do the gentlemanly thing and clean up the kitchen while you two go relax or take care of the swamp tour business if needed."

"I don't have but one tour scheduled this afternoon and my helper Evan is handling that. Won't take me but a minute to clean up the kitchen, and if you get more than one person working in that tiny space we'll be bumping into each other."

"And I'm only one person," Hunter said, "so that's why my offer stands."

"I have a better idea," Eulalie insisted. "You should show Helena around the area. Take the pirogue and give her a personal tour."

Hunter started stacking the dessert plates. "Have you ever been on a swamp tour, Helena?"

"Not since I was about ten years old when Mia thought it would be a capital idea. It wasn't. The tour guide got out of the boat, waded to a patch of dry land and picked up a baby alligator. He got back on the boat and handed it to me. I had nightmares for years about the mother alligator coming after me."

"I leave the gators alone," Eulalie said. "They don't bother me. I don't go getting them all riled up. You can trust Hunter to keep you safe. Cory's been bringing Romeo and Hunter up here to fish and hunt for years."

Robicheaux's words came to mind. At the time, Helena had thought visiting the bayou near where Elizabeth had been killed was the last thing she'd want to do this afternoon. Now the idea intrigued her.

She needed to know as much about Elizabeth's killer as she could before he called again. The more she knew, the better her chance at helping to bring him down.

"A personal tour sounds like a good idea if Hunter has time."

"Are you sure?" Hunter questioned. "We'll likely see an alligator or several."

"Alligators won't bother you," Eulalie said. "They aren't aggressive unless you try to hurt them or their babies."

"Which I definitely won't do," Helena said.

"All right then," Hunter said. "If you're game, I'm in."

The bayou was a fifteen-minute walk, due south from the B and B. Again, she tugged on the swamp stompers.

Within five minutes, she was thankful for them no matter how unbecoming they were. The earth became squishy beneath her feet. A few yards more and an inch or two of standing water greeted every footfall.

The feeling of isolation was overpowering. Helena spooked at every rustle of the tall grasses and the branches above her. She imagined slithering snakes, rats, giant spiders or even scorpions crawling inside her boots or up the legs of her trousers.

Finally, they approached the muddy banks of the murky bayou. The waterway was wider than she expected, a good fifteen feet across at this point. She had no idea how deep it was since the dark murkiness of the water prevented her from seeing anything below the surface.

Scrawny cypress trees canopied the slow-moving water. Crows cawed as if warning they were invading their space. She startled a stately gray heron who took flight.

Helena scanned the area for a pirogue without luck. She did see what was left of a gray, deteriorating cabin with a partly missing tin roof a few yards down the bayou. It had apparently once rested on stilts, but it was leaning so badly now that the one weathered chair that leaned against the front wall looked as if it would collapse if sat in.

Helena took a couple of quick steps to catch up with Hunter. "Please tell me no one lives in that disaster."

"No, not for years, anyway. It's survived strictly from Eulalie's occasional intervention."

"Why would Eulalie want to save it?"

"It's a hit with the tourists, especially the youngsters. They get excited when she has one of her workers dress in a pair of ripped and faded overalls and sit in that warped chair. Her handy man Joe Bob is especially popular. His wiry white beard and corncob pipe don't hurt any, either. He waves, and the tourists snap pictures like crazy."

"Sounds like a production."

"Like nothing you can imagine," Hunter said. "When Eulalie starts telling those old Cajun tales about growing up on the bayou and wrestling alligators with her grandpa, she has them in the palm of her hand. Plus, she always locates a few alligators for them to take pictures of so no one leaves disappointed. It's hard to be out here very long without spotting a gator."

"In that situation, I prefer disappointment." She scanned the area again. "Where is the pirogue you talked about?"

"Just a few feet away." Hunter disappeared into a cluster of thick brush and cypress trees. Once he was out of sight, an eerie fear gripped her, and she was almost sorry she'd agreed to this.

And yet if the theory was correct, Elizabeth Grayson

had willingly come with a killer who'd brought her to a scene much like this one.

Or had she been forced here, screaming for help with no one to hear her, by the monster who was now trolling Helena by phone?

Helena struggled to push that image from her mind as Hunter approached with a narrow, flat boat on his back.

"Let me help you with that," she called.

"No need. It's not heavy, just awkward."

"Is it safe to leave a pirogue just stashed in the swamp?"

"It can't walk off by itself, especially when it's chained and locked to the trunk of the biggest tree around here. Not likely to get stolen, anyway. If you got here by bayou as most do, you have your own boat."

"Makes sense. What can I do to help?"

"Hold this rope so the dang thing doesn't go floating off without us while I get the pole and paddles."

Minutes later, they were floating deeper into a world that a lot of Louisianans had only seen in pictures and movies.

"Glad you suggested this," Hunter said. "No place is as soothing and peaceful as this. Listen to those tree frogs. That's as calming a serenade as you can get in any concert hall."

Soothing and peaceful were not the words she would have chosen, but it felt far less intimidating with Hunter so near.

A snowy white egret looked up from its fishing stance on the bank of the bayou and watched them float slowly by. The only time Hunter used a paddle was to steer them away from an occasional clump of vegetation that clogged part of the waterway.

They came to a fork, a wider stream of water opening up to their right. Hunter steered the pirogue straight ahead.

"How do you keep from getting lost out here?"

"I've been down here enough with Barker that I could probably navigate these waters in my sleep."

"What do you do down here?"

"Duck hunting is great in these parts. Good fishing, too, if you know where to go. Frogging is fun and good eating."

A splash to her left made her jump. She turned to see a large dog-sized rodent join a few buddies in the water."

Helena shuddered. "Are those rats?"

"Nutria, but basically they are large rodents. They're a real nuisance in these parts. They tear up the banks and cause unnecessary erosion."

"Don't the alligators eat them?"

"Yep and so do some people—no one I know, but a few adventurous souls."

Helena gagged. "I doubt I could ever eat again if I looked down and saw one of those giant rats on my plate."

"I'm with you. Check out the snake slithering across the water in front of us."

She sucked in a gulp of muggy air. The snake was at least five feet long and black or at least it looked dark-colored in the water.

"Please give it lots of room," she said.

"That's just a water snake. It won't hurt you. You gotta watch out for water moccasins, though. They make terrible company."

"Thanks for sharing that with me."

"Just pointing out the facts. No need to worry when I'm around. I do know how to shoot."

"Do you have a gun with you now?"

"Unless I'm asleep or making love, I'm toting. Even then the weapon is within arm's reach. It goes with the job."

Helena felt something on her neck and swatted a large mosquito.

"Had enough?" Hunter asked.

She'd had more than enough, but she wasn't quite ready to go back. "Is this near the place where Elizabeth was killed?"

Hunter paddled them past the snake without even glancing at it. "So that's why you wanted to come out here. Sometimes Romeo talks too much."

"I get phone calls from a serial killer, Hunter. I think I can handle a crime scene."

"The two don't actually equate, but fair enough. Evidence indicates Elizabeth was killed and dragged into the bayou about ten minutes from here by boat."

"Then she didn't drown?"

"Are you sure you want to hear the gory details?"

"I'm a big girl. I can handle the truth, I think. Stop if I start to lose my lunch."

"The body was found not far away, tangled in the roots of cypress trees, but according to forensics she was already dead from slash wounds on her chest before she landed in the water."

"Were all four of his victims killed near here?"

"No. Just Elizabeth. The others were killed in Algiers swamps."

"Why do you think he changed his crime scene for Elizabeth?"

"We're not sure, but the killer made several changes in his modus operandi for Elizabeth. Look, I know you're tough, Helena, but I don't think we should take this conversation any further. What sounds like objective facts in the middle of the day can become fodder for nightmares when the sun goes down."

"I'm merely trying to get a handle on what my caller is truly capable of doing. It's hard to believe a man could function and pass himself off as human in the real world with that much evil in his heart."

"The bright side of all of this is that most people are truly good and have never even considered what it would be like to take someone's life."

"Yes, but I'm starting to understand how Mia became so fascinated by the workings of a serial killer's mind."

"Your grandmother had amazing insight. I swear she might have figured out who the killer was if she'd gotten the chance to talk to him a few more times."

"Don't count on that happening with me."

"I'm not."

Hunter paddled for a few more minutes before taking a fork to the left. He laid his paddle beneath the seat and took out the long pole to help guide him through some heavy vegetation that almost totally clogged the waterway.

"The crime scene is just to your right. Take a quick look while I turn the pirogue around so that we can start back."

"I don't see any crime scene tape."

"It's been six months and several tropical storms ago."

"Then how can you be sure this is the exact location? Everything we've passed seems almost the same to me."

"There are lots of landmarks. You just have to know what to look for."

He pointed to a garden of cypress trees. "That bald cypress is one of the tallest trees in this area. If you look in the top branches, you'll see the nest of a Southern bald eagle."

"You're right. I see it."

"What you can't see from the water is that there is an old logging road that runs almost to the bayou. We believe that the killer may have brought her here via that road instead of by boat. Easy in, easy out, for him."

"If he drove down here, couldn't you match tire tread?"

"We might have garnered a clue if we'd gotten here before heavy rains washed them all away."

The murky water rippled as Hunter slid the paddle beneath the surface and began to turn the small pirogue around. This time she didn't object.

Before they reached the B and B, Hunter got a call that he was needed back at the precinct ASAP.

There had been a foiled abduction in broad daylight in the French Quarter.

The killer may have attempted to strike again.

Chapter Twelve

Hunter dropped Helena off at home and went directly to the hospital where Cory Barker was waiting for the medical staff's permission to question today's victim. He found Barker in the hospital cafeteria nursing a cup of coffee.

"Still waiting, huh?"

"Yep. The nurse has my cell phone number and she promised to text me the second the doc says I can talk to his patient—Celeste Fountain. In the meantime, I decided to come down here, feed my need for caffeine and touch base with the crew handling the even stickier parts of the investigation—like locating the suspect."

"I talked to Lane Crosby on the way here," Hunter said. "He's questioning the two men who came to her rescue. He says the way they describe it, this was a purse snatching that went badly when she fought back."

Barker sipped his coffee from a disposable cup. "Coffee's out of a machine since the cafeteria's not open for dinner yet, but it's not too bad. Want me to grab you a cup?"

"Not yet. What's your take on the situation?"

"I figure we'll have the suspect in jail within twenty-four hours, but he's not the French Kiss Killer unless he's having a mental breakdown. Every move in today's attack was careless or downright stupid."

Hunter nodded. "Which is why we need to arrest today's would-be abductor as soon as possible and keep the hype that he might be the French Kiss Killer to a minimum."

"You're right," Barker agreed. "But wouldn't it be a roaring shocker if it turned out he was our guy?"

"Yep," Hunter said. "Be nice if I won the lottery tonight, too, but I won't start spending my winnings just yet."

Barker got a text from the nurse and the two of them headed to Celeste Fountain's third-floor hospital room. The doctor was standing outside her door to greet them. He introduced himself, then pulled off his glasses and slipped them into the pocket of his white coat.

"Mrs. Fountain has only minor injuries, a few bruises and scratches on her hands and knees. Nonetheless, she has been through a very traumatic experience this afternoon. She's convinced that she barely escaped a serial killer."

"We have no evidence of the serial killer aspect," Barker said. "But witnesses verify she was attacked in a public parking lot by an unknown assailant."

Hunter took a step in the direction of Celeste Fountain's room. "The most important thing right now is for us to get a description of the suspect so we can get him off the streets."

"She understands that," the doctor said. "Just don't push her too hard."

"Definitely not," Barker said.

The doctor left. The nurse ushered them into the victim's room and introduced them. The first thing Hunter noted was that Celeste looked nothing like Elizabeth or any of the other victims attributed to the serial killer.

Her hair was straight and coal black. She appeared slightly overweight and wore excessive makeup especially around her eyes.

Barker pulled a hand-size recorder from his pocket. "Do you mind if I record our conversation? I have a rotten memory and worse handwriting."

"I want to be recorded," Celeste said. "I have important things to say." She pushed a button and raised her bed until she was in a sitting position. "Are you going to read me my rights?"

An odd question. "We don't need to," Hunter explained. "You're the victim and we don't suspect you of doing anything wrong."

"I didn't," Celeste said. "I was just getting out of my car to go to my job."

"Where do you work?" Hunter asked.

"Well, I wasn't exactly going to my job. I got fired last week. I was going to look for a new job. I heard the Aquarelle Hotel was looking for waitresses and I've had lots of experience at that."

"For the record, can you give us your name, age, address and phone number?" Baker said.

She did. She was twenty-eight, divorced, the mother of a three-year old daughter who was currently in the father's custody. She lived in Gretna, a small town in the Westbank area.

"Take your time and tell us exactly what happened," Hunter said.

The gist of her explanation was that she had just parked and was getting out of her car when a slow-moving black sedan drove past her. She thought nothing of it since she figured he was looking for a parking space.

"Did you get a good look at the driver when he drove by?"

"Not the first time, but I saw plenty of him when he drove by again, that time at a crawl. He stopped right by me and lowered his window a crack like he had something to ask me.

"I couldn't hear what he said, so I approached his car."

Barker stepped over to the head of her bed. "What happened then?"

"First thing I knew, he jumped out of the car and grabbed me. I started screaming for help and the driver pulled a large black gun. He aimed it at me and told me to shut up or I was a dead woman."

This was the first Hunter had heard that a gun was involved. "What did you do?"

"I started kicking and scratching at his arms and face like a wildcat. I was scared but I'm no pushover. If he was going to shoot me, he'd have to do it in that busy parking lot."

"Did he try to force you into the car?"

"He didn't have time. Two young men heard the commotion and came running. Dirty coward saw them and shoved me hard to the concrete. Miracle he didn't run over me."

"Did the attacker take your handbag?"

"He tried when he shoved me to the ground. Like I said, I put up a fight."

"Describe the attacker for us," Hunter said. "Give us as much information as possible. Take your time."

Her description was detailed. She said he was about the same height as Hunter, which would have made the man about six-two. Around a hundred and eighty pounds. He had spiky black hair and was wearing ripped jeans.

Barker asked the right questions to keep her going. If her description was dead-on, it shouldn't be hard to identify her attacker from a mug shot.

"I'm the one who saw him best," Celeste said. "Those guys ran him off, but they didn't get a good look at him. You can't trust what they say."

"You are a great help," Hunter assured her.

"If you catch him, does that mean I get the money?"

"What money is that?" Barker asked.

"That hundred thousand dollars I'm supposed to get for leading you to that Kiss Killer or whatever you call him. It'll go to me, won't it? They said it on TV. A hundred thousand dollars to anybody who helped them catch the killer. They can't lie on TV."

That was a new one to Hunter. "You did a brave thing to fight off your attacker," Hunter said, choosing his words carefully. "We haven't arrested anyone yet, but if that guy you fought off turns out to be the serial killer, I figure you're entitled to at least some of that money."

"*All* of that money," Celeste emphasized.

This wasn't an argument he could win. "Do you think you can pick him out of a lineup?"

"I'd know that creep if I saw him coming from a block away."

They stayed with her another thirty minutes. Hunter had no doubt they'd apprehend her abductor and zero confidence he would be their French Kiss Killer.

But he'd been wrong before.

HELENA SAT ON her balcony in one the two semi-COMFORTABLE CHAIRS THAT went with a bistro set Mia had bought for her years ago. She sipped her white wine while her mind struggled with the shooting range conversation she'd had with Hunter.

Six years was a long time. So long, she'd almost convinced herself she'd moved on. She'd survived the heartache and become stronger and wiser for it.

In many ways, she had moved on. She'd finished her education, spent a year in France studying under an elite watercolorist. She'd taught a fine art class at Boston U and worked as a museum curator in a famous museum.

Now she'd sold a painting for seven thousand dollars. That was next to nothing compared to the estate that Mia had left her, but it had special meaning. Someone thought her painting was worth it and wanted it to hang in their house or office.

But no matter what strides she'd made, she'd never wanted a man more than she wanted Hunter. She couldn't imagine that she ever could.

Passion raged inside her, a hunger for him so strong she felt it in every cell of her being. If anything, it was stronger than it had been before he'd run out on her.

She'd been caught up in a dream of forever with Hunter. He'd been twenty-five then, the same age she was now. A cocky young cop who took her breath away the first time she saw him patrolling their neighborhood.

She and her college friends blatantly flirted with him while he tried to avoid them like any good cop would. Eventually the chemistry overpowered him, too, and he agreed to go with her to an art show at Tulane where she was a freshman.

Back then there had been no dreams of making it big in the art world. No thoughts of Boston. Her idea of success had been showing her work at local galleries and teaching art at the high school level.

She still loved New Orleans. The money from the estate was enough to open her own gallery, though it wouldn't have the clout of the gallery she'd be working for in Boston.

Would she be willing to give up the new dream to take a chance on a man who'd walked out on her once before? Would she ever regain the trust she'd lost when he'd dumped her with no credible explanation for his leaving?

A piercing ring interrupted her troubling thoughts. It was her wiretapped phone, which meant it was Elizabeth's killer again. She shuddered, then jumped from her chair and rushed into the bedroom to answer it.

"Hello."

"Hello, my sweet."

The childish voice ripped through her.

"I guess you've already heard. Some idiot made a huge mistake. Tried to steal my thunder. He'll pay for that."

"Who made a mistake?"

"A nobody in a parking lot. Doesn't matter except he screwed up my timing with his foolish behavior. It's full speed ahead now. You should kiss Hunter goodbye."

"How did…"

The connection broke.

An icy chill settled bone deep as the madman's confusing words echoed in her brain.

Was he calling Hunter an idiot? Was he planning to kill him? Why else would he say she should kiss Hunter goodbye?

Another ring of a phone, this one emanating from the cell phone *not* being monitored. She checked the caller ID and answered quickly, her pulse still racing.

"Hello, Hunter."

"Are you okay?"

"Getting there. You?"

"So angry it's rattling my brain. I can't believe that psychopath had the gall to call you and threaten me."

"You heard the call?"

"Barely. I was on my way to my car and being followed by a noisy pack of reporters when I felt the vibration in my pocket."

"Why the reporters? Is there a new development I should know about?"

"The woman whose attack I rushed home to investigate is insisting to the media that her attacker is the French Kiss Killer and when they arrest him, she wants all the reward money."

"Do you think it actually was the serial killer who attacked her?"

"Not one iota of evidence of that."

"I guess that's what the caller meant by an idiot stealing his thunder."

"It's difficult to understand what's going on in his sick mind, but I figure he's mad that his fearful public may think he was the one who fouled up the abduction attempt this afternoon—if it actually was an abduction attempt."

"But you are convinced it wasn't him?"

"Close to certain, but we haven't identified a suspect as yet."

"But he said I should tell you goodbye." Her voice trembled. "He must be planning to kill you?"

"Don't worry, Helena. I plan to see that he doesn't. He's not going to hurt you, either. I'll see to that. There's a cop watching your house and gate right now. Go back to enjoying your wine on the balcony."

"But who is watching out for you?"

"My buddies Smith & Wesson."

"Okay, but I'm calling Romeo in the morning. No cameras in my private spaces but the rest of his ideas are a go. If Mia could afford it, then I guess I can, too."

"Good thinking. Look, babe, I gotta run. Take care."

"Stay safe," she whispered. And then he was gone. No mention of when she'd see him again.

She had the horrible gut-wrenching feeling that it might be never.

ALYSSA SAT GLUED to her chair as the anchor on a rerun of the ten o'clock news gave details of an armed attacker trying to kidnap a young woman in broad daylight. The victim's name was being withheld but the assault had occurred only a few blocks from Alyssa's studio.

The victim was able to provide a detailed description of her attacker to the detectives, but the suspect was still on the loose.

There had been some speculation that the suspect might be the infamous French Kiss Killer, but that idea had not been substantiated by the NOPD.

She'd had a steady stream of customers from noon until she'd closed about thirty minutes ago. Several had mentioned concern about today's attack.

Alyssa backed up the feed and ran it again. Attack in the French Quarter—possible failed abduction. No one had died or been seriously injured. But someone could have been. Her heart pounded, and an eruption of acid pooled in her stomach. She ran for the bathroom, knowing she was about to lose her dinner.

The anxiety wasn't new. She'd lived with some level of it ever since her first visit with Helena on Tuesday night. Meeting Lacy had only compounded the problem.

There was no logical explanation for her practically

crippling apprehension, yet she couldn't shake it. She stood and walked over to the counter. Hunter Bergeron's card was still there where she'd left it when he'd come to talk to her about Lacy.

She glanced at the kitchen clock again. Too late to call, she thought, as she punched in his number, anyway. Her breath was coming hard and fast.

"Bergeron," he answered. "At your service."

"Hunter, it's Alyssa Orillon. I'm sorry if I woke you but this is sort of an emergency."

"What's wrong? Do you need an ambulance or a police officer?"

"Nothing like that. I just saw the evening news. I don't need the name of the young woman who was attacked this afternoon. Just tell me it wasn't Helena Cosworth or the tourist who looks like Elizabeth Grayson."

"It was neither Helena nor Lacy Blankenship. They're both safe."

Air rushed into Alyssa's lungs and she started to tremble. "That's all I needed to know."

She thanked Hunter and tried to assure him she'd be all right even though she didn't believe that herself.

There was only person who might be able to help her get past this. Her grandmother claimed she had lost all her psychic powers with age. Her memory was dimming, the distant past becoming more available than what she had for breakfast. But if anyone could help Alyssa understand what was going on, it was Brigitte.

The nursing home was across the Lake Pontchartrain Causeway, near where Alyssa's mother lived in Covington. It would take her at least an hour to get there in light traffic. It might be a wasted trip, but it was the only option she had.

The chances of it helping might improve if she could talk Helena into going with her. It was worth a try.

LACY SLIPPED HER magnetic hotel key into the slot, opened the door and tiptoed to her side of the bed. If she could wiggle out of her dress and bra, she might be able to slide beneath the crisp white sheets without waking her roommate. It was a long shot. Brenda was a very light sleeper.

But Lacy's lies were starting to become confusing even to her. She kicked out of her high-heeled sandals and twisted until she could reach the dress's back zipper.

"You don't have to sneak in. I'm not your mother."

"I woke you? Sorry, Brenda."

"I wasn't asleep. I worry when my best friend is out past midnight with a stranger."

"We're on vacation. Besides, he's not a stranger. He's a nice guy I've met several times."

"Ever heard of the French Kiss Killer?" Brenda asked sarcastically. "Everyone else in this town has. They say he's probably fun to be with, too, until he kills you."

"The odds of getting killed by a serial killer are lower than being abducted by an alien from outer space."

"You made that up."

"Sounds good, though, doesn't it?" she teased in an effort to get Brenda to lighten up.

"If you're not going to listen to me, then pay attention to our new friend Courtney. She lives in New Orleans, and she says never go off alone in this town with someone you don't know well."

"I didn't. I went off with a perfect gentleman who I've run into around the hotel several times. He didn't even try to put the make on me. How's that for class?"

"Oh, geeze. It's that guy who manages the restaurant, isn't it? No wonder he's always stopping by our table."

"Could be."

"I give up. You're going to do what you want to, anyway."

"And what I want is to spend the whole day with you tomorrow. How about visiting the Mardi Gras Museum?"

"I like that idea," Brenda said.

"Laissez les bons temps rouler," Lacy said as she sashayed to the bathroom to brush her teeth.

Brenda groaned. "Now you're speaking French."

"It's a Cajun expression for 'let the good times roll.' You gotta love this town."

IT FELT LIKE Helena had just fallen asleep when her alarm clock woke her with its piercing peal. She reached over to turn it off and realized it was her phone. She picked it up and read the time and caller ID display.

One fifty. Hunter.

"Hello."

"You sound as if I woke you."

"It is a wee hour of the morning," she said.

"Then I guess I should let you get back to sleep."

"Wake me up just to say goodbye? Nice try, Detective. Where are you?"

"Standing in front of your house."

"It's a little late for stalking me. There's room on the couch."

And here she went again, her body coming to life at the prospect of seeing him and possibly watching him do something as unremarkable as sleep. Her pulse raced as she pulled on her robe and ran down the stairs to let him in.

"You look beat," she said when he ambled through the door.

"Feel beat, too. Worse, I've spent every minute since I left here this afternoon running in frantic circles, chasing my tail."

"I take it that means you didn't arrest the parking lot villain."

"We can't even get a straight story on it. The victim says the guy had a gun. The young men who came to her rescue say they never saw it and that they had a good look at what was going on. The victim says he was trying to force her into his car. The same witnesses say he was trying to grab her handbag."

"The woman who was attacked should know," Helena insisted.

"She appears to have ulterior motives."

"Such as?"

"She claims her attacker was the French Kiss Killer, and since she described him to Barker and me, she deserves all the reward money."

"Did you explain to her it doesn't work that way? The info has to lead to the serial killer's arrest before there's a payoff."

"Yes, but I'm just one of those corrupt cops trying to keep the reward for myself or so she's complained to every reporter who'll talk to her. That's most of them."

"But you don't think he's the serial killer?"

"Nope, but we can't prove that until we arrest him. That reminds me. I'm supposed to tell you that Natalie Martin, the profiler on our team, wants to talk to you sometime today."

"Really? I thought your task force members didn't even want me to hear Mia's messages from the killer."

"Seems at least one of them is having a change of

heart. Natalie has some ideas for how you can get more helpful responses and also keep the lunatic on the phone longer."

"I'm willing to meet with her, but from the way he talked tonight, that may have been his last call to me."

"Which would suit me just fine," Hunter said. "You've done enough."

"None of us have done enough unless we stop him before he kills again, and he sounds as if that is imminent."

"Again, that is not your responsibility."

Easy for him to say. "Exactly who is on the task force?"

"Detectives Cory Barker, Lane Crosby, Andy George, Natalie and me. And then we have Robicheaux to call on when needed. We also have a lot of help from other guys in the department when the situation calls for it."

"If this goes on long enough, I guess I'll meet them all. Do you want something to eat or drink?"

"I could be persuaded. What do you have?"

"We'd best go to the kitchen and check it out. I haven't had a chance to grocery shop since I've been here. I'm still making do on the basics Ella bought for me before I arrived."

Hunter kicked out of his shoes and followed her in his stockinged feet. She went to the pantry.

He opened the fridge. "Ummm. Butter. Eggs. Creamer. And half a croissant. Can you top that?"

"I'll see you a loaf of wheat bread and raise you a box of tasteless-looking, healthy cereal," she joked. "Wait. I may have hit the mother lode. A small bottle of maple syrup and a box of pancake mix that says just add water. Pretty sure we have that."

"And I've discovered a half-pound package of bacon in the freezer right next to a pint of chocolate chip ice cream," Hunter said. "The makings of a feast. Can you cook?"

"No, but I can stir water into a box of mix."

"I'm impressed. I'm dynamite with a spatula," he claimed. He pulled one from Mia's utensil holder and twirled it like a baton before dropping it to the counter.

In minutes, the front of Helena's pajamas was sprinkled with the pancake mix. Hunter grabbed a dish towel and wiped it away. When his fingers brushed her nipples through the soft fabric, desire hummed through her.

What a difference a few hours could make. No, it wasn't the hours, it was all Hunter. Right after the phone call from the killer, Helena had felt as if she was on the verge of disaster, apprehension choking the life right out of her.

Hunter showed up and within minutes, the gloom had given way to teasing, laughter and the inevitable sensual tension. Cooking had never been this much fun. All the problems she'd been faced with earlier were still there, but they were coated with raw craving now.

Hunter defrosted the bacon in the microwave and then fried the slices until they were crispy, just the way she liked it. In between flipping her pancakes on the griddle, Helena brewed a pot of decaf coffee in case she ever got around to going back to bed tonight.

By the time they were ready to eat, the sensual tension was sparking like electricity. It was bound to lead to trouble. She dropped her fork while trying to take the first bite.

"Let me help you with that," Hunter offered. He speared a bite of his pancake, dragged it through a puddle of syrup and fed it to her. A drop of the warm, sweet syrup settled in the corner of her mouth.

She reached for her napkin, but not before Hunter leaned over and captured the syrup with his napkin. She felt light, frothy, as if gravity might not be able to anchor her to earth.

"I better get my own fork," she whispered, "or we may never get around to consuming our feast."

"Would that be so bad?" he asked.

She ignored the loaded question. There was no doubt in her mind that she was falling in love with Hunter again—if she'd ever been out of love. But this wasn't just love for the man he used to be, it was for the man he'd become. He was brave and confident, more sure of himself than when they'd been together. She'd never felt more protected.

But had he really changed? Was he capable of a forever commitment this time—if she got to that point herself? Or was she already there and only fooling herself?

Hunter devoured his food. She picked at hers. By the time they'd finished eating, her sensual excitement level had cooled but not by much.

It was late. Hunter had to be exhausted and who knew how much sleep he'd get before he felt compelled to get back on the job?

He insisted on helping her clean up the kitchen. He was rinsing the syrup from their plates when his phone buzzed. He picked it up. "Have to take this," he said. "Police work."

He set the plates in the sink and answered the phone as he walked out of the kitchen. She couldn't stop the thought from entering her mind—being married to a homicide detective probably meant a lot of nights of eating and sleeping alone.

But then being single did, too. She was used to that, but she doubted any spouse of a cop ever got used to the dangerous risks.

"Good news or bad?" she asked when he rejoined her in the kitchen.

"Semi-good. Another witness who was also in the parking lot at the time of the incident called in with what he says is the suspect's license number."

"I'd think that deserved more than a semi-good," she said as she wiped down the counter.

"It would be except the witness mainly wanted to know about the award money, so the license number could be a hoax."

"Don't they know you'll figure it out quickly if they lie about something so easy to check?"

"I think they have so many dollar signs in their eyes, they can't see anything else. But it's a busy parking lot so it wouldn't be unusual for someone to see trouble and jot down the license number."

"Hopefully that's true in this case."

"I should be going," Hunter said. "Sorry I woke you, but I really wanted to see you tonight. I had to make sure you were okay after visiting the crime scene in the swamp and then dealing with that bizarre, disgusting phone call."

"I'm glad," she said. "It's late and you must be exhausted. The couch is still available if you want to crash there again."

"Sounds good." Instead of making a move in that direction, he walked over, poured himself another cup of coffee and sat down at the table. He looked serious and even a little apprehensive, which spiked the air with tension, no longer sensual.

"You asked me what happened to make me walk out on you just before our wedding."

Now she recognized the awkward aspect of the tension. It was dread.

"I wasn't completely honest with you," he admitted. "I think I owe you that."

So did she, but she wasn't sure she was ready to deal with the truth. "Was it another woman?"

"In a way, but not what you're implying."

"Then how?"

"I don't know if you remember, but I had killed my first person since becoming a member of the NOPD. Everyone assumed that was what had me so upset. They were wrong. My regret was that I hadn't killed him sooner."

"I know you were temporarily suspended, but then all charges were dropped when the shooting was ruled self-defense. I must be missing something."

Hunter stood and began to pace. "My partner and I were sent out to respond to a 911 call from an eight-year-old who said his daddy was drunk and was about to kill his mother. When we got there, the father came to the door. His wife and the kid were standing behind him."

Helena didn't interrupt. It was almost as if Hunter were no longer in her kitchen talking to her but had slipped back into a troubling past.

"The man had been drinking. The curses he hurled at my partner and I were slurred. He assured us there was no problem. He might have gotten a bit rowdy, but he would never harm his wife and boy.

"The woman backed him up, but we knew she was lying and so frightened of the guy she was shaking. She put her arm around the boy's shoulder and encouraged him to lie, as well.

"The boy insisted he made the call, but he knew his daddy wouldn't hurt them. His voice broke. Clearly, the kid was scared to death.

"I tried for thirty minutes to persuade the mother to press charges. She refused over and over, insisting they'd only been arguing and the boy had gotten upset. Finally, the man ordered us off his property."

"And by law you had to go?"

"By law and by policy, but even then, I'd turned around and was heading back to the house when we heard gunfire. We kicked in the door and found the man standing over his wife who he'd shot through the head. The boy was stretched out over his mother's bleeding body."

Tears filled Helena's eyes. No wonder that had hit Hunter so hard. She'd not known these details.

"You tried to save her," Helena said. "It was out of your control. The man must have still held the gun."

"He didn't," Hunter said. "He was unarmed. He'd tossed his weapon to the floor. When we burst through the door, the kid picked it up and pointed it at his dad."

Hunter stopped pacing but still avoided eye contact with Helena. "I couldn't let him do it. Not because I gave a damn about the man. My first impulse was to shoot him myself so the boy didn't have to live with that."

"But you didn't?"

"No. I jumped the kid and wrestled the gun from his hands. In the process, his drunken father was killed from a ricocheting bullet."

"No wonder you were hurting. I just wish you'd have told me that back then."

"I couldn't."

"Because you didn't trust me?"

"Because that boy was me, Helena."

Chapter Thirteen

Hunter's words made no sense to Helena. "I don't understand."

"I lived through that very same horror, except I was only six at the time. I called the police and then lied to them just like my mother told me to do. If I hadn't, he would have beaten both of us like he did almost every night, at least that's how it seemed to me then.

"That night he didn't beat her. Instead, he blew out my mother's brains. And then he came after me, beat me until I was unconscious."

"What happened to your father?"

"He went to prison. I never saw him again. I tried to find him when I finally started dealing with this after our breakup. He'd been released years before. He'd never come looking for me."

Things were starting to make sense and Helena's heart ached for the boy of six who'd faced such tragedy. But then she looked at the brilliant, dedicated detective standing in her kitchen and she knew he'd faced the worse and made it through.

"What happened to you after that?"

"I went from one foster home to another. Nobody let me stay for long. I had a giant chip on my shoulder and I was a troublemaker."

"Who later became a cop and then a Marine and is now a fantastic homicide detective."

"It took me years to get to this place. The problem was I never faced what I'd been through. I don't remember ever crying. I told friends at the new school I had to attend that my mother had died of cancer and that my dad was a fatally wounded war hero. The first time I remember weeping for my mother was the day I ran out on you.

"That's why I couldn't marry you then. I had nothing to offer you until I came to grips with my past. I had to prove to myself I could face the truth and move past it. I had to understand that I would never become the monster my father had been.

"As a kid, I had wanted to kill my dad and as a cop, I had wanted to kill the man who blew his son's mother's brains out. The past was destroying my future. I couldn't pull you into that."

"And you feel you've moved beyond that?"

"I do. It may sound corny, but the Marines did make a man of me. The intensive counseling I finally got helped, too."

She walked over and put her arms around his waist. "Welcome back, Hunter Bergeron. You were always that man to me."

He held her without talking for long minutes. "This is the real me," he whispered. "As good as it will likely ever get. Lots of faults, but I'm crazy in love with you. Always have been. Always will be. No pressure, I just wanted you to know."

She had never loved him more.

"Now, does that offer still stand to sleep on your couch?"

"No. I don't think so. You're not couch material. But there's room in my bed for two."

HELENA CHANGED INTO a teal-colored satin cami pajama set in lieu of her flour-splattered ones while Hunter showered in her bathroom. The sliding doors to her balcony were already closed and locked; the heavy, noise-trapping drapes were pulled tight.

She plumped both their pillows and dimmed her bed-side lamp to a soft glow. Anticipation swirled inside her, as she slid between the sheets.

The bathroom door opened, and Hunter stepped into the bedroom, only wearing one of her white, fluffy towels knotted at the waist. She stared at his broad chest as if seeing it for the first time.

In a way, she was. The ex-Marine at thirty-one was more muscular, his pecs and abs far more defined than they'd been the last time she and Hunter had shared a bed.

She thought his body was perfect then. Now he'd taken masculinity to a whole new level. If he didn't make a move on her soon, she'd explode.

He stepped closer to the bed then loosed the towel and let it fall to the floor. He was already hard, his erection proof that he was not too fatigued to feel the same desire that was vibrating through her.

Instead of climbing into bed with her, he lifted the top sheet and pulled it to the foot of the bed. She reached over to turn off the lamp.

"Please don't," he whispered. "Just let me look at you and drink all this in. You've walked through my dreams for six years, but it was never like this. You were never more beautiful, never more ravishing than you are at this minute."

She slipped her fingers beneath the spaghetti straps of the cami and slowly tugged them off her shoulders one at a time. Her breasts swelled above the fabric until she lifted the top over her head and tossed it to him.

"Want to help?" she tempted.

"I'm not sure I can and keep control."

Keep control. She was so caught up in the moment that she'd lost control. "I don't have any protection," she blurted out.

"I do," Hunter whispered, "though I haven't been intimate with a woman in almost a year. And only in my wildest dreams did I imagine a moment like this."

He removed a condom from his wallet and slid it onto her bedside table. Then without another word, he slid into bed beside her, raised up on one elbow and worked his hand beneath the elastic waist of her shorts.

His fingers brushed her coppery triangle of hair, finally dipping inside her. When she grew slick with desire, he slid the damp pajama shorts down her legs then twirled and shot them across the room.

He kissed her mouth, softly at first and then hard and relentlessly until her lips felt ravaged yet hungry for more. The kisses grew deeper still, stealing her breath until they both came up for air.

His hands cupped her breasts, his thumbs massaging her nipples before taking one at a time into his mouth. He nibbled gently and sucked until she moaned in voracious pleasure.

Then, trailing her abdomen with sweet kisses, his lips reached the erogenous area that took her to the edge of orgasm. Her body writhed and arched toward him.

He rolled away and raised on an elbow again. "I'm human, you know, and you're making it impossible for me to hold off until you're completely satisfied."

"I'm ready, so ready. I want you now. All of you."

He took a minute to encase his desire in the condom, then straddled her and fit his erection inside her. He thrust faster and faster, driving her delirious with desire.

Helena moaned and bit her lip, giving in to the thrill as they exploded together in savage release.

Hunter stayed on top of her for glorious minutes, his face flushed, his breathing coming in quick gasps. She closed her eyes, letting the perfection of the moment caress her soul.

"I love you, Helena Cosworth," he whispered, as he pulled her back into his arms.

"I love you, Hunter Bergeron." At that moment she knew she always would.

Hunter was soon fast asleep.

Helena lay awake, relishing the sound of his rhythmic breathing and the warm glow of her body after the loving.

The contentment was short-lived. Quivering tremors attacked in the dark as the killer's words came back to haunt her.

Please, God, don't let me have to say goodbye to Hunter or let him be forced to say goodbye to me.

The promise of happy-ever-after was within their grasp. *Don't let it be stolen from us now.*

SAYING GOODBYE ON a sticky note after the most memorable night of his life was a damned shame. Walking away from the bed where Helena lay sleeping was pure torture.

But he'd chosen this life and felt honored to be one of the youngest homicide detectives with the department. Having been named to head up the serial killer task force was lagniappe.

The task force was organized shortly after the third victim and gained momentum after Elizabeth Grayson's murder. They'd covered every angle, questioned hundreds of people, delved into the backgrounds of everyone who had a shred of evidence against them.

The killer had outsmarted them at every turn. He seemed to know what they were thinking before they acted. He was knowledgeable about their limitations within the law and made fools of them repeatedly, as he was doing with the repetitive phone calls.

They were desperate for a break and they may have just gotten it. Or they might be dealing with another kook.

Hunter finished writing his note.

Sorry I had to cut out like this. A new lead just in that might go nowhere. Don't go away. I'll be back. Love you.

It didn't even touch on what last night had meant to him. No room on the small paper square. No time to write it. Mainly, he'd never been good at putting his emotions into words.

He'd work on that.

He leaned over and let his lips brush Helena's. She stirred but didn't open her eyes. As much as he ached to crawl back into her bed and into her arms, he tiptoed away and left her sleeping.

HELENA WOKE TO a gentle ache in her thighs and heart-stopping memories rambling through her sleep-dulled brain. She rolled over and reached for Hunter. Her hand swept across empty sheets. The house was silent.

He was gone.

For a second she thought it might all have been a

dream. And then she saw the yellow note attached to his pillow. She picked it up and flicked on the lamp.

She read the short note twice, hoping to find some hidden hint of how their lovemaking had affected him. "Love you" was as close as it got but she'd settle for that. She knew *love* wasn't a word he threw around carelessly.

The house seemed incredibly empty with him gone. Mia's absence magnified the feeling. It was as if the home where she'd spent so many happy hours was revolting against her.

After all, she'd come here to close this chapter of her past and turn Mia's beautiful house over to strangers.

Only houses didn't think or feel, and the real estate possibilities were at least temporarily in limbo. Besides, she'd be crazy to let anything distract from the ecstasy she'd shared with Hunter last night.

She stretched and luxuriated in the sensation of her nakedness against the sheets, reminding her of all the ways Hunter had explored and titillated her body last night.

The thrill of their lovemaking stayed with her through her first cup of coffee and shifted to anticipation for more of the same while she showered and dressed in a pale pink sundress with a halter neckline.

And then the dread and fear crept in, followed quickly by the urge to change into one of her painting smocks and take her easel into the courtyard. She needed an outlet for her joy and a calming for her soul.

Instead she decided to settle for taking a walk through the Quarter and stopping at Sophia's Bakery near her house for a chocolate croissant before the unforgiving heat claimed the day.

She waited until she was ready to walk out the door

before making a call to Robicheaux and telling him she was ready to sign a contract for the proposed project. He made an appointment to meet at her house at three.

She started to call Hunter but hesitated. He'd ordered her not to leave the house without letting him know exactly where she'd be. On the other hand, she hated to interrupt him.

She decided on the latter. Better interrupted than angry at her. Her pulse quickened as she punched in his number.

"Is anything wrong? Are you okay?" His usual greeting when she called. He was protective to the core.

"The only problem I have to report is that a sexy detective broke out of my house in the wee hours of the morning."

The comment was met with laughter. Lots of laughter.

Her cheeks began to burn. "Was I on speaker?"

"Yeah. My bad. A group of us are in an online meeting with the chief. Speaker's off now."

"How's the new lead working out?" she asked.

"Too soon to say."

"That's better than 'nothing there.'"

"Yeah." He sounded distracted.

"Sorry that I caught you at a bad time," she said. "You said I should call when I leave the house so…"

"Where are you going?" he interrupted.

"For a walk around the neighborhood with a stop at the bakery. I don't need a police stalker. I just wanted you to know where I'll be."

"When are you leaving?"

"Right now."

"Wait ten minutes, and remember, no alleyways or shortcuts."

"I'll stay right here in the heart of the Quarter. I'll be fine."

"Okay. I'll call you later," he said.

He'd said okay, but she figured he'd still alert the cops in the area to keep an eye on her. As long as the killer was contacting her, she'd be considered high risk.

Her phone rang as she stepped into the courtyard. She closed and locked the door behind her and walked over to the fountain before answering.

"Hello."

"Is this Helena Cosworth?"

"Yes."

"It's me, Alyssa."

"Are you already up and working this early?"

"Up but not working. I'm taking the day off and driving across the lake to visit my grandmother. She's living in an assisted living center near my mother."

"Good for you. I'm sure she'll be glad to see you."

"You never know. Some days she's sharp enough to converse with me on almost any topic I bring up. Other days, she seems totally disoriented or not interested in anything I have to say. She'll fall asleep while I'm talking."

"How old is she now?"

"Ninety-two. But she drives her walker like a race car. The reason I called is that I'm hoping you'll ride over there with me."

Now things were starting to add up. "This wouldn't be the grandmother who used to be the famous medium, is she?"

"Yes, it's Brigitte, but I'm not counting on her advising you in any way. She claims her mind and body retired from all things psychic."

"Yet somehow, you hope she'll suddenly recover her skills and explain your bloody vision of me and Lacy?"

"I'm not expecting miracles. But what could it hurt to visit her?"

"No. I'm not going to pull a ninety-two-year-old woman into this. Please, let it go, Alyssa. You don't believe you have extrasensory skills yourself, so the visions are meaningless."

"You can ride out there to keep me company. If nothing else, you can meet Brigitte. She's a character worth knowing."

"I have an appointment here this afternoon at three with Romeo."

"With whom?"

"Real name, Antoine Robicheaux. He's a friend of Hunter's. Used to be an FBI agent but owns an apparently very successful security company now. Not sure if he's making me safe or a prisoner with all the locks he's installing, but the only way in for a criminal will be by helicopter."

"It would be cheaper to move Hunter Bergeron in with you."

"Are you staring into that fake crystal ball again?"

"Just a thought. But I'm serious about needing company on that long drive across the Causeway. If we leave here around eleven, we can easily be back by three."

"You're not going to give up, are you?"

"No," Alyssa said, "but I promise not to harp on the bloody images."

"In that case, I'll ride over with you."

"Great. Pick you up at eleven."

It was only half past eight now. Helena would still have plenty of time for her walk.

She heard her name called and looked up. Ella was

on her balcony, picking dead blooms from her Mandevilla plant and letting them parachute to the pebbled courtyard below.

"Do you have time for a cup of coffee?" Ella called.

Helena hated turning her down, but now she was primed for a morning walk and one of Sophia's flaky chocolate croissants.

"Why don't you come take a walk with me? I'll treat you to a cup of coffee at Sophia's bakery."

"I'd love to. Mia and I used to walk almost every day. I've tried doing it without her but it's not the same."

"I know. I miss her, too. Come on down. I'll wait."

There went her opportunity to do nothing but think of Hunter and the bizarre turns her life had taken over the past few days. But it would also help her avoid thinking of the killer and what he'd meant by his latest horrifying comments.

Ella was at the gate in less than ten minutes wearing a pair of athletic walking shoes, trousers, a colorful tunic and a large-brimmed straw hat.

"I sure do appreciate your asking me along," Ella said. "Sometimes I think I'll go bananas in that house thinking about poor Elizabeth. I can't even turn on the TV the past couple of weeks without hearing some reporter bantering about how it's right around the six-month mark and there's going to be another killing any day now. And I'm not just talking about the local channels, either."

"I'm sure it's been hard on you. All I can tell you is that the police are determined to make sure that the killer doesn't strike again."

"For sure, Hunter is," Ella agreed.

At seventy-two, Ella could still walk almost as fast as she talked and that was saying a lot. Several friends of Ella's and Mia's stopped to say hello. All of them were curious about what Helena was going to do with the carriage house and the adjoining property.

Helena had no answers for them. Hunter had told her he loved her. He hadn't said anything about the future. How could she make any definite plans without knowing where their relationship was heading?

The bakery was crowded when they arrived. She and Ella found a table for two near the left back corner but with a good view of everyone entering.

"This is the best people-watching area in the French Quarter," Ella said. "You see everything here. Look at that young woman who just walked in. Why in the world would she think having her hair two completely different colors would be becoming?"

"It's the style among the younger set," Helena offered.

"I suppose so. We didn't do that in my day."

The waitress stopped by their table and took their orders for coffee and chocolate croissants.

The bell over the door tingled again. Two young women stepped inside and scanned the area for an empty table before heading their way. Lacy and her friend.

It would be hard to bypass a catastrophe unless by some miracle, Ella didn't see the likeness between Lacy and Elizabeth. Only judging from Ella's pained expression, she already had. Her face was ashen as the young women found seats just two tables down from them.

"The blonde who just came in looks just like my Elizabeth." The timbre of Ella's voice was practically bloodcurdling. "You must see it, too."

"There's a likeness," Helena agreed. She reached over and took one of Ella's shaking hands. "This is making you uncomfortable. Why don't I have the waitress change our orders to takeout?"

"No," Ella said emphatically. "I'm not ready to go."

Helena couldn't believe sitting here and reliving the heartache of Elizabeth's death could be good for Ella but forcing her to leave could be even more devastating.

Lacy left her table after ordering and walked back to the restroom area. While she was gone the waitress brought Helena and Ella's order. Before Helena had time to stir cream into her coffee, two groups of women stopped by their table to say hello to Ella and Helena.

Ella barely spoke to any of them.

"Did you and Mia come in here often?" Helena asked when they were alone again.

"Every Tuesday and Thursday."

"You were a regular. No wonder so many of the customers know you."

"Mia knew and talked to everybody everywhere we went. Elizabeth was like that, too. I should have warned her more often not to trust strangers."

"Don't go blaming yourself, Ella. Elizabeth had a beautiful spirit. People young and old were drawn to her. That's all."

Ella was about to take a bite of her croissant when Lacy sat back down at her table. The pastry slipped from Ella's shaky fingers and fell back to the saucer. A few drops of coffee spilled over Ella's fingers as she pushed the mug away.

"I'm sorry."

"Nothing to be sorry about." Helena dabbed up the spill with her paper napkin.

A few minutes later Connor Harrington stepped into the coffee shop. Judging from his clothing and sweat, he'd likely been to the nearby gym.

He went to the counter for a coffee and then headed toward Helena's table. He never made it. Instead he joined Lacy and her friend.

"Lacy and Brenda, a nice surprise running into the two of you," he greeted loudly enough for Helena to catch the friend's name.

In seconds he and Lacy were involved in an animated conversation. Brenda looked annoyed. Connor left a few minutes later with his coffee. He never noticed Helena or else he chose not to acknowledge her.

Ella continued to stare at her full cup of coffee and untouched croissant while Helena finished hers. "I hate to rush you, but I have an appointment at eleven," Helena said.

"I have no appetite today. We can go now," Ella agreed.

Helena paid the tab and left a tip.

Ella stopped next to Lacy as they were leaving and put a hand on the young woman's shoulder.

"I don't mean to upset you, dear, but you could be the twin of my great-niece who was murdered last spring."

Lacy looked perplexed. "I'm sorry."

"Nothing to be sorry for. You're beautiful. I only said this to warn you to be careful."

Lacy stared at Ella as if she was totally confused by the unusual comments from a stranger.

"Sure," Lacy said. "I'll stay out of trouble."

"Don't go off alone with anyone you don't know," Ella continued. "The serial killer who stole my niece's life may be looking for someone exactly like you."

Thankfully, Ella walked away after that. Lacy didn't say a word.

Her friend didn't stay silent. Brenda's words were loud and clear.

"If you don't heed Courtney's warning about hanging out with strangers, I don't suppose you're going to listen to that poor old lady who lost her niece, either."

Helena waited until they were outside before texting Hunter about seeing Lacy and Connor together.

Hunter's response was an emoji indicating he'd gotten her message. He was obviously busy, but Helena would have loved to know if Courtney was the undercover police officer who was supposed to be looking out for Lacy. If so, she might need to step up her efforts.

The killer's last phone call had warned he was moving full speed ahead.

LUNCHTIME FOR THE residents was finishing up when Helena and Alyssa arrived at the assisted living center. Brigitte had finished her meal and was dawdling over a bowl of what looked like caramel pudding.

Brigitte seemed glad to see them and suggested they go the center's atrium to talk, explaining that it felt almost like being outside but without the heat and humidity.

Alyssa offered to get her a wheelchair. Brigitte acted insulted. For good reason, Helena realized when they started walking. As promised, Brigitte was a Hells Angel behind that walker.

They stopped at a vending machine as they left the cafeteria and Alyssa got soft drinks for herself and Helena to tide them over until they had time to grab lunch.

"Are you sure you don't want anything from the machine, Grammy?" Alyssa asked.

"I'm sure unless they've added vodka."

"No vodka. I can get you an orange juice and you can pretend it's a vodka screwdriver."

"It's hard enough pretending you drove all the way

over here in the middle of a work day just to chat. I'm sure you are looking for some type of interpretation."

Brigitte's wavery voice gave away her age as much as her wrinkles and nearly translucent skin did. On the other hand, her attitude and ease with words revealed she hadn't lost much in the intellect and wit departments.

But it was her extrasensory abilities they were about to put to the test. Helena grew more uneasy as Brigitte led them to a spot in the corner where three club chairs were placed around a small round table.

Alyssa brought up the subject of her frightening visions.

The only comforting aspect of this was that Brigitte showed no indication that she envisioned Helena splattered in blood.

Next, Alyssa spent a few minutes trying to engage Brigitte in small talk. Brigitte wasn't buying it.

Brigitte reached over and put a bony, vein-stitched hand on Helena's arm. "It's great meeting you, but I'm out of the psychic game. My brain and body won't hold up to constantly living inside other people's problems."

An odd way of putting it. Giving up the game rather than losing the ability.

"My sweet granddaughter here is much smarter than me. She's convinced herself she's a fraud so that she doesn't have to take on the responsibility of saving everyone around her. I pray she stays on that path, but today's visit makes me fear otherwise."

"I am a fraud, Grammy, except..."

She hesitated. Helena and Brigitte stayed quiet and waited on her to finish that pronouncement.

"Except that sometimes I let my imagination take off on its own and leave my reasoning ability behind.

I don't trust what I see in my subconscious, but I can't always brush it off."

Brigitte leaned back in her chair and closed her eyes as if fading off to sleep. Helena felt terrible. They'd not only infringed on her peace of mind, they were interfering with her naptime.

A second later, she opened her eyes again and stared at Alyssa. "If you're here for me to interpret your imaginings, you're wasting all our time."

"We shouldn't have bothered you," Helena said. "Alyssa, please don't say more about the hallucinations."

Brigitte went on as if Helena hadn't jumped into the conversation. "If you're here for advice, Alyssa, I'd warn you to trust your instincts. Go where angels fear to tread if you must, but don't bury yourself in regrets when you realize you haven't changed anything. The future is not in your hands."

Helena was awed by Brigitte's wisdom. As Mia had always said, the passing years might rob one of a few brain cells, but the lessons living taught more than made up for that.

"Don't you even want to hear about what I'm dealing with, what my friend Helena is facing?" Alyssa asked, disappointment bleeding into her words.

"No. It wouldn't help, Alyssa. Even when I was at the top of my game, I could never absorb meaning from secondhand interpretations. Talking about it is only going to upset all of us."

"I was hoping meeting Helena would spark your own vision."

"I'm sorry, sweetie. I've spent the past few years learning to block those revelations. Now, I don't know what exciting plans you ladies have for the rest of the day, but it's nap time for me."

"We'll walk you back to your room," Alyssa said.

"I'm not an invalid. You're my guests. I'll walk you to the door."

Brigitte was not one to argue with, so they followed as she led the way.

They shared goodbyes and hugs but for some reason Brigitte suggested Alyssa get the car and pick up Helena at the door.

The second Alyssa was out of earshot, Brigitte reached for Helena's hand. The calm Brigitte had exhibited inside the building transformed into drawn facial muscles and anxiety clouding her eyes.

Helena suddenly realized why Brigitte had sent Alyssa on without her. Brigitte was about to go herself where angels feared to tread. Helena was pretty sure she was not going to like what she was about to hear.

Chapter Fourteen

Helena waited in dread for Brigitte Orillon to speak her mind. She didn't have to wait long.

"I don't know what Alyssa saw or thinks she saw in her phantasms."

"She thinks someone is out to kill me, but she can't decipher who," Helena said, keeping it simple. "In any case, we were wrong to intrude on you like this."

"No. You were right to come. Alyssa is right about your being in danger."

"But you wouldn't let her talk about it."

"I needed to focus on my own reactions and I don't want her to get drawn into the danger. That can happen, you know. It's another reason I've never encouraged her to develop the gift and follow in my footsteps. Much better for her to think she has no extrasensory perception, though she clearly has a great depth of feelings."

"I understand."

"Listen close to what I have to say. Someone is coming after you, but you will not be his only victim."

"Who will be the second victim?"

"I don't know."

"Who is the man who wants me dead?"

"I don't know that, either. I sense what I cannot see,

but his heart is as black as a moonless night and evil consumes his soul."

Alyssa drove up in the circular drive and stopped a few feet from them.

Brigitte squeezed Helena's hand. "Nothing is what it seems. Trust no one."

Helena's blood ran icy cold as she climbed into the passenger side of Alyssa's compact car. She reached into her handbag and fumbled for her phone. She needed to talk to Hunter, needed to hear his voice. Needed his strength.

But she couldn't say all of that in front of Alyssa and disturbing Hunter on the job wouldn't help.

Besides, Brigitte was ninety-two years old. What could she possibly know about the killer that Hunter and his task force, including his brilliant FBI profiler and past FBI agent Romeo, didn't know? Helena could not be in safer hands.

It was ten after three when Hunter and Barker walked out of the chief of police's office. The latest finding was newsworthy and the mayor was eager to share any good news having to deal with the serial killer. Unfortunately, it didn't mean they had an ID on the suspect who might strike again at any minute.

They had two hours before they had to be at the mayor's office for a press conference.

"One of us should call and give the news to Robicheaux," Barker said. "He'll flip if he hears the bombshell developments from the chief on TV before he hears it from us."

"He does like to be on the inside," Hunter said, "and he did call this right from the beginning—more or less."

"Yeah, yeah, I know," Baker said. "And I'm the one who argued he was wrong."

"You'll owe him a couple of beers for that."

"Speaking of having a drink, we don't have but two hours before we have to be back here. Do you want to grab a coffee and a slice of pie?"

"I would except I need to check in with Helena. Robicheaux is supposed to be there designing a new security system for her house and rental property. I can kill two birds with one stone."

"Things seem to be getting serious awfully fast between you and Helena. I know she's cooperating with the investigation and times are tense. Just remember that emotions can get all mixed up in the heat of danger."

"I've got my head on straight."

Not actually true. He'd never had his head on straight where Helena was concerned, but he wouldn't let his emotions interfere with his main focus—keeping her safe.

Nothing they'd learned today had decreased the danger. If anything, it may have upped it.

"I might as well tell you now, Barker. I haven't mentioned this to Helena or to anyone on the task force yet except Natalie Martin, but I've decided to block her from taking any more calls from the lunatic."

"Where in the hell did that idea come from? You know that as faulty and unsuccessful as that's been, it's our only contact with the suspect."

"He can still call. He just won't get through to Helena. I'll take the calls and I'll do the talking to him."

"Do that and he'll quit calling. You know we still have Elizabeth Grayson's killer out there. He's unhinged. The calls make that clear. He could strike again any day now."

"More reason I don't want her exposed to his threats any longer."

"I can almost guarantee you Robicheaux will balk at that idea. Even if he doesn't, it damn sure won't get my vote."

"Sorry, but it's not up for a vote. Helena is not bait."

"Okay. Your call, at least for now. See you at five."

"I'll be there."

There was a good chance Elizabeth's killer would be watching the breaking news bite that would be broadcast on every local channel and likely picked up by some twenty-four-hour news channels, as well.

With luck, he'd realize the odds were turning against him and decide to surrender.

Bad thing about luck was you simply couldn't count on it.

HELENA DIDN'T TELL Alyssa about her private conversation with Brigitte. Actually, the two of them had talked very little on the way home. When they were back on the south shore of Lake Pontchartrain, Alyssa offered to buy her lunch.

Helena was certain she couldn't hold down a spoonful of food. She took a rain check, claiming she had some tasks to take care of around the house before Robicheaux arrived.

There were no tasks and if there had been, Helena would have been too shaken to do them. Brigitte's words had upset her even worse than the monster's phone calls.

She'd never taken mediums or any kind of psychic phenomena seriously. It was ridiculous that she was so upset by it now. It was the constant living with the reality of a madman calling and possibly stalking her that had her beginning to accept the murderously inexplicable as truth.

Once inside the house, Helena walked through every room checking the locks on the few windows and doors that opened to the outside. Hunter had said there would always be someone nearby to hear her if she screamed for help. She was tempted to test him on that.

She took a deep breath and exhaled slowly. Her paranoia was getting out of hand. Nothing had changed. Hunter had promised he'd let nothing happen to her and she had no reason to doubt him.

Helena walked into what had been Mia's bedroom, crashed on top of the coverlet and chose a book from the stack of nonfiction crime selections. She opened it to a random page and began to read.

Common and not-so-common traits of serial killers.

She scanned the page. There was nothing unexpected or shocking in the list, but a couple of traits piqued her curiosity.

A desire to improve their expertise with every murder. A fascination with death and watching someone die.

She turned the page and found notes that Mia had entered on the margins from the top to the bottom of the page. One sentence stood out in her mind.

Be careful whom you trust.

It was the trust element again. Trust no one. Be careful whom you trust. How many times and in how many different ways had she heard that warning in the few days she'd been here?

The doorbell rang. She closed the book and returned it to the stack before hurrying to the door.

She hoped it would be Hunter. Instead it was Robicheaux.

"You look beautiful, as usual," he quipped once she'd ushered him inside.

"You don't look so bad yourself."

"Thanks."

He grinned at her compliment. She had no doubt he knew how handsome he was and made use of that in selling his security services.

"Glad you decided to go with at least some of the items we talked about," he said. "It's the latest technology—top of the line. Might not be as good as having a sharpshooter like Hunter hovering over you every second, but it doesn't snore."

"Ah, honesty in packaging."

"I do deliver perfection."

"Modest, too."

"When you're good, flaunt it. Speaking of that, I hear you're a terrific artist."

"Don't believe everything you hear. We should probably get down to business before you get me started on my art."

"Whatever you like."

His relaxed and flirty attitude made it almost seem the serial killer situation was faraway fiction. It felt good even though she knew the attempts at normalcy on both their parts was only temporary escapism.

"I know we discussed a lot of this already," Helena said. "But I need you to go over exactly what will be installed, the cost and how it works. Then I'll make a decision on which options I want to go with."

"Absolutely. Can we do this in the kitchen? It's easier if I can lay everything out visually for you."

"Sure."

He followed her to the kitchen. "Would you like

something to drink?" she asked. "Coffee, iced tea, a soft drink?"

"What, no booze?"

"No hard liquor. I might be able to come up with a cold beer."

"I'll go with that and next time I stop by, I'll see your bar gets restocked. It's the least a friend can do."

She got a beer from the fridge and sat it in front of him while he laid out his multipage proposal.

"What made you leave the FBI for the security business?" she asked.

"I liked the idea of being rich. And the FBI has too many stifling rules that I never liked to follow."

"They must have been upset when you resigned. I heard you were a superstar."

"I think they were glad to see me go so that they could get a rule-follower in my place. And don't believe the superstar bit. That was more a case of being in the right place at the right time—more than once. Jimmy Gott Terlecki was a good example of that."

The name sounded vaguely familiar. "Who was Terlecki?"

"A serial killer who preyed on young strippers and prostitutes in the DC area just under eight years ago. I was following where the clues led when I caught him in the act of strangling a prostitute in the back seat of his car."

"Is he still in prison?"

"Never spent a day in prison. He pulled a gun on me. I was faster than him. I put a bullet through his head."

The doorbell rang. "That's probably Hunter," she said.

By the time she reached the door he'd already let himself in. He pulled her into his arms for a kiss that sent tremors of desire from her head to her toes. She felt relieved. And safer. She always felt safe when Hunter was nearby.

"Is Robicheaux here yet?" he asked.

"He's in the kitchen."

"Good. I need to fill him in on the latest developments."

"I guess that means you want privacy."

"No. You may as well hear this, too. The mayor, chief of police, Barker and I are making a statement to the press at five."

Her pulse raced. "You've arrested the French Kill Killer?"

"The news is not quite that big, but it's positive."

In minutes the three of them had moved from the kitchen to the comfortable sitting room. Hunter sat down by her on the sofa where he'd fallen asleep what now seemed like ages ago. Robicheaux sat in a club chair opposite them.

"So, what is this major development?" Robicheaux asked.

"To start with, you were right when you said Elizabeth's killer was a copycat and not the same man who'd killed the first three victims."

"Always good to be right," Robicheaux said. "Is that a sure thing or a theory?"

"As of about two hours ago, we have confirmed DNA evidence to back it up."

Helena listened as Hunter explained how a man named Eric Presserman who was recently released from prison saw information about the reward money that Mia helped raise and came forward to tell what he knew.

"He claimed that while he was serving time at Angola, one of his cell mates, Samson Everson, who was in on armed robbery, bragged to him about killing two young women in swamps near New Orleans and throwing their bodies to the alligators.

"Samson didn't just tell him the basics, he provided all the gory details. Told him how he tied the victims' panties to tree branches and the bizarre pattern of slash marks left on their breasts. Information that was never released to the public, so Presserman would have had to get it from the killer."

"Crazy that when a man gets away with murder, he can't keep his mouth shut," Robicheaux said. "What else did the fool brag about?"

"He said he still dreamed of killing beautiful young women and couldn't wait to get out of prison and do it again. He already had his next victim picked out."

"Where is Everson now?" Robicheaux asked.

"Dead. What was left of his body was found in his torched and totaled car a few days before the third murder. No one tied him to the murder of the earlier two women."

"And they didn't check the DNA at the time?" Helena asked.

"They should have," Hunter agreed. "If they did, the results were never flagged and have since disappeared from the system."

"That sounds a bit suspicious," Helena said.

"Screwups happen sometimes," Hunter said.

"Son of a bitch," Robicheaux said. "A greedy ex-con spits out more information in one day than the task force has collected in almost six months. Guess I'm losing my touch."

"Thank goodness that sooner or later most criminals make mistakes," Hunter said, "like not being able to refrain from bragging about what they got away with."

Helena turned to Hunter. "But you still don't know who killed the third victim and then Elizabeth—or why. Or who is calling me on the phone claiming to be the killer. Now I wonder if that's even related to Elizabeth's murder. The caller might be some fruitcake trying to get in on the act, too. Another copycat. Perhaps he's not even dangerous. Except the killer talked about Elizabeth's red panties in one of his calls to Mia."

"Right. We still have every reason to believe your caller killed Elizabeth and likely the third victim, too."

"Once you kill someone and watch them die, it can get in your blood," Robicheaux said. "That's one thing I learned while working at the FBI."

Helena cringed.

"Not always," Hunter said, "but too often."

"The new developments provide the chief of police and the mayor something to dangle in front of the citizens as a sign of progress, but it doesn't lower the danger risk," Robicheaux said.

Hunter laid a hand on Helena's. "The good news is that you no longer have to worry about talking to the suspect. His calls will go straight to my phone and to the police tracking device."

"No," Helena said, without hesitation. "The caller thinks he has some connection to me. Even if you're not able to locate and arrest him via the call, he may slip and confess something to me just like Samson Everson did to his cell mate."

"It's not worth the risk," Hunter insisted.

"It will be if it stops a murder."

"Helena's right," Robicheaux said. "Once this new information hits the airwaves, things will change. If he gets nervous enough, he may give her something—anything—to help us identify and arrest him."

"Helena's not bait," Hunter said.

"I am if that's what it takes," Helena said. "Besides, I have complete trust that you'll protect me."

Complete trust. The one thing people kept warning her not to have.

"I like the way you think, Helena," Robicheaux said. "And once I get the new security system up and fully operating, I can guarantee you that no one will come into this house unless you let them in."

Helena wrapped her arms about her chest. "Which is close to what Elizabeth did when she went with her killer willingly."

Robicheaux rubbed the back of his neck as if his muscles were too tight. "There's no one hundred percent way to know that's exactly how that went down."

"True," Hunter agreed. "Everything we were sure of before is now suspect in my mind since we found out we're dealing with a copycat killer."

"I think it's someone close to home—too close," Helena said. "Possibly someone Ella sees as a friend. But then he must have been someone who'd heard Samson Everson's story, too."

"If Everson talked to Presserman, there's a good chance he talked to others," Robicheaux said.

Hunter and Robicheaux talked for another ten minutes, but Helena stopped trying to follow the conversation when the police jargon started to flow. She kept thinking of Elizabeth who'd been killed by a crazed copycat who treated life and death like a game.

Brigitte's warning echoed through her mind. She doubted either of the men would put much stock in the words of an elderly psychic in a senior living center, yet Helena couldn't ignore Brigitte's alarm.

She turned to face Hunter. "I never got a chance to

tell you what Brigitte Orillon said when Alyssa and I were leaving the assisted living center where she lives today."

"Brigitte Orillon?" Robicheaux repeated. "Isn't that the psychic who used to claim she could solve crimes?"

"Supposedly she used to be a medium," Helena said.

Robicheaux frowned. "If she's the same one I've heard of, she must be a hundred years old by know."

"Not quite." Helena left it at that.

"What did Brigitte say?" Hunter asked.

"That the killer is coming after me but that there will be two victims."

"Don't let her frighten you with that ballyhoo," Robicheaux said.

"I'm just repeating her words."

Hunter took Helena's hand and squeezed it. "I'm doing my best to see that there are *no* victims. And even if there are, no matter what the Orillons conjure up, you are not going to be one of them."

Robicheaux nodded. "And I'll be right there to see that Hunter has all the help he needs even if it means me moving in with you to be here when Hunter can't."

"I trust you with her life, but not anywhere near her bed," Hunter quipped.

Helena wasn't sure he was joking.

Hunter stood. "I hate to leave such good company, but I've got to go now. If I'm late, I'll catch hell from the chief."

Helena walked Hunter to the door. He held her in his arms and the thrill of being near him rocked her to her soul. Still she couldn't help thinking about Brigitte's words. Two victims.

"Does Lacy have full-time police protection?" Helena asked.

"She will now, as a precaution until she leaves the area. But she won't be aware of it."

"Thanks. That eases my mind. Will you be back tonight?" she asked, trying not to sound needy or afraid.

"I'll be back if you want me."

"I do."

"I'm not sure when. Barker and I will probably be working into the wee hours of the morning with all the new information we have to check out."

"I can go to the store and pick up something for dinner," Helena offered. "It's finally cool enough we could eat on the balcony by candlelight."

"How am I supposed to resist an invitation like that?"

"I was being quite selfish and hoping you couldn't."

"Barker won't like it, but I can probably get away for an hour or so around eight. You light the candles. I'll bring wine and dinner from my favorite steak house."

He trailed kisses from her earlobe to her lips.

And then he was gone, leaving her hungry for more of him.

Robicheaux took his time, hanging around until the press conference started. She had no choice but to invite him to watch it with her in the sitting room.

She would have preferred watching it without his commentary so that she could fully appreciate how intelligent, professional and gorgeous Hunter looked giving his spiel.

When the press conference was over, she practically pushed Robicheaux out the door. She went upstairs and was just stepping out of her clothes to shower when her phone rang.

She grabbed the phone and checked the caller ID. Randi. Terrible timing, but it could be important.

"I've got great news for you," Randi said as soon as they got past the hellos.

That, Helena wasn't expecting. "What kind of news?"

"I think we have a buyer and from what I hear, he's willing to pay the full appraisal price and possibly more."

Helena swallowed hard. A promising, prospective buyer. That's what she'd come back to New Orleans for. She should be jubilant. Instead anxiety settled like lead weights in her chest.

"Who is the interested party?" she asked.

"I'm not sure. I'm talking to the man's Realtor agent at this point, but it sounds like we're dealing with a celebrity of some sort or perhaps foreign royalty. He doesn't want his name revealed and he doesn't plan to use it for rental property so either he has a huge family or expects a lot of visitors."

Last Tuesday Helena would have been thrilled with this offer. That was before she'd reunited with Hunter, before he'd turned her world upside down. Before they'd made love.

She better understood his reasons for leaving before, but his miserable past was still his past. Could he promise and deliver forever, or would he walk away and break her heart again?

If he did, how would she ever get over that?

"I can request an appraisal tomorrow," Randi said. "Get that and then we'll see how serious our mystery buyer is."

Helena couldn't say yes—or no. "I need time to think this over."

"I don't recommend waiting around long," Randi said. "Real estate offers can go from hot to icy cold fast. Getting an appraisal doesn't obligate you to sell."

"You're right. I suppose an appraisal couldn't hurt."

"Agreed. I'll order one tomorrow and ask for a rush. I'm surprised you don't sound more excited, though. Are you having second thoughts about selling your late grandmother's beautiful home?"

Second thoughts. Third thoughts. All of them wrapped up in Hunter. "Perhaps," Helena admitted. "Let me know when you get the appraisal."

"Will do."

What she wanted was a lifetime of loving Hunter Bergeron. But it had to be all or nothing. No walking out when the going got tough. No crushing her heart and all her dreams again.

She needed commitment.

Chapter Fifteen

Hunter's spirits were plunging fast. With time of the essence, he and the rest of the task force seemed to be running in circles.

He pushed back from the table and walked over to their map of where each previous murder had taken place. "The first two victims no longer matter in the immediate scheme since their killer is dead. Presserman couldn't be the copycat killer since he was in prison during the third and fourth murders."

"The way I see it is our web grows smaller," Lane Crosby said. "I think we should narrow this down to a killer who knew Elizabeth and probably knew Mia Cosworth and possibly Helena, as well, before trying to figure out anyone's connection to Samson Everson or Presserman."

"So now we're looking for the man who killed victims three and four and then started making bizarre phone calls to first Mia and now Helena Cosworth," Barker said.

"And he's playing us like a well-tuned Stradivarius," Hunter said.

"Top of suspects on my list has always been Pierre Benoit," Barker said. "The guy's the perfect suspect and not just because I don't like his attitude. He speaks fluent French."

"He knew Mia, Ella and Elizabeth fairly well," Hunter said. "Plus, he's good-looking and suave enough that young women would be attracted to him."

"And he has an airtight alibi," Crosby reminded them.

"Or maybe not," Hunter said. "He was out of the country for the first two murders but not for Elizabeth's. Barker, how about you recheck which continent he was on at the time of the third murder?"

"How about we also put a tail on him for the next couple of days?" Barker said. "If he's Elizabeth's killer, he may lose his cool and try to skip town now that this new evidence is out."

"What about Connor Harrington?" Andy George asked. "I say we take another look at him, too."

"No reason not to." Hunter checked his watch. Eight o'clock. He expected an argument when he suggested they break for dinner. He didn't get it. Everyone was weary and hungry and needed some time with their family, but no one was ready to call it a night.

All five of the task force members agreed to meet back at ten to pore over the files for something they might have missed when they thought they were dealing with a serial killer who'd killed all four women.

Hunter called in a to-go order for filet mignons and salad from his favorite steak house. He'd make a quick stop at the liquor store, splurge for a bottle of good red wine and then he'd head straight for Helena's.

For the first time since he was a kid cowering from a drunken father, he was afraid. Afraid that he wasn't doing enough to protect Helena, though he had her house watched 24/7 and had her followed wherever she went.

But the brazen copycat killer was both incredibly evil and cunning. Hunter should never have let Helena take the phone calls from a maniac. He should have encouraged her from the first to go back to wherever home was until the killer was arrested.

It wasn't too late. Getting out of that house and out of New Orleans was surely the safest course of action. She wasn't one to take orders, but he'd do his best to persuade her to leave right away.

Her safety was all that mattered.

THE CRESCENT MOON floated in the night sky surrounded by brilliant stars that put Helena's fluttering candle to shame.

She sat across the iron bistro table from Hunter sipping her wine on what should have been one of the most poignantly romantic moments of her life. Instead anxiety and tension flooded the space between them.

Her perfectly grilled filet was barely touched. Hunter's plate was clean, amazing considering the deep worry lines that furrowed his brow.

His kiss when he'd arrived had been both tender and strained. Conversation since then had been almost non-existent. But unspoken or not, the tension dominated the night and let heartbreaking memories sneak into her consciousness.

It was stress and fear brought on by his job that had ripped them apart before. That time the situation had hit too close to home for him. She understood that better after hearing about his tragic childhood, but still his drawing away now troubled her.

"Is there something you're not telling me?" she asked.

"I'm just thinking you must be wishing that you'd never come back to New Orleans even temporarily."

"I don't regret coming back, though I admit the timing is bad."

"Do you still have a house in the Boston area?" Hunter asked.

"Yes. And a new job starting in November."

"The job of your dreams. The life of your dreams."

"Who told you that?"

"Mia." He turned to face her, then reached across the table and took both her hands in his. "I've given this a lot of thought, Helena. I think you should take the first flight back to Boston either tonight or in the morning."

She swallowed hard. "Are you that eager to get rid of me?"

"I'm that determined to keep you safe until the killer is off the streets. Hopefully that will be soon. Don't tell anyone you know around here where you are going. No one, not even Ella."

"Ella's not a killer."

"No, but she's a talker."

"Then you think the killer is someone she's close to?" Helena asked.

"I've never ruled that out."

Helena's resolve swelled. "I appreciate your concern, but I'm not going anywhere, Hunter. I'm the only personal contact you have with the French Kiss Killer. One more phone call might give us that breakthrough moment."

"I've gone along with you until now," Hunter said, "but the game has become too deadly. Even in Boston, you'll need a bodyguard. Robicheaux can hook you up with one."

"I'm not going anywhere. You do your job—I'll be here waiting for the bastard's call."

Hunter pushed back from the table. "There's a law against ignoring a policeman's orders."

"Really? Then arrest me."

"I'm considering that. Until I do, I'm moving Doug Conn into the carriage house with you tonight. He's not a member of the task force but he's one of the best detectives in the department. No one will get by him."

"If that's what it takes, then bring him on."

HELENA WAS EVEN more stubborn than Hunter remembered. It was an exasperating trait and weirdly he loved her all the more for it. She'd always gone after what she wanted.

At one time that had been him. He'd blown that. Now it was apparently a career in Boston she needed. Somehow, he couldn't imagine himself fitting in her art world.

Mia had suspected that all along. She hadn't specifically pointed out that Helena's life was better without him in it. Her words had been more tactful, but the message had been clear. Clearer yet had been her conviction that he'd broken Helena's heart once and that she didn't deserve that from him again.

He agreed. He loved Helena too much to ever put her through any kind of pain again. How could he ask her to give up a life she loved, one that challenged her great talent, to be with him?

And how in the world could he ever give her up again?

His phone vibrated, and he took a call from Barker.

"What's up?"

"I told you I wanted to put a tail on Pierre Benoit."

"Yeah. Did the chief balk on that?"

"No, but so far we haven't been able to locate him. A neighbor said she saw him leaving with a suitcase a couple of hours ago. I managed to get in touch with his supervising attorney at the law firm where he works. He said Pierre came in right before he left work today and requested a week's emergency leave."

"Did he get it?"

"He did. If I can't locate Pierre soon I'll put out an APB as a person of interest."

Robicheaux and Barker had considered Pierre Benoit a serious suspect from the beginning. Maybe he should have paid more attention to their hunches all along.

THE CLANGING OF garbage cans and the odor of fresh brewed coffee woke Helena from a restless sleep. She rolled over and experienced a sinking feeling when she realized that Hunter wasn't in bed with her. Evidently Doug Conn had brewed the coffee.

The grandfather clock on the landing chimed six times as she stretched and kicked off the top sheet. The air-conditioning was already cranking away even though thunderstorms and a dip in the temperature were forecast for late afternoon.

There had been no call from the killer that night. Weirdly, she regretted that, even though a madman's call in that spine-tingling child's voice tore her apart. But at least a call from him offered one more chance to locate him before it was too late.

Hunter had stayed until Doug Conn arrived for duty last night. Helena had hated to see him leave, but Doug had proved to be super nice and very professional.

He'd set up his laptop on the seldom used dining room table and assured her he was armed and ready to protect. She'd only seen the pistol he wore at his waist but suspected he had another weapon or two on him somewhere.

She slid her feet into her slippers, stepped over to the sliding glass door and opened the lightweight privacy drapes. The gloomy gray of predawn was depressing.

The two chairs pushed away from the table were bitter reminders of how quickly last night's dinner had gone from promising to a clash of wills. But the evening had still ended with a kiss at the door.

She walked to the bathroom, splashed her face with cold water and tamed her hair with a few strokes from her hairbrush.

She slipped into a full-skirted cotton dress and a pair of sandals and started down the staircase toward the inviting odor of coffee.

It was still impossible to descend the stairs without thinking of her grandmother and how much she missed her. She didn't doubt that Mia had discouraged Hunter from looking her up when he'd moved back to New Orleans.

She knew better than anyone how long it had taken for Helena to get her life back on track after their breakup. Nonetheless, the final decision not to contact Helena had still been Hunter's.

That was all in the past. The issues now were more confusing. Was the magic she felt with him lasting, or was it the danger that intensified their emotions to a fever point? Did he want her to leave because he thought their relationship was moving too fast, or was it purely for her own safety?

"Hope I didn't wake you," Doug said as she joined him in the kitchen.

"No, I'm an early riser—even when my life is normal. Have you heard from Hunter?"

"A couple of times during the wee hours of the morning and again about thirty minutes ago," Doug said.

So Hunter had no doubt had little or no sleep last night. "Are there any new developments in the case?"

"A couple, but I'll let him tell you about them. He asked that you call when you woke. He didn't want to disturb you. Coffee's fresh if you want some."

"Thanks." She poured herself a cup. "I can cook you some bacon and pancakes after I talk to Hunter or there's my standby of yogurt and granola that you can help yourself to."

"Actually, I'll be leaving as soon as my replacement gets here. Hunter will fill you in on that."

"Then if you'll excuse me, I'll take my coffee onto the private courtyard patio and call Hunter."

"Is that the one off the downstairs bedroom?"

"Yes."

"I'll walk out with you and secure the area and then give you all the privacy you need."

In many ways this level of protection was more frightening than being on her own, a constant reminder that she was living under a time bomb of danger.

But if Brigitte had been right, there would be two victims. Was there some young woman right now going about her life with no hint that someone was stalking her and planning her murder?

Five minutes later, Helena had settled in a dark green Adirondack chair with a view of the privacy fence that surrounded her, pots of late-blooming asters and lantana and a male cardinal who perched on the top of a standing bird feeder. Hunter's phone rang twice before he answered.

"Doug said you wanted me to call."

"Yeah. I did. Can I call you right back, ten minutes or less?"

"Certainly."

He sounded weary and a little edgy. Hopefully it was not because the killer had struck during the night. She finished her coffee and set the empty cup on the table beside her chair, scaring off a gecko who tumbled to the stone floor.

She grabbed the phone when it rang. "Hello."

"Sorry about that, but I was on the phone with Barker and it couldn't wait."

"A new development?" she asked, praying it was a good one.

"Pierre Benoit was picked up for questioning in Dallas, Texas, a couple of hours ago."

"Pierre? Questioned about what? You surely don't think he killed Elizabeth."

"That hasn't been ruled out completely, but apparently his sudden departure from his home and job here is a result of his mother having a stroke yesterday."

"Oh, dear. I'm sorry to hear that."

"We all are. He was released immediately."

"Anything else happen while I slept?"

"Several more leads phoned in after the publicity yesterday. We're checked them out, but so far nothing is jelling."

"I was almost sure the killer would call last night," Helena said, thinking out loud. "He seems to enjoy the game of cat and mouse so much."

"About last night," Hunter said. "I know I came on strong, but you have to understand that it's not some unreasonable cop machoism. It's that I can't do my job here unless I know I'm doing everything possible to protect you."

"I know that and I appreciate it."

"Did things work out okay with Doug?"

"Perfect. He's super professional."

"One of the most trusted guys on the force in my mind. So is his replacement today. Ralph Bellinger. You'll like him."

"Do you really think it's necessary I have someone in the house with me during the daylight?"

"Humor me."

"I will. You outrank me. Just one more quick question. Do you know how much longer Lacy and her friend will be in New Orleans?"

"They are flying home tomorrow afternoon."

"That makes me feel better. Will I see you again today?"

"I was afraid you might not want me to after last night."

"I very much want to. Please take care of yourself, Hunter." She wanted to say more, like I love you. The timing seemed all wrong.

"See you the first chance I get. Until then Ralph will look after you, but I want you to seriously consider leaving town."

And though she hated to admit it, right now she did desperately miss her safe, peaceful life in Boston.

RALPH BELLINGER WAS as professional as Doug, staying out of Helena's way and leaving her to wander the carriage house as the hours dragged by. She tried cleaning out her grandmother's bedroom closet, but each item she touched brought her spirits even lower.

Thankfully, Ella walked over at noon and joined Helena for a sandwich and a glass of iced tea. Ella avoided talk about the new findings in Elizabeth's murder investigation in spite of the fact that it was all over the news.

Instead she relied on talk of the weather. Thunder rumbled in the distance and layers of dark clouds were rolling in.

"I know it sounds strange," Helena said, "but I've always liked thunderstorms. Not hurricanes or tornadoes, mind you, just the ferocity of an average New Orleans thunderstorm. They seem to wash away the staleness and revive the earth."

"It stormed the night Elizabeth was abducted."

"I didn't know that," Helena said.

"No reason you should."

There was no rage in Ella's voice. It was a statement of resignation, acknowledgement of a grief that would never be washed away.

Ella pushed away her half-eaten sandwich and wiped her mouth on the cloth napkin.

"It wasn't raining when Elizabeth left the house," Ella continued. "The sudden squall from the Gulf blew in around ten. I worried that she was cold and wet, never knowing that she was in the hands of a monster."

"I'm sorry." The expression was pathetically inadequate, but Helena couldn't think of anything that would ease Ella's pain.

"Your grandmother stood by me through it all. I don't think I would have survived without her."

"I know Mia was glad she could be here for you."

"She was amazing. She was always claiming she was close to identifying Elizabeth's killer. Bless her heart, I think she really believed that."

"But you didn't?"

"No. She sat around and read those books about serial killers until all hours of the morning. They put weird thoughts in her head. In the beginning, she'd actually suggested Hunter might be the killer because she figured he was mentally unstable when he called off your wedding. Then she got to know him and realized how smart and dedicated he really is."

Thunder rolled in the distance and the first streak of lightning split the clouds.

"I better get home before the monsoon hits," Ella said. She carried her plate and tea glass to the sink.

Helena walked her to the door and gave her a warm hug. "Call if you need anything," Helena said.

"I will. I know this is none of my business, but I don't think you should sell this house or the property. You belong here. You belong with Hunter."

Helena couldn't argue that.

She considered delving into the books on Mia's nightstand again but decided against it. Instead she walked upstairs and turned on her laptop.

She typed in French Kiss Killer and watched as a choice of articles popped up. She surfed down to one written by Antoine Robicheaux.

"Living in the Head of a Serial Killer."

She scanned the article, hitting only the main points. It emphasized that to identify and apprehend a serial killer, one had to think like the killer. Understand how he sees his world.

She skipped to another article by Robicheaux. This one described how he'd assisted in apprehending several serial killers in states across the country.

She could see why Hunter thought so highly of him. She just hoped he came through this time.

ALYSSA ORILLON CLOSED the door behind a customer and staggered to her chair, suddenly so dizzy and disoriented her feet couldn't find the floor.

She'd been fine earlier in the day when Lacy Blankenship and two of her friends had stopped in, but within minutes after they'd left, she'd developed a case of vertigo. She'd had to lie down for a half hour to regain her equilibrium.

That was over an hour ago. Now, she was developing a brain-crushing headache to go with her nausea.

And still she couldn't get Lacy Blankenship off her mind.

Lacy was the only one who'd wanted a psychic session. She was positively giddy as she'd described her obsession with an older man she'd met in New Orleans. She wanted Alyssa to offer assurances that this sophisticated charmer she'd fallen in love with at first sight loved her as much as she loved him.

Alyssa didn't have to be a medium to realize the vacation affair with an older pursuer wasn't likely the real thing. Even in Lacy's love-crazed description of him, he sounded like a player.

She'd delicately warned Lacy not to invest too much of herself into the relationship until she'd known the man longer. Separation wouldn't tear them apart if he was the right man for her. Alyssa seriously doubted her words had affected the impressionable young woman.

Now all Alyssa could think of was Lacy and her likeness to Elizabeth, who had also trusted the wrong man.

Alyssa put her head back and closed her eyes. Her head begin to spin and then the dark, bloody images from the other night struck like waves of neon lights crashing into her brain.

Only now it was Lacy and Helena on the run, sloshing through mud and standing water, the man with the knife chasing them through the fog.

The images zoomed in and out, faster and faster. Her stomach retched. She made it to the bathroom just in time to lose her lunch. Shaking and weak, she went back to the chair where she'd been sitting, picked up her phone and punched in Helena's number.

Chapter Sixteen

But occasionally a successful serial killer defied all odds, his skill coming from his superior intellect and his motivation via the thrill of power. That made him almost impossible to track down and apprehend.

HELENA'S PHONE RANG as she finished reading the disturbing words from one of her grandmother's collection of articles.

"Hello."

"Helena. It's Alyssa." Her voice was so shaky Helena could barely understand her.

"What's wrong?"

"I need to talk to you. Can I come over now?"

"No. You sound ill. I'll call 911."

"No. It's the images again, the ones from the other night. I'm so afraid for you. I think the killer is about to strike."

Alyssa was clearly shaken. Her fear was real. Her facts were sketchy. "Stay put. I'll be there as fast as I can."

"You can't come alone. It's too dangerous."

"Rest assured. There's no chance of my doing this solo. My bodyguard won't allow it."

She broke the connection and stepped onto her balcony. The air was still muggy, but dark clouds had rolled in. A lightning bolt streaked across the sky followed by a deafening clap of thunder. The full force of the storm would hit any minute.

Helena grabbed an umbrella and raced down the stairs. Ralph heard her approach and was waiting for her at the foot of the staircase.

"Whoa there. Where do you think you're rushing off to with that umbrella?"

"My friend Alyssa Orillon just called. She's hallucinating about the serial killer and is practically hysterical. I have to calm her down."

"I have strict orders from Hunter that you're not to leave the house. If you try, I have to contact him."

"You do what you need to. I'm doing what I have to."

Helena had no doubt that Ralph would follow her or that he'd contact Hunter who'd have someone follow her.

Ralph's footsteps sounded behind her, keeping up with her fast pace even though she could hear him talking on his phone. She unlocked the gate, shoved it open and took off at a jog.

An elderly couple had stopped on the sidewalk and were struggling to open a stubborn umbrella in preparation for the deluge that would hit soon. Any other time Helena would have stopped to help and encouraged them to seek shelter before the inevitable torrents of rain arrived.

Another lightning and thunder duo hit as she reached the corner. The sidewalks were mostly empty now, though a group of millennials, likely tourists, were dancing around across the street from her and sipping daiquiris from red to-go cups as if the storm was reason to party.

Helena glanced around. Ralph was a mere step behind her. If anyone had noticed them, they might have thought he was chasing her. She was two blocks from Alyssa's when the first fat drops of rain pelted the top of her head and her face.

A gust of cold wind whipped her hair into her eyes and sent the rain flying at her sideways, prickling her skin like needles. She slowed enough to open her umbrella before crossing the street in the middle of the block to reach the side with more store awnings for protection.

As she stepped onto the curb, an even stronger gust of wind hit, reversing her umbrella and almost blowing it from her hands. Trying to control it threw her off balance. She tripped, and her feet went flying from beneath her.

Two strong arms wrapped around her a second before her butt hit the sloshing water. She turned around, expecting her rescuer to be Ralph. It wasn't.

"Hunter. How did you get here at that exact moment?"

"I'm like Superman. I sense when a lovely damsel is in distress."

"More like a half-drowned, clumsy damsel."

"I never said I was picky."

He led her to a storefront of a souvenir shop and they huddled close to the glass, protected by the large awning. Her damp hair dripped down her face and tickled her eyelashes. His arm was around her shoulders.

Her gaze met Hunter's. His fingers trailed a path down her wet cheeks until he slid his thumb beneath her chin and nudged her mouth to his. His lips found hers and she melted into his sweet, poignant kiss. In the midst of a storm, her life in danger from a madman, she had never felt so protected or loved.

The rain continued to fall in deluges for several minutes, finally slowing to a shower as the ferocity of the storm gave way to the first cool front of autumn.

"Tell me what's up with Alyssa," he said, his deep voice more gravelly than it had been before their kiss.

"She's seeing those visions again and they have thrown her into a state of hysteria."

"I thought you told me she doesn't claim to have any clairvoyant powers."

"That's what she says, but still she's unable to dismiss the images as being irrelevant."

"Then I guess we better go check her out."

"You don't have to go with me," she said. "I know how busy you are. I didn't tell Ralph to call you."

"I'm busy looking for a killer who's playing me for a fool. I've spent hours upon hours chasing rabbits. What can I lose by spending a few minutes with a psychic?" He ran his hand across her shoulder blades and let his fingers tangle in her hair. "Besides, I'm not about to turn down a legitimate reason for spending some time with you."

"I like that." She turned around suddenly realizing her previous bodyguard was nowhere in sight. "Where's Ralph?" she asked as Hunter raised his umbrella.

"Taking a break before going back to the carriage house. I told him when I caught up with him that you're in my hands for now."

"Very good hands," she agreed as they started sloshing through and around puddles toward Alyssa's.

HUNTER HAD TO admit that talking to psychics made him uncomfortable. He figured to each his own when it came to making a living as long as it didn't hurt anyone else, but he couldn't buy into the sixth sense business.

Nonetheless, the minute they walked in her door, he could see that she was shaken. He listened and let Helena do the talking at first but joined in the conversation when they got down to the direct facts of the matter.

"It started as soon as Lacy and her friends left," Alyssa explained. "Well, actually, I was uncomfortable talking to Lacy about this man she'd met while here on vacation. It got worse from there."

"Who were the friends that were with her?" Hunter asked.

"Her friend Brenda who was with her when she came originally, though I didn't know her name on that first visit. And a slightly older woman named Courtney."

If Courtney was with them, there was much less to worry about. "Tell me again what Lacy said about this man and try to leave nothing out."

The story Alyssa told about falling for a gorgeous stranger could probably describe hundreds of tourists a year. "Did Lacy tell you his name?"

"No. I asked, but she said she'd rather keep that a secret. That's not why I think she's in danger," Alyssa insisted. "It's the phantasms that haunt me."

"Phantasms? Not sure I know what those are," Hunter admitted.

"Ghostlike creatures. Only they weren't ghosts, they were bloody images of real people. Lacy and Helena and a man who's always too blurry to recognize."

"I know the idea of a serial killer right here in the French Quarter is frightening," Hunter said. "But remember that we have zero evidence that the serial killer has ever seen Lacy, much less that she's his target."

"But Lacy looks so much like Elizabeth," Alyssa argued. "If he merely ran into her on the streets, he'd have to see that. Whatever attracted him to Elizabeth would attract him to Lacy, too."

"That's possible, which is why I'll check on Lacy. Is there somewhere private I can make a phone call?"

"Yes, in my studio." She crossed the room and opened the door for him. One step inside and he felt like he'd entered the inner realm of some magical Greek goddess.

A bowl of fragrant vapors, dim lighting, a glowing crystal ball, a set of cards spread out on the silk-covered table. And creepy background music that he'd only heard before in haunted houses at Halloween.

He made a call to Courtney to verify that Lacy was safe.

She answered on the first ring.

"Thanks for calling me back so soon, Hunter."

"If you called me earlier, I didn't get the message. I was just calling you to make sure everything is going okay."

"I just left the message at the precinct. We have a problem."

Not what he wanted to hear.

"Lacy has disappeared."

"Do you have any idea where she is or who she's with?"

"I do."

His insides took a hit as he listened to the details. He prayed his worst fears were all wrong and wished to God he didn't have to tell this to Helena. But she deserved the truth. There wasn't enough sugar in the world to fully coat this but he'd damn sure try.

Chapter Seventeen

Hunter didn't give any verbal indication the news was bad when he rejoined Helena and Alyssa, but Helena knew that was the verdict from the extended veins in his neck and his strained facial expression.

He tried to reassure Alyssa that things were under control. He was good at that and she did seem to be feeling a little better when they left.

Helena waited until they were out the door before she confronted Hunter. "What's the real story?"

He reached down, took her hand and squeezed it. "Nothing you want to hear."

"I know you only want to protect me, Hunter, but I don't want to be protected from the truth. Did you talk to Courtney or just to one of the other officers involved in the investigation?"

"I talked to Courtney."

"Is she still with Lacy and Brenda?"

"She's with Brenda. Lacy seems to have disappeared."

"Disappeared from where? The hotel?"

"The city."

Panic painted ugly pictures in her mind. She struggled to stay reasonably calm.

"The three of them were having lunch and a beer

at the Crescent City Brewhouse. They were almost through eating when Lacy excused herself to go the restroom and didn't return."

"So she just walked out on them. Did they have an argument?"

"According to Courtney, everything seemed to be going great except that Lacy was even livelier and more animated than usual."

None of this made sense. Surely no one abducted her in the middle of the day. "When did this happen?"

"Approximately a half hour ago. They started to worry after about ten minutes. They searched the bathroom and outside the building. There was no sign of her. The rain had started by then so it was very unlikely she stepped outside to make a phone call or write a text."

"Did they try to text her?"

"They called her and then they answered her phone. She'd left it on the table with them so they couldn't possibly reach her."

"Did they see her talking to anyone who looked suspicious either inside or outside the restaurant?"

He shook his head. "Don't jump to the worst conclusions, Helena."

"You mean like the fact that the French Kiss Killer told me it was full speed ahead or that Lacy looks enough like the last young woman he'd murdered that they could be twins?"

"Or more likely, she's slipped off to see her new love interest that she told Alyssa about."

"Do they know who that is?"

"Brenda has strong suspicions. She thinks Lacy has been sneaking out to meet Connor Harrington after he goes off duty at night."

"Connor, my engaged tenant? What a jerk. Lacy is years too young…"

She stopped midsentence as a terrifying possibility rushed her brain. "Oh my God. Surely he didn't kill Elizabeth. He's not planning to kill Lacy."

"More likely he's a jerk who two-times his fiancée, but I'm heading over to the Aquarelle Hotel now to question him about his relationship to Lacy and see if they're up to a little afternoon delight or if he knows where she is."

"And if he's not there?" she asked, her fears multiplying even with no real evidence.

"If he's not there, we'll find him. I had hoped we could grab a quick lunch before I had to jump back into the fray but looks like that's out of the question. I'll walk you home. It's barely out of the way."

"I'll save you the trouble," Helena said, the plan forming in her mind as she spoke. "I'm going to the hotel with you."

"This is police business. I can't take a civilian into that situation."

"Then I'm going without you. As a friend of Lacy, I have every right to talk to him myself."

"You're not a friend of Lacy's."

"Close enough." She started walking.

Hunter tried to grab her wrist. She shoved him away and kept walking.

"At least let me do all the talking," Hunter ordered.

She made no promises.

Fifteen minutes later Helena and Hunter were seated in Connor's office, sipping hot coffee from deep blue mugs that had been brought in by one of his waitresses. Connor sat across from them, tapping nervously on the table.

"This isn't the best time for me to chat," Connor said, "but since you insisted we meet, I assume this is police business."

"It is," Hunter said.

Connor nodded toward Helena. "So why is she here?"

"She's concerned about a young woman who's a guest in your hotel."

"It's not my job to keep up with the guests. It's my job to make sure they're comfortable and satisfied."

"Have you been satisfying Lacy Blankenship this afternoon?" Helena asked, letting the reproachful words slip out before she could stop them.

Hunter glared at her.

Connor ignored her question and kept facing Hunter. "What is this about? Are you accusing me of something?"

"No," Hunter answered. "We're just trying to track down Miss Blankenship. It seems she's lost her phone and no one can reach her."

"Have you contacted her friend Brenda who's traveling with her? You can usually find the two of them together."

"Not this time. Brenda is the one who brought her sudden disappearance to our attention."

"I'm sorry, but I can't help you with that."

"Brenda seems to think you've been hanging out with Lacy after closing time," Hunter said.

"Is that against the law these days?"

"No," Hunter said.

"Regardless, I haven't seen her after work or any other time except to speak to her inside the hotel common areas. I'm engaged to be married to a beautiful and wonderful woman. I love her and there is no way I'm going to mess up what we have with a fling. Besides, it would be against company policy and I'm not doing anything to blow this job."

Helena had to admit he sounded sincere, and she wanted to believe him. She'd always liked Connor. But the anxiety burning in her chest wouldn't quit.

"Do you have security cameras in the hallway?" Helena asked.

"Antoine Robicheaux's company installed all of our security features," Connor assured her. "They're the best in the business. I'd need a warrant to release private information on my guests."

"No warrant at this point," Hunter said. "I would like to check her room to make sure she hasn't injured herself and can't call for help."

"Good idea," Connor agreed willingly. "I'll check her room number and walk you up there."

In case she'd been injured or met with foul play. Helena knew exactly what he really meant.

"You'll need to wait here, Miss Cosworth," Connor said. "Company policy when I open someone's room for the police."

"No problem."

Apprehension ran ragged races along her nerves until they returned ten minutes later. The room search had revealed nothing. Suitcases and clothes were still in the closets and there was no sign of foul play.

"So, that's it?" Helena questioned as they left the hotel.

"I can't exactly arrest him due to rumors he may be having a consensual affair."

"But what if he knows where Lacy is? What if…"

Hunter interrupted her with a finger to her lips. "I'm a good cop, Helena, with great instincts. I think Connor was telling the truth."

"But if you're wrong?"

"Then we're still covered. I'll have a tail on him until Lacy shows up."

"I'm sorry," she said. "You're the detective. I'm not. But this is all so frightening and nerve-racking."

"I know. For all of us. I'm just trying to do my job the best I know how. I'll put my life on the line in a heartbeat to save an innocent life—the same way everyone on the investigative force will. But just so you know, keeping you safe is the most important thing in my life right now."

He pulled her into his arms and touched his lips to hers. She trembled, not from fear, but from the intensity of the emotions coursing through her veins.

"Thanks for being a hero," she said when he let her go. "Thanks for looking after me."

"Always."

Always would be almost long enough for her.

THE RAIN HAD slowed to a mist when he spotted Lacy, waiting for him in the narrow alleyway where he'd told her to meet him. He scanned the area to make sure no one was watching and then stopped next to the dumpster.

He reached across the seat and opened the passenger side door. She smiled and climbed in.

"I was afraid you weren't coming," she said, leaning over for a kiss as he drove to the corner.

"I'm right on time," he said, just as he'd planned it. "Have you seen anyone since you got here?"

"No people. I was checked out by a calico cat and a couple of roaches large enough to give the curious cat a ride on their backs. This disgusting alley stinks."

"Sorry about that but it can't be helped."

"How long do we have to keep our feelings for each other a secret?"

"One more night, and then you can tell the world."

"You're so mysterious."

"That's what you love about me." He chuckled as he reached over and ran his right hand between her legs. This would be so easy. He turned right at the corner.

"Where are we going?" Lacy asked.

"To a hideaway in Algiers."

"A hotel?"

"Nothing that boring," he teased.

"I don't even know where Algiers is, but I can't wait."

"Only a short drive away, I promise. And then we'll have the whole night together."

"I'll need to use your phone to call Brenda before dark and let her know I'm safe."

"Of course, my sweet. We can do whatever you want." Tonight would be his grand finale, the end of his career as the French Kiss Killer.

Two more murders and then he'd have to let this dark side of him die with the murderous legend. Part of being a successful serial killer was knowing when to let the identity fade into oblivion. Even he couldn't outsmart everyone forever.

Tonight, he'd have the ultimate orgasm as he watched two beautiful women fighting for their last breaths before he tossed them overboard to the hungry gators who lived in the swampy waters.

And no one would ever guess that the killer had been in their midst all the time.

HELENA RECEIVED A phone call from Hunter at ten o'clock that evening. He gave her a quick update on the quickly emerging situation.

Lacy Blankenship had not been found. Her friend Brenda was an emotional train wreck and was talking to every reporter who'd listen to her. She'd also called Lacy's parents.

It was the first they'd heard of the French Kiss Killer. They were desperate and had booked the first flight to New Orleans the following morning.

"I'd hoped I could get back there to at least tell you good night in person, but that looks impossible now."

"I understand. I'm in good hands with Cory Barker tonight, but what happened to Doug Conn? Did he have enough of me already?"

"He's taking the second shift tonight," Hunter said. "Rest assured, no way is anyone getting the best of Barker."

"I'm convinced," she said. "Don't worry about me. I'm more concerned about you."

"Don't be. I plan to still be alive to celebrate when the French Kiss Killer goes down. Tell Barker I'll get back to him later. Gotta run now, but…" He hesitated. "About the other night when I said you should go to Boston. That was only about keeping you safe. I hope you know that."

"Let's save the subject of Boston for another night."

They said their goodbyes and she walked back into the kitchen. Barker was spooning vanilla ice cream over a slice of apple pie Ella had brought over at dinnertime.

She filled him in on the latest news about Lacy. Neither of them mentioned that she might be in the hands of the serial killer, but the possibility silently overrode the conversation and the mood.

Barker wiped his mouth on a paper towel he'd taken from the counter. "You can tell me it's none of my business if you want, but what's the deal between you and

Hunter? I know you used to date, but what broke you guys up? You seem to have a lot of chemistry going on between you now."

She started to evade a direct answer to Barker's question the way she usually did, but what was the point? It was fact.

"He left me at the altar."

"Hunter? Man, that doesn't sound like him."

"He had his reasons."

"That's a shocker. I figured it was the other way around. Your grandmother said you were a very talented artist with a promising career in Boston. Hunter doesn't seem like much of a fine arts connoisseur kind of guy so I figured you were too sophisticated for him."

"I am an artist and I do love everything about the art world and Boston, but that's not what broke us up."

"They have art in New Orleans—or so I've heard," Barker said. "I haven't actually seen any of it, well, except for the statues in the park and in St. Louis Cathedral. Any chance you'll move back here permanently and take over your grandmother's property?"

"There's always a chance." If she had something to come back for.

BY THE TIME Helena went to bed, the rain had stopped completely, and the clouds had thinned to the point where a few stars and a crescent moon found an occasional opening.

She'd left the curtains open, preferring a glimpse of moonlight to darkness tonight. Better to see the shadows creeping across her ceiling than to fight the nightmarish images flooding her subconscious.

It was past midnight the last time she'd checked the phone. The monster had still not called.

HELENA WAS WAKENED by the shrill ringing of her phone. Startled, she sat up in bed, heart pounding. The monster had finally called.

She reached for the wired phone but let her hand slide across it without picking it up when she realized it was her personal phone that was ringing. It must be Hunter calling with another update.

She stared out the sliding glass door and murmured hello in her sleep-heavy, husky voice.

"Bonjour, mademoiselle." Spoken in a soft, disguised voice.

Her heart jumped to her throat. The monster was always a step ahead.

"Who are you?" she begged. "Where are you?"

"Turn around and see."

Chapter Eighteen

Fear gripped Helena as she stood, turned and stared into the steel-gray eyes of Antoine Robicheaux. Only a few feet away. Smiling as if this were all a very sick joke.

"Not you. The monster can't be you."

Her pleadings of denial sounded brittle even to her own ears, as if fighting their way through a scream that was stuck in her throat.

"Don't be so surprised. No one is what they seem. Not even you. Given the right circumstances, everyone can kill."

"You're right. I could kill you right now and enjoy it."

But could she or would she hesitate even if the pistol Hunter had given her was in her hand?

"Did you kill Elizabeth Grayson?"

"No. That was the work of the French Kiss Killer." He smirked. "I'm part of the good guys team. Just ask Hunter."

"Do you have Lacy?"

"Are you jealous? Don't be. She's waiting on you in the swamp. We should hurry. The gators will be getting hungry."

In one quick movement, she yanked open the drawer of her bedside table and went for the gun she'd never expected to fire. Before she could take aim, Robicheaux knocked the gun from her shaking grasp and slammed a fist into her stomach.

She doubled over in pain and finally the scream escaped. Shrill, loud, tearing from her throat like ripped tissue. There was no way Barker couldn't have heard her, but there was no response.

Robicheaux must have already killed him. She was on her own. She was no match for him physically, but if she could make it onto her balcony, some late-night partyers on the street might hear her scream.

But the bed was between her and the balcony and Robicheaux was between her and the stairs.

There was no exit. She had to fight. Still struggling to breathe after the punch in the stomach, she went for the bedside lamp.

Before she could tear the plug from the wall, he was on her again. She felt a sharp, piercing stab in her neck. She saw the needle as he pulled it from her flesh. She kicked and swung her fists, connecting only with air.

The room began to spin. Pinpricks of light went off inside her head like bottle rockets as Robicheaux bound her legs and wrists. She knew what he was doing, but she had no control of her body. No feeling of pain or movement.

Hunter would kill Robicheaux for this. Somehow, he'd find out the truth and Robicheaux would pay. But it would be too late for Helena and Lacy.

I love you, Hunter. I haven't moved on. I couldn't. You never let go of my heart.

HELENA FADED IN and out of the comatose condition, unsure where she was even when she was partially alert, unable to scream or to speak, her body being bounced around as if she were on a carnival ride.

She had no idea how long she'd been floating in and out of consciousness. A moment? An hour? A day?

Finally, the movement stopped. She opened her eyes as metal clicked and could tell that she was lying in the trunk of a vehicle, a man staring down at her.

Romeo. Antoine Robicheaux. The monster. Confusion diffused enough that she remembered being abducted. She had no idea where he'd taken her. Her wrists and hands were bound in duct tape.

He lifted her roughly as if she were a sack of potatoes and then propped her against the back fender of a pickup truck. Her bare feet sank into a boggy quagmire.

He dragged her through an area that became continuously swampy as they went downhill toward a gray, weathered, ramshackle house like the ones Hunter had pointed out to her when they'd visited Eulalie.

But the area looked different. More trees with branches that canopied the dark water. A bayou that seemed to finger out in every direction.

She heard a splash and turned to watch an alligator slide from the muddy bank and into a strand of slowly moving water.

When they reached the half-rotted steps to the front porch, Robicheaux picked her up, carried her inside and then dropped her onto a stained and dusty sofa.

Lacy was propped into a straight-backed chair a few feet away. Her wrists and feet were bound as well, and she was tied to the chair. A dirty rag had been stuffed into her mouth, no doubt to keep her from screaming while he had gone back for Helena.

Robicheaux walked over and yanked the rag from Lacy's mouth. "Scream and the party's over. You get me."

She nodded.

"You two enjoy your visit to the bayou. It's all part of the Louisiana adventure, Lacy. Helena can tell you all about it while I get your little surprise ready. I'll be back soon, but I want both of you to be fully alert for our next adventure. If you guessed it's a boat ride, you get the prize. We'll take the pirogue down the bayou and then we'll stop. I'll slice your breasts and your throats and watch while you choke to death on your gurgling blood. Then I'll toss you overboard."

Fury temporarily overrode Helena's fear. "You won't get away with this. Hunter will track you down. You'll see death from the other side and we'll see how brave you are then."

Lacy began to cry. "I thought you loved me. Why are you doing this?"

"Because I have no choice."

He stood silent for a long time and for the first time Helena thought she saw a trace of regret in his eyes.

"Why did you call my grandmother?" Helena asked the question that had burned in her mind ever since she'd arrived back in New Orleans.

"Because I liked her. If she hadn't fallen and died when she did, she might have been the one person who could have dragged me out of the darkness."

"It's not too late. You can walk away from this hell."

"I'll walk away when you two are dead."

He was truly mad.

Helena had to find a way to escape. Her wrists and ankles were still bound, but she could crawl and scoot across the floor. There must be something inside this house she could use as a weapon.

"Wait," Robicheaux said as he started to walk out the door. "I almost forgot, and it only takes one little mistake to take a killer down."

He walked back over and tied Helena's hands to a giant meat hook that hung from an iron overhead beam.

He was the devil himself.

"One more question," Helena said.

"Anything to make this good for you but make it quick."

"How did you know the man who had killed the first two women was dead before you killed the third woman and Elizabeth Grayson?"

"Because I'm an expert at what I do. I had tracked Samson Everson down. I was watching when he killed the second woman and I knew when he'd been released from prison and selected his third target. I killed him first."

The truth was sickening. "You could have saved the second victim, couldn't you? Instead you let her die and then you became the monster yourself. No wonder you know so much about how the brains of serial killers function. You are one."

"And now he's going to kill us." Tears rolled down Lacy's cheeks. "Please don't kill us," she begged. "I'll never tell anyone what you've done. Just let me live."

"It's too late for that now," Robicheaux said. "I have to see this through."

Helena waited until he was out of earshot before she tried to comfort Lacy. "Don't give up yet. As long as we're breathing, we have a chance. The smartest, bravest detective I know has promised to keep me safe. All we have to do is stay alive until he gets here."

She had no idea how he'd ever find them, but she had to hold on to something. She loved Hunter even more now than she had six years ago.

She had to live to tell him that.

Chapter Nineteen

Hunter was at a dead run when he reached the door to the carriage house. He'd tried to reach Barker and Helena on his way over. Neither had answered.

He couldn't imagine that anyone could have gotten past Cory Barker, but that didn't reduce the rising panic. He unlocked the door and rushed inside, Smith & Wesson in hand.

"Barker! Helena!" His frantic calls echoed through the house. The only response was a coughing noise as if someone was trying to clear their throat.

He followed the noise to the sitting room. He saw the blood splattered over the furniture and walls before he saw Barker. Barker was facedown in a pool of crimson.

Hunter fell to his knees and checked Barker's pulse. Almost too weak to be alive. He looked at the chest wound. The blood was starting to clot. "Where's Helena?" Hunter asked.

"He took her." Barker's voice was weak, the words whispered.

"Who took her? Who did this?"

"Romeo."

Curses flew from his mouth. "I'll kill him."

"Get on it."

"Do you know where they went?"

"Algiers. Swamp. First victim."

Fury and dread roared through Hunter as he called for an ambulance for Barker.

"Hold on. Help is coming, old buddy," Hunter said.

The French Kiss Killer had finally made a mistake. He'd thought Barker was struggling for his last breath when he couldn't resist bragging about his plan.

He should have known Barker was as tough as they came.

Hunter knew exactly where the first victim had been killed. He'd checked out the crime scene several times after the murder.

He didn't wait around for the ambulance. Barker needed a lot more help than he could give him.

He had to reach Helena in time.

Time was running out for Helena and Lacy. Helena knew it, but still she cursed Robicheaux as he tucked her and Lacy into the hull of the long, narrow pirogue. With their wrists and ankles still bound, there was no way to roll into the water and try to swim to safety.

Their only chance of escape would be for Helena to get her hands on the hunting knife Robicheaux wore in a scabbard like a sword. Robicheaux stood in the back of the boat and poled them away from the muddy bank.

Their boat ride to hell had started.

Lacy screamed for help but there was no one to hear. Helena used her body to rock the boat, hoping Robicheaux would fall on top of them and she could get her hands on that knife. It was a long shot. It was the only shot.

Robicheaux didn't fall. Instead, he dropped the pole inside the boat and unsheathed the knife. He raised it over her, ready to bury it in her chest or to slice her throat.

Her last thoughts were of Hunter and all the years they'd wasted.

Chapter Twenty

Hunter dodged branches, tangled vines and massive palmetto fronds as he raced toward the leaning, crumbling fishing cabin he remembered well. He'd parked uphill, above the worst of the swamp. He didn't want to be spotted until he was ready to spring into action.

The house was dark. Hunter's spirit plunged. He pushed himself to run faster, ignoring the pain in his chest and the cold, slimy snake he had to brush from his face after colliding with the branch of a cypress tree.

And then he heard the scream. Not coming from inside the house. He followed the sound, away from the house and toward the murky bayou.

He couldn't understand what had driven Robicheaux to this madness. It was of no concern now. All that mattered was stopping him before he killed Helena and probably Lacy, as well.

Hunter had lived through watching his father kill his mother. He didn't think he could live through losing Helena. Life couldn't take his world away again.

HELENA HELD HER breath as Robicheaux hesitated. He stared into the distance as if he'd heard or seen something that startled him.

She rocked the boat again. He fought to maintain his balance and then swung the knife at her face.

Gunfire cracked like fireworks. Robicheaux grabbed his chest with one hand and tried to bury the point of the knife inside her chest with the other. He missed by inches.

He collapsed and fell into the water, overturning the boat and dumping Helena and Lacy into the bayou. The whir of helicopters drowned out their cries for help.

Seconds later she and Lucy were surrounded by the most beautiful sight she'd ever seen. A NOPD rescue crew. Hunter was barking orders.

Someone pulled a deathly still Robicheaux from the water. A SWAT team member waded in to save Lacy. Hunter's arms encircled Helena as he pulled her to the bank.

Hunter cradled Helena in his arms, holding her as if he'd never let her go.

"I let you down," Hunter muttered. "I promised to protect you and I let you down."

"You saved my life. I kept telling myself you'd come but I don't think I believed it."

"I've never been that frightened before," he admitted. "I don't know how I could have gone on if I lost you."

"I love you, Hunter. I always have. I always will."

"Well, I guess that settles it then. Time for a move. What's the weather like in Boston this time of year?"

"Who needs Boston? Everything I've ever wanted is here."

Epilogue

Three months later

Helena adjusted the skirt of the simple white wedding gown she'd purchased six years ago. She stepped into the courtyard on a beautiful, unusually warm December morning. She looked up and spotted Hunter standing beside the minister at the flower-bedecked altar.

He smiled. Her heart sang.

She walked past the rows of guests seated on folding chairs. She had no one to give her away. She needed no one. Mia's spirit accompanied her all the way.

Cory Barker sat with his wife and two daughters. Healing had been slow and painful, but he'd make a full recovery in time.

Ella had the seat of honor on the first row of folding chairs.

Alyssa was Helena's maid of honor.

Everything was perfect and yet Helena's hands grew clammy when the minister began the vows. Tears welled in her eyes as she whispered her "I do."

When it was Hunter's time to state his vows, the love in his eyes convinced her that nothing would ever tear them apart again.

He said "I do" and the minister presented them as husband and wife.

"You may now kiss the bride."

Hunter did. The way all perfect weddings should end, as if a thousand brushstrokes had painted her world with love.

This time he was here to stay.

* * * * *

COLTON 911:
BABY'S BODYGUARD

LISA CHILDS

For Marie Ferrarella, Carla Cassidy and
Beth Cornelison—it was an honor to work on this
Colton series with such amazing authors!

Chapter One

Her eyes were wide with fear and death. She stared up at him as if appealing to him for help. She wasn't the only one.

"Come on, Forrest," his brother Donovan implored him. "Whisperwood PD needs your expertise."

Forrest gestured at the body lying amid the piles of dirt where Lone Star Pharma had intended to expand its parking lot. The drug company had had to put its plans on hold once the asphalt crew had dug up the body. "This isn't a cold case."

She couldn't have been buried that long; the body had barely begun decomp. Not that he was that close to the scene, which the techs were still processing. He'd wanted to stay out of the way, but his brothers had urged him closer.

"This isn't the only body that turned up recently," Jonah, the oldest of his brothers, chimed in on the conversation. He and Donovan had picked up Forrest from their parents' ranch and brought him out here. Now he understood why. They were trying to get him involved in the investigation.

They stared at him now. And even though Donovan wasn't biologically their brother, he looked more like Jonah than any of their biological brothers did. They were both dark haired and dark eyed, whereas Forrest's hair was lighter brown and longer than their buzz cuts, and his eyes were hazel.

"Unfortunately she isn't the only recent casualty," Forrest agreed.

A dozen people had lost their lives due to the flooding and wind damage Hurricane Brooke had wreaked on Whisperwood, Texas. Despite being early in the season, the storm had been deadly.

"That's why we're here—to help out because of the natural disaster," he reminded his brothers. They were part of the Cowboy Heroes, a horseback rescue organization formed years ago by ranchers and EMTs. Forrest had volunteered to help the Heroes' search-and-recovery efforts—not the police department. "And this isn't a natural disaster."

Though this person might have been one of the people reported missing since the hurricane, the storm hadn't caused her death. From what Forrest could see in the lights that the Whisperwood PD's forensic unit had set up to illuminate the crime scene, the young woman had bruising around her neck and on her arms and legs. She hadn't drowned or been struck by a fallen tree.

She'd probably been strangled and maybe worse.

A chill raced down his spine despite the warmth of the August night. The death had happened recently.

"This is murder," Jonah said. He must have noticed what Forrest had. "Just like the body that Maggie and I found last month." He shuddered now. "And that one definitely falls within your area of expertise."

Forrest shook his head. "Not anymore."

A shooting had forced his early retirement from the Austin Police Department's cold-case unit. That shooting and the pins that held together the shattered bones

in his leg were why he'd had to retire with disability
and why, as a volunteer with the Cowboy Heroes, he
was consigned to a desk, operating the telephones. He
took the calls about what people were missing: loved
ones and livestock. But he'd rather be out in the field
with his brothers, actually searching for those missing
people and animals. Hell, he'd rather be back on the
job. And they knew him so damn well that they were
aware of that.

Jonah lowered his voice to a gruff whisper and murmured, "Not because you don't want to."

Sure, he would love to go back to the job, but there
was no way in hell that he could pass a physical now.
Not with his leg.

As if he'd read Forrest's mind, Jonah continued, "But
you can now. The chief will give you a special dispensation to help out as an interim detective."

The "special dispensation" pricked his pride, and
he clenched his jaw. "I don't need you all doing me
any favors."

"You'd be doing me the favor," Donovan said. "I was
just about to leave on my honeymoon when this call
came into the department." Donovan helped out only
part-time with the Cowboy Heroes; he was a full-time
K9 cop with Whisperwood PD.

"It's a mini honeymoon," Forrest reminded him.
"You're not going to be gone long."

"But even when we get back, I'm going to be distracted," Donovan claimed. "Bellamy's pregnant."

Jonah chortled and slapped their brother's back.
"That's great! That's wonderful news."

And with everything that had happened since the
hurricane, good news was more than welcome.

"Congratulations," Forrest said, and he reached out

and squeezed his brother's shoulder. Donovan and Bellamy so deserved their happiness. They'd been through so much recently.

"Thanks," Donovan said with a big grin. But then he glanced down at the body and shook his head. "She deserves someone's full attention, and the police department and the chief are just stretched too damn thin right now, dealing with the aftermath of the hurricane."

And the other dead body.

The chief's sister. Had someone else really murdered her? Or was serial killer Elliot Corgan messing with everyone from beyond his grave?

Forrest wouldn't put it past the sadistic son of a bitch. When he'd been on the job, he'd dealt with quite a few serial killers. They got nearly as much enjoyment playing mind games with law enforcement as they did killing.

He glanced down at the dead girl. At least one thing was for certain: Elliot hadn't killed her. He wouldn't have been able to manage that from beyond the grave. Unless...

"You're already on the case," Jonah said with a slight smile. "I can see your wheels turning."

Forrest glared at his big brother, but he didn't deny it. Too many thoughts flitted through his mind. Was she one of the people presumed missing because of Hurricane Brooke? Had someone taken advantage of the storm to murder her, thinking that law enforcement would assume she'd been lost in the flooding that had followed the storm?

Chief Thompson had been moving around the crime scene, talking to the techs and officers guarding the perimeter. Ignoring the reporters who shouted questions at him from the other side of the police tape, Whisperwood PD's top cop walked toward Forrest and his brothers. Thompson had been doing this job for a long time, and his experience showed in the lines in his face and the way his shoulders sagged when he looked down at the body. He shook his head and sighed, and his Stetson slipped lower over his face.

Forrest had realized some years into his career that it would never get any easier to see someone dead, especially *murdered*, and the chief just proved that to him. He let his own hat slide down to shield his face.

Thompson turned away from the body to focus on Forrest now, his blue eyes sharp with intelligence and determination. "So, you going to do it? You going to take the job?"

His brothers stared at him, nodding and smiling to encourage his acceptance. They probably figured this would be good for him, would get him back doing the job he loved. But when he'd been shot, the job hadn't been the only thing he'd lost that he loved.

That experience had taught him never to risk his heart again. So the job was all he had—even if it was just a short-term assignment.

He nodded. "Yes, I'll take it."

Not for his sake, though, like his brothers obviously wanted. But for hers.

He stared down at the dead woman, determined to make sure she got the justice she deserved and that the killer would not hurt anyone else.

"HE'S SO CUTE," Bellamy cooed as she cradled the baby against her chest and kissed the top of his head. He'd been born with a full head of soft brown hair, the same chocolaty color as his mama's. He also had her big brown eyes.

Rae's heart swelled with maternal pride. "Yes, he is," she said just as a yawn slipped out. He'd also been keeping her up nights with a bout of colic, and Bellamy's bed was so comfy, Rae was tempted to take a nap right there amid the pile of clothes and the suitcase.

"Hey, you need to finish packing," Maggie told her sister as she pried the baby from Bellamy's arms. "You're supposed to be leaving for your honeymoon."

"I will," Bellamy said. "As soon as Donovan gets back from the crime scene."

Rae shuddered. "So another body's been found?" Twelve people had died in the hurricane, but she'd thought all of the missing had been accounted for— thanks to the Cowboy Heroes' rescue-and-recovery efforts.

Maggie had been one of the missing. Fortunately she had been found alive. Jonah Colton hadn't just rescued her, though; he'd also fallen in love with the former beauty queen. A pang of wistfulness tugged at Rae's heart, not that she wanted anyone falling in love with her.

She was too busy with her two-month-old son and her law-school classes and her new job as a paralegal to fit a man into her life right now. Or ever.

Connor was the only man for her. She smiled as he clutched his fingers around a lock of Maggie's pretty blond hair. Like every other male in Whisperwood, he was drawn to the former beauty queen.

Rae might have been jealous if Maggie wasn't as beautiful inside as she was on the outside. She twisted her pretty features into comical faces as she cooed at the fascinated baby. Then she glanced up at Rae and a frown pulled down the corners of her mouth. "From what the chief told Jonah, it sounds like the death had nothing to do with the hurricane."

Rae gasped. "Was it…like the body you and Jonah found?"

Maggie shuddered. "I hope not."

That body had been mummified. Rae hadn't seen it, but just the thought of it had given her nightmares. She couldn't imagine what Maggie had gone through because of that and the threats to her life.

All of the crime in Whisperwood was what had compelled Rae to take the LSAT to try to get into law school. Nobody had probably been as surprised as she'd been that she'd done so well that she'd had her pick of schools. Of course she'd chosen to stay in Whisperwood with her friends. With her mom gone, they were the only family she had now—except for Connor. She'd already been pregnant with him when she'd taken the exam.

Bellamy nipped her bottom lip with her teeth. "Maybe Donovan and I shouldn't go away right now."

"No!" Rae and Maggie both shouted.

Connor, startled, began to cry. Rae jumped up from the bed and took him from Maggie. Holding him close, she rubbed her hand up and down his back and murmured, "It's okay, sweetheart. You're okay."

He settled down with a hiccuping sob. Then the tension drained from his tiny body and he began to drift off to sleep like Rae had longed to.

"You're so good with him," Maggie said with a smile.

"You are," Bellamy agreed. She looked more like Rae, with dark hair and eyes, and with as long as they'd known each other, they were more like sisters than friends. "You're amazing. I can't believe how much you're doing all on your own."

Rae smiled with pleasure and pride. But then she reminded her friend, "You've done the same."

Maggie's mouth pulled down into another frown, and regret struck a pang in Rae's heart. She hadn't meant to cause any issues between the sisters. They'd already had too many.

"I was never alone," Bellamy said. "I had you, Rae." She turned toward Maggie and smiled at her sister. "And you... I just didn't realize what all you were doing for me."

"Rae's right," Maggie said. "You did all the heavy lifting on your own." Taking care of their ailing parents. "You deserve this honeymoon. You deserve every happiness. Don't let Donovan back out of going."

Bellamy smiled. "Not a chance. He's determined to go. He and Jonah are going to work on convincing Forrest to step in and take over the murder investigations."

Maggie nodded. "Oh, that's what big brother is up to." She'd fallen for the oldest of the Colton brothers. "He said he was going to pick up Forrest."

Another little pang struck Rae's heart at the mention of that particular Colton brother. It was probably just regret again. She shouldn't have asked him to dance at Bellamy and Donovan's wedding. But as one of two maids of honor, she'd wanted to make sure every guest enjoyed the celebration. That was the only reason she'd asked—not because he was ridiculously good-looking, with his chiseled features and his brooding intensity.

He hadn't had to be so curt with her, though. Sure, she'd known he had a limp from an injury in the line of duty. But he still worked with the Cowboy Heroes, so she hadn't thought he was really disabled. He could have held her and just swayed from side to side. It wasn't as if she'd asked him to two-step or line dance with her. But she shouldn't have asked at all. The only reason she had was because of how alone he'd looked…even among all of his family.

And that loneliness had called to hers. Because even with her son and her good friends, she sometimes felt alone like that, too. That was better, though, than falling for someone only to have him leave.

"I didn't think Forrest was going to stick around much longer," she said. "Won't he move on to the next natural disaster, with the rest of the Cowboy Heroes?"

"Whisperwood needs them for more than rescue-and-recovery efforts right now," Maggie said. She shuddered again. "There's a killer on the loose."

"That's why we should postpone our honeymoon," Bellamy said.

"No," Rae and Maggie said again, their voices soft this time, though.

Bellamy sighed. "Okay, but you both need to promise me that you'll be extra careful."

"Of course," they agreed, again in unison.

"I know Jonah won't let anything happen to you," Bellamy told her sister. "But you…"

Rae smiled. "I can take care of myself." She'd done it for most of her life.

Bellamy took the sleeping baby from her arms and snuggled him against her. "But you have Connor to worry about, too, and your classes. I'm really concerned about you living out there in the country, alone."

"I'm not alone," Rae reminded her.

Bellamy pressed another kiss to the soft hair on Connor's head. "He's not going to be much protection against a bad guy—at least not for a few more years."

"Like twenty," Maggie added with a chuckle.

"I don't need a man to protect me," Rae said. She'd never had one. Her father had been more likely to put her and her mother in danger—at least financially—than to protect them. "I don't need a man at all."

"You proved that by having this little guy on your own," Maggie said. "I admire you."

"Me, too," Bellamy added. "Although I think I had more fun conceiving mine the way we did."

Rae stared at her friend. "What?"

"I'm pregnant," the new bride announced, her face glowing with happiness and love.

Tears rushed to Rae's eyes. "That's wonderful."

"So wonderful," Maggie agreed as her eyes filled with tears, too. "I'm thrilled for you."

"Me, too," Rae said. "You and Donovan are going to be amazing parents."

"I'm going to drive you crazy," Bellamy warned her, "with all the questions I'll be asking you." Bellamy's mom was gone, like Rae's was.

Rae missed her mom every day. They'd been so close; Georgia had been more of a friend than a mother to her. Now that she was a mother herself, she'd never needed her more.

"You won't drive me crazy at all," Rae assured her. "I'm not sure I'll have all the answers, though." Mostly she felt as if she was stumbling around in the dark, blindly finding her way as a parent and as a student again at thirty-five.

"You'll have more than I'll have," Maggie said. "You're the smartest, most independent person I know."

The tears already stinging her eyes threatened to spill over, but Rae blinked them back to smile at her friend. "I'm not sure about smartest. Law school is tougher than I thought it would be."

"Because you just had a baby two months ago and you're working," Bellamy reminded her as she stared down at Connor, who was sleeping so peacefully in her arms.

If only he slept that peacefully at night…

"It'll get easier," Rae said. That was what she kept telling herself.

Bellamy chuckled softly. "You're smart, but I think it's your stubbornness that keeps you going."

A smile tugged at the corners of Rae's mouth. She couldn't deny that.

"Just don't be so stubborn and independent that you put yourself in danger," Bellamy advised. "Promise?"

Rae sighed. "Of course I'm not going to put myself or Connor in danger," she assured her. "Stop worrying about me. And let's get you ready for your honeymoon!"

"Since she's already pregnant, I think she knows about the birds and the bees," Maggie teased.

They all laughed, rousing Connor from his impromptu nap. But he didn't cry when he awakened; he just groggily looked up at Bellamy, who was holding him. She was like an aunt to him, and Maggie was fast becoming like another. These women and her baby were the only family that Rae needed.

She didn't need a man for protection or for anything else. But when she left Bellamy's cute two-bedroom house and headed home with Connor safely buckled into the back seat, an odd chill passed through her despite the warmth of the August night. Fear.

Maybe it was all of the talk about bodies and killers.

Or maybe it was her postpartum hormones.

She preferred to blame the hormones. Because she had nothing to fear.

THE TELEVISION SCREEN illuminated only the area of the dark room around the TV. From the shadows, he watched the evening news report from the crime scene at Lone Star Pharma.

Her body had been found. His hands clenched into fists as rage coursed through him.

Damn it...

The news crews had been kept back, behind the police barricade. But the camera zoomed in on the scene and captured the people investigating the discovery. The Cowboy Heroes.

What the hell were they doing there?

He unclenched one fist to turn the volume up.

"Chief Thompson has enlisted the help of former Austin cold-case detective Forrest Colton," the reporter announced. "Colton has been given special dispensation from the Whisperwood Police Department to lead the investigation of this murder and the body discovered last month in a mummified condition. Colton holds the highest clearance rate in the Austin Police Department, so an arrest seems imminent."

He cursed again.

No. An arrest was not imminent. Forrest Colton might have gotten lucky in Austin, but his luck was about to run out in Whisperwood. And maybe his life, as well.

Chapter Two

A week had passed since his brothers had ambushed him at the crime scene. A week of frustration that gripped Forrest so intensely, he wished he'd never accepted the position no matter how temporary it was going to be.

The hurricane had caused so much damage, and not just physically. Emotionally people were dealing with the loss of loved ones and their homes or their livelihoods. The Whisperwood Police Department was stretched thin. The crime-scene techs were understaffed and overworked, so nothing had been processed yet from either scene. And the coroner…

She hadn't even taken the bodies from their refrigerated drawers yet, let alone begun the autopsies. And until he had more information, Forrest didn't want to parade in the family members of every missing person to see if the dead woman was their loved one. He didn't want to put every family that was missing someone through that kind of pain.

Hell, he didn't want to put one family through that kind of pain. But it was inevitable. Once they figured out who she was.

Everybody expected miracles from Forrest, but his

hands were nearly as tied as the poor victim's hands had been—bound behind her back.

He wrapped the reins around his hands and clenched his knees together as the quarter horse he rode scrambled over the uneven ground. Despite taking the detective position, Forrest continued as a volunteer for the Cowboy Heroes. The team was not done with Whisperwood and the surrounding area, which had been hit particularly hard with flooding after Hurricane Brooke.

The water had begun to recede, though, leaving only muddy areas like the one in which the horse's hooves now slipped. His mount leaning, Forrest nearly slipped off it and into the mud. Ignoring the twinge of pain in his bad leg, he tightened his grip.

"Whoa, steady," Forrest murmured soothingly. When the horse regained its balance, a sigh of relief slipped through Forrest's lips. This was why he usually handled the desk work for the rescue agency and not the fieldwork. But like his brothers, he'd been born in the saddle. He couldn't *not* ride.

He wasn't able to help with the rescues as physically as he would have liked, though. Sometimes his leg wouldn't hold his weight, let alone the weight of another person or animal. He sighed again but this time with resignation. It was what it was.

He'd accepted that a while ago. And he helped out where he could—like riding around to survey the areas. There were still some people missing, and maybe the floodwater had hidden their remains.

Not that he wanted to find any more bodies.

But that was the purpose of the recovery part of the Cowboy Heroes' rescue-and-recovery operation. Survivors needed that closure of knowing what had happened to their loved one and having that body to bury.

That was why he needed the body in the morgue identified, so he could give her family some small measure of peace.

Until he found her killer.

And he would.

His frustration turning back to determination, he urged the horse across the muddy stretch of land. Heat shimmered off the black shingles of a roof in the distance. He'd started out early from his family ranch, before the sun had even risen much above the horizon, and it wasn't much higher now. So it was going to be another hot August day, which was good.

The last of the water should recede and reveal whatever secrets it has been hiding. Whatever bodies…of animals and people.

So much livestock had been lost, too. A pang of regret over all of those losses struck his heart. Then another pang of regret struck him when he realized whose house he'd come upon in the country.

Hers.

Rae Lemmon. His new sister-in-law's best friend, and quite the beauty. He hadn't lived in Whisperwood for years, but he remembered this was her family home. And maybe he'd subconsciously headed that way.

But why? Sure, she was beautiful, but because she was beautiful, she wouldn't want anything to do with a disabled man. She'd asked him to dance at the wedding, but that must have only been out of pity or maybe just a sense of obligation to her friend.

And maybe that was why he'd come this way, to check on her place—out of a sense of obligation. She was his new sister-in-law's best friend, so that almost made her family, too. And as much as the Coltons took care of everyone else, they took extra care of their own.

He knew that because of how everybody had taken care of him after he'd been shot. Well, everybody but one person. But she hadn't been family yet, and after he'd been shot, she'd returned his ring.

He flinched as the memory rushed over him. Not that he could blame her. As she'd said, she hadn't fallen in love with a cripple, so he really shouldn't have expected her to stick around for him. It wasn't as if they'd said their vows yet either, and now he expected those vows would not have included "in sickness and in health."

While the old memories washed over him, the horse continued across the muddy field, toward the back of the house. The field was higher than the yard, so he could see into it, could see that a tree had toppled over into the water pooled on the grass. Maybe the roots had turned up a mound of dirt, or maybe something else had made the hole. The pile was almost too neat, as if it had been shoveled there.

Maybe she'd thought the hole would drain away the water.

But as Forrest drew nearer, he peered into the hole and discovered it wasn't water filling it. Something else lay inside it, something all swaddled up in linen material smeared with mud and grime.

"What the hell…?" he murmured.

He swung his leg over the saddle and dismounted. His boot slipped on the muddy ground, but he used the horse to steady himself. Like all of the horses for the Cowboy Heroes, Mick was well trained and helpful. Forrest patted his mane in appreciation before stepping away from his mount and turning toward the hole. He leaned over and peered inside it, and his boot slipped again.

This time he didn't have the horse to steady himself, so his leg—his bad leg—went out from beneath him. As he began to fall, he reached out to catch himself. But like his boot, his fingers slipped on the mud, too, and he slid into the hole, knocking the loose dirt into it with him. It sprayed across that weird material.

Whatever it was, it had contoured to the shape of the object beneath it. But it wasn't an object.

It was a body with arms and legs and a face.

A mummy…like the one his brother Jonah had found. But unlike that body, Forrest suspected the storm hadn't turned up this one. Someone else had either dug it up or dug the hole to bury it here, like someone had buried the woman by the pharmaceutical company.

But why here? Why in Rae Lemmon's backyard?

Forrest reached into his pocket and pulled out his cell phone. He needed to call in a team to process the scene. Hopefully he could remove himself from it without compromising any evidence. After he called the coroner and some crime-scene techs, he shoved his phone back into his pocket and tried to pull himself out of the hole. Using his good leg, he dug his boot into the side of the hole and climbed out. As he pulled his boot free, some dirt tumbled down into the hole, next to the body, and the sun glinted off it.

It wasn't just dirt. There was something shiny beneath the mud and grime. Something metallic. Like coins or…

Buttons?

Had those belonged to the victim or the killer?

RAE CLOSED HER eyes and savored the silence. She would have to get up soon for work, but she had a few minutes to rest her eyes and relax. And after Connor had spent most of the night crying inconsolably, she needed some peace. He'd finally fallen back to sleep.

The pediatrician suspected the baby had colic, for which Rae blamed herself. The stress of law school, her job and single parenthood had affected her ability to produce breast milk and she now had to supplement with formula. When she'd called the doctor's service last night, she'd been told to switch to a soy-based formula, which she would do today on her way to bring Connor to day care.

Exhaustion gripped her, pulling her into oblivion. But she had been asleep for only a moment when a noise startled her. It wasn't the light *beep* of the alarm, but a loud pounding at a door. Worried that the knocking would wake up Connor, she rushed out of her bedroom without bothering to grab a robe. The only people who visited her were Bellamy and Maggie. Maybe Bellamy was back.

But she probably would have just let herself in; she had a copy and knew where the spare key was hidden. Disoriented for a moment from lack of sleep, Rae rushed to her front door and opened it. But nobody stood on her porch. If someone was there, they probably would have rung the bell.

The back door rattled as that fist pounded again. And a soft cry drifted from the nursery. Connor wasn't fully awake, but he was waking up. She ran across the living room and kitchen to pull open the door. "Shh," she cautioned her visitor. Then she gasped when she recognized the man standing before her. "What—what are you doing here?"

What the hell was he doing there? Especially now? She had to look like death—after her sleepless night—with dark circles beneath her eyes, and her hair standing on end. And her nightgown…

She glanced down at the oversize T-shirt an old boyfriend had left behind. At least she'd gotten something comfy out of the relationship. But she hadn't expected much. Her experience with her father had taught her to never count on a man to stick around, and every boyfriend she'd ever had had reinforced that lesson.

That was why she'd chosen to be a single mother. She didn't need a husband to have a family. She didn't need a man. But this one…

He was so damn good-looking, even with mud on his clothes and smeared across his cheek. A fission of concern passed through her. "Did you get thrown?" she asked. Over his shoulder—his very broad shoulder—she caught a glimpse of a dark horse pawing at the muddy grass. "Are you okay?"

"I did not get thrown," he said, his voice sharp as if she'd stung his pride.

Or maybe that was just the way he always talked. He'd sounded that way when he'd told her that she couldn't be serious about asking him to dance.

Her face heated with embarrassment, but she didn't know if it was because of what had happened then or how unkempt she looked now. And with the way he kept staring at her, he couldn't have missed it. He was probably horrified.

"Then what are you doing here?" she asked again.

"I've called the police."

"I thought you were the police," she said. She knew, from the news reports and the gossip around Whisperwood, that the chief and his brothers had successfully talked him into investigating the murders.

"I am," he said. "That's why I called. I need to tape off your backyard. It's a crime scene."

Despite the heat of the August day, a cold chill raced down her spine and raised goose bumps on her skin. "Crime scene?" she asked. "What are you talking about?"

"I found something in your yard," he said.

"Why were you searching my property?" she asked. "Did you have a warrant?"

His face flushed now.

"I know my rights," she said. "If you didn't have a warrant, your search was illegal."

"I was surveying the flood damage," he said, "and your yard was in plain view from the field behind it."

Which was his family's property. In Whisperwood, the Coltons' ranch was second in size only to the Cor-gan spread.

"So you weren't even acting as a lawman when you performed this illegal search?" she asked. "You were just riding around your own property?"

His brow furrowed, and he opened his mouth to answer her, but she cut him off with a, "How dare you!"

She'd thought she'd let it go—her embarrassment over how he'd rejected her request to dance. But now that embarrassment turned to anger, which she unleashed on him.

Or maybe her exhaustion had made her extra irritable.

"You're trespassing on my property," she continued. "And when your fellow officers arrive, they will be obligated to issue you a citation."

"Rae—"

"You're not above the law," she said, "just because you're a Colton."

"I know I'm not above the law," he said, his face still flushed, but with anger now. It burned in his hazel eyes, as well. "And neither are you."

"I am a law student," she said. "And I'm already working as a paralegal. I probably know the law better than you do."

He snorted then. "I've been a police officer for years," he reminded her. "I know the law. Why did *you* switch from managing the general store to law?"

She narrowed her eyes and studied his handsome face. He'd barely talked to her at her friend and his brother's wedding, so why was he curious about her now? Especially since he seemed to know more about her than she'd realized.

She was proud of her decision to go to law school, so she answered him, "I want to do something about all the crimes happening around Whisperwood."

"Then you should want me to investigate what I found on your property," he pointed out.

Now she was curious, which she probably would have been right way if she wasn't so damn exhausted. "What did you find?" she asked.

"A body."

She gasped in shock and shook her head. "No." It wasn't possible. Someone couldn't have been murdered in her backyard, where she'd imagined her son playing as he grew up, just like she had played there as a child. She shuddered and murmured again, "No."

Forrest nodded. "I'm afraid it's true."

"But—but I didn't hear anything." Wouldn't she have heard something if someone had been murdered in her backyard? But with work and school, she was gone so much that she probably hadn't even been home when it had happened. "I didn't see anything amiss."

"Have you missed anyone?" he asked. "Somebody staying with you that suddenly disappeared?"

She shook her head. Somebody had disappeared years ago on Rae, but that had been his choice to leave. Nobody had murdered him, although she'd sometimes wished she would have...when she'd watched her mother suffer.

"So you didn't notice anything in the backyard? Any digging?" he asked, persisting with his questions.

She shook her head again. "Why the hell would someone bury a body in my backyard?"

"I'm not sure if they'd just buried it, or if it was just uncovered," Forrest said. "It could have been there awhile."

"Like the body that Maggie and Jonah found after the hurricane?" she asked.

They had just stumbled across the body—the mummified body. She shivered with revulsion. What if that was what Forrest had found in her backyard? Another mummy?

"I'll know more once the coroner arrives," he continued.

The wail of a siren grew louder as it came closer to her house. Maybe the coroner was arriving now, along with the squad cars with the flashing lights that were pulling into her driveway.

Connor cried out now, and it wasn't a sleepy little cry but a wail almost as loud as the siren.

"What the hell is that?" Forrest asked in alarm.

And Rae bristled all over again with outrage. "*That* is my son," she replied as she hurried off to the nursery.

TENSION GRIPPED THE chief, and he tightened his grasp on his cell phone before sliding it back into his pocket.

Behind him, sitting on the porch of his two-story farmhouse, Hays Colton chuckled. "Forrest has always had good timing," he said of his son. "You drive out here, looking for him, and he calls you like he somehow knew."

Chief Thompson shook his head. "That's not why he called." And he could have pointed out that Forrest's timing wasn't always perfect, or young Colton wouldn't have taken that bullet in his leg. But if his instincts weren't as strong as they were, he might have taken that bullet in his heart or his head instead of his leg.

He had survived.

His shooter had not.

"What's wrong?" Hays asked, his blue eyes wide with alarm. "Is he all right?"

Thompson nodded. "Yeah, he just called to give me a heads-up."

"Did he find out the identity of that poor girl found at the pharmaceutical company?"

The chief shook his head. "I wish that was why he called. Or better yet, to tell me he caught the killer." Because it would probably hit the news soon anyway, Archer Thompson shared, "He found another body."

Another person for the already overworked coroner to identify.

"I'm sorry," Hays said. He rose from the porch swing, set his coffee cup on the railing and reached out to pat Thompson's shoulder.

They'd known each other for a long time, but Thompson didn't need any more sympathy. He needed answers—about his sister's murder and about these bodies that had recently turned up. He uttered a ragged sigh as he pushed himself up from the rocking chair in which he'd been sitting. He didn't move as fast as he once had, his bones aching now with age and overuse. He didn't stand quite as straight and tall as he once had either.

Neither did Hays, though, who had spent too many of his seventy-some years in the saddle, working his ranch. "My son will find out who really killed your sister," Hays assured him.

Thompson wanted to believe the killer was Elliot Corgan, because then he would have the satisfaction of knowing the sick bastard had died in prison. But Elliot had denied killing his sister, and there was no way he could have killed that woman whose body had been discovered in the Lone Star Pharma parking lot.

There was another killer in Whisperwood.

And until he was caught, the chief had a feeling that bodies would keep turning up.

Chapter Three

Cries emanated from the house, drawing Forrest's attention back to the one-story ranch structure and to *her*. A shadow passed behind the windows as if she was pacing in her kitchen. She had a baby.

Somebody had probably mentioned it to Forrest, but he didn't remember. He'd been preoccupied with the hurricane damage and now with the murder investigation. He surveyed the crime scene. Techs worked on bagging those corroded coins or buttons he'd uncovered, while the coroner worked on removing the body from the hole. They knew what they were doing; they didn't need his supervising their every move. In fact they'd probably resent it if he did.

So he headed back to the house. He raised his fist to the frame around the glass in the back door but hesitated before knocking. The cries were louder now, so he wasn't at risk of waking the baby.

The little guy was already awake and squalling. Seeing through the glass that Rae had her hands full with the baby, Forrest reached instead for the knob, turned it and let himself back into the house.

She gasped at his bold intrusion, but then she didn't seem to like anything he did. The invitation to dance had definitely been extended out of obligation or pity.

Probably obligation…because she didn't seem to like him enough to pity him.

She glared at him over the baby's head. "Why did they have to come here with the sirens blaring?" she asked. "It doesn't look like an emergency."

"No," he agreed. The body was far beyond help. Rae Lemmon looked as if she needed help, though, as she rocked the baby's stiff little body in her arms.

Dark circles rimmed her brown eyes, but instead of detracting from her beauty, they highlighted it. She looked both vulnerable with her delicate features and sexy as hell with the old T-shirt molded to her generous curves.

"He had just finally gone to sleep," she murmured with a little catch in her voice, "when the sirens woke him up."

A pang of regret struck Forrest. The officers hadn't needed to put on the sirens. It would have been better to draw less attention to the scene than more.

Fortunately no reporters had followed them. Forrest had never enjoyed dealing with the press. So he definitely should have advised the police not to use the sirens when he'd called in what he'd found. He opened his mouth to apologize, but before he could, chimes rang out.

Was that the sound of her doorbell?

Maybe a reporter had picked up on the call after all. He grimaced—just as Rae held out the baby toward him.

"That's my phone," she said, as she handed him the crying infant.

Because he had no experience with babies, he didn't know how to hold him. But he reacted instinctively, closing his hands around the baby's midsection. Was he supposed to cup his head or something? He moved one hand to the baby's neck, and the little guy's head swiveled toward him.

The face that had been scrunched up with cries froze with shock, and his dark eyes widened as he stared up at Forrest. Was he scared?

His crying stopped, though, so that was a good thing. Forrest could hear himself think again. He could also hear the soft murmur of Rae's voice as she spoke to someone—maybe the baby's father. She must have left the phone in another room, since in order to answer it she'd left him alone with her baby.

Forrest was as frozen with fear as the little guy was. What if he was holding him wrong? Or he dropped him?

Rae would hate him even more then.

And Forrest would hate himself. But the kid was light and easy to hold. Maybe he could do this. And if he figured it out, he would actually be able to hold Donovan and Bellamy's baby once it came, and not harm his little niece and nephew.

He crooked his arm and eased the baby into that, so the kid could stare up at him more comfortably. And he kept staring like he had no idea what the hell Forrest was, let alone whom. Keeping his deep voice to a low rumble, he murmured, "I'm Detective Colton."

Not that the baby could actually understand him. But he stared up at Forrest's face as if he was listening.

Maybe Forrest reminded him of his father. Where was the guy? Forrest didn't remember seeing anyone hanging around Rae at the wedding. But then, as one of the maids of honor, she'd been busy. Not too busy to ask him to dance, though.

But that must have been just part of her duty as a maid of honor—to look after the guests. Maybe that was why the baby's father had made himself scarce. Or maybe he'd stayed home to watch the baby, since he probably would have been newly born at the time of the wedding.

She hadn't looked like she'd recently given birth then, though—not with how well her navy blue maid of honor's dress had fit her.

Forrest had so many questions about Rae Lemmon, so much curiosity. It was that curiosity that had drawn him to her house this morning and to the body in her backyard. That—more than anything—should have proved to him that she was going to be trouble.

He had to restrict his curiosity to professional only, since his broken engagement had convinced him that personal relationships were not for him. The only personal relationships he was going to allow himself was with his family.

Being around this little guy might help him prepare for the new baby so that he would be able to help Donovan and Bellamy when they needed it. So that he could be a good uncle to the little cowgirl or cowboy that the newlyweds would have.

"What about you?" Forrest asked the baby. "Are you going to be a cowboy? You want to learn to ride?"

Despite having no experience with kids, he realized this one was too young to answer any of his questions, but the baby seemed fascinated by his voice. Those already wide brown eyes widened even more. With those enormous eyes, delicate features and brown hair, the baby looked so much like his beautiful mother.

A little bubble floated out of the baby's lips as he gurgled. And Forrest tensed with concern. Was something wrong?

And where had the baby's mother gone?

Forrest had felt more comfortable finding that mummified body in her backyard than he did standing in her kitchen, holding her child. That body was beyond saving; the only thing he needed to do for her was find her killer.

But the baby…

He could screw up. He could cause him harm, and that was the last thing he wanted to do.

WHY HAD THE crying stopped?

What had Forrest Colton done to her baby?

Rae peered through her open bedroom door at the man standing in her kitchen. He'd moved Connor to the crook of his muscular arm, and her child lay there, staring up in adulation at the man holding him.

Connor hadn't looked at her that way in a while— with fascination. Frustration, instead, scrunched up his little face when he stared up at her. He'd been so fussy lately.

For her.

But not for Forrest Colton.

What the hell had the man done to him?

"Rae? Are you there? Are you okay?"

It wasn't his deep voice rumbling in her ear as she pressed the cell phone into the crook of her shoulder and tried to dress while peering through the crack of her door. "Yes, Kenneth, I'm fine," she assured her caller, who was one of the lawyers at the firm where she worked as a paralegal.

"Do you need me to come out there?"

"No," she automatically replied. She'd been saying that to him a lot since she'd been hired at the firm—no to an offer of coffee or dinner. Not that he was harassing her. He'd made it clear that he was happily married and that his offers were only intended to make her feel welcome at the firm.

"I just wanted to be available in case any legal issues arise out of this search of your property," he explained. "You're one of the family here at Lukas, Jolley and Fitzsimmons." He was more family than she was because he was related by marriage. His father-in-law was Fitzsimmons.

"I'm actually going to leave soon." Even though this was her home, she didn't want to stay here while Forrest Colton was on her property. "I'll drop off Connor at day care and come into the office."

Kenneth blew out a ragged breath of relief. "That'll be good for you to get out of there."

He'd called because he'd heard on his police scanner that the coroner and a crime-scene unit had been dispatched to her address. He used the scanner to drum up business for the firm—chasing ambulances.

"Yes," she agreed. It would be good for her to get away from Forrest Colton. And to get him away from her child. "I'll see you soon," she said as she clicked off her cell phone.

While juggling the phone, she'd managed to replace her nightgown with a long summer dress. She'd even managed to rub some concealer over her dark circles and cover it up with a dusting of powder. A swipe of mascara across her lashes finished her makeup routine.

She stepped out of the bedroom and rushed into the kitchen. Forrest looked up from her son and focused on her face.

Did he notice the makeup? Did he think she'd put it on for him?

The heat of embarrassment rushed up now, probably

flushing her face under that thin dusting of powder. "I had to take that call," she told him.

"Was it your husband?" he asked.

A chortle slipped through her lips at the thought of her being married. "Not mine," she said.

"Somebody else's?" he asked.

She grimaced. "Don't make it sound like *that*. He's one of my colleagues. He heard the call and was concerned."

Forrest's brow furrowed. "How did he hear it?"

She shrugged. It wasn't illegal to own a police scanner, but since starting law school, she'd already grown tired of the ambulance-chaser comments.

"What about you?" he asked. "Did you hear anything last night?"

"I already told you I hadn't," she reminded him. Then she pointed toward the baby, who'd actually fallen asleep now in Forrest's arms. "He's the only one who's been making any noise around here at night."

The detective looked down at the baby again, and his lips curved into a smile, which was quite a turnaround from the grimace of horror that had crossed his face when she had first handed him her son. "What's his name?" he asked.

"Connor."

He glanced up at her as if waiting for more.

So she added, "Lemmon."

"You're not married?" he asked.

"I thought I already established that," she said. When she'd asked him to dance at that wedding.

She was old-fashioned enough that she wouldn't have asked a single guy to dance if she was married. But apparently she wasn't as old-fashioned as he was.

"You know you don't have to be married to have a baby," she said.

"The father didn't want to marry you?"

Both outraged and offended, she gasped. Forrest Colton wasn't just old-fashioned; he was a jerk. "The father doesn't even know me."

He gasped now.

And she laughed at the shock on his face.

Her son tensed briefly in Forrest's arm, but he moved him in a rocking motion, and Connor settled back to sleep. How could the man soothe her son while he riled her up? She'd never met anyone who'd infuriated her as much as Forrest Colton did.

"I chose to have my son on my own," she informed him. "I used a sperm donor." And before he could jump to another unflattering assumption about her, she added, "From a sperm bank."

"Oh," he murmured.

Not everyone understood or appreciated what she'd done. But she didn't care. She loved Connor so much— even when he kept her awake. She moved closer to Forrest and brushed a fingertip along Connor's cheek. He was so perfect.

"You chose to be a single parent," he murmured.

And she couldn't tell if he approved or disapproved. But she didn't give a damn what he thought anyway.

"He's the only male I need or want in my life," she informed Forrest, just like she'd told her friends a week ago. She didn't want anyone to answer to, anyone to disappoint or abandon her.

"That's too bad," he said.

And she gasped with surprise yet again. Was he… interested in her after all? She glanced from Connor's face to his, which was flushed now.

"I meant…because it would be safer for you and Connor if you weren't out here alone," he said quickly, as if he was worried she'd misunderstood him.

She sighed. "You sound like Bellamy and Maggie," she admitted.

"They're concerned about you, too?"

She nodded. And that had been before Forrest's discovery in her backyard. She couldn't imagine how much they would worry now. She was surprised that he was concerned, though.

Why?

He barely knew her. And if he was interested in her, he wouldn't act like such a jerk. Maybe it was just the lawman in him that had him worried about her safety.

"Your friends are wise to worry about you being out here all by yourself," he said.

"They're my friends, so they should know better than anyone else does that I can take care of myself and my son without the help or protection of any man," she informed him.

"I'm not saying you need a man," Forrest told her. "I'm saying that you need someone, though. You're training to be a lawyer, not a police officer."

She tensed. "You really believe I'm in danger?"

He shrugged, which jostled the sleeping baby into opening one eye and peering up at the man holding him.

If she was in danger, Connor would be, as well. So she had to ask, "What do you think?"

"I think there's a killer in Whisperwood," he said. "So nobody's safe."

She reached for her son, taking him from the detective's arm. When her fingers brushed across his muscular forearm, a tingling sensation rose from her fingertips to her heart, jolting her.

And Connor.

He awoke with a cry of protest. Apparently he'd preferred Forrest Colton holding him over his mother holding him. But then he had to be frustrated with her; she hadn't managed to comfort him last night, hadn't managed to make him feel better, like her mother had always made her feel better.

Even when Mama had been so very sick, she'd offered solace to Rae, had held her and soothed all of her fears. She missed her mom every day. And she needed her now more than she ever had.

Because Rae was scared…and not just of the killer on the loose. She was scared that she may have taken on more than she could handle alone.

She was alone.

He had watched the house all day, had watched the police collect their evidence, had watched Rae Lemmon leave and then return later, after the police had already gone for the day. So she was the only one near the house now.

She and her baby.

He waited outside, watching the house until all of the lights flickered off inside, leaving it dark. Then he moved away from the tree against which he'd been leaning, and he headed toward the house.

Beside the sidewalk leading up to the porch, a big iron pot overflowed with red geraniums that matched the flowers overflowing the window boxes of the little white ranch house. He bent over, tipped the pot and fumbled beneath it.

Then a grin curved his lips, and his fingers closed around a key and tugged it free from beneath the pot. A magnet glued to the key had kept it stuck to the bottom. With the key in hand, he climbed the short steps up to the porch. As he moved across it to the front door, boards creaked beneath his weight. He unlocked the door, and it creaked as he opened it.

He tensed, waiting for lights to flash on inside, but everything remained dark and quiet.

The house was small, just two bedrooms off the living room, with a bathroom in between them. The door to the first bedroom was mostly closed, so he walked past it and the bathroom to the second bedroom. Moonlight streaming through the window reflected off the glow-in-the-dark stars painted on the ceiling. That light shone down on the face of the baby sleeping in the crib.

He crossed the room to the crib and stared down at the sleeping child. Something twisted in his chest, and he sucked in a breath.

He hated to do this.

But he had no choice.

Not anymore.

His hand shaking, he pulled a switchblade from his pocket and popped out the blade. Then he leaned over the railing of the crib, with the knife in his hand extended toward the sleeping child…

Chapter Four

Chief Archer Thompson was in over his head. He knew it. That was why he'd hired the detective from Austin— Forrest Colton. He hadn't done that just because Hurricane Brooke had stretched the department so thin that it was nearly transparent. He'd hired Forrest because Archer was too close to one of the murder victims.

His hand shook as he reached for the picture on the bookshelf in his home study. Emmeline at sixteen. So beautiful...

So sweet.

The first body Hurricane Brooke had uncovered was his sister's. Missing for all of those years...

Was it the same situation with the body that Forrest had found out at the Lemmon house? Had her family been wondering for decades where she was?

And what about the woman in the parking lot?

She hadn't been dead long, but somebody was probably already missing her, wondering where she was, if she'd been hurt and stranded in the hurricane.

He didn't need the coroner's report to know that she'd been murdered like the others. Elliot Corgan was dead now, so he couldn't have hurt her.

And he claimed he hadn't hurt Emmeline.

But if not him, who? Who else would want to harm the sweet young woman his sister had been?

Yeah, he was in too deep—too emotionally invested in finding the killer. Forrest Colton wasn't. He would be able to examine everything with objectivity. He wouldn't have had all of the success he'd had solving those cold cases in Austin if he got too involved. So nothing and nobody should be able to distract Forrest from finding this killer.

HE WAS DISTRACTED, so distracted with thoughts of Rae Lemmon and her sweet baby. Despite her insistence that she didn't need any protection, Forrest should have insisted on leaving an officer at her house. He could have convinced her that it was protocol—to protect the crime scene.

But it wasn't the crime scene he was worried about.

Her house was so far from town, so far from any other homestead. While some of his family's ranch touched her property, the closest other dwelling belonged to the Corgans. And one of them had been a serial killer. How the hell had Elliot Corgan's family kept the fact that he was a murderer out of the press for so many years?

Judicial order?

They must have paid the judge for that order. Had they paid for anything else in town? For someone else to start up the murders to try to make Elliot Corgan look innocent?

His blood chilled as the thought occurred to him. But why bother now after another Corgan had already been arrested? James Corgan had tried to kill his ex-wife, Maggie Reeves-Corgan, and Forrest's brother Jonah, who was now Maggie's fiancé. Fortunately James hadn't been as successful at committing murders as his great-uncle had.

Those old case files sat atop Forrest's desk, the top folders nearly sliding off the mound of records and onto the floor of his cubicle area of the Whisperwood Police Department. He'd looked through everything in those case files and was as convinced as the jury had been that Elliot had been responsible for all of those murders.

But one.

There had been one victim all those years ago that had been strangled but hadn't had a scarf stuffed in her mouth like the others. She'd also been the only one of those bodies that had been mummified.

Like the chief's sister...

Like the body found in Rae's backyard...

No. Even back then, before Elliot had been arrested, convicted and sentenced to life in prison, there had been two killers. Were there two killers now? Or had that one just started up again?

Had his first recent murder been Elliot's? After Jonah and Maggie had interviewed the serial killer in prison, he had supposedly committed suicide, but Jonah had had his doubts. And knowing serial killers as well he did, so did Forrest. Had this killer somehow gotten to Elliot to prevent the inmate from revealing *his* identity?

And if this killer could get to someone in a maximum-security prison, he could certainly get to someone who lived in a little ranch house outside town.

Forrest shivered despite the fact that the air conditioner barely worked in the big open area that was divided only by the short cubicle walls. Out of all of the cubicles, his was the only one currently occupied. The officers on duty had gone out on patrol hours ago. Except for the 911 area and the front desk, the building was pretty much deserted.

He needed to head home or his parents would worry. Despite all of the years he'd been gone or maybe because of them, his parents worried about him like he was a teenager staying out past curfew. Not that he ever stayed out late. It wasn't as if he had anyplace—but work—to go. And maybe that was why they worried.

He touched his bad leg, which was stiff from all of the time he'd been sitting at his desk. They were probably worried that he was going to get hurt again—like he'd been hurt before. Like he still was…

His leg shook, threatening to fold, but he locked it and walked stiff-legged around his desk. He'd just stepped outside the dingy fabric walls of his cubicle when the phone on his desk began to ring. Dispatch probably didn't realize he was still in the office, so the call hadn't come through them. It must have come into his direct line.

Dread gripped his stomach, churning it, as he hobbled back to his desk and picked up the receiver. "Detective Colton."

"This is Dr. Bentley from the medical examiner's office," the caller identified herself. "The ME wanted me to let you know that we're pretty certain of an identification for that murder victim."

Shocked, Forrest sucked in a breath. "That was quick."

"For the one in the parking lot," Dr. Bentley clarified. "Despite how well it was preserved, the other body may take a long time to identify."

The body in Rae's backyard.

His mind flitted to Rae Lemmon and to her son—to the two of them being alone in that house where the body had been buried just a few yards from their back door. And that dread gripped his stomach again.

He was more worried about her than he was about notifying the family of the murder victim from the parking lot. But he owed them his full attention; they'd already lost too much.

"Are you still at the office?" he asked the doctor.

"Yes, Detective."

"I'm going to come down and take a look at the full report," he said. Her family was going to want more than her identification; they were going to want to know what happened to her.

They were also going to want to know who did it to her. He couldn't give them that person's name. Not yet.

But he would. He had to stop this sadistic killer before he killed again. Before he hurt anyone else.

And again an image of Rae's pretty face flashed through his mind. She'd said she could take care of herself, so she was strong and resourceful. To get into law school, she also had to be smart. Too smart to take dangerous risks. He really had no reason to be worried about her.

But those other women had probably thought they could take care of themselves, too, that they needed no protection. Now they were lying in the morgue. He did not want Rae Lemmon to wind up there.

DESPITE HOW EXHAUSTED she was from all of her sleepless nights, Rae couldn't rest. Sleep continued to elude her. And it wasn't because Connor was crying.

He was quiet—so quiet that she felt goose bumps of unease lift her skin. Why was he so quiet now?

He was exhausted, too, though. Probably even more exhausted than she was, since he was the one who'd done all of the crying the past few nights. He must have just been sleeping soundly.

Like she wished she could sleep.

But unlike Connor, she wasn't blissfully unaware of what had been discovered in their backyard earlier that day. A body.

Whose?

Who had been killed, and had that murder taken place right here? In Rae's backyard? Or in her house?

She shivered at the thought.

Would Forrest come back? Would he want to bring his crime-scene techs into her home?

She'd left before they'd finished up in her backyard. But they'd been gone when she'd returned, leaving behind only that yellow tape that had cordoned off her backyard.

Not that she wanted to go out there ever again.

When she'd left, she'd locked up the house, so unless Forrest had found the key under the flowerpot, he wouldn't have been able to get inside without breaking and entering. And she'd found no evidence of that.

Unlike the backyard, her house had seemed undisturbed—or at the least just as messy as it had been when she and Connor had left. Would she have even been able to tell if Forrest had searched it?

Of course he must have realized he would need a warrant before she would allow that. She'd made it clear to him that she knew her rights and had no intention of letting him violate them or anything else.

But he'd violated her sleep. Thoughts of him—as much as thoughts of that poor corpse—had kept her awake. Why did he irritate her so much?

What was it about him that bothered her in a way she couldn't remember anyone else ever bothering her?

She turned to flip to her left side from her right, but the sheets twisted around her, prohibiting her from moving. A curse slipped out from between her lips.

And she tensed. Hopefully she hadn't awakened Connor. But she heard something else—a strange creaking noise, like something or someone moving across the floorboards.

Then Connor did awake with a cry. But this wasn't like the nights before, when colic had brought him out of an already fitful sleep. This sounded more like a cry of terror—but it might have held pain, as well.

Jerking at the tangled sheets, Rae fought her way out of the bed. Tripping and stumbling over the ends of the sheets, she picked herself up from the floor and ran from her bedroom into Connor's. If she'd met anyone between her door and his, she would have plowed them over; she was so desperate to get to her son.

But nobody crossed her path. And nobody stood inside the nursery, but there was something, some lingering presence, some scent...

And she knew that Connor had not been alone the entire night. Somebody had been in his room. She scrambled toward the crib and peered over the railing.

Connor's feet and arms flailed as he lay on his back, kicking and screaming. She reached down and picked him up, checking his tiny body for wounds or whatever was hurting him as she did.

He was stiff, but nothing felt wounded. She soothed him by rubbing her hand up and down his back, which was damp with perspiration from his exertion, and a few hairs stuck to her palm. Had he been thrashing so violently that he'd pulled out some hair?

Maybe she needed to call a doctor. Or take him to the emergency room.

She held him tightly against her and murmured soothing words as she continued to stroke his back and rock him. Her heart pounded frantically, and his smaller heart echoed that beat…until finally it slowed. And his terrified sobbing quieted to soft, shaky cries.

And with his crying no longer ringing in her ears, she could hear other things. Like that creak again…

But it wasn't a floorboard this time. It was the creak of a door opening, then the distinctive click of it closing again. She shuddered. Somebody had been inside the house, inside the nursery…with Connor.

She needed to call the police.

She'd been so anxious to get to Connor that she'd left her cell in her bedroom. Had the intruder been in there? Had he taken her phone? Her purse?

She didn't care if he'd taken everything she owned—as long as he didn't harm her son. Or her.

She had to make sure he didn't return. With Connor still clasped in her arms, she rushed out of his room and back to hers. Her fingers trembling, she flipped on the switch next to the door and illuminated the room with the ceiling light.

Her phone lay on the bedside table, connected to her charger, so she rushed over to it. But as she reached for it, she noticed something fluttering on her pillow in the breeze that blew in through the open window. A piece of paper.

But it wasn't just paper.

When she picked it up, short strands of brown hair rained out of it, onto her tangled sheets. She touched the strands, which were baby soft, and panic gripped her heart.

It was Connor's hair. She inspected his little head and found where the piece had been cut, just above his left ear. But it looked like only his hair had been cut, the ends left jagged.

No blood smeared his pink skin.

He hadn't been hurt. But he could have been.

Or he could have been taken from her.

Someone had been inside her house. Inside the nursery and close enough to Connor to cut a lock of his hair.

She shivered with fear and revulsion.

Her poor baby…

Why? Why would someone have broken in to…?

What?

Remembering the note, she held it up to read the words crudely scrawled across the lined paper. *Get rid of the cop, or you'll lose your kid. For good.*

Get rid of the cop?

Forrest?

Or all of the police who'd been working the crime scene in her backyard?

That wasn't her fault. She hadn't found the body. She hadn't called them.

She glanced down at her phone. She couldn't call now for help. Whoever had left that note, whoever had been inside her house, might be outside—waiting, watching…

Seeing if she would ignore his warning.

And what would happen if she did?

Would he break back into her house? Would he come inside and steal Connor?

Or kill him?

Chapter Five

She had a name now. The body found during the parking-lot excavation belonged to twenty-year-old Patrice Eccleston. Patrice's family had reported her missing shortly after Hurricane Brooke had struck the Gulf Coast.

They weren't sure when they'd talked to her last, though, and couldn't pinpoint an exact moment when she had disappeared. Nobody knew what she would have been doing anywhere near Lone Star Pharma.

Forrest had come back to the crime scene. He needed to release it so that the construction could continue on the parking-lot extension. But first he needed to make sure nothing had been missed—nothing that might lead them to Patrice's killer.

Her body had been found late in the afternoon, so the scene had been processed into the night. Something could have been missed.

Not bandages and embalming fluid, though. She hadn't been mummified like the other bodies. But he wondered… Was that because the killer had been interrupted? Or because he was too old to handle the bodies as he once had?

It would have taken strength to strangle Patrice. She

was young and very fit. She would have been strong, too. She would have fought.

The coroner had confirmed signs of a struggle in the bruises and scratches. Poor Patrice had fought for her life. But she'd lost.

Forrest needed to find who had won. Who had taken the young woman's life way too soon?

The yellow tape sagged between the thin metal posts that had been planted between the mounds of dirt and the backhoe that had dug up those mounds and the body. The body of Patrice Eccleston.

Why here?

And why her?

Had she known the person who'd murdered her? Or had a stranger chosen her at random?

So many questions...

But even though he now had her name, Forrest still had no answers to those questions. To the ones that would give Patrice's grieving family true comfort.

Forrest lifted his stiff leg and stepped over the sagging tape, his boot sinking deep into the soft earth on the other side. The freshly dug up soil reminded him of the crime scene at Rae Lemmon's house. Hurricane Brooke hadn't brought up that body like she had the corpse of the chief's long-missing younger sister. Someone else had brought up that body, had dug it up just like this one had been dug up.

But Patrice had been inadvertently dug up during the parking-lot extension. The body in Rae's backyard had appeared to have been intentionally dug up.

What the hell was going on?

Forrest walked around the crime scene, moving closer to the hole where Patrice's body had been. Had something been missed? Was there a clue here like those old coins or buttons or whatever he'd discovered at Rae's?

He pulled out one of the posts holding up the sagging tape and began to poke through the mounds of dirt. A soft metallic clink rang out as his makeshift tool struck something within the dirt. Using the pole as a shovel, he moved the soil aside until he uncovered a trio of coins. Or buttons.

Leaning over, he peered closer to inspect them. These were caked with dirt and grime like the ones he'd found in Rae Lemmon's backyard. Exactly like the ones he'd found in Rae's backyard despite this being a recent crime scene and that an old one.

Or was it?

Had the body just been moved there?

He needed to find out why these scenes were linked. And how Rae Lemmon's property and Rae figured into these murders if at all.

DESPITE LOCKING ALL of the windows and barricading the front door, Rae hadn't been able to fall back to sleep the night before. She'd felt *him* out there.

She didn't know who *he* was, but she'd had no doubt that he was somewhere close enough to watch her, to see what she would do. If she would disregard his warning.

She'd wanted to so badly. She'd wanted to call the police. Or at least her friends.

But her friends would have insisted that she call the police or, worse yet, Forrest Colton. And she hadn't been willing to risk it—to risk her son's life—for anything.

Maybe she would have fallen back to sleep if she hadn't stayed in his room, curled up in the chair next to his crib. Despite his late-night haircut, Connor had

had no issues falling back to sleep. Maybe what had happened had seemed just like a bad dream to him.

Rae wished that it had been. But the note and that little clipped lock of hair proved that it hadn't been just a nightmare. It had happened.

It could not happen again. No stranger could get that close to her son.

An image flitted through her mind—an image of Forrest Colton holding Connor so easily and comfortably in the crook of his strong arm. The baby had been so content after such a fussy night. Connor obviously hadn't felt as if Forrest was a stranger.

But he would have to be one now. He would have to stay away from her and her child.

While Connor had slept in, she'd showered and dressed for work—not that she had any urge to go. But as a single mom, she was the only one who could pay the bills—for day care, for food, for utilities…

She didn't have to pay for the house. Her mother had left it to her when she'd passed away last year. Mama had bought the house before she'd met Rae's father, and she'd always refused to put him on the deed. She'd probably worried that if she had, he would have lost it somehow. Instead she'd lost her husband. When she'd gotten sick, he'd just taken off.

That had proved to Rae that men couldn't be trusted, and she vowed to never need anyone. Which was good because none of the guys she'd dated had chosen to stick around either.

She leaned over the crib railing and brushed her finger across Connor's cheek. But she needed this little guy. Even though he'd been in her life only for a short time, she couldn't imagine her life without him.

And she vowed now that she would never have to because she would make damn certain that nothing happened to him.

An engine rumbled outside the closed window as a vehicle pulled up to the house. Why hadn't she heard that last night? Had the intruder arrived on foot? Or horseback as Forrest had the morning before?

Connor must have heard the engine, too, because he opened his eyes and stared sleepily up at her. Had he seen the person last night? He must have, because he'd cried out with such fear. He'd seen whoever had broken into their home. If only he could talk.

She picked him up from the crib and clasped him close to her before walking through the house to peer out at the driveway. And a curse slipped out of her lips when she spied the police SUV and the man who stepped out of it.

Forrest Colton.

She glanced around the SUV, around the driveway and front yard. But she couldn't see anyone lurking out there now. Maybe he'd gone with the dawn, since he'd had no shadows left to hide in. Or maybe he was still there.

Still watching her.

And now he would see that Forrest was here despite his warning. He would think that she had ignored it.

That she didn't care.

Fear gripping her, Rae clasped Connor so tightly that he tensed and began to cry. If not for his crying, she would have pretended that they weren't home. But Forrest knew they were, and he rang the bell.

Keeping Connor against her with just one arm holding him now, she used her other hand to jerk the chair from beneath the door handle. Not that she intended to let Forrest in.

She opened the door but stood inside the jamb and coldly asked him, "What do you want?"

His brow furrowed for a moment with confusion and then he glanced at Connor, who continued to cry. "Oh, did he keep you awake last night, too?"

Too? Did he know about the intruder?

Then she remembered that he knew about her sleepless night before he'd discovered that body in her backyard. "No, not him."

He raised a brow, as if silently asking who.

But she wasn't about to tell him about the reason she really hadn't slept. So she just shook her head and reminded him, "It's none of your business."

"Actually, it is," he said. "Your property is a crime scene. I need to know who's had access to it. Who has been visiting you?"

She wished she knew. "My friends come by—you know them, Maggie and Bellamy."

That eyebrow arched again. "Nobody else?"

"I don't know," she answered honestly. "I haven't seen anyone else."

But she knew someone had been there. She had proof of it—not that she was going to show it to Forrest. No. She had to get rid of Forrest as soon as possible. So she began to close the door. "If that's all, I really need to get ready for work."

Somehow his foot had crossed the threshold, and his leg pressed against the door, stopping her from closing it on him. "You look dressed," he murmured gruffly, and something like disappointment flashed through his hazel eyes.

He couldn't have actually found her sleep shirt sexy, though. Or her.

She wore black dress pants now with a blouse buttoned all the way to her neck. The partners at the law firm were very conservative—even Kenneth Dawson, despite his ambulance-chasing tendencies.

"I need to get Connor ready to bring to day care," she said.

His cries had quieted, but he squirmed against her. Awake now, he had to be hungry. Fortunately he felt dry or she might have had to change herself again with as closely as she'd been holding him.

Forrest's eyes narrowed now as he stared at her. "Is something wrong?" he asked.

Heat climbed to her face, but she shook her head. "No. I'm just busy—so busy that I don't have time to keep telling you that I don't have any information to help you. I don't know anything about how that body wound up in the backyard. I can't help you!" She put her shoulder behind the door now, trying to squeeze Forrest out.

"You need help," he said.

And she froze. What did he know?

"Don't go getting all defensive," he said. "I know you think you can handle everything all by yourself."

She did get defensive now, as her pride smarted from his remark. "I can."

He pointed toward the chair next to the door. "You're obviously scared."

"A body was found in my backyard," she reminded him.

"You weren't scared yesterday," he said.

"I didn't have time to think about it," she admitted. Or she would have realized that he was right—that she was in danger and vulnerable out here on her own.

"Think about reaching out for help," he advised her.

She shook her head. "I don't need or want your help!"

"I wasn't volunteering," he said. "I was thinking about your friends, Maggie and Bellamy."

Her face got hotter with embarrassment. Of course she should have realized that he wasn't offering his personal protection or help. He hadn't even wanted to dance with her. If she told him about what had happened the night before, about the warning, he would probably assign another officer to her case. He had bigger cases to solve than finding out who had threatened her.

"Bellamy is on her honeym—"

"She and Donovan get back today," he interrupted. "And Maggie hasn't gone anywh—"

"Without Jonah," she said. And while he wasn't actually a police officer, he was one of the Cowboy Heroes, and maybe her intruder considered him law enforcement, as well.

"Don't you like my brother?" Forrest asked, and he seemed defensive now.

She sighed. "I like Jonah. I especially like how happy he makes Maggie. I don't want to intrude on their new relationship." That was very true. She was so happy for her friend that she didn't want to dump her worries on her, especially after everything Maggie had just been through with her crazy ex-husband.

"I know my brothers wouldn't consider your reaching out to your friends to be an intrusion," he said. "And while I don't know Bellamy and Maggie that well yet, I doubt they would be your friends if *they* considered your asking for help an intrusion."

"They wouldn't," she admitted. Hell, they would be happy to help if she reached out. Too happy.

And once they knew what had happened last night, they would insist that she report it to the police and probably to Forrest in particular, since his investigation in her backyard must have been what had precipitated the threat.

Why?

She wanted to know who had been buried back there. More important she wanted to know who had done it and for that person to be brought to justice. But she wasn't willing to risk her baby's life for it or for anyone.

"I need to get to work," she said as she leaned against the door again, trying to push it closed—on Forrest. "So you need to leave." Before anyone saw him here. "Now!" Her voice cracked with desperation.

He kept his boot planted on her threshold, and his body planted in the doorway, and he was too big, too muscular, for her to move. His hazel eyes narrowed again, and he leaned closer to study her face.

She sucked in a breath as an intense feeling gripped her. It wasn't fear this time. It was…

The same thing she'd felt when she'd asked him to dance at the wedding. Sure, she'd felt sorry for how alone he'd seemed that night. But that wasn't the only reason why she'd asked him to dance. She'd been attracted to him. Then. And now.

Forrest Colton was so damn good-looking, so sexy…

But she couldn't give in to that attraction—even as he leaned closer, so close that his lips could have brushed across hers. If she rose on tiptoe, if she lifted her mouth.

Temptation tugged at her. But the last thing she wanted the intruder to see was her kissing Forrest Colton…even if she wanted so badly to do it, so badly that a cry of frustration slipped out between her lips.

"Please," she murmured. "Please leave me alone."

As if she'd slapped him, he jerked his head up and stepped back. And finally she was able to slam the door between them. She slammed it with such force that Connor began to scream.

Regret gripped her now as powerfully as that attraction had. And she wasn't just regretful that she'd upset her son. She regretted not kissing Forrest Colton. But maybe he hadn't intended to kiss her at all.

Maybe she'd just imagined his intent, just like she wished she'd imagined that man breaking into her home the night before. When she left the house moments later to leave for work, Forrest was still parked in her driveway. And there was no trace of attraction on his face, just irritation...with her.

"Why are you still here?" she asked.

He held up a piece of paper. "I got that warrant you told me I needed," he said.

Her brow furrowed. "Warrant? But you already searched my property without it."

"Not the house," he said.

"You want to search the house?" She tensed.

He nodded. "And this piece of paper gives me the legal authority to conduct that search."

She only glanced at the paper, which must have been printed from one those mini printers officers used to issue citations in their vehicles. Then she shrugged. "Whatever. You won't find anything." She stepped back onto the porch and unlocked the door for him. He wouldn't find the note. She'd tucked that into her purse, sealed in a plastic bag, along with that lock of hair. "Just lock up when you leave."

As if that mattered.

The intruder had gotten in easily enough last night that she hadn't even heard him until Connor had cried out. Was he out there now?

Watching?

And what would he do about Forrest's being here again? Over his staying to search the house?

Would he make good on his threat?

Tears rushed to her eyes, and she blinked furiously as she turned away. But Forrest must have seen them, because he caught her arm, the one from which Connor's car carrier swung. He turned her back toward him.

"Are you okay?" he asked, his deep voice sounding even deeper with concern.

She closed her eyes and willed the tears away. "I…" She couldn't tell him.

As if he'd read her mind, he implored her, "You can tell me."

But she shook her head. "I have to go." She jerked away from him and rushed toward her small SUV. Hopefully her intruder had seen that and realized that she was doing everything she could to get rid of Forrest.

Unless…

Unless he didn't just want the detective to go away. Maybe he wanted him dead.

Chapter Six

She had been on his mind since she'd left him alone that morning to search her house. Hell, she'd been on his mind even before that, even before he'd found that body in her backyard. She'd been on his mind since he'd seen her, looking so damn beautiful, at Donovan and Bellamy's wedding.

Maybe that was why he was here. Not just to welcome the newlyweds back but to get insight into the woman who confused and fascinated and aggravated Forrest.

He'd nearly kissed her that morning. His skin heated and his pulse quickened just thinking about it, about how close his mouth had come to hers—so close that he'd nearly tasted her minty breath.

He wished he'd tasted her mouth, wished that he'd given in to temptation and kissed her, even though he knew that would have been wrong. Or at the very least unprofessional.

Not that he considered her a murder suspect. But he had found a body in her backyard. And he had a feeling she knew more than she was admitting, that there was something she was keeping from him. And that was why she seemed so damn scared.

Not that she didn't have reason to be, though. There was a killer on the loose in Whisperwood.

Forrest had to find him.

"I guess we bored him into a stupor," Bellamy remarked with a giggle.

Donovan snorted. "Forrest usually gets like this when he's working a case, so single-minded that solving it is all he can think about."

He did get that way—until now, until this case. Now he kept thinking about Rae Lemmon instead of the case. His mind was totally focused on her. And how the hell was he going to catch a killer like that?

Unless she knew who the killer was. Was that why she'd been so anxious to get rid of him that morning? Was she trying to protect someone?

"And he's not working one case but two." Donovan continued to talk about Forrest as if he wasn't even there.

"Two?" Bellamy asked and then nodded. "You mean the chief's sister and the body found in the parking lot. Of course with so many years between the deaths, it's unlikely the murders would be related."

Forrest wasn't so sure about that, but he wasn't about to share his suspicions with Bellamy when she obviously didn't have all of the facts yet. They had just returned from their honeymoon and were currently in the kitchen of Bellamy's house, unpacking groceries they must have just picked up from the store.

Forrest had called Donovan and informed him of the body he'd found in Rae's backyard, but obviously he hadn't shared that news with his bride yet. And apparently she hadn't learned about the body from anyone else either.

Like Rae.

Why was she so damn stubbornly independent that she refused to reach out even to her friends? Why was she so determined to do everything on her own?

"What?" Bellamy asked as she looked from him to Donovan and back. "Has something else happened?"

"I didn't want to upset you," Donovan began, "especially now."

"I'm pregnant," Bellamy said, "not fragile. I can handle getting upset, which is lucky for you since I'm getting pretty upset right now."

"Uh, maybe I should go," Forrest murmured as he started to rise from the chair he'd taken at the kitchen table.

But Bellamy shoved him back into his seat. "What's going on?" she asked him.

He looked to his brother, who just nodded at him. "I found another body."

She shuddered. "Oh, no."

That wasn't the worst part of it, and she needed to know, so he added, "In Rae's backyard."

She turned back to her husband. "And you didn't tell me?"

Not wanting any trouble between the newlyweds, Forrest jumped in to explain, "It just happened yesterday."

"You weren't feeling well," Donovan reminded her.

"I was tired," she said. Then she touched her belly, which had swelled. She was showing now. "We were tired."

Donovan slipped his arm around her and kissed her forehead. "I was going to tell you but then this guy showed up." His brother focused on him again. "Why did you show up? I'm not thinking that it was just to welcome us back and hear about the amazing time we had."

"I did want to make sure you had a good time," Forrest said. His brother and Bellamy certainly deserved their happiness.

"But…" Donovan prodded him. "What else?"

Forrest turned toward his new sister-in-law again. "I wanted to ask you about Rae."

"She's my best friend."

"So there's no one who knows her better?"

She shook her head. "We grew up together. We've been friends since kindergarten. But I think we grew up even more later in life, when we had to deal with ailing parents. Rae's dad took off when her mom was diagnosed with cancer, leaving her holding the bag to take care of her. Georgia Lemmon was tough, though. She survived *that* time."

"But it came back," Forrest guessed.

She nodded.

"What about her deadbeat dad?"

She shook her head.

No wonder Rae had decided that she didn't need a husband to have a family. Not after the example her father had given her.

But that propensity to take off on a sick mate wasn't exclusive to male partners. While Forrest had been working with physical therapists so that he would be able to walk again, his fiancée had taken off. He'd gotten a text.

Sorry, I didn't sign up for this.

Newly engaged, they hadn't worked on their vows yet, but it was clear that she wouldn't have included "in sickness and in health" in hers. And apparently Rae's dad hadn't in his either.

"Could it be her father?" Bellamy asked. "Could his be the body you found in the backyard? Maybe he didn't take off after all."

Forrest shook his head. "This body was like the chief's sister—female and looks as though someone tried to preserve her, too."

Bellamy shuddered again.

Donovan tightened his arm around his wife and assured her, "Forrest will find the sick bastard who did it."

His brother had more faith in him than Forrest probably deserved. He didn't even have a clue right now—just those weird metallic things he'd found and had sent off to the lab.

"I'm worried about Rae," Bellamy said with concern darkening her dark eyes even more. "How is she?"

"Stubborn," Forrest automatically replied.

Bellamy's lips curved into a slight smile. "You're getting to know my best friend well."

Not well enough.

Not as well as he would have liked. He wished again that he'd kissed her. But that was a line he could not cross—for both their sakes.

He could not be distracted right now, not when he had a case—or cases—to solve.

"I don't know her at all," Forrest said. "And she won't talk to me. She won't answer my questions." Like what was going on with her, and why she was scared.

She had seemed afraid of him, but she had no reason to fear him…unless she was hiding something from him. Like the killer.

Bellamy tensed and pulled away from Donovan. "What questions could you have for Rae? You can't suspect her. You can't think that she has anything to do with the murders."

"Of course he doesn't think that," Donovan answered for him.

Forrest frowned at his brother. "I don't want to think that, but I can tell she's holding something back." Or at least that was the way he'd felt that morning when she'd been so anxious to get rid of him.

Maybe she'd just been busy getting ready for work and all. But Forrest had sensed something else— something that had to do with him or at least with the investigation.

"It's hard for Rae to trust people," Bellamy said. "It's hard for her to let anyone in."

"Sounds like someone else I know," Donovan said with a grin at his brother. "This guy has a problem trusting people, too."

"I guess that would come with the territory of being a detective," Bellamy mused.

Donovan shook his head. "That's not the only reason."

Shannon was one of the reasons. Donovan knew that Forrest had lost more than his job when he'd been shot. He must have shared *that* with his bride, because she sighed and murmured, "Of course." Then she reached out and grabbed Forrest's hand. "I'm sorry."

"I'm not," he said, and for maybe the first time since he'd received that text, he meant it. "Better I find out before we were married." And losing her hadn't upset him nearly as much as it should have, if he'd truly loved her like their brother Dallas had loved his late wife. His loss was really a loss. Ivy had been awesome. Shannon, on the other hand, hadn't been whom he'd thought she was.

Bellamy sighed again but nodded in agreement.

"You're better off without her," Donovan heartily agreed. "She was selfish. You deserve someone better, someone like Bellamy."

She smiled and leaned back against her husband. "Or like Rae," she added as she arched her dark brows.

Forrest snorted. "She's made it clear she has no interest in me."

But for a second there this morning he'd thought she'd been staring at his mouth as intently as he'd been staring at hers. That she'd leaned forward as he'd leaned down.

That she'd been as attracted to him as he was to her. But then she'd jerked back. And that look on her beautiful face had been so fearful.

Of what?

Him?

Donovan's heart rate quickened as the door closed behind his brother. "Are you mad at me?" he anxiously asked his bride.

"You shouldn't have kept that news from me," Bellamy said. "You should have told me about Forrest finding the body in Rae's backyard."

"Yes," he agreed. Yet the pang that struck his heart wasn't of regret but of concern when he remembered how tired she'd been the past couple of days. He'd been so damn worried about her and the baby.

And that sense of helplessness that had gripped him then gripped him again. He wanted to be able to help her through this pregnancy, but the only thing he could do was try to protect her, to protect *them.* He closed his arms around her—around them both—and held her tightly.

She sighed and leaned against his chest. They were

so close that she must have sensed his protectiveness. "You don't have to worry about me. I'm tough. You know that."

"Yes, I do," he agreed with a ragged sigh. "I just didn't want you worrying about Rae."

"I always worry about Rae," Bellamy said with a ragged sigh of her own.

"She's tough, too," Donovan reminded her.

"I know. She's been through so much already, though, and that body turning up in her backyard..." She tensed in his arms. "What if it had been out there as long as the chief's sister was missing? Rae and I used to play in that yard..." She shivered despite the warmth of the day.

Donovan rubbed his hands down her back, trying to warm away her chill. But he suspected the only thing that would put them all at ease would be catching this killer. It was a damn good thing he'd come back.

"Do you think Forrest could be right?" he asked her. "Do you think Rae could know more than she's admitting?"

Bellamy pushed her palms against his chest and pulled away from his embrace. "Absolutely not. Rae can't have anything to do with those murders."

"But could she have some idea who might have committed them?"

"If she did, she would tell Forrest or the chief," Bellamy insisted. "She's going to law school because she wants to help stop some of the crime going on in Whisperwood. She would never protect a killer."

"Not even if that person was a friend?" he asked. "Or a relative?"

"The only person Rae would break the law to protect would be Connor," Bellamy said, "and that sweet baby has nothing to do with any of this."

Donovan smiled. "Of course not."

"And neither does Rae."

Bellamy had known the other woman since kindergarten, so she knew her well. But Donovan knew his brother very well. Usually Forrest's instincts about a case were right—not so much when it came to women, though.

So which was it? Was he seeing Rae Lemmon as a suspect or as a romantic interest?

No matter which, after what Forrest had been through with that flaky fiancée of his, he was unlikely ever to trust her. And Rae didn't trust any man.

Yeah, it was good that he and Bellamy had come home—if only to keep the peace between Bellamy's best friend and his brother.

DROPPING CONNOR AT day care that morning had been harder for Rae than it usually was. And it was usually very hard. But letting him out of her sight after what had happened last night had been especially difficult.

And spending all of these hours away from him, stuck at her desk in a windowless room at the law firm, had made her physically ill. Her stomach churned with anxiety and fear. She just wanted to be with her son, to make sure that he was safe. She knew that she didn't need to worry, though.

The day care was very well staffed with maternal types who were even more overprotective than she was, including the male owner, Bob McCauley, who was a former football player. Nobody would be able to get one of the babies past him without one hell of a fight. But even knowing that...

She couldn't shake her fear for her son. Had she put him in danger that morning, talking to Forrest Colton? She never should have opened the door to him.

Would her note writer punish her for disregarding his warning?

She wanted to be with Connor, but maybe he was safer at the day care than he would be with her. Bob would protect him more effectively than she could. Maybe that was why she was still at work this late.

Sure, she'd had piles of research for a pending case for one of the partners. She could have gotten through it faster, though, if she hadn't been so distracted.

She had been so distracted that she hadn't even realized what time it was…until she noticed the digital numbers on the corner of her computer monitor. She gasped and then sucked in a breath as the sound echoed eerily in her small office. No other noise drifted beneath the door like it usually did.

Everybody else must have already left for the day. And she should have, too. Bob wouldn't be worried; the day care center had a second shift for parents who worked later or had classes after work, like she did a couple of nights a week. But now that she knew what time it was, she was anxious to leave the office.

Especially since it felt so forebodingly empty.

She shut down her computer and gathered up her stuff, shoving it inside the purse with the note and lock of hair she'd sealed in a plastic bag, like evidence.

Should she have given it to Forrest?

The thought lifted goose bumps on her skin, though, as a chill rushed through her blood. She couldn't risk it—no matter how much she wanted the person who'd threatened her son to be caught.

And the killer.

Were they the same?

They must have been or why the threat? Only the killer would want Forrest out of the way. Well, she and the killer. Even if she hadn't received the threat, she wouldn't want Forrest Colton around her. She had too much going on—she was way too busy to deal with him and that annoying attraction she felt for him. And that was all it was: an annoyance.

That annoyance surged through her now as she threw her purse over her shoulder and stepped out of her office into the dark hallway. Like her office, it had no windows, and someone had shut off the lights already.

Hadn't they noticed the light under her door? Hadn't they realized that she was still at work? Or had that been the reason for shutting off the lights? To spook her even more?

Goose bumps rose on her skin as that chill chased through her again. But would the person who'd broken into her house know where she worked, as well?

Whisperwood was a small enough town and so gossipy that everybody knew everybody else's business. It would be easy enough for anyone to track her down at home and at work.

She hurried down the hall toward the elevators, rushing past the closed doors of other offices along the way. A loud *thump* emanated from beneath one of those closed doors, and she gasped in shock at hearing the sound. Then a giggle followed her gasp, and her fear eased.

Apparently she wasn't the only one working late... although the *thump* and the giggling didn't sound much like work.

The doorknob to the closest office rattled as the door opened slightly. Kenneth Dawson peered out through the crack, his thin blond hair slightly mussed. "Oh, Rae, I didn't realize you were still here."

Which explained why the lights had been shut off. With her office farther down the hall than his, he wouldn't have noticed the light under her door.

"I'm leaving now," she assured him.

"Worked late like I am," he said.

His flushed face made it look like he had been working out—physically and not mentally.

"My wife brought me dinner," he added with a smile.

Rae smiled and nodded. "Oh, that was very sweet of her."

"Yes," he agreed, but he didn't open his door any farther and offer to introduce his wife to Rae, which was odd since he'd once invited her to join them for dinner at his house.

Of course Rae was always in a hurry to leave and get Connor from day care, so he probably didn't expect her to want to linger. And she didn't.

"Enjoy your dinner," she said. "Good night." And she rushed off toward the elevators again. An elevator car came quickly—since everybody else had probably already left the building for the night. She stepped inside and as the doors began to close, that giggle rang out again.

Mrs. Dawson sounded so happy and youthful. Rae wished she would have taken the time to meet her. But she needed to get to Connor. So she rushed from the building, to her SUV and then to the day care center, and as she did, she kept glancing around her, checking for anyone looking at her, watching her.

But nobody and nothing stuck out to her. Of course she was learning to be a lawyer, not a cop—just as Forrest Colton had pointed out to her. She didn't know how to accurately assess who might pose a threat to her or to Connor.

"Everything okay?" Bob asked as the burly middle-aged man carried the baby carrier to the car for her.

She nodded.

"I heard about another body turning up out at your place," he said.

She shuddered.

"If you need anything…"

She thought about telling him about the threat, but like her friends, he would probably also want her to call the police. And the last thing she needed was the police—particularly Detective Forrest Colton—coming around her place again.

Hopefully he had concluded his search quickly that morning and was long gone. When she pulled into her driveway a short while later, she didn't notice any vehicles. But a light did glow inside the house.

Had one just been left on? Or was someone inside?

Leaving Connor in the back seat in his carrier, she headed cautiously toward the house. The door was shut, but behind the curtains pulled across the windows, a shadow moved. Someone was inside her house.

Forrest?

Or the person who'd snuck in last night to threaten her son?

Chapter Seven

Forrest hadn't expected a warm welcome. Hell, he hadn't expected a welcome at all—just questions and confusion and pain.

So much pain.

But neither man cried. They hadn't when he'd notified them of Patrice's death either. Her brother and her widowed father had been in shock then, so he hadn't asked them many questions. That was why he'd returned tonight, to talk to them after they'd had some time to process the news of their loss. But they were more inclined to ask their own questions than they were to answer his.

"What are you doing to find her killer?" her father, Atticus Eccleston, asked.

"Is her murder your primary focus?" her brother asked. "Or do you only care about the old bodies?"

Forrest furrowed his brow in confusion. "What?"

"We heard all the news reports about you," the father explained. "That you're a cold-case detective."

"My last assignment with the Austin Police Department was in the cold-case unit," Forrest admitted. That was his position when he'd been shot. "But I worked in the homicide unit for a long time before that."

And he'd been so damn good at solving murders that

they'd moved him to the cold-case unit. Bragging about his past wouldn't give these guys what they needed. Only finding Patrice's killer would give them the justice and closure they wanted.

"Stopping this killer is my top priority," he assured them. Before he killed again.

An image of Rae's face, pale with fear, flashed through his mind. With a killer on the loose, she had every reason to be afraid, but a feeling nagged at him, making him wonder if she had another reason. But what?

"It's too late for my sister," Ian Eccleston said. "Too late to do anything to save her or bring her back." But still he didn't cry; his face just flushed with rage. And his fists were clenched, as if he was tempted to take a swing at Forrest.

He'd been attacked during plenty of other investigations, but usually the suspect tried to fight him, not the family member of a victim.

"I am very sorry for your loss," he told them both— as he had the other night. They hadn't acknowledged his comment that night. They'd been too shocked. Too numb.

Unfortunately that numbness had worn off to leave anger and pain.

"We don't want your sympathy," Ian scoffed, and he walked over to open the front door of the house he shared with his father. "We want results. If you can't get them, we'll find the bastard ourselves."

"Give the lab time to process all the evidence from the scene," Forrest said as he stepped out that open door. "And if you remember anything that might help our investigation—"

"We would have already told you," Ian said, and he

slammed the door in Forrest's face—just like Rae had that morning.

And both instances had Forrest feeling again like he wasn't being told everything—like these people knew more than they were sharing with him.

He wasn't going to get anything else out of Ian Eccleston. But he might be able to get Rae to tell him more, if her friends were right that she could be trusted.

But then, his experience with Shannon had taught him that it was better to trust no one, at least not with his heart. He was damn sure Rae Lemmon didn't want that anyway, though, or she wouldn't have jerked back before he'd been able to kiss her. Not that he'd any business kissing her.

But her backyard was a murder scene, so he definitely had business with her.

And right now that business was unfinished.

SHE HADN'T KNOWN what to do when she'd seen that shadow pass behind her living room curtains. Rae hadn't known if she should call the police.

But before they arrived, the intruder could have made good on their threat to hurt Connor. Or her. So to protect her son, she'd turned and run back to her vehicle. But when she'd opened the door, someone had stopped her—with a hand on her arm. And she'd screamed in terror...until Bellamy had spoken.

"I'm sorry I scared you," she said again—as she had when she'd first approached Rae on the driveway.

Rae forced a smile. "It's fine. I'm just so tired that I'm jumpy."

"Are you sure you're just tired?" Maggie asked. She'd showed up moments after Rae had with the pizza her sister had been craving. It sat mostly untouched in the middle of the kitchen table.

They had probably already eaten with their significant others and had really bought the pizza for her. But Rae wasn't hungry, not with all of the knots of dread and fear filling her stomach.

"Or is Forrest right and you're scared of something?" Bellamy asked.

She tensed. "Forrest? He talked to you?" she asked. "About me?"

Bellamy nodded.

"He had no right to interrogate you," Rae said. "You're not a suspect and neither am I."

Bellamy glanced down at the table, as if she couldn't meet Rae's eyes.

Horrified, Rae asked, "Am I a suspect?"

Bellamy looked back up now, her gaze intent on Rae's face. "He doesn't think you're a killer, but he thinks you know something you're not telling him."

"Are you interrogating me now?" Rae asked defensively. But now she couldn't meet her friend's eyes. She jumped up from the table and began to collect the plates.

Maggie said, "I can get those." But she was holding Connor on her lap, and the both of them looked so content.

Connor hadn't looked like that last night. He'd looked terrified. And that terror passed through Rae as she remembered the intruder's threat.

Tears stung her eyes, blurring her vision. She blinked furiously as she turned away to carry the dishes to the sink. But someone grabbed her arm, holding her in place.

"You are scared," Bellamy said.

"A body was found in my backyard," Rae reminded her. "Of course I would be scared."

"Anybody would be," Maggie agreed with her with a shudder of revulsion.

But Bellamy shook her head. She'd known Rae too long and too well. "Not you," she said. "Forrest is right. There's something else that has rattled you." She narrowed her eyes and tilted her head. "Is it him?"

"H-h-him?" Rae sputtered. "Does he think that?" Had he guessed that she was attracted to him? Since she'd just about risen up on tiptoe and pressed her lips to his, he'd probably guessed—not to mention that she'd asked him to dance at the wedding a few weeks ago.

Bellamy smiled. "No. Not Forrest. Not after what his fiancée did to him."

Rae gasped. She hadn't known he was engaged. If she had, she never would have asked him to dance or nearly kissed him. "What did his fiancée do?"

"Ex-fiancée," Maggie chimed in.

So she'd known about his engagement, too.

"When he got shot, while he was still recovering, she took off with his ring," Bellamy said.

Rae sucked in a breath. "She left him?"

Bellamy nodded. "He had to endure months of physical therapy before he could even walk again, and instead of helping him through that, she took off."

Just like Rae's dad had taken off when her mother had been diagnosed with cancer. She flinched. So it wasn't just men who couldn't be counted on to stick around.

"She hurt him badly when she abandoned him," Bellamy continued. "Not just his heart but his self-esteem. He doesn't think you're into him. He thinks you're lying to him."

"About what?" Rae asked.

"About the killer," Bellamy continued. "He thinks you know something about him, that you're protecting him."

Could it really be the killer who had left that note for her? She'd pretty much already concluded that it had to be, though. Who else would want the detective out of the way, besides her?

"Is that why you're here?" Rae asked. "Do you think that, too?"

"Of course not," Bellamy assured her as she jumped up from the table to put an arm around her. "I told him that the only person you would lie to protect would be Connor."

Rae sucked in a breath and tensed. And Bellamy must have felt that tension. She turned Rae toward her. "That's it, isn't it? Someone has threatened Connor."

Maggie jumped up from the table, too, with the baby cradled protectively in her arms. Both of these women would protect her child as fiercely as she would.

Rae trusted them. Tears rushed to her eyes as she nodded. "Yes." Her voice cracked with the fear that bubbled up inside her. She shouldn't have come back here. But she was glad that she had, glad that Bellamy had been waiting for her.

"Who?" Maggie asked. "Who's threatening you?"

"I don't know," Rae admitted. She grabbed her purse from the counter, where she'd dropped it, and she pulled out the plastic bag containing the note and Connor's hair. "Someone was in the house last night—in Connor's room."

"Why didn't you call the police?" Bellamy asked.

"Because the note told her not to," Maggie pointed out.

"But I should have," Rae admitted. By not calling the

police, Rae had let the person get away with what he'd done—breaking in and threatening her son.

"You should have left the minute it happened," Maggie said, and she tightened her arms around the baby as she looked fearfully out the kitchen windows.

She'd been glad her friends had been here, but now she realized that their being here put them in danger, too. A danger that they hadn't even known about, because she hadn't been open and honest with them about what was going on with her.

"You should have come to one of us," Bellamy said.

Rae nodded. "I know but I knew you guys would want me to call the police, that you'd want me to report it. And I was worried that the note writer would come back, that he'd make good on his threat." The tears spilled over, running down her face as sobs bubbled up from her throat.

Bellamy held her tightly. "You and Connor are not going to be alone from now on. We'll protect you. We'll all protect you."

Rae loved her friends too much to put them in danger, especially now with Bellamy pregnant and Maggie so happy. She pulled back from Bellamy's embrace. "No, you won't. I'll call the police."

It was their job to protect people. Of course their presence would also put her and her son in danger.

More danger.

They were already in danger.

"Call Forrest," Bellamy told her as she drew her cell from her pocket...as if she intended to call if Rae refused.

She knew what she had to do, what she should have done right after she'd found the note. But she'd been so scared then, so terrified that someone had so easily gotten to her son. Without protection, that was bound to happen again.

Yet she couldn't help but worry that Forrest's involvement would put them in more danger, not just from the killer but from that attraction she felt for him. She couldn't fall for another man who wasn't going to stick around when she needed him.

And once Forrest solved these murder cases, he would leave Whisperwood. The hurricane was the only reason he'd been here in the first place.

"Chief, Chief," reporters called out from the television screen that sat on the bureau at the foot of his bed.

He—along with all of the other viewers—watched Archer Thompson turn toward the reporters gathered outside the Whisperwood Police Department.

"Was Elliot Corgan an innocent man? Or is there another serial killer on the loose?"

As part of his plea deal, Elliot Corgan's name had not been released as the Whisperwood killer. That had probably been more his family's doing than his, though. They hadn't wanted anyone to know the biggest landowners in Whisperwood had a killer among them.

He snorted. Elliot hadn't been their only disgrace, though. Even the younger generation had proved to be a disappointment. But Elliot had definitely been their biggest.

Why hadn't he just claimed the sheriff's sister as one of his victims? Then all of this would have been done. But hers wasn't the only body that had turned up. Why the hell couldn't the dead stay buried?

He focused on the chief again, who declined to answer any questions. "This is an ongoing investigation," he said, "so I'm not at liberty to comment on it."

"Is that because you've turned over the investigation to Forrest Colton?" another reporter asked. "Why did you do that, Chief? Because it was too close to home for you?"

Archer turned fully toward the cameras and the television viewers now. The man was older, but age didn't affect his tall body. He stood straight and strong. "I did that because Forrest Colton gets results. He closes cases. He finds killers. And he will find this one."

Not if the killer found him first and got rid of him.

Chapter Eight

Forrest was in the morgue. Again.

Over the course of his law-enforcement career, he'd spent entirely too much time in the morgue. Other detectives accepted the coroner's report without question. Forrest wanted to see the wounds himself; it helped him connect to the victim and to the killer.

What kind of killer preserved his victims as the chief's sister and the body of the woman in Rae's backyard had been preserved?

And why not Patrice?

Had there just not been enough time for him to process her body as he had the others?

Or didn't he have the energy anymore?

No. The bruises around her neck certainly showed the strength of her killer. He didn't lack energy. So it must have been time he'd lacked.

Poor Patrice.

She had been so young, so vital. The sheriff's sister and the other victim had once been young, too. The killer had tried to keep them young with the way he'd preserved them. But they had died long ago.

Unlike Patrice.

Since she was the most recent victim, her murder

should be the easiest to solve. But Forrest was drawn to the other body, to the one he'd found in Rae's backyard.

Hell, he was just drawn to Rae and to her son. And he had no damn idea why. He had a case to work, which was something that, after the shooting, he'd thought he would never have the opportunity to do again. This was his chance to prove himself, to prove that he was still capable of performing the job he loved.

So he couldn't afford any distractions like Rae and her beautiful brown eyes and her curvy figure and her soft skin and her full lips.

Lips he wished he'd kissed.

"See anything I missed?" the coroner asked, her voice sharp with sarcasm.

Forrest sighed. "That's not what I'm looking for," he assured her. "And as I told you, you didn't need to be here." In fact he would have preferred to be alone, so he could think. But even with her present, he'd been able to think only of Rae Lemmon, of how she'd looked that morning.

Scared.

Was that because she'd guessed he was about to kiss her? Was that what had scared her?

He was a little scared of how badly he'd wanted to kiss her, of how much of an attraction he felt for her.

"I want the killer caught, too," the coroner said.

"I know," he said.

"I have daughters this age," she continued with a catch in her voice. "I hate to think of them out there with a killer."

Maybe that was why he kept thinking of Rae—because she was so alone out there, where he'd already found one body. Well, she had Connor. But he was no protection. He needed her; he was totally dependent on her.

She had to stay safe. Didn't she realize that?

"Tell them to be careful," he advised.

She snorted. "They will tell you that I already nag them quite enough. They are careful. But these women probably thought they were being careful, too."

He nodded. They probably had.

Just like Rae Lemmon thought she was being careful, that she could take care of herself and her son without any help. Hopefully she had at least reached out to her friends, since she clearly had no intention of reaching out to him.

And his reaching out, albeit theoretically, to these victims hadn't given him any new clues to the killer's identity. "You be careful, too," Forrest advised the medical examiner. "I'm sorry you came down here for nothing."

She sighed. "I wish you had found something I missed," she said. "Something that would lead us to this monster."

He nodded. But he had nothing else to say, so he turned to leave. He'd just stepped into the hall and closed the door when the cell in his pocket began to vibrate.

If it was the coroner, she would have just opened the door and called him back. It had to be someone else, so he drew out the cell. But he didn't recognize the number on the screen. It could have been a reporter; several of them had been calling him to comment on the investigation, especially since they weren't getting much out of the chief.

He stared down at the screen, though, hesitating before pressing that decline button. Something compelled him to press the accept button instead.

"Colton here," he said.

"Uhh…" a soft voice stammered in his ear. "This—this is Rae Lemmon."

He hadn't imagined that fear this morning. He heard it now in her voice. "What's wrong?" he asked.

"I—I need to talk to you," she said.

"Are you home?" he asked.

"Yes," she said. "And my friends refuse to leave until you get here."

She was definitely in danger.

"Should I send out a police car?"

"No!" she quickly rejected the offer. "Just you. Please come alone."

Come alone?

He had agreed to that stipulation before—when a potential witness had set up a meeting with him. That *witness* had started shooting the minute he'd turned up to the warehouse where they'd agreed to meet. The "come alone" stipulation had been the trap that had nearly taken his life, as well as his livelihood and so much else.

But this was Rae, so once again he found himself agreeing. "I'm on my way." He clicked off the cell but the sound of her voice, with the fear cracking it, still rang in his ears. He tried rushing up the stairs, from the basement to the lobby, but his leg had stiffened up and refused to bend, forcing him to hobble. Maybe it was because it had been a long day of being on his feet, or maybe it was because he needed the reminder—the warning—to be careful.

ONCE SHE WAS alone, Rae wished her friends would come back. But she was the one who'd convinced them to leave, who'd assured them that Forrest was on his way and she would not be alone for long. But every second that they were gone felt like an hour, an hour of her tensing with fear over every creak of the house and every whisper of the wind outside the windows.

Even Connor had left her alone with her thoughts, since he'd fallen asleep in his crib. He must have forgotten all about the night before. She wished she could forget, too, but that note and that lock of hair would haunt her for a long time.

She held them in her hand now, still sealed in that plastic bag. She couldn't wait to hand them over to Forrest Colton. Maybe that was why she was so on edge waiting for him to arrive. She was scared to be alone, but her senses hummed with excitement at the thought of seeing him again.

Lights flashed in her windows as a vehicle turned into her driveway. Her pulse leaped. But she wasn't afraid that her intruder had returned. She doubted he would have just driven up to her house, since he hadn't done that the night before. She knew who had arrived, and it was why her pulse leaped, why her skin heated, why her heart pounded.

Forrest was here.

She met him at the door. He must have jumped out of his SUV before he'd even shut it off, because he'd taken no time to get from it to her porch despite his limp.

"I thought your friends were going to stay until I got here," he said. "I would have driven faster if I knew they were gone."

"They just left," she assured him as he stepped inside the house. He couldn't have arrived any faster than he had—even if he'd been at his parents' ranch where he'd been staying since his volunteering with the Cowboy Heroes had brought him home to Whisperwood. But she suspected he hadn't been there, since he was still wearing the dress pants, with his boots, that he'd had on that morning. If he'd been home to the ranch, he probably would have changed into jeans.

She closed the door behind him and, with her hands trembling, turned the lock. Locking the door had done no good the night before, though.

"They should have waited for me to get here," he said. "Are you okay? What's going on?"

His concern touched her—so much that tears overwhelmed her, filling her eyes and her throat. In reply to his questions, she handed him the plastic bag.

"What the hell...?" he murmured as he stared down at the handwritten note.

"I found this lying on my pillow last night," she managed to say around the emotion choking her.

"And the hair?" He stared at her now, as if trying to see where it had been cut.

"Connor's," she said. "I woke up because he started screaming. When I was in the nursery with him, I heard someone walking out of the house and closing the door. I ran back into my bedroom for my cell phone, and I found this." She shuddered at the memory.

"And then you didn't call the police to report the break-in," he said. "And that's why you also tried to get rid of me in the morning."

"I want to protect my son," she said.

"That's why you should have called right away," Forrest admonished her. "Or told me when I arrived this morning. We could have checked for fingerprints and for signs of a break-in."

"I couldn't find any," she admitted.

"Hadn't you locked the door?"

She bristled with defensiveness. "Of course I did." She hadn't always, but after he'd found that body in her backyard, she'd checked the lock twice before she'd gone to bed that night.

He was looking at the lock now, inspecting it from the inside and then from the outside, after he unlocked and opened the door. "Nobody forced it. Do you have a spare key hidden outside?"

She nodded and gestured at the gardenia plant. "Under the flowerpot."

He studied the pot now, where dirt had spilled over the rim of it onto the porch. Before he touched it, he pulled the sleeves of his suit coat over his hands. Then he tipped it and peered beneath it. "There's no key."

"There was," she insisted. But her head began to pound as she tried to remember the last time she'd seen it. "Bellamy might have left it out when she'd used it earlier." That was how she had probably let herself in, unless Forrest's team had left her doors unlocked. "She has her own, though, so she might not have used it. She's the only one who knows it's there besides me. And I always use the one on my key chain." When she remembered to lock the door at all.

Forrest snorted. "A flowerpot next to the door? It's the first place I'd look if I was trying to get inside."

Heat rushed to her face as she realized it hadn't been the best hiding spot. But until recently crime hadn't been much of a concern in Whisperwood—at least not that she could remember. She wouldn't have been much older than Connor was when Elliot Corgan had been killing women.

He was dead now, though. He couldn't be responsible for these murders.

It had been there a long time, and her property was

close to Corgan ranch land. He could have buried one of his victims in her backyard.

Forrest touched his hand to the small of her back and guided her back into the house. The heat of his touch warmed her again. He closed the door behind them.

"You need to get your locks changed," he said. Then a curse slipped out of his lips. "Hell, you need to leave this place. It's a crime scene."

She glanced around the place, but like when she'd returned home earlier, she saw no signs of his search—no evidence of his finding any evidence inside her house. "Did you find something?" she asked. She then shuddered before asking, "Blood? DNA?"

He shook his head. "Nothing to indicate that a person was murdered inside the house."

She uttered a ragged sigh of relief. "Then it's not a crime scene."

He held up the plastic bag. "It is. Do you have any idea who left you the note?"

She shook her head now. "No, no idea."

He stared at her, his hazel eyes narrowed as if he considered her a suspect. She hadn't left herself the damn note, though now, like the note's writer, she was wishing the detective was gone.

"What about you?" she asked. "You're the one he wants out of the way, so you must have some idea who it is."

He grimaced. "I wish I had an idea, a suspect, something." A curse slipped out between his lips. "I'm sorry."

She wished she could blame the note on him. But he wasn't the one who'd threatened her. None of this was his fault—except for how he made her feel.

She had been so focused lately on just being a mother and a student and a worker that she'd nearly forgotten she was a woman, too. He'd reminded her, which was probably why he irritated her so much. Or maybe he wouldn't irritate her so much if he actually returned the attraction. For a moment that morning she'd thought he'd been about to kiss her, but she must have imagined that, because he was all business now.

"You were smart to seal this in a bag," he said. "I'll have it dusted for prints."

"Maybe you'll find some on Connor's crib, too," she suggested. "He must have leaned over it to snip that piece of hair from his head." Tears rushed to her eyes again as she relived the horror of how close somebody had been to her son, how easily he could have been hurt or worse.

"Is he okay?" Forrest asked, and his free hand moved to her shoulder.

The weight of it felt good, felt comforting somehow, while also unsettling her. She nodded. "Yes, he's fine. He's sleeping soundly, while I don't think I'll ever be able to sleep again."

"Not here," Forrest agreed. "You need to get out of here. Go stay with Bellamy and Donovan or Maggie and Jonah."

She shook her head. "That's not an option."

"They're your friends. They would let you stay with them if you asked."

"I don't have to ask," she said. "They already offered."

"Then—" he glanced around the floor "—where are your bags?"

"I'm not going to impose on my friends," she said. "Not with a baby who still doesn't sleep through the night."

"I don't think they would mind," he assured her.

"They wouldn't," she agreed. "But I would. I don't want anyone else losing sleep because of me or my son."

"Then you need to book a room at a hotel—preferably one with good security."

Heat rushed to her face. With the costs of day care and law school, she didn't have an extra dime to spare. She couldn't afford to stay in a hotel with bad security, let alone one with good. But she was too proud to admit that to him, so she just murmured, "I can't."

"Then I'll stay here," he offered.

A twinge of panic gripped her heart. "No. You can't. The note writer wants you out of the way."

"Yeah," Forrest agreed. "So he can terrorize you. That's why I should be here."

Scared, she shook her head as tears rushed to her eyes again. "No. You can't. It's too dangerous."

"It's too dangerous for you and Connor to be here alone," he said. His hand on her shoulder turned her toward him and then pulled her closer. "I will protect you."

But she had a feeling that he might be the one from whom she needed the most protection—because she wanted him so badly.

His hand moved from her shoulder to her face. His fingers brushed across her cheek and along her jaw before he tipped up her face. "I will keep you safe."

Staring at his handsome features, at the intensity in his hazel eyes, Rae felt anything but safe. She felt everything…a desire she hadn't felt in so long, if ever.

His eyes darkened, and he suddenly lowered his head to hers. But he paused—with just a breath between their lips—and she was the one who rose up on tiptoe, who pressed her mouth to his.

A jolt shot from her lips straight to her heart, making it pound madly against her breast. His lips were still—for a moment—before they moved hungrily over hers. He kissed her with a passion she hadn't suspected him to be capable of, that she hadn't expected that she was capable of feeling until it coursed through her. She raised her arms and threw them around his neck, holding his head down to hers—holding his long, tense body against hers.

A kiss had never affected her as much, had never made her want as much, as she wanted Forrest Colton—and not just for protection.

WHAT THE HELL *is she doing?*

Hadn't she heeded the warning at all? The note had specifically said to get rid of the detective. Maybe she hadn't called Detective Colton out to the house, but she hadn't thrown him out like she had the last time he'd showed up, that morning.

And with the way their shadows moved behind the curtains, she had no intention of getting rid of him. She held him as if she never intended to let him go.

And that wasn't good. It might wind up costing her so much.

So damn much.

Chapter Nine

Who was in the most danger? The baby? Rae? Or Forrest? He wasn't sure. While the threat had been made against little Connor, Forrest wasn't as worried about the baby as he was about himself.

But he had a job to do—at least that was his excuse for staying at Rae's house. It had also been his excuse for pulling away from her earlier that evening, when everything inside him had been urging him to lift her up in his arms and carry her off to her bed. Then he'd remembered that if he'd tried, his leg would have probably folded beneath their combined weights and sent them both crashing to the floor.

Embarrassed and angry at the thought, he'd pulled away from her then.

Her face flushed with embarrassment, she'd stumbled back and murmured, "I'm sorry."

"*I'm* sorry," he'd said, correcting her. He'd started to kiss her first—before he'd stopped and waited to make sure she'd wanted this, too. But even though she'd closed the distance between them and pressed her lips to his first, he had been taking advantage of her—of her fear and vulnerability.

"I'm sorry," he'd repeated. "I know the only reason I'm staying here is to protect you and Connor."

And he couldn't do that if he was distracted with his desire for her. He'd gone into the nursery then to stand guard over her son, and she'd gone to bed.

Alone.

His body tightened at the thought of Rae, tangled in her sheets, wearing only the old T-shirt that molded to her curves. She'd looked so sexy in it, so sexy that he couldn't help but imagine how she would look out of it, with nothing but the flush of desire on her skin. She had seemed to want him as much as he'd wanted her.

So maybe he hadn't been taking advantage of her vulnerability. But he had been neglecting his job, which was to protect her and her son.

From the killer?

That had to be who had left the threat. Who else would want him out of the way? Besides Rae? She hadn't been happy to see him the past couple of days—until earlier tonight. Tonight she had been relieved when he'd showed up, but only because she was afraid.

That was why she'd kissed him. Out of fear and maybe gratitude. She couldn't actually be interested in him; that would mean that she was willing to take on another responsibility for her already overburdened shoulders. Shannon hadn't wanted the responsibility of caring for someone with an injury, and she'd once loved him. Why would Rae want to deal with his disability?

Not that he saw a future with her—with them. He wasn't sure he was even going to stay in Whisperwood after he solved his case or cases. He wasn't sure yet if the murders were connected or not.

Hell, he wasn't sure of anything anymore.

What the hell was he even thinking by staying here, trying to protect them? He should have called in a uniformed officer for that duty.

But Rae had been so frightened…

That he hadn't been able to leave. And so he stood watch in the nursery now.

Connor had been sleeping peacefully, just a whisper of breath escaping his little nose and rosebud lips. But a soft cry slipped through them now, and the baby tensed in his crib.

Forrest glanced toward the doorway. He didn't want to wake up Rae, didn't really want to see her wearing only that T-shirt, or he was going to wind up in more trouble than if the intruder attempted to get inside again. So he reached inside the crib, slid his hands beneath the little body and lifted Connor from his bed.

The baby blinked open bleary eyes and stared up at Forrest. His mouth opened, but instead of letting out a louder scream, a little burp slipped between his lips. And a little bubble floated out.

Forrest chuckled. "A little gassy, huh?"

Those little rosebud lips curved into what looked like a smile, but that was probably just gas, too. Forrest found himself smiling back anyway. Then his palm grew damp where he cupped the little guy's pajama bottom, and he swallowed a groan. The baby was wet.

He needed a diaper change, or he was probably going to start crying for real.

Forrest glanced toward the doorway again. Maybe it would be better for Rae to handle this. Forrest wasn't squeamish—not after all of the crime scenes he'd investigated—but he had never changed a diaper before.

How hard could it be, though?

And with Bellamy expecting his niece or nephew, he was going to need to learn—if he ever intended to help out with babysitting.

Connor's face twisted into a little grimace, as if he'd

just noticed the wetness, too, and another cry slipped out of his lips.

"I've got this," Forrest assured him. "I'll change you." At least he would give it a try.

He carried the little guy over to the piece of furniture that looked like a low dresser that had been painted blue and decorated with sheep. The pad on the top of it also had little sheep on it. A couple of disposable diapers had been left on top of it, as well. Forrest breathed a sigh of relief that he wouldn't have to deal with pins—just tape and the little guy's flailing feet in those damp pajamas.

Forrest unsnapped the onesie thing but getting Connor's feet out with all his kicking was not an easy task. He didn't want to hurt him. "You gotta help me out here, buddy," he murmured. "We have to get this thing off you."

He was able to tug on the pajamas until Connor's kicking legs slipped out. Then he ripped off the sodden diaper, pulled it from beneath him and wadded it up before opening the blue pail next to the changing table and dropping it inside. "Okay, we got that nasty thing off."

Forrest reached for the wipes and the powder. After cleaning him, he sprinkled some powder, which wafted up like a cloud. He sneezed, and something gurgled out of the baby again, something that sounded like a giggle.

Probably just gas again. But Forrest smiled down at him anyway. "You think this is funny?" he asked.

The little feet kicked again.

Forrest slid a clean diaper beneath him and secured it around him with the tape on each side. Or he hoped he had secured it. When he lifted Connor from the table, the diaper didn't fall off, so he hadn't done too badly.

Except that he didn't know where the clean pajamas were. "Do you need new pj's?" Forrest asked as he cradled the baby against his chest. The little body was warm, and so was the house and the night outside it. He wasn't going to freeze if Forrest couldn't find him dry clothes. But a twinge of guilt struck him that maybe he wasn't doing this right.

Connor gurgled again and now his little fists flailed against Forrest's chest. He wasn't fighting to get away, though; he was just restless and wide-awake.

"How do I get you back to sleep?" Forrest wondered aloud. "Do I sing? I don't know any lullabies."

But to be a good uncle, he should probably learn some. At the moment all that came to his mind were the words to the old Guns N' Roses song "Sweet Child o' Mine."

As he sang, heat rushed to his face—not that singing to Connor should have embarrassed him, but he had a sensation that the baby wasn't the only one listening to him. And this time when he glanced to the doorway, someone stood there in that old, thin T-shirt.

"Don't stop on my account," she said, her voice husky with sleep. "This is the first time I've heard a heavy metal lullaby."

His face grew even hotter. "It was the only song I could think of." But now he could think of nothing but her looking so damn beautiful and sounding so damn sexy with that sleep in her voice.

SWEET CHILD OF *mine*...

The words to the song, sung in his deep voice, resonated throughout her head and her heart.

Sweet child of mine...

Connor wasn't his child. But he was caring for him like he was. She'd watched while he'd changed the baby's diaper and then sung him back to sleep. While she had miraculously managed to fall asleep even after that kiss they'd shared, she'd awakened the minute she'd heard Connor's cry.

And fear had pierced her heart like the blade of a sharp knife. Then she'd heard the deep murmur of a familiar voice, and her fear had subsided. Forrest Colton was here, protecting them.

But he'd done even more than that; he'd taken care of Connor in a way no one had but her since the baby's birth. He'd changed him and cuddled with him and sung to him.

Warmth flooded Rae's heart, which felt as if it had swelled in her chest, as she stared at the two of them: the big man with the tiny baby clasped against his heart. This warmth wasn't just for her son.

Forrest was so much more than he'd seemed when they'd first met. When he'd turned down her invitation to dance, she'd thought he was cold and bitter, but that wasn't who he was at all. There was nothing cold and bitter about him now as he gently cradled the baby.

She'd thought she'd wanted to do this alone, that being a single parent was the best for her and for her son. She didn't want Connor to have a father who would just let him down and leave like hers had. But now she'd gotten a glimpse of what it could be like if Connor had a father—for him and for her.

Now the warmth spread to her face with embarrassment that she was fantasizing about a man she barely knew. She liked his brothers a lot, but just because his last name was Colton, too, didn't mean that he was a good man. There were other branches of the Colton family tree, branches that were as dangerous as the Corgans had proved to be.

But Forrest was a lawman, so she doubted that he

was at all like his dangerous relatives. At least he wasn't a physical danger to her. But emotionally...

He was making her long for something she'd already given up on ever finding: love. A man who would stay.

He was only here because it was his job, though.

"I didn't realize diaper duty was part of the service," she said.

"If you'd known, would you have called me last night, when the intruder left the note?" he asked.

She shivered as she remembered how different last night had been from this one. She'd been so terrified—so alone. Maybe it wasn't all that different, though. She was scared tonight, too, but of what she was beginning to feel for Forrest Colton.

Attraction and something deeper, something that would cause her pain if she gave in to it, but she couldn't—she *wouldn't*—give in to her feelings. He wasn't even sticking around Whisperwood. He was only here because of the hurricane, because he was a volunteer for the Cowboy Heroes. He probably would have been gone already if he hadn't been hired to help out the Whisperwood PD with the murder investigation.

Rae had to protect her heart. She couldn't be like her mother, who'd fallen for a man who hadn't stuck around. While Georgia hadn't realized that about Beau Lemmon at the time she'd met him, Rae knew Forrest wasn't staying.

"I'm not sure I should have called you at all," she admitted. She knew she definitely shouldn't have kissed him—because now she wanted to kiss him again, so badly.

"You're worried about the threat," he surmised. "That the intruder will come back and make good on it."

She nodded. But with Connor clasped in Forrest's

arm, he was safe. She was the one in danger, because she wanted to be clasped in Forrest's arms, too.

"I'll make sure you and Connor have twenty-four-hour protection," he assured her. "There's no way the person who left that note will hurt either of you."

He sounded so determined that some relief eased the tension that had been gripping her. "Thank you," she said.

His face flushed. "I'm just doing my job."

After she'd kissed him, he probably wanted to make that clear to her, so that she didn't misconstrue his protection as affection for her or for Connor. But the way he'd kissed her...

And the way he held her son, so gently.

She shook off the wistfulness that had suddenly come over her. "I know," she assured him, but her lips curved into a teasing smile. "Although, I'm not sure diaper duty is part of being a detective."

He smiled back at her. "I didn't want him to wake you up."

She couldn't help but wonder why. Out of consideration? Or because he hadn't wanted to see her again?

"I—I should call in a replacement for me for the morning," he said. Clearly he didn't intend to be her twenty-four-hour protector. He had a job to do, and babysitting her and Connor was not part of that job.

He carefully placed the sleeping baby back in his crib before pulling his cell phone from his pocket. "I'll make my call outside," he said. "So I don't wake him again."

But he hesitated over leaving the room, as if reluctant to pass her in the doorway. When he neared her, his body tensed, and he sucked in a breath and held it.

She stared up at him as he passed her, and his hazel eyes darkened with desire. Or maybe that was just wishful thinking on her part, because he continued past her as if she hadn't tempted him at all.

But she was tempted to follow him out, to kiss him again. The crib sheets rustled as Connor moved in his bed and a little cry slipped through his lips. His cry brought Rae to her senses. She couldn't throw herself at Forrest again; he obviously didn't want her.

"I WANT HER," Forrest Colton said.

The chief blinked away the bleariness of sleep, jerked fully awake and focused on the cell in his hand. "What?" he asked.

"I want Rae Lemmon to have around-the-clock protection," Forrest said.

Maybe that was what he'd said the first time, but Archer had been partially asleep and hadn't heard him correctly. Or maybe what Forrest really wanted had unconsciously slipped through his lips. "Why would she be in danger?" Archer wondered aloud.

"I told you about the note," Forrest said.

Maybe he had, but again the chief hadn't been paying much attention yet. He couldn't wake up as quickly as he used to. "Tell me again."

When Forrest did, Archer still wasn't certain how threatening it was. "So somebody was in her house, but he didn't hurt either her or the baby when he'd had the chance?"

"He scared her," Forrest said.

Detective Colton sounded scared, too.

"He threatened her baby," Forrest continued.

"But he didn't hurt him," the chief said. "Of the bodies, we've found none of them was a baby. No baby has been hurt."

"No, it's women who are winding up dead," Forrest said. "So Rae Lemmon's the one in danger."

"We don't have the extra manpower to provide around-the-clock protection for her," Archer said. And he wasn't certain how necessary it was. Sure, someone had been inside her home, but she hadn't been hurt.

If the killer had intended to make her his next victim, he'd had the chance. Now that she'd been warned, she would be more aware, more careful. She didn't need the already limited police resources, and Archer proceeded to tell his new detective this.

"She does," Forrest insisted. "I promised her that she and her son would be protected."

"She can stay with friends or get out of town," Archer suggested, "and she'll be safe."

"No," Forrest said. "The only way she'll be protected is if I do it myself."

Archer cursed. "I need you focused on solving these murders," he reminded him. "That's why I hired you. Not to play bodyguard to a single mom and her infant son."

"I know," Forrest said. "And I'll figure out a way to do both."

Before the chief could say anything else, Colton broke their connection. Not that there was probably anything Archer could have said to change the young detective's mind. Forrest Colton seemed pretty damn determined to play guardian to Rae Lemmon and her baby.

Why?

Was he just concerned about the threat and worried that some harm might actually come to her child or to her? Or was there something else making Forrest Colton so protective?

Was he falling for the single mom?

If that was the case, and that threat was as serious as Forrest believed it was, then she and her baby weren't the only ones in danger. Forrest was in danger, too.

Hell, since the threat was about getting rid of the detective, he was in the most danger—and maybe not just from the person who'd left that note, but from that single mom and her baby, as well.

Chapter Ten

He could work anywhere—even in Rae Lemmon's kitchen, even with her wearing just that T-shirt while she slept in her bed just a few yards from where he worked. After his call, he had returned to the nursery to find her already gone.

Which was good because he hadn't wanted to admit to her that the chief hadn't seen the same need for her protection that Forrest had. Was he overreacting?

Not at all.

Somebody had invaded her home. Even if he'd used the key under the flowerpot or found the door unlocked, he had still entered her house without her permission. He had also snipped a piece of hair from Connor's head and left that threatening note.

That was some kind of sick individual to scare a single mom like that. Maybe he was even a killer.

So she and her son absolutely needed protection. Forrest could protect them most if he figured out who the hell had left the note and who had killed those women.

Were they the same person?

He stared down at the pictures he'd spread across her kitchen table. In the light from the pendant hanging over the table, he studied each of the crime-scene photographs for a clue he might have missed, like those buttons had been missed on the first pass through at the drug company's parking lot.

He'd sent those off to the FBI's crime lab because he'd wanted results back faster than he'd been getting them from the Whisperwood crime-scene technicians. But the FBI's lab was backlogged, too. If only solving crimes was as easy as TV shows made it look, then he could have investigated everything and wrapped up all of the cases within an hour.

He'd been staring at these damn pictures for more than sixty minutes, and he hadn't discovered anything new. Hell, he hadn't discovered anything at all. Maybe if Rae wasn't so close...

And so sexy and beautiful that she kept distracting him from his job. But he wasn't even sure what his job was at the moment—to be a detective or a bodyguard.

His physical exhaustion and the weight of his concern for Rae and Connor settled heavily on his shoulders, so heavily that he closed his eyes for a moment. Just a moment...before a soft gasp jerked him fully awake, so awake that he scrambled up and knocked over the chair he'd been using and nearly struck Rae.

She stood next to the table, her brown eyes wide with horror as she stared down at the pictures spread across the white painted surface. "Oh, my."

"I'm sorry," Forrest said. For so many things...

Sorry that he'd let his guard slip long enough for her to sneak up on him.

What if she'd been the intruder?

He was also sorry that she'd seen the gruesome photos of the victims and the crime scenes. With his hands shaking slightly, he swept the pictures back into the folders.

"It's fine," she said despite the catch of emotion in

her voice. "I'm going to need to get used to seeing photographs like that with the profession I've chosen."

"Does Lukas, Jolley and Fitzsimmons handle criminal cases?" he asked.

Her eyes went wide again with surprise. "You know where I work?"

He shrugged. "Bellamy must have mentioned it." And he'd paid attention despite himself, because he was so damn curious about Rae Lemmon.

She smiled at his comment. "Bellamy likes to brag about me."

"She does," he agreed. Was that because Rae was her best friend or because she was playing matchmaker?

The same thought might have occurred to Rae, because her face flushed with embarrassment. "To answer your question," she continued, "no, they don't. But after I pass the bar, I'd like to work in the district attorney's office."

"You want to be a prosecutor?" he asked. Every damn thing she did fascinated him and appealed to him.

She nodded. "Yes. There's been so much crime in Whisperwood lately that I feel compelled to try to help stop some of it."

"That's why you're going to law school while working and raising your son alone?"

She nodded.

"And here I thought you were just a masochist."

She smiled again, and a strange warmth spread throughout his chest. She had a beautiful smile that lit up her chocolate-brown eyes. "That, too," she said, and as if to prove her point, she took the folder from his hand and started flipping through the photographs. The smile left her face, and her eyes darkened with sorrow.

"You don't have to look at those," he said. She probably shouldn't be looking at them, not that she was a potential suspect or anything. But she might know a suspect.

Why else would she have been threatened like she'd been?

"But since you have seen them," he continued, "what are your thoughts? Could these murders have been committed by the same person?"

She shivered even though she wore a light robe over her T-shirt. That must have been for his benefit. But he would have preferred that she'd skipped the robe.

Hell, he would have preferred that she'd skipped the T-shirt. Heat flushed his face and his body at the thought of seeing her naked, of touching her.

He drew in a deep breath and pushed the image of her, like that, from his mind. He pointed toward the folder. "There was no attempt to mummify the body that was found in the parking lot."

"Maybe he didn't have time," she said. "Maybe he was interrupted. Or not as physically able as he once was."

Forrest sucked in a breath, awed by her insight. "You're going to make a damn good prosecutor."

She smiled and spread that warmth through his chest again. She was so beautiful that he found himself leaning toward her. But before his lips could brush across hers, a cry rent the air between them.

Had someone gotten inside the nursery? Panic replaced the warmth in his chest, pressing heavily against his heart as he ran toward the nursery and Connor.

He would never forgive himself if something happened to the baby because he'd let himself get distracted—because he hadn't been paying close enough attention.

And he was pretty damn certain that the baby's mother would never forgive him either.

SHE WOULD NEVER forgive him for making her fall for him. And she knew she was falling when she watched him once again pick Connor out of his crib and cradle him against his muscular chest. He cuddled her son as if he was the baby's father rather than just his protector.

That was the only reason he was here—to protect them. She had to remind herself of that. But the reminder didn't ease her attraction to him, didn't cool the desire she felt for him, the desire that had kept her from falling back to sleep after she'd left the nursery.

Forrest patted Connor's little bottom. "He's dry," he said. "Why's he crying? Is he hungry?"

She shook her head. "I fed him after you left to make your call." And that had been just a little over an hour ago. Even Connor couldn't be hungry again so soon.

Forrest tensed. "Did you overhear any of that?"

She shook her head. She'd been focused on her son and had also been reluctant to eavesdrop. "Let me take him," she said as she reached out for the baby. Maybe she hadn't burped him well enough before she'd put him back down to sleep.

Forrest had moved his hand from the baby's diapered bottom to his back, and as he patted, Connor spit up all over the front of Forrest's checkered shirt. The detective's hazel eyes widened with shock and horror.

"That's why I wanted him," she said. She hadn't wanted her son to spit up on his protector. "I was afraid that might happen."

Forrest arched a brow over one of his eyes. "You sure you didn't put him up to it?"

Since he'd turned down her invitation to dance, she

hadn't been very friendly to him, and her face flushed with embarrassment that he'd stung her pride so much.

"Of course not," she said, but her lips curved into a slight smile. "He's too young to be trained to do stuff like that." Weariness tugged her lips back down. "And if I could train him to do anything, it would be to sleep through the night."

"Don't you know your mama needs her beauty rest?" Forrest asked the baby as he jostled him in his arms.

"Don't—" Rae began. But it was already too late.

The baby threw up even more on Forrest's shirt.

"How much did you feed him?" Forrest asked.

She sighed. "Apparently too much." His bout of colic wasn't helping his digestion any either.

But throwing up must have because his lids began to droop over his big brown eyes, and he nodded back to sleep. She stepped closer and lifted him away from Forrest's chest. "I'll put him down. You can go change your shirt."

"I didn't bring anything to change into," he said. "I didn't realize I was going to wind up staying."

"You didn't have to," she said.

"You wouldn't go to a hotel or your friend's house, so yes, I had to," he said.

He could have left her and Connor alone, to fend for themselves, if the intruder had returned, but he had refused to do that. He was a good man.

After cleaning up a sleeping Connor and settling him back into his crib, she turned toward Forrest, and a gasp slipped through her lips as she discovered that he'd taken off his soiled shirt.

He was a sexy man, too.

So damn sexy...with his heavily muscled chest that was lightly dusted with golden-brown hair.

Her mouth watered, forcing her to swallow down the desire that nearly choked her. She couldn't remember ever wanting anyone the way she wanted Forrest Colton. What the hell was wrong with her? Was it the lack of sleep? Her fear over the threats?

Or just hormones?

With the shirt dangling from one of his fingers, he asked, "Where's your washing machine?"

Leaving Connor asleep in his crib, she walked on suddenly trembling legs toward the doorway Forrest's big, half-naked body filled. She swallowed again and cleared her throat before replying, "I'll wash it for you." But when she reached for the shirt, he held tightly to it.

"I can do it," he said. "You should go back to sleep."

She doubted that she would be able to sleep now, since she hadn't been able to earlier. Having him in her house had some strange restlessness coursing through her, making her hot and achy in places where she hadn't been hot and achy in a damn long time...if ever.

"Fortunately I function well on small amounts of sleep," she said as she tugged again on the shirt.

"You don't have to," he said.

She smiled. "Just like you didn't have to stay here."

Or change Connor's diaper, or try to comfort him when he was crying...

Damn Forrest Colton. He was definitely making her fall for him. And she knew better than that; she knew he wasn't sticking around Whisperwood. His assignment here was only temporary.

"I have to," he said. "And when I called the chief, he refused to put anyone else on protection duty for you and Connor."

She tensed. "He doesn't think I'm in danger?"

"He doesn't have the resources," Forrest said. "That's

how I got tapped to investigate these cases. Because of Hurricane Brooke, Whisperwood PD is just spread too thin right now."

"And murder investigations would take precedence over the note left on my pillow," she said with a sigh. "You should be working on those cases and not baby-sitting me and my son."

"I promised I would make sure you and Connor stay safe," he said, and his deep hazel eyes filled with intensity as he stared down at her. "And I keep my promises."

She smiled but shook her head. "You won't if you make promises that you can't keep."

"But I—"

She pressed her fingers across his lips before he could finish his protest. "You can't be with us 24/7. You have a job. A life. And so do I. I need to go to work and to my law-school classes."

His lips moved beneath her fingers. "But the threat—"

"Isn't going to stop me from living my life," she said.

"That's exactly what might happen," he pointed out. "If you're not careful."

She smiled again. "I am always very careful." That was why she had used a sperm donor to have a baby—because she was too careful to trust a man to stick around for her and most especially for her child. She didn't want her son to be as disappointed as she had been so often.

"You're not being very careful right now," he murmured, and using their hands on his shirt, he tugged her close, so close that she pressed against his bare chest.

And her breath caught as desire overwhelmed her. His skin was so hot, his body so hard. "Forrest…"

He was right—damn it—because she wasn't being

careful. And she was probably going to wind up hurt and disappointed, but she figured she might be even more disappointed if she didn't act on her desire for him.

She would deal with the fallout later.

She dropped his shirt and eased her hands between them, sliding her palms over his bare chest. Soft brown hair covered well-developed muscles that rippled beneath her touch.

He groaned and stumbled back when she pushed him. Then he shook his head and, breathing hard, murmured, "I'm sorry."

She wasn't. Yet.

She pushed him again, out of the nursery, and he stumbled back another step.

"I'll leave you alone," he promised.

"That's not what I want," she said.

"What do you want?" he asked.

"You."

Instead of pushing him, she pulled him now, tugging him toward her bedroom. But he didn't budge, his big body frozen with tension that radiated off him and to her. It gripped her, spiraling inside her with such intensity that she knew she needed to release it. If she didn't, she might explode into a million pieces.

"Are you sure?" he asked, his voice gruff with passion and something else.

Something like vulnerability.

Clearly Bellamy and Maggie had been right; his fiancée had done a number on him when she'd taken off like she had—the same number Rae's deadbeat dad had done on her.

"I'm sure," she said, and to convince him, she rose on tiptoe and pressed her lips to his.

His arms closed around her, holding her against him

as he kissed her back. But then he pulled away and murmured, "This is a mistake."

And she tensed. "I'm sorry." Tears stung her eyes; this time his rejection hurt more than just her pride. "I need to stop throwing myself at you."

He chuckled, a deep chuckle that rumbled in his naked chest. "You're not throwing yourself." His chuckle turned to a groan. "But even if you had, I would catch you and not let you go." His arms tightened around her.

She pulled back, staring up at his handsome face. His jaw was so tightly clenched, a muscle pulsated in his cheek. "I thought it was a mistake."

"It is," he said. "I need to stay focused on protecting you. But I want to do so much more."

Her breath escaped in a gasp of relief. He wasn't rejecting her. "We're safe," she said. "Nobody has tried to get inside." And she doubted that they would with his police vehicle parked outside. "Nobody's out there."

"I hope you're right," he said, and he lowered his head and kissed her again.

HE WAS OUT there—watching the shadows behind the curtains, watching as they moved together toward that front bedroom.

She hadn't heeded his threat. Hell, it wasn't his threat. It was the threat of a killer—a killer who wanted this detective off the murder cases so badly that he would do anything.

Even kill again.

The baby? Or him?

If he didn't get the detective to back off, would he,

despite trying to get rid of the lawman, be the next victim? It was a chance he couldn't take—even if he wound up becoming a killer himself.

Chapter Eleven

The law office of Lukas, Jolley and Fitzsimmons wasn't far from the Whisperwood Police Department. Forrest wanted to continue driving past the brick building without letting out Rae or Connor, but she reached across the console of her SUV and gripped his knee.

His entire body reacted just as it had last night. Tension filled him, and his erection throbbed behind the fly of his wrinkled dress pants.

"This is it," she said. "Where I work."

"You shouldn't be going to work," he said. "It's too dangerous."

But it would have been more dangerous had they stayed inside her house together because they would have given in to the attraction between them, just as they had the night before. Or had that really happened?

Or had he only dreamed it?

He had been so exhausted that he might have nodded off at the table and only imagined they'd made love. But he hadn't awakened at the table; he'd awakened in her bed, with her naked body clasped in his arms, and her head nestled between his neck and shoulder.

How had he been so irresponsible? So reckless? The intruder could have returned when they'd been making love or when they'd fallen asleep.

Forrest had rushed out of bed then to check on Connor, to make sure nothing had happened to him. The baby had been fine. But Forrest was not.

He would never be fine again. What had happened between them…

Rae tightened her grip on his thigh. "Forrest, please."

She'd said that last night, when he'd kissed his way from her lips down her entire body. She'd begged for more. But she hadn't been the only one.

He had worried that he might not survive the onslaught of emotion when she'd returned his favor and kissed him all over, including the scars on his wounded leg. Shannon had been so horrified of his injury that she'd run away. But Rae…

Rae was different. She'd stuck around after her father had taken off and had cared for her sick mother. Rae was caring and compassionate.

And passionate and…

"Forrest," she said again.

With a sigh of resignation, he turned around in a parking lot a block past the law building and headed back to her work. Finally she moved her hand from his leg, and he sighed again, but with regret. Despite the tension it caused, he wanted her touching him—like she'd touched him last night.

But she'd turned around to peer into the back seat, where the baby carrier was secured. "We should have dropped off Connor first."

"You're sure he will be safe at the day care?" Forrest asked as he had the first time.

She smiled. "Yes, there's no way Bob McCauley would let anything happen to him."

"Bob McCauley?" The name sounded vaguely familiar to him but not as a day care owner. "Didn't he play professional football?"

She smiled. "Yes, he did. So you know that nobody would try anything with Bob protecting Connor."

Even though Forrest recognized the name, he didn't know the man, so he wanted to talk to him before determining if he trusted Connor in his care. Rae hadn't wanted to be late for work, though, so she'd asked to be dropped off first. He also wanted to make sure she would be safe before he left her, so he parked her SUV and insisted on following her up to her office, while carrying the handle of the carrier with the sleeping baby over his arm.

An odd chill swept over him, despite the heat of the Texas sun bearing down on them already. He glanced around the lot, looking for someone watching them, and his free hand moved toward his holster. Had someone followed them from the house? Or had the person been waiting here, at her work, for Rae's arrival?

The morning sun glinting off all of the vehicles' tinted windows made it impossible to see inside, to see if anyone was inside, watching them. But that sensation prickling Forrest's skin and raising the short hairs on the nape of his neck confirmed to him that someone was there.

Maybe not the person who'd left the threat for Rae, but someone.

He tightened his grip on the baby carrier and stepped closer to her. Rae's body tensed as he did. Did she feel it, too? Had last night affected her like it had him?

She'd been acting all morning like it hadn't happened, though.

Maybe that was why he kept wondering if he'd only

dreamed it—because he seemed to be the only one who remembered it. Or wanted to remember it.

She hastened her step as if trying to create some distance between them. But he lengthened his stride and, despite his limp, managed to keep close—for her protection. But she didn't look as if she felt safe.

Hell, she wouldn't look at him at all. She pushed open the door to the foyer and rushed toward the bank of elevators. When the doors to one of the elevator cars opened, she stepped inside and hurriedly pressed a button as if she was trying to escape him. He—and Connor—joined her before the doors closed. Despite already pushing the button for her floor, she kept staring at the panel as if she preferred looking at it to looking at him.

Since they'd awakened that morning, she really hadn't looked at him, as if she couldn't bear to face him. Or face what they'd done?

Did she regret making love with him? Had it only been a moment of weakness—of vulnerability—for her?

Guilt settled heavily onto his shoulders that he'd taken advantage of that vulnerability, of her fear. Sure, she'd insisted that wasn't the case, that she'd really wanted him.

And that had seemed true with the way she'd touched him, the way she'd kissed him, the way she'd cried out with pleasure when she...

Now heat rushed to his face and suffused the rest of his body. He drew in a shaky breath to settle himself, to control the urge for him to lean closer to her and press his lips to hers. To remind her of the heat of the desire between them, the passion.

As he began to bend toward her, though, the elevator lurched to a stop and the bell dinged. The doors slid open, and she stepped out of the car. Only then did she turn back to face him. "You don't have to come any farther," she told him. "I'm on my floor. I'm safe."

As if the matter was settled, she crouched down to peer into the carrier at her baby. "Be good," she told the sleeping infant.

Love glowed on her beautiful face, warming her brown eyes. She loved her son so much that it radiated from her. Then she lifted her gaze to Forrest and the warmth left her eyes as her guard went back up. "Please make sure he gets safely to day care."

"I will," he promised. "I'll protect him." Or die trying.

Her lips tugged down at the corners. "I warned you about making promises you can't keep."

"I will keep this one," he vowed. "I will."

She sighed and stepped back, and the doors began to close. A sense of panic rushed over him, and he slapped his hand against them, holding them open. "I should make sure you're safe here," he said.

Her smile flashed. "I am fine. I can take care of myself."

She was Bellamy's age—thirty-five—so she'd been taking care of herself for a while now. So he believed her.

That didn't make him feel any better, though. Somehow it made him feel worse—like he had personally put her in danger. But all he'd done was find that body in her backyard; someone else had put it there.

Someone she knew?

She pushed his hand back from the door, and his skin tingled even from that slight contact. "Take Connor to day care and get back to your real job," she told him. "You don't need to babysit either of us now."

She lifted the hand that had touched his to her lips and pressed a kiss to it. And his heart caught when she blew that kiss...until he realized she was blowing it at her son. Not at him.

After she blew it, she turned on the wedge heel of her sandal and started down the hallway. A man stood in an open doorway to one of the offices, staring at her. Forrest could understand why he stared. She looked beautiful in a yellow dress that clung to her shapely curves and sleek legs.

Something tightened in his chest, like someone was squeezing his heart. While he understood it, he didn't like how that man looked at her. And he wondered how she would look at him. The doors closed before he could witness their interaction, but it left him wondering.

What kind of threat had that note been?

A serious one?

Or one designed to manipulate her into reaching out to help from a friend? Or someone who wanted to be more than a friend?

Forrest couldn't be certain, though, if it was his detective instincts that had come up with that possibility or his jealousy. Despite what had happened between them last night, he had no right to feel jealous or possessive of Rae Lemmon. Hell, he'd never felt jealous over anyone before—not even his fiancée.

No. He was probably just concerned—because when he left he had that feeling again, like someone was watching him. Was it the person who'd threatened Rae or someone else?

ONCE RAE TURNED away from the elevator, a sudden panic struck her, stealing her breath away and making her knees tremble. She turned back, but the doors had already closed. And the button above them showed that it was descending, taking her son and Forrest away from her.

Just for the workday.

They would come back for her. Forrest had promised that he would keep Connor safe. That he would protect her son.

She really didn't want him making her any promises, though. Her father had made her more than enough of those, promises that Beau Lemmon had never managed to keep. Had he even intended to when he'd made them?

Rae doubted it. He'd probably only been telling her what she'd wanted to hear, that he would come back.

That he would get his act together so that he could be the husband her mother deserved and the father she deserved. But that was a promise he had never kept.

Forrest clearly intended to keep his promise, to keep her and Connor safe. But she didn't know if that was a promise he would be able to keep or if the person who'd left that threat was more determined than he was.

"Who was that?" someone asked.

Rae turned back to find Kenneth Dawson standing in the open door to his office. She forced a smile. "Just a friend."

But images of the night before, of how Forrest had kissed her, touched her, pleasured her…rushed through her mind. Her pulse quickened, and her flesh heated—just as it had the night before. She'd never experienced anything as powerful as making love with Forrest. Last night had been amazing. Forrest Colton had been amazing.

His fiancée had been an idiot to leave a man like that. His injured leg hadn't hindered him at all—in the bedroom or in life. In fact, it had probably only made him stronger and more resolved.

So when he made a promise, he would do everything he could to keep it. But would it be enough?

"Must be a good friend for you to trust him with your baby," Kenneth murmured. "Or is he the father?"

Rae wished that Connor had a man like that in his life for more than protection. But she would be enough for her son. Just like her mother had been enough—more than enough—for her.

"Rae?" Kenneth prodded her. "Is he?"

She turned back toward the man, and as she drew in a deep breath, she reminded herself that he was one of her superiors at the firm, even though his name wasn't technically on the sign. She could not reply as she wanted—to tell him to mind his own damn business. Forcing a smile, she shook her head. "No. He isn't. That was Detective Colton with the Whisperwood Police Department."

"He's the one who found the body in your backyard," he said.

She wasn't certain how he would know that unless the media had mentioned it. But in every news report she had seen, Forrest or the chief had refused to answer questions about an ongoing investigation.

As if he'd noticed her suspicion, he reminded her, "I heard it on the police scanner."

She suppressed a little shiver of revulsion over his being such an ambulance chaser. It was lawyers like Kenneth Dawson who had earned the profession the bad reputation.

That was why she wanted to work on the other side—for the prosecution. For law and order, and not financial gain.

But Kenneth had always been nice to her, so she forced another smile for him. "That's right. Well, I better get to my desk. I'm sure I have a lot of work to do."

He stepped out of his doorway just as she headed toward her office, and she accidentally brushed up against him when she passed. Another shiver of revulsion coursed through her. Wasn't he the nice man she'd wanted to believe he was?

Or maybe it was just that damn note that was making her suspicious of everyone. Except Forrest.

She knew that he would do his best to protect her and Connor—even though the chief hadn't taken the threat as seriously as he had.

Forrest had done more than protect them last night, though. He'd made her feel things she hadn't felt in so long—if ever. So much damn pleasure that it had overwhelmed her.

Even thinking about it now overwhelmed her. The way he'd kissed her, touched her, moved inside her...

Heat coursed through her body now as she remembered how he'd made her feel. Her hand shook as she turned the knob on her door and pushed it open. Her legs trembled as she crossed the threshold and headed toward her desk.

Forrest was such a thorough lover. He'd made certain that she'd found her pleasure—many times—before he'd taken his own. She'd never known so generous a man. Most of them she'd known had been selfish.

Could she really trust that Forrest was that different, that he might actually stick around? She doubted it. His only interest in her was protecting her and Connor. Well, maybe not his only interest.

But she couldn't give in to that desire again. She

would only fall for him more deeply than she had already.

She dropped into the chair behind her desk and reached for the mail the clerk had left on the corner of it. She handled a lot of the incoming correspondence. So she began rifling through it. One of the envelopes bore only her name, though. No address. Nothing to do with the law firm at all.

Who would have sent something to her at the office?

It must have been an interoffice message from one of the partners. Maybe from Kenneth, although he usually liked to come and talk to her personally.

She sliced the envelope open and dumped out a single folded sheet of paper. When she unfolded the note, she found the same scrawled block letters that she'd found on the slip of paper on her pillow. The message was a little different, though.

It was more threatening.

Get rid of the detective, or your kid won't be the only one who suffers.

"Oh, my God," she murmured. She needed to call Forrest to warn him. Somebody really wanted him gone, so much so that they were willing to hurt a baby and her to get to him. She fumbled her cell phone out of her purse and punched in the contact Bellamy had given her for Forrest.

"This is Forrest Colton, interim detective with the Whisperwood Police Department, please leave a message and I'll return your call."

Why had it gone directly to voice mail?

Why wasn't he picking up?

She left a message. "Call me back. I just got another threat."

But would he be able to return her call?

Or had she tried to warn him too late?

THE CELL PHONE sitting on the table at JoJo's Java began to vibrate, and the screen lit up with a number Jonah Colton didn't recognize. His beautiful fiancée leaned across the table between them, her blond hair sliding across her cheek as she glanced down at the screen.

"Probably a telemarketer," he commented as he left the phone lying there. He would rather focus on Maggie than an offer for new windows, cable or a way to reduce his nonexistent credit-card debt.

She shook her head, though, so she must have recognized the number. "You need to get that. It's Rae."

Jonah furrowed his brow. "Why would she be calling me?" Maggie had filled him in on what had happened to her friend—about the threatening note and that Rae had called Forrest to report it.

Forrest would have handled the threat. Despite his injured leg, he was every bit the outstanding lawman he'd always been. It was too damn bad that, because he hadn't been able to meet the physical requirements of his job, Austin PD had forced him to retire on disability. That limp didn't slow down Forrest at all.

So, why would Rae be calling Jonah?

Had something happened?

He grabbed up the phone and hit the accept button. "Rae, is everything all right?"

"No," she said, her voice tremulous with fear. "I don't know what Maggie told you—"

"Everything," he interjected. He and his fiancée had no secrets. Only love and understanding.

Her shaky breath of relief rattled his phone. "I got

another threat—at the office—about Connor and For-rest," she said.

"Did you show it to Forrest?"

"He left with Connor," she said, and her voice cracked again. "And he's not picking up his phone."

Her fear filled him now, and he jumped up from his chair. "I'll find him," he said.

"Hurry," Rae implored him. "This threat was left in my office."

According to Maggie, the other one had been left on a pillow on her bed. The person threatening her had to be someone close to her.

Rae had apparently come to the same conclusion, be-cause she added, "If he knows where I work and where I live, he probably knows where Connor's day care is. Forrest was going there with my son when he left me at the office."

And now she couldn't reach him.

She had to be terrified about her child. "Please find them," she pleaded.

It was clear that Connor wasn't the only one she was worried about; she was worried about Forrest, as well.

So was Jonah. "What day care?" he asked.

"I know," Maggie said. She'd jumped up from her chair as well, forgetting her coffee. "I'll go with you."

He shook his head. If Forrest was in danger, and it certainly sounded as if he was, then Jonah had no in-tention of putting his fiancée in danger, too.

But she headed out the door ahead of him, straight for their vehicle. From the urgency in Rae's voice, he didn't have time to fight with Maggie. So he just hur-ried after her. "I'll let you know when I find them," he told Rae before clicking off his cell.

He only hoped when he had found them that he

would have good news to share with her. As one of the Cowboy Heroes, unfortunately he usually had more bad news to share than good.

Chapter Twelve

He hadn't been wrong. Someone had been watching him and Rae arrive at her office. Fortunately that someone had followed him from the lot instead of staying behind to stalk Rae.

But then again the threat had been against her child—not her—and Connor slept peacefully in the back seat. Peacefully but not exactly safely, not with the big cargo van following them. The van windows were tinted, so Forrest couldn't see the driver or even how many passengers might be inside with him. Was Forrest outnumbered?

He reached for his cell, but when he pulled it from his pocket, the screen was black. He hadn't brought a charger to Rae's last night, and the battery must have died. A curse slipped through his lips, followed by a twinge of guilt striking his heart. He glanced back at Connor, but the baby was still asleep. Even if he hadn't been, though, he probably wouldn't have understood what Forrest had said, and he certainly couldn't repeat it. Yet.

Forrest had to make sure that Connor would have the chance someday to talk, to curse, to grow up.

He had to make sure he kept his promise to Rae and kept her son safe. The van edged closer, as if the driver was no longer worried about Forrest's noticing him.

Another curse burned his throat, but he forced it down. Swearing wasn't going to help him, and with his dead phone, he couldn't call for backup. He had to protect Connor himself.

As he pressed down on the accelerator, he glanced into the rearview mirror. He wasn't looking at the van behind him, though. He was trying to see the car seat, to make sure he'd secured it like Rae had showed him. She'd been adamant about how to install it so that the baby would be safe.

But he'd removed it at her office and had then put it back in without her supervision. Had he done it right?

Would Connor be safe at this speed?

He glanced up from the baby to the back window, where he saw the van was now so close that its grille was all Forrest saw. He pressed on the accelerator again just as the van brushed the back bumper of Rae's small SUV. Then he jerked the wheel and took a sudden turn onto a side street. The van passed it, but the brakes squealed as it stopped and backed up.

The driver was determined. But so was Forrest. He'd grown up in Whisperwood; he knew all of the streets well. Using his knowledge, he led the van around the city. But the driver must have known the city well, too, because Forrest didn't lose his tail.

The van also had a more powerful engine, because it easily kept up with the speeding SUV. Where were the police officers? Why had nobody stopped them?

But that was why Forrest had been hired, despite his disability, because the department was spread so thin—too thin obviously to patrol the streets. Too bad the day care had been in the opposite direction from the police department, or he would have been closer to Whisperwood PD.

He headed there now, though, but the driver sped up. If he knew Whisperwood as well as he seemed to, he might have guessed where Forrest was heading. And he was determined that he and Connor would not make it there.

The driver closed the distance between the vehicles and struck the back of the SUV hard. Connor awoke with a scream. Forrest cursed as he gripped the wheel, struggling not to lose control.

But the van struck again and again.

And Forrest worried that Rae had been right not to trust him. He shouldn't have made the promise to her—because he wasn't going to be able to keep it after all.

RAE HAD EXPECTED a call back. She'd hoped for a quick assurance from Forrest that he and Connor were all right, that he'd just been too busy talking to Bob Mc-Cauley to answer his phone.

But she knew that if he'd been able, Forrest would have taken her call. He wouldn't have wanted to worry her, and he would have been worried about her. She didn't take that personally, though, even after last night. He was just doing his job. He wasn't just a detective; he was a lawman who'd sworn years ago to serve and protect. And he'd promised to protect them, as if the threat was somehow his fault.

But he'd only been doing his job when she'd received that threat. A job that someone obviously didn't want him doing. It had to be the killer leaving the notes. Who else would want to get rid of Forrest?

She'd once thought she had when he'd showed up at her back door that day he'd found the body. Now she didn't want him gone. She just wanted him to be all right.

He and Connor had to be okay.

He'd promised.

The phone call she wanted never came. Instead Jonah Colton showed up in her office doorway. She'd been staring at it since she'd called him. But his wasn't the face she'd wanted to see looking in at her.

And even if she had, she wouldn't have wanted to see him like this—his jaw tense, his face pale with concern or fear. Heart pounding, she jumped up from her chair. "What is it? What's wrong?"

She peered around him, looking for Forrest. Maybe he'd just moved slower due to his limp; maybe that was why he wasn't in the doorway, too. But she knew—she just knew—there was another reason.

"There's been an accident," Jonah said, confirming her fears.

"Accident?" She shook her head in denial. "It was no accident." She reached back and grabbed her purse from her desk. Then she shoved past him in the doorway. "Where are they? Where are Connor and Forrest?"

"At the hospital," he replied, his voice soft with sympathy and that concern that pinched his handsome face.

Panic nearly buckled her knees, making her stumble as she headed toward the elevator. Jonah reached out and steadied her with his hand on her elbow.

"I'll bring you there," he said.

Her son was in the hospital. He was so little, so fragile...

What the hell had happened?

She wanted to know the details about that, but more important she wanted to know that he was all right. She had to make sure that he was all right.

Jonah pushed the button for the elevator, and the doors immediately opened. They stepped inside, and he pushed the button for the lobby. He was in as much of a rush to get her to the hospital as she was. If he hadn't offered to drive her, she would have run to the hospital. Nothing and nobody would keep her from her child.

And Forrest.

Her stomach pitched as the elevator stopped in the lobby. What had happened to him?

Tears stung her eyes as fear overwhelmed her. If only she had listened to him and hadn't gone to work.

He could have kept her and Connor safe at their home, as he had last night. But Forrest hadn't just kept them safe; he'd made love to Rae and had made her start to fall in love with him.

If something had happened to him…

If something had happened to either of them…

She would personally track down the person who'd hurt them. And that person would pay for what he'd done.

"You're going to pay up one way or the other," his caller said.

He didn't recognize the voice emanating from the phone any more than he had recognized the handwriting on the notes that had been left in his motel room for him. But he didn't have to know who his caller was to know what he was: a killer.

And now he might be the same. Regret and self-disgust churned his stomach, making bile rise up in his throat.

"So you damn well better have done what I ordered," his new boss continued.

"I did," he said. "I did what you wanted."

"You got rid of the detective from Austin?"

"Yeah…" And probably not just him.

A memory ran through his mind, of Colton carrying the baby seat through the parking lot at the law office. Of him securing it into the back seat of Rae's SUV.

How secure had it been?

"You damn well better have," the person continued, his voice gruff with disgust. "You owe me a hell of a lot of money."

He flinched. That wasn't the way it had started out, or the way it should have wound up. But nothing in his life had ever wound up the way he had expected it to.

Not his career.

Or his family.

Not one damn thing about his life.

His luck had run out a long time ago. He was the only one who hadn't realized it, though. Everybody else had just kept collecting IOUs from him—until his debt had become insurmountable.

What about Forrest Colton? How lucky was he? Had he survived the crash?

If the detective had survived this attempt, he would not be able to survive the next. Or *he* was going to wind up repaying his debt with his own life.

Chapter Thirteen

Fury coursed through Forrest. "I don't care that I'm not the baby's legal guardian," he said. "I want to know how Connor is doing."

The nurse at the desk remained stone-faced as she just shook her head in reply to his questions. He'd been able to crack hardened criminals easier than this woman.

"You need to return to the examination area, Mr. Colton," she said, "while we're awaiting the results of your CAT scan."

He touched his forehead. "It's just a bump." That throbbed like hell, but he knew enough to know it wasn't serious. Neither was the pain reverberating from his hip down his leg. That was because of the seat belt and the bump on his knee that matched the one on his head.

Because of a faulty airbag, the dashboard had done more damage to him than the crash had. But he didn't give a damn about his own injuries.

"I am responsible for that baby," Forrest said.

"I thought you admitted you're not the father," the nurse reminded him, her brow furrowed as she studied his face.

Forrest cursed his own damn honesty, wishing he'd

lied now. At least then they would have let him be with Connor. Had they allowed Maggie back to see him?

"I am a detective with the Whisperwood Police Department," Forrest said, and he pulled out his temporary badge to show her. "I am responsible for Connor Lemmon because I was protecting him."

But he hadn't done a very damn good job. He hadn't been able to outrun the van, which had kept ramming into them until the SUV had crashed into a parked car.

Forrest didn't know what had happened next. He might have blacked out for a couple of seconds—because the van was gone when he opened his eyes. And Connor had been screaming hysterically.

Forrest had forced open the crumpled door of the SUV, but when he'd stepped out, he'd nearly collapsed on the street from the pain radiating throughout his bad leg. Even now it threatened to buckle, so he leaned more heavily on the edge of the nurses' station.

"I need to know how he is," he persisted. He needed to know how badly he'd broken his promise to Rae.

The baby had looked fine when Forrest had forced open the back door and unclasped his carrier from the seat. The harness seemed to have held him mostly immobile.

But babies were fragile.

The little guy could have had internal injuries, wounds that Forrest hadn't been able to see. Fortunately someone had witnessed the crash and called 911, so an ambulance, with sirens blaring, had roared up at the same time Jonah and Maggie had. They'd followed the ambulance, with him and Connor inside, to the hospital. But once in the ER, he and the infant had been separated for treatment.

He'd thought he would be able to see Connor again, but the damn staff had refused to reunite them. Why?

"What's wrong with him?" he asked the nurse. Maybe that was why she wouldn't tell him, because it was so bad. Panic gripped him as he considered how bad it could be.

Fatal.

Rae had already suffered so many losses: her father's abandonment during her mother's illness, and then her mother's death. But losing her son...

How would someone ever recover from that?

Forrest had known the infant for only a few days, and he was in pain—a pain that was so much more debilitating than physical injuries. His heart ached with it.

"Mr. Colton," the nurse said as she came out from behind the desk.

He turned toward her, and as he loosened his grip on the counter, his leg shook beneath him, nearly dropping him to the floor.

"You need to return to the examination table," she said. "You probably have a concussion, and your leg—"

"It's a mess," he finished for her. "It's been a mess since I was shot. I don't have any injuries from the crash." None that compared to the gunshot wound that had shattered bone and left him permanently disabled. "What I do have is a responsibility to the person I was protecting and a right to know how he's doing."

She uttered a weary-sounding sigh. "You are persistent."

Not persistent enough to have kept his promise to Rae, though.

"Return to your examination area at least until we get back the results of your CAT scan, and I'll—" she lowered her voice and whispered "—tell you about the baby."

A moment of panic struck him. Now that she'd agreed to share Connor's condition with him, Forrest wasn't sure he wanted to know.

What if he'd broken his promise?

What if he'd failed Rae?

She would never forgive him.

And neither would Forrest ever forgive himself.

RAE CLASPED CONNOR'S limp body to her madly pounding heart. He seemed so lifeless, but for the soft breaths escaping his lips. He was alive.

Tears of relief coursed down her face.

"He's fine," Maggie assured her. "The doctor just told us that he has no injuries—no effects—from the accident at all."

Rae had heard him, too. But she hadn't believed it until she'd held Connor, until she'd felt his warmth and heard the sounds of his soft breathing.

"He must just be exhausted," Maggie said as she stared at the baby, too. Her beautiful blue eyes were damp with either tears of relief or of the fear she'd felt when she'd realized that he'd been in an accident.

Rae nodded in agreement with Maggie's assessment. Connor got like this—limp with exhaustion—after he cried, and she imagined he must have been crying during and after the crash. That he must have been terrified.

"What happened?" she asked. Now that she knew he was all right, she wanted those details. But before giving Maggie a chance to answer, she added, "How is Forrest?"

"Sorry," a deep voice said, and then the curtain

around Connor's examination area was pulled aside to reveal Forrest. A red bump swelled on his forehead, and he leaned on one crutch for support.

A twinge of pain struck her heart over his injuries. He had not escaped as unscathed as Connor had. "Are you okay?" she asked.

He nodded. "I'm fine." He didn't look fine. His jaw was clenched and his hazel eyes were dark with concern. He gestured at Connor. "How is he?"

More tears welled in her eyes—more tears of relief—that Forrest had survived, as well. Emotion choked her, and she couldn't speak for a moment.

Maggie answered for her. "He's really fine. Not even a bump or a bruise—unlike you."

"That nurse wouldn't give me any information about Connor's condition, but she told you about mine?" Forrest asked.

Maggie pointed at his head. "She didn't need to say anything. It's clear you didn't escape without any injuries like Connor did."

A ragged breath of relief escaped his lips. "He's really okay?" He wasn't looking at Maggie, though. He was looking at Rae.

She nodded. "Yes, he is."

"I'm sorry," he said again. "I had a feeling there was someone in the parking lot of the law office. And then he started following us to the day care center."

He hadn't just followed them, though.

"I tried to lose him," Forrest said.

"Him?" Rae asked. "You saw him?"

He shook his head. "The windows were tinted, so I couldn't see who was behind the wheel. And after he forced us off the road, he drove off. He got away."

She shivered and clutched Connor tighter in her

arms. He had gotten away, so he could come back. To her house. To her office. Here.

She shuddered. "We need to get Connor out of here," she said.

As if he'd read her mind, Forrest assured her, "He's safe. This place has some pretty tough security, and that's just the nurses."

One of them had followed him inside the curtained area, and she glared at him now. "Mr. Colton was quite concerned about your son," she told Rae. Then she turned back toward him. "But you can see that he's fine. You, on the other hand…"

"What?" Rae asked. "Isn't he okay?"

The nurse ignored her as she continued to speak to Forrest. "We got back the results of the X-rays on your leg and the CAT scan on your head."

"And I'm fine," Forrest insisted.

But the nurse didn't confirm this. All she said was, "You need to speak to the doctor, Mr. Colton."

And the crushing panic returned to Rae's chest, pressing down on her lungs and heart so that she had to struggle to breathe. "Forrest…"

But the nurse was already leading him away from her.

Maggie stepped closer and wrapped her arm around Rae's waist. "I'm sure he's fine," she said.

"Then why wouldn't she tell him that?"

Maggie shrugged. "Privacy rules. She wouldn't give us any information about Connor until you got here, and then the doctor had to do it."

Rae nodded in agreement. "That's right. That has to be what it is."

But would Forrest's results be as good as Connor's?

With the bump on his head and the crutch under his

arm, he had obvious injuries. How severe were they? And were there any other ones?

Concussion? Broken bones? Internal injuries?

He'd promised to protect them, but at what cost to himself? His life?

JOSEPHINE COLTON STUDIED her husband's face as he held his phone to his ear, listening. The color had left his skin, and there was a slight tremble along his jaw. "You'll let us know how he is and if we need to come."

It wasn't a question. He was informing his caller that it was required. While always diplomatic and polite, her husband had a backbone of steel, and anyone who'd worked for him or that he'd raised would attest to it. The steel was bending a bit with age and worry over those kids they'd raised.

The minute he clicked off his cell, she asked, "Who is it?"

But there was a part of her that knew already. The minute he'd accepted the interim position with the Whisperwood Police Department, she'd begun to worry that this would happen again, that he would be wounded in the line of duty.

Hays had worried, too. And he was worried now, with deep grooves beside his mouth and between his brows. "Forrest."

Her fears confirmed, she gasped. "How badly?"

"According to Jonah, he's conscious and pissed off," Hays replied with a smile he mustered for her sake.

She smiled back at him, like he wanted her to, but her fears did not subside. He'd been conscious and pissed off after he'd been shot in the leg, and that injury had been so severe, the doctors had thought they might have to amputate.

"What happened?" she asked.

He shook his head. "Something to do with Bellamy and Maggie's friend Rae."

The pretty brunette. Josephine had seen her talk to Forrest at the wedding, but he'd walked away from her then. "Is she all right?"

"She wasn't in the car with him," Hays replied, and his brow furrowed more as he added, "but her baby was."

Josephine gasped again with fear for the infant. He was so young, so fragile. "Is he all right?"

Hays shook his head. "I don't know."

"We should go to the hospital." She glanced around the farmhouse kitchen. Where had she put her purse? Hell, she didn't need it. She just needed to make sure her son was all right and that Rae Lemmon's son was, too.

"Jonah said he would call back once he knew more," Hays said, and he walked over and put his arm around her. "You know how tough Forrest is. By the time we'd get there, I'm sure he would have already checked himself out."

"With or against doctor's orders," she murmured. Because he was that stubborn.

And that stubbornness would probably be the death of him. Or of her.

Josephine loved all of her boys, but she didn't love worrying about them like she did. And since they'd all chosen to be lawmen or military men or rescuers, she was constantly worrying about their physical and emotional well-being.

Dallas was still devastated from losing his wife, and Forrest over losing his job. Only Donovan and Jonah were truly happy now. She wanted that kind of happiness for all of her children.

Chapter Fourteen

The front door closed behind Jonah and Maggie, leaving Forrest and Rae alone in the living room. Connor, exhausted from the ordeal, slept peacefully now in his crib. Forrest and Jonah had searched the house the minute they'd arrived, looking for any more notes or signs of another intrusion.

But they had found nothing here.

"I have an officer picking up the note from your office, along with all of the building's security footage from the morning," Forrest said. "Hopefully we'll be able to figure out who left that note on your desk."

They already knew why. Someone wanted him out of the way.

Either because of the investigation or because of her.

That was why Forrest had returned to her house when he'd really wanted to assign the young officer to protection duty instead. He hadn't talked to the chief yet, but surely the guy had to see that Rae was in real danger. Or at least her son was, and who wouldn't deem security necessary for a defenseless infant?

Forrest sucked in a breath as he relived those interminable moments when he hadn't known how Connor was, if he'd survived the crash without injury.

And he remembered that he needed to call his folks.

Unfortunately Jonah had told them what had happened, and they were worried. Now he understood some of what they must be feeling.

Not that Connor was his kid. But he cared about the little guy. And he cared about Rae. Too much.

Too much to stick around if it was his presence that was putting them in danger. But was the reason someone wanted him gone more to do with Rae than the murder investigation?

Did she have some admirer or stalker who wanted her all to himself?

Another memory flitted through his head of that lawyer watching Rae from his doorway. The way he'd looked at her...

It hadn't been like a boss should look at an employee, or a colleague at a coworker. It had been how a man looks at a woman he wants.

The way Forrest looked at Rae.

He wanted her.

Maybe that was the real reason he'd come back to the house with her instead of assigning that young officer. Not that he intended to be as selfish as he had been the night before.

He couldn't act on his desire for her. He couldn't risk being distracted, not after someone had tried and nearly succeeded to kill him and Connor.

"You're right," she said.

He tensed. Had she read his mind? Did she know what he'd been thinking—about what they'd done the night before, about what he wanted to do to her now?

"It's too dangerous for me to go to the office, to bring Connor to day care," she said, and she shivered. Wrapping her arms around herself for warmth or comfort, she added, "I don't want to think about what might have happened if you and Connor had made it to the day care, if something happened to him there or to the other children." She shivered again.

His chest ached with the need to wrap his arms around her, to comfort her. But he knew that his comforting her might lead to more, like it had the night before.

"I'm sorry," she continued. "I should have listened to you." She stepped closer then, and after unwrapping her arms from around herself, she reached for him.

But he stumbled back a step, to avoid her touch.

She flinched and murmured again, "I'm sorry. I'm sorry you got hurt."

"I'm fine," he said.

She narrowed her eyes and studied his face with suspicion. "The ER doctor seemed concerned about you leaving the hospital."

He shrugged. "He was worried that I might have a slight concussion." He touched the bump on his head and winced. "Because of this. But my head is hard as a rock." The gnawing ache in his leg that radiated out from the bump on his knee to his ankle and up to his hip bothered him more. But he'd refused to take any painkillers for it.

He needed to stay sharp in order to find out who the hell was threatening her and her son. And because he needed to stay sharp, he needed to fight his attraction to her. But she looked so beautiful in that sunny yellow dress that skimmed over her curves.

"What about your leg?" she asked, and her gaze ran down his body.

His traitorous body hardened in reaction to just that look, and it was one of concern, not desire. But then she sucked in a breath as if she'd noticed how the fly of pants was strained now.

"My leg is fine, too," he said, and it was, since that ache had moved to another part of his body. He turned away from her and peered through the nursery doorway.

"Did I hear something?" he asked despite the silence. Connor needed to wake up so that Forrest would come to his senses, so that he wouldn't be tempted to act on his attraction again.

Rae glanced toward the outside door instead, and her brown eyes widened with fear. "Did you? Do you think someone's out there?"

He stifled a groan. "No," he assured her.

But could he be certain?

He didn't necessarily think the person who'd threatened them was out there, but he wondered about Jonah. Had his brother really left?

Forrest wouldn't have put it past him to stick around. Ever since he'd been shot, his brothers had been extra concerned about him. So had his parents.

He needed to check in with them as Jonah had suggested, to make sure that they weren't too upset. He was upset enough for all of them. But he wasn't concerned about his life; he was worried about hers and about Connor's.

If he was worried at all about himself, it wasn't about his life but about his heart. He'd had it broken too recently for him to trust it with anyone else yet. Even Rae.

Maybe most especially Rae, who had already declared her determination to raise her son alone. She wasn't looking for any man, least of all a disabled one who had already put her new family in danger.

"I'm the one who's sorry," he said. "I'm the reason you started getting those threats." And by sticking around, he wasn't necessarily protecting her and Connor but was probably putting them in more danger. "I'm the one this person wants gone."

Yet here he was. He'd insisted that Jonah bring them all back to her house.

"So maybe I should leave," he suggested.

She shuddered. "Whoever he is, he doesn't want you just to go away. He wants you dead. He tried to kill you today."

"And Connor could have been hurt in the cross fire," Forrest said, guilt churning his stomach into knots. If anything had happened to her baby, he never would have forgiven himself. And neither would she have.

"That's why I should go," he continued. "And why I should stay away from you."

For Connor's sake, for hers and for his, too.

He couldn't risk his heart again—not even for Rae. Not that she probably wanted him to. All she'd wanted from him was protection, and all he'd done was put her and her child in more danger.

BLOOD STAINED THE crumpled dash of the SUV. The chief flinched as he studied the wreckage. "I want this processed right away," he told the tech from the crime lab.

The young woman's eyes widened with surprise. She had to be wondering why a traffic accident would take precedence over all of their other cases. But this hadn't been an accident.

Forrest had been right to take the threat to Rae Lemmon's child seriously. Detective Colton had paid for protecting them with his own blood. Jonah and Donovan had assured him that their brother was fine. But now that he'd seen the crash for himself...

It could have been so much worse. The baby could

have been hurt, as well. Despite his sleepless night of surveillance, Forrest had done a damn fine job of minimizing the risk to other drivers on the road and to that child. Maybe Austin PD shouldn't have been so damn quick to retire him with disability. The detective was more physically capable than his previous department and maybe he himself knew.

"We're also looking for a white van," he told the tech. "If one turns up—"

"Over there, Chief," the tech interrupted as she pointed to another corner of the police impound lot.

Smoke rose yet from the burned-out skeleton of a vehicle, and a groan slipped through his lips.

"I'm not sure it was white," the tech said. "It was already fully engaged when the fire department was called to an alley not far from the hospital."

Had the driver followed the ambulance to the ER? Had he wanted to make certain that Forrest or the baby hadn't survived the crash?

"We need that processed ASAP, as well," he said.

"We'll have to wait until it cools off, Chief," the tech pointed out.

He nodded. "Just until…" He needed a damn lead to whoever had threatened his new detective. He couldn't lose Forrest yet, but he suspected that he would eventually—to another, longer-term job.

His cell phone vibrated in his pocket. He pulled it out and expelled a sigh when he saw the screen. It was Forrest. Was he already leaving?

After Archer hadn't taken his concerns seriously, he might be compelled to quit. He walked back to his SUV before clicking the accept button. "Colton, how are you?" he asked.

"So you know," Forrest said.

"I'm at the impound lot now," he admitted. "You're lucky you walked away from that crash." Then he flinched at his insensitivity. He'd been told that it was lucky that Forrest could walk at all—after the shooting that had nearly ended his career and his life.

"That's not the only thing I should walk away from," Forrest said.

And Archer swallowed a curse before asking, "You're quitting?"

"Yes," Forrest replied.

"But I thought you wanted to find the killer, too." Not as much as Archer did, though. Nobody wanted to find the killer as much as he did. All those years he'd spent wondering what had happened to his sister...

Was her killer the same one who'd buried the body near the parking lot of the drug company, though? Or were there two of them?

And if so, he needed Forrest Colton now more than ever. "You can't give up yet."

"I'm not giving up on finding the killer," Forrest assured him. "I'm giving up protection duty."

Archer glanced over at the wreckage and sighed. "Of course. I don't blame you." Not after that crash. Even though his offer came too late, he said, "I'll send over an officer to replace you."

"Who?" Forrest asked.

"I don't know yet," Archer said. "I'll have to see who's coming on duty, so they can stay through the night."

"Only send someone who's done this kind of thing before," Forrest suggested.

Or was it an order?

Forrest unwittingly answered the chief's unspoken

question when he added, "Whoever you send will need to meet my approval."

He clicked off before Archer could comment further, leaving the chief wondering if anyone he sent would actually meet Forrest's approval. Just how attached had the young detective gotten to Rae Lemmon and her baby?

RAE SUCKED IN a breath at the sudden jab of pain in her chest. It was as if Forrest had plunged a knife into her heart. He was leaving just like every other man she'd ever known.

How could he? But then how could she think that he would stay after he'd been hurt? After his sleepless night? After what he'd said about putting her and Connor in more danger with his presence?

He must have felt her presence, because he turned away from the back door and the window he'd been staring through while he'd spoken to the chief.

"You're really leaving," she murmured.

He nodded. "Once my replacement arrives."

Her skin heated with a sudden surge of anger. She wasn't as angry with him, though, as she was with herself. Last night never should have happened; she never should have trusted him enough to make love with him.

"So much for your promise," she bitterly remarked.

"I will make sure you and Connor stay safe," he assured her. "And the most effective way for me to do that is to stay away from the two of you."

A twinge of pain joined her anger. "So leave then," she told him. "We don't need you." But her words echoed hollowly back to her. How had she, in such a short amount of time, become reliant on him?

She had always been so independent. That had begun out of necessity, but it was her choice now. To be alone.

"Leave," she ordered him.

His vehicle was here, since they'd taken hers that morning because the baby carrier had already been buckled into the back seat. And hers was the one that had been wrecked.

"I'm not leaving until my replacement gets here," he said. "I'm keeping my promise."

She snorted. "You're keeping your distance. What? You get scared today?"

"Yes," he said.

She wasn't sure if he was talking about the crash or something else.

Her?

"I was scared that something had happened to your son," he said. "That I had broken that promise you didn't even want me to make to you. And that scared me. It scared me that I care about him, about you."

She gasped now, as shock surged through her, replacing the anger. "Forrest..." She stepped closer to him, but like when she had reached for him earlier, he moved away from her.

It was as if he couldn't bear her touch anymore.

That hadn't been the case last night.

Last night he'd uttered a ragged groan every time she'd touched him, kissed him...

"It's because I care that I have to stay away from you," he said.

Realization dawned. He wasn't talking about just protecting her; he was talking about making love to her.

He didn't want to do it again.

He considered last night a mistake.

So should she—because it had made her want something she should have already known wasn't possible. Someone she could count on.

Chapter Fifteen

The young officer seemed capable enough. Since he'd worked as a security guard while putting himself through college and the police academy, he had experience with protection duty. He also looked like a body builder, so he was probably a hell of a lot more capable than Forrest was. But the thought of leaving churned his guts so much that he felt physically sick. He wasn't ready to leave yet, so he'd sent the young officer outside to patrol the yard.

That was probably the best place for him to be with the sun setting. It had taken the chief a while even to send someone out and a while longer for Forrest to interview the man. During that time he had seen very little of Rae.

Connor had awakened, and she'd busied herself by taking care of him and ignoring Forrest's presence. Or at least that was how he felt: ignored. Like she wanted to pretend he'd already left, like her father had left.

Was that why she'd gotten so upset about his turning over her protection duty to someone else? Because she figured he'd broken his promise like her dad had broken his promise to stand beside her mother through sickness and health?

He didn't want to be compared to a person like that,

to someone who reminded him so much of his own ex-fiancée. Shannon certainly hadn't wanted to stick around during his sickness.

But Rae and Connor weren't sick. They were in danger. Because of him.

The best thing he could do to protect them was to stay away from them. Surely, she had to see that was why he'd chosen to turn over the duty of guarding them to someone else. Someone like the capable, young officer outside.

He glanced out the window, but it had gotten so dark that he couldn't see Officer Baker anymore. He could have called him, made certain he was still out there and then he could have left. But thinking about her father had made him curious about the man.

How long ago had Mr. Lemmon taken off?

Around the time that body had been buried in his backyard? Since it had been mummified, it could have been there for decades, like the chief's sister's body had been. It could have been there before Rae's parents had even moved into this house. But what if it hadn't been?

What if that body had had more to do with Rae's dad taking off than his wife's illness? Maybe he'd been running away from the scene of his crime.

Crimes?

Had he known Emmeline Thompson, too?

Wanting to ask all those questions, Forrest glanced toward the closed door to Rae's bedroom. That must have been shut as a message to him, because she hadn't closed it the night before. But then he'd been in that bedroom with her for much of last night. He'd been in that bed with her.

He longed to join her now in her bed, but he doubted she would welcome his presence. Or even the questions now swirling through his head. So instead of looking for answers from her, he began to look for them around the house.

This was where Rae had grown up, where she'd lived with her mother, and her father had lived there, too—before he'd taken off. Frames held photos of her mother and of Rae at different ages. But where were the photos of her father?

Forrest rose from the kitchen chair, grimacing over the pain shooting up and down his stiffened leg. He stood for a long moment before he trusted it to hold him as he walked. Then he headed out of the kitchen and into the living room. On the wall opposite to Rae's closed bedroom door was a row of bookshelves. He hobbled toward those because he'd spied earlier, among the spines of books, a couple of photo albums.

Leg still aching in protest of his weight, he dropped onto the sofa next to the bookshelves and flipped open the first album. Dust fell off the top of the plastic folders and settled onto his dark pants.

Rae must not have looked at these photos in a long time. Then he realized why when he saw the man in the pictures. He had to be Rae's father—not that they looked much alike, but in some of the photographs, he was holding a baby that looked like Connor in a pink blanket, and in a few others, he was holding the hand of a little girl with big dark eyes and brown hair who gazed adoringly up at him.

There were also photos of him with a woman who looked like a taller, willowy version of Rae. But he looked distracted in some of those photos, as his attention was either on the television or something in his hand.

Forrest leaned over the album, peering at the slips of

paper. In other photos, those pieces of paper were either sticking out of his pocket or wadded up in his hands.

Betting slips?

But what did that mean?

Had Beau Lemmon been a bookie or a gambler?

And how did that relate to the mummified body in his backyard? Had that person owed him a debt? Or had he owed one to her?

Had Beau Lemmon killed that person and buried her in his own backyard, where his adorable little girl had played?

Forrest had already pegged the guy for a loser, taking off when his wife got sick, but now he wondered if he was more than that.

A killer.

WAS HE GONE? She'd heard the other officer arrive, had heard them speak and then a door opened and closed. Had Forrest turned over Connor's and her security to another bodyguard?

After the day he'd had, she couldn't entirely blame him. The anger she'd felt earlier with him had faded now to disappointment and disillusionment.

She'd made a mistake being intimate with him last night. Just as she'd had in the past with other men. Having sex didn't lead to true intimacy, not the kind her friends had found with their Colton men.

She'd thought he might be worth risking her heart on.

A twinge of pain struck it now. How had she already let herself start falling for him?

She knew better. She knew that—at least for the women in her family—love didn't last, if it had ever really been love at all. And in her case—with Forrest— she hardly knew him. So of course it wasn't love.

It was appreciation for how sweet and protective he'd been with Connor. That was all it was.

And desire.

Her body ached with that now, so much that she couldn't sleep. Not without him.

Resigned to another restless night, she threw back the thin sheet and rolled out of bed. She should have introduced herself to the officer. Actually, she should have been the one who'd interviewed him. After all, he was assigned to protect her and Connor. Not Forrest.

He was going to stay away from them.

For their sakes?

Or his?

She suspected it was as much for his as it was for theirs. Was he afraid of getting hurt physically again or emotionally?

That fear of his getting hurt flickered through her. The note writer wanted him gone to the extent that he'd tried to take Forrest's life.

Maybe his staying away was for the best—for him. Maybe he should leave Whisperwood entirely. Maybe he already had.

She grabbed her robe from the back of the door and shoved her arms into the sleeves. After securing the tie around her waist, she pulled open the door and stepped into the living room.

A wave of relief rushed over her. He hadn't left. He sat on her couch, a lock of light brown hair falling across his forehead as his head bent over something on his lap. When she identified what it was, her relief fled, leaving only panic and pain.

"What are you doing?" she asked.

He didn't jump or tense. He must have noticed when she'd opened the door, but he hadn't looked over at her.

He didn't even look up at her now. Instead he was totally focused on those old photographs.

"Why are you looking at those?" she asked with a shudder of her own. She didn't like looking at them, at the past. The only photographs she wanted to see were the ones hanging on her walls or sitting in frames on the shelves. Maybe she should have tossed out the old photo albums, but she'd figured that one day her children might want to see pictures of her past, to learn more about it.

Why did Forrest?

"Do you know where he is?" he asked, and he pointed toward a picture of her father.

She sucked in a breath and shook her head. But because he still wasn't looking at her, she replied shortly and succinctly, "No."

"No idea?"

"I don't think about it," she said. "I don't think about him."

He looked up at her then, his deep hazel eyes filled with skepticism of her claim.

With good reason, she had lied. She thought about him, about how he'd taken off on her and her mom, every time she considered risking her heart on someone. Like Forrest.

She remembered how Beau Lemmon had hurt her mother and her, and she realized that falling in love wasn't worth the inevitable pain that followed the fall.

"Let's just say I don't know, and I don't care," she said.

He tilted his head, and his eyes narrowed. "Have you heard from him?"

She shook her head.

"Nothing?" he asked. "Not even when your mother died? Didn't he try to inherit the house or—"

"Mom was sick for a long time. She divorced him during that time and made sure I was her sole beneficiary," she explained. Her mother hadn't been bitter about Beau, but she'd been realistic.

"Why?" he asked. "Did she think he would just gamble it all away if he inherited?" And he pointed to something in the picture, a slip of paper.

"Lottery ticket?" she asked.

He shook his head. "More like a betting slip— serious gambling."

She snorted. "Serious? I don't think that's something my father ever was."

Not even when he'd made those promises that he would come back to them a better man. If he'd been serious, he would have come back. If he'd been able...

"I think he might have been serious about gambling," Forrest said. "Maybe he went to Vegas or Reno when he left Whisperwood."

She shrugged. "I don't know. He didn't leave a forwarding address."

"And he's never sent a letter or postcard?" Forrest persisted.

She snorted. "My father isn't like yours. He wasn't a good man or a..." She trailed off as she realized the reason for his questions. "You think he buried that body in the backyard?"

"I do consider him a suspect," Forrest admitted.

She appreciated his honesty even as she felt a flash of shame. "When I said my father isn't a good man, I wasn't implying that he's a bad man. That he's evil. He's just flawed."

Most people were.

As if thinking of his flaw, Forrest rubbed his palm over his wounded leg.

She'd run her lips over it, over the scars from the bullets and from the surgeries that had pieced his leg back together. But that wound wasn't a flaw. There was nothing flawed about Forrest Colton.

He was so damn good-looking with that chiseled jaw and cheekbones and those deep-set hazel eyes. He stared up at her again, and his eyes darkened even more as the pupils dilated and swallowed up all of the gold and green.

As if he'd read her mind, he murmured, "You're not flawed." Then, despite the obvious discomfort of his leg, he surged to his feet. "You're absolutely flawless."

When he looked at her the way he was looking, the way he'd looked at her last night, she believed that he found her as irresistible as she found him. And he was irresistible. So irresistible that she heaved a heavy sigh before she stepped closer to him and wrapped her arms around him. Then she rose on tiptoe and brushed her mouth across his.

He sucked in a breath. "I thought you were mad at me for leaving."

Her lips tugged up into a smile as she pointed out the obvious, "You're still here."

He heaved a heavy sigh now that feathered through her tangled hair. "I know."

"Why?"

"Because I can't bring myself to leave."

He would. Eventually. She knew that. Everybody had left Rae—whether they'd intended to, like her father and some ex-boyfriends, or they hadn't intended to, like her mother, who'd fought so hard to beat the cancer. But it had kept coming back for her.

She closed her eyes as a wave of pain washed over her. Forrest must have seen it, because he closed his arms around her and softly asked, "Are you okay?"

She gestured at the couch. "That—those pictures—just bring up painful memories."

He moved one hand from her back to her face and ran his fingers along her jaw. "Then let's make better memories—like last night. That's all I've been able to think about. You. Being with you. Being *inside* you."

She shivered even as her flesh heated and her pulse pounded. "Yes," she murmured.

"I haven't asked a question," he said, and he was smiling now.

"You will," she said. He'd made certain last night, several times, that she really wanted him. To save them time, she told him, "I want you. I want you with me, inside me."

He groaned and bent forward slightly, as if she'd kicked him. But then he straightened up and lifted her into his arms as he did.

"Forrest," she protested. "Your leg—"

"I don't care," he said. "I don't care about anything but getting you to that damn bed."

She giggled despite her concern. She giggled at his eagerness. He clearly wanted her as badly as she did him. Despite his injury and his limp, he carried her easily and quickly to the bedroom and to the bed.

Maybe he dropped her a little abruptly onto the mattress, so abruptly that she bounced once, but she only giggled again. He hadn't dropped her because he was hurting—at least not over his leg or his head. He'd dropped her because he was tearing off his clothes to join her. To join them.

As he laid his holstered gun on the table beside her

bed, he murmured, "There's a police officer outside. You and Connor are safe."

She couldn't help but wonder if he was trying to convince her or himself. She didn't care, though. She cared only about being with him, as naked as he was now. So she shrugged off her robe and pulled her T-shirt over her head.

He sucked in a breath as his pupils dilated and his nostrils flared. "You are so damn beautiful."

Her hair was a mess, and her makeup all washed off, but he didn't seem to care—not with the way he stared at her, as if awed.

He made her feel beautiful. She smiled as pride swelled within her. But then she looked at him, standing so gloriously naked beside the bed, and she was suddenly humbled. He was all sculpted muscles—but for the scarred leg. But that only made him more attractive, since it was a badge of his courage and his determination. He was a hero.

Her hero.

She reached out for him, tugging him down onto the bed with her. She wrapped her arms around his neck and pulled his head down to hers. She kissed him with all of the desire raging inside her.

He kissed her back just as hungrily, his mouth moving sensually across her. His lips nipped at and nibbled hers. Pulling her bottom lip between his, he nipped at it lightly with his teeth before sliding his tongue across it and then into her mouth.

He made love to her mouth like she wanted him to make love to her body.

She arched up, rubbing her hips and breasts against him. His erection throbbed against her belly, pulsating with his passion.

"Forrest," she murmured against his mouth.

Then he moved his mouth, sliding his lips down her throat to the point where her pulse pounded madly with desire. Her heart racing, she nearly sobbed at the tension building inside her.

His soft hair tickled her skin as he moved his head lower, to her breasts. He kissed the full mounds before closing his lips over a taut nipple.

She cried out with pleasure as he tugged on it. Then he slid his tongue across it, and that pleasure flowed from the tip of her breast to her core, which pulsated with need. "Forrest…"

But he was moving again, his mouth sliding across her belly and over her mound. Then he touched her core, his tongue stroking over the most sensitive part of her.

She cried out softly as she came. But it wasn't enough.

She wanted more.

She wanted him.

All of him.

Filling her, like he had last night. Filling the emptiness she hadn't even realized she'd had, the hollow ache that she hadn't been aware of until he'd filled her, until he'd completed her.

He pulled back and fumbled around beside the bed. She spied the packet in his hand and took it from him. After tearing it open, she rolled the condom onto his throbbing erection.

He groaned as cords stood out in his neck and along his temple. "Rae, you're killing me."

She didn't want to do that, but someone did. Someone had tried…

She could have lost him. The thought filled her with horror and dread. And she reached out for him, clasping him closely, pressing kisses to his mouth and then his neck and his shoulder and his chest.

A growl emanated from his throat, and he lifted her as he crouched on the bed. Then he guided himself inside her.

As he filled her, she came again, her inner muscles clutching at him. He groaned and thrust again and again until he joined her in pleasure.

So much damn pleasure…

She'd never felt anything so intense, never known such pleasure existed. But he wasn't done—even though they'd both climaxed.

He kept touching her, kissing her, making her fall deeper and deeper in love with him. And now he was killing her—with pleasure.

FORREST COLTON WASN'T dead.

He should have been furious that his order hadn't been carried out. But just that attempt on Colton's life and the threats against the woman seemed to have distracted him from his cases.

So those threats and those attempts would have to keep happening to keep Detective Colton distracted. And if one of those attempts happened to succeed…

A grin curved his lips. He wouldn't give a damn about another life lost, since he hadn't given a damn about the first.

The only life he wanted to protect was his own.

Chapter Sixteen

A week had passed of Forrest keeping his distance from Rae and Connor. It was for the best—for them and for him. And probably for Whisperwood, as well. He could focus on his cases again.

He could focus on finding a killer who was probably the same person who'd run him and Connor off the road. The person who'd left those threats for Rae.

Her father?

Why would he have been gone for all of these years only to return and threaten her? It made no sense. But still…

He'd put out an APB for Beau Lemmon to be picked up for questioning. Forrest had a hell of a lot of questions for him. Like how he'd walked out on his sick wife and daughter, and how much he knew about that body buried in his backyard.

Rae's backyard now. The house was hers, along with whatever other estate her mother had left her. Would her father resent her over that enough to threaten her?

Realizing he was grasping at straws, Forrest sighed and focused on the other files on his desk. Patrice Eccleston's file. He wished it was thicker than it was, but the leads and clues were slim.

He still hadn't gotten back the lab results on those buttons, coins or whatever the hell it was he'd found at both crime scenes. The presence at both of them should have proved that the same killer had murdered the victims. But why had one body been mummified and the other not?

His head began to pound, and it had nothing to do with the yellowing bruise on his forehead. The bump had gone down, like the one on his knee. Frustration, not physical wounds, caused his aches. And not just frustration with the murder cases.

He was frustrated over not seeing Rae, over not being with Rae. He missed Connor, too, missed the innocence of the infant and the warmth and even the scent of him.

Powder and soap and...sometimes things that weren't all that sweet. His lips curved into a slight grin as he remembered the baby's spitting up all over his shirt.

And what that had led to.

He and Rae making love.

God, he missed her. So damn much.

"What the hell are you doing?" a voice demanded to know. "Daydreaming? You should be out tracking down my sister's killer, not snoozing behind your desk."

Ian Eccleston loomed over the partition wall of Forrest's cubicle in the Whisperwood Police Department. He didn't have a private office. Since he was only temporary, he was probably lucky he'd even been given a desk.

He snapped the folder shut and flipped it over so Ian wouldn't see the label that had the victim's name beneath the case number. He didn't want Patrice's brother to see how little information they had.

He also had a strange feeling about Ian Eccleston.

Maybe his anger was just one of the stages of grief. Or maybe it was something else.

"Do you have anything to share with me?" Forrest asked him. "Something you've remembered about your sister?"

The guy's face flushed as his temper grew hotter yet. "That's your job. I'm not doing your job for you."

"You want your sister's killer caught, don't you?" Forrest asked.

The guy jerked his head in a quick nod. "Yeah, but I ain't the detective. You are—though I checked you out, Colton, and all you do is cold cases."

"That was my last assignment with the Austin Police Department," he reminded the guy. "Not my only one."

"But you're probably focusing on those cold cases—those old bodies—not my sister's fresh one." He flinched as he said it, so maybe the guy really cared that his sister was dead. Or maybe this was all an act to throw suspicion off him.

Forrest flinched now at his own cynicism. When had he begun to suspect everyone? Why couldn't he look at people the way Rae did? Just because someone wasn't necessarily good didn't mean they were bad. They were just flawed. Maybe Ian Eccleston was just flawed, or maybe he was justifiably furious that his sister's killer was still running around free.

And she was dead.

Forrest tapped his fingers against that turned-over folder with the photos inside of her crime scene, of her corpse. No. Her brother didn't need to see the contents of her file, whether he was grieving or the killer.

He wasn't old enough to have committed the other murders, though. But he could have heard enough about them recently to try to copycat one.

Was that what Patrice's murder was? A copycat or the killer's comeback murder?

Had Beau Lemmon come back to Whisperwood?

"What are you doing to find Patrice's killer?" her brother asked.

"I'm not at liberty to discuss ongoing investigations," Forrest said.

Ian snorted. "That's the answer you and the chief keep giving in interviews," he said. "I'm not some nosy reporter. I have a right to know what you're doing to find my sister's killer."

Bracing his hand against the folder on his desk, Forrest used it to push himself up from his chair. Maybe he would need to walk Ian to the door. But before he could move away from his desk, a young female officer rushed up to them.

"Everything all right?" she asked as she glanced toward his unannounced visitor.

How had Ian gotten back to his cubicle?

Forrest nodded. "Mr. Eccleston was leaving."

"I'm not going anywhere until you give me some answers," Ian stubbornly insisted.

Forrest regretfully admitted, "I don't have any answers to give you."

Ian snorted. "And you're supposed to be some hot-shot Austin detective."

"I do have that information you requested on Beau Lemmon," the officer said, as if in Forrest's defense. "I emailed it to you."

"Do you know where he is?" he asked.

She shook her head.

"Beau Lemmon?" Ian asked, his forehead furrowed with confusion.

"Do you know him?" Forrest asked. "Did your sister know him?"

"No." Ian cursed. "This has nothing to do with her, does it?"

"We have several open cases," the officer answered for Forrest.

She might have thought she was helping him, but she only made Ian more furious. His face flushed an even brighter shade of red.

"And every one of those cases is more important to you than my sister is," Ian angrily exclaimed. He cursed both of them then before rushing out of the department.

"I'm sorry," the officer said.

He shook his head. "Not your fault." It was his for not finding Patrice's killer. "You weren't able to find Beau Lemmon yet?"

She sighed. "No, I'm sorry. But I did find some arrests on his record, which will give you an idea of where he's been and what he's been doing."

Forrest tapped his keyboard and pulled up his email. He found hers and opened the attachments, the arrest reports from Las Vegas PD and Reno PD and Atlantic City.

He sure as hell had pegged Beau Lemmon right. The guy was a gambler. But his arrests weren't for gambling—at least not directly. The money he'd stolen as a pickpocket and through breaking and entering had probably been to finance his gambling or to pay off debts.

If he was desperate enough to steal, what else might he be desperate enough to do? Kill?

THE OFFICER PULLED out his gun and pointed it at the door as someone stepped onto the porch.

"You can put that away," Rae said. "It's just one of my bosses from the law office."

Kenneth Dawson tapped his fingers lightly against the glass in the door before turning the knob. Rae gasped at his audacity. Maybe she shouldn't have had the officer re-holster his weapon. Catching the knob in her hand, she held it tightly, got behind the door and pulled it open just a few inches. But Kenneth pushed against it, trying to open it wider as he peered inside her house.

"What are you doing here?" she asked. She'd been working from home, but all her assignments had been emailed to her, not personally delivered.

"We're missing you at the office," he said. "Wanted to make sure everything was okay."

Maybe that was why he seemed so nosy. Or maybe that was just his personality—since he was the only one at the firm who fit the unflattering description of lawyers being ambulance chasers. Had he chased one here?

Had someone found another body nearby? She couldn't see around him, though, since he blocked the entire doorway, trying to force his way inside.

Knowing the officer was close, she stepped back and let him in the door. He tensed as he noticed the young officer standing behind her. She was glad that it was Officer Baker's shift; the guy was bigger than some body builders.

"Looks like I was right to check up on you," Kenneth said. "Is everything okay?"

Officer Baker didn't say anything. Maybe he wasn't allowed to comment.

Rae had already told the law-firm partners about the threats and that she didn't want to put anyone else at work in danger with her presence. Hadn't they shared that information with Kenneth?

And if not, why not?

Didn't they trust him?

Should she?

He had never actually done anything that had made her uncomfortable, though, until the other day. Something about the way he'd looked at her, and the questions he'd asked her about Forrest—it had all felt inappropriate to her.

Like his showing up here.

"Detective Colton is concerned about my safety," she said.

"Detective Colton," he repeated the name, his voice sharp with something like resentment.

But why would he resent Forrest? He was older than Forrest—probably at least a decade older—so they hadn't grown up together. Their paths could have crossed in law enforcement, though.

"Where is Detective Colton now?" Kenneth asked, and he glanced around her house, as if looking for him.

She flinched. Forrest had said he was going to stay away for her and Connor's safety. But she suspected he was just avoiding her. While he desired her, he obviously didn't want the responsibility of a ready-made family.

When she'd chosen to become a single mother, she'd known that some men might be turned off by the prospect of raising a child that wasn't theirs. But she'd figured she wouldn't be interested in those men anyway. That wasn't the case with Forrest. She was more than just interested in him; she was infatuated.

"You and the detective aren't on a first-name basis?" Kenneth asked, a smirk twisting his thin lips.

Heat rushed to her face, but she was not about to discuss her relationship with Forrest with a colleague. Not that she had a relationship with him. She hadn't even heard from him over the past week.

But he always called whatever officer was guarding her at the moment. Predictably this officer's phone rang. Baker pulled it out and, as he glanced at the screen, remarked, "This is Detective Colton now. I should take this."

He hesitated, though, before clicking the accept button. "Will you be okay if I step outside?" he asked.

She wanted to tell him no, but she didn't want to offend Kenneth. His father-in-law was one of the partners. Because of that, surely she could trust him not to try anything with her. After all he was married to his boss's daughter.

She nodded. "Sure, I'll be fine."

"Of course she will," Kenneth told the officer, using his hand to wave him off.

The young man's brow furrowed, but the phone continued to ring, so he opened the door and stepped onto the porch. As the door closed behind him, panic settled on Rae's chest. Maybe it was just that she hadn't been without security the past week, or maybe it was that something about Kenneth scared her now.

Before she could figure out the reason for her uneasiness, a cry emanated from the nursery. She nearly breathed a sigh of relief as she hurried toward her son. As she leaned over the crib railing to pick him up, she heard a strange noise and turned around to find that Kenneth had followed her.

And he was staring at her ass as she leaned over her child. Too bad she was wearing shorts instead of jeans.

She hurriedly picked up Connor and turned so that her son was a shield between her and her colleague.

But Kenneth stepped forward and reached for one of Connor's kicking feet. "Look at you, you're so cute," he cooed.

Connor stiffened and cried louder with either fear or dislike. He was apparently not a fan of Kenneth's either. Not that she hadn't been...until that day she'd found the threat on her desk and Forrest and Connor had been run off the road. But maybe that had just made her paranoid.

"He's not a happy baby, huh?" Kenneth remarked.

"Usually he is," she said. With the exception of those colicky nights he'd kept her awake. He'd never cried when Forrest had touched him; in fact he'd stopped crying for Forrest.

But Forrest wasn't here. And he probably wasn't coming back—even after he caught the killer. Because once the killer was caught, he would be able to leave. Return to his job in Austin or find a permanent job somewhere else.

She pushed that thought from her mind as she focused on her child. She changed him into a dry diaper and onesie, but he didn't stop crying.

"Is he hungry?" Kenneth asked. "Do you need to breastfeed?" His gaze dropped to her chest, as if he expected her to start right now, right in front of him.

"I don't breastfeed anymore," she said. Just because of the stress of her busy schedule, she hadn't been able to produce much milk. And now with the stress of those threats and the danger she and Connor were in, she hadn't been able to produce any at all.

"Poor little guy," Kenneth said with a smirk. "No wonder he's unhappy."

She couldn't suppress the shudder of revulsion over

his comment. "I need to take care of him," she said, "so you should probably leave."

"But I came all this way to check on you," he said.

"And I'm fine," she said. Thanks to Forrest's making sure she had protection.

But now Forrest's phone call had drawn that protection away from her. She had a feeling she might need him back...because Kenneth kept coming closer.

She didn't want to lose her job, but she wasn't going to tolerate any harassment either. "I can't remember— do you and your wife have children?" she asked.

He shuddered now. "God, no."

She sucked in a breath.

"I just mean—we're too young," he said.

He was older than she was.

"And too busy," he added.

His wife didn't work. Neither of them was as busy as Rae was. But she wouldn't judge him for not wanting children any more than she wanted people judging her for wanting them so much that she'd chosen to raise her son alone.

"I know you're busy," she said. "So I appreciate you stopping by to check on me. But I wouldn't want to keep you."

His blue eyes narrowed now, as it must have finally occurred to him that she was trying to get rid of him. "What's the matter, Rae? Don't you want me in your house?"

She suspected that wasn't where he really wanted to be. He wanted to be where Forrest had been—in her bed. But Forrest had left her bed and never returned.

She didn't want any other man in it, though. Especially after that.

She was never going to trust another man to get that close to her. But Kenneth was leaning closer, over Connor.

With a silent plea for forgiveness, she thrust her son into his arms. "You want to hold him?"

The baby squirmed and screamed in his awkward embrace. And he hurriedly handed back her son. "No, no, I don't want to hold him."

Forrest hadn't reacted like that when she'd thrust Connor into his arms that first morning he'd showed up in her backyard. He'd held him and soothed him better than she'd been able to.

He was so good with Connor. And with her.

But it didn't seem like he was ever coming back. She didn't want Kenneth to come back either.

"You're lucky he didn't throw up on you," she said with a slight smile. "He has a tendency to do that."

Kenneth recoiled even more. "Well, I better be going then." He walked out of the nursery, but instead of heading to the front door, he walked to the back door and peered into the yard.

"Your car is out front," she reminded him as she followed him into the kitchen.

"Crime scene's out there," he murmured, as he stared at the hole in the ground. Yellow tape dangled from posts that had been pounded into the ground around it. "So that's where the body was found."

Again, it wasn't a question. He knew.

From what he'd heard on the police scanner? Or for another reason?

Even though the air-conditioning wasn't doing much to cool the house, she shivered. She hated this, hated suspecting everyone around her.

But there was just something so damn creepy about Kenneth now. But was he creepy enough to be a killer?

Chapter Seventeen

Maybe it was Ian's visit earlier that day that had unsettled Forrest. Or had it been his phone call to the officer on protection duty that had done it?

What the hell had Kenneth Dawson been doing at Rae's house? He could have been bringing her work. But wasn't most office work done electronically now? Forrest suspected work wasn't why Kenneth had stopped by; he'd wanted to see Rae.

Forrest did, too. Maybe that was the reason for his current state of restlessness. A week was just too damn long for him to go without seeing Rae and Connor, without personally making sure that they were all right. Without touching her, kissing her…being with her…

Not that he expected her to welcome him back into her arms or her bed. She probably felt that he'd abandoned her, the way her father had abandoned her mother when she'd needed him most. But Rae didn't really need Forrest.

Nobody did.

Other—more able-bodied—officers would do a better job protecting her and Connor. Forrest couldn't chase down a suspect—couldn't run off a threat—the way the more physically capable officers could.

And those other officers weren't in danger like Forrest was either. They wouldn't endanger her and Connor with their very presence like he did.

But nothing else had happened to him after he and Connor had been run off the road. Nobody had made another attempt on his life. So maybe the person just wanted him out of Rae's and Connor's lives.

But why?

So he could insinuate himself there? Like Kenneth Dawson might have tried this afternoon? Had that been the purpose of his visit? Or had he been scoping out the situation to return later?

A chill chased down Forrest's spine with the horrific thought. Maybe no more attempts had been made in the past week because the killer had been taking his time to plot his next attack so that he would succeed.

But what was his goal? To get rid of Forrest or of Rae and Connor?

NOBODY KNEW THIS place better than he did. Hell, he was the only one who knew the body had been buried here. Well, not the only one.

The discovery of that body should have served as a big enough distraction, should have kept the damn police department busy trying to figure out who the victim was and what had happened to her. But it hadn't been enough.

At least not to the person who now held his debt. He—whoever the hell he was—wanted more from him. Wanted blood.

Murder.

He'd almost pulled it off when he'd forced the detective to drive into that parked car. But somehow Detective Colton had survived. So had the baby.

Not that he'd wanted to hurt the baby. He hadn't. But he didn't want to get hurt either.

And that was going to happen if he didn't do more to get rid of Colton. He had to send the stubborn detective a real message. A message that no matter what Forrest Colton did—or how many people he had protecting the house—Rae and the baby weren't safe.

Nobody was.

Keeping to the shadows, he moved closer to the back of the house. The plastic tape strewn around that hole fluttered in the slight breeze. He didn't need the tape to know where that hole was; he'd dug up most of it himself. And a few other damn holes before he'd remembered where it was.

Rae hadn't seen him then. She hadn't seen him once since he had returned to Whisperwood. Maybe that needed to change.

Maybe he needed to talk to her—to make her understand...

But to get close to her, he had to get rid of her protection. The moonlight illuminated most of the yard, enough that he could see a rock lying among the mound of dirt. He picked it up in his gloved hand and tossed it, not at the house, but at the barbecue grill sitting on the back patio.

Metal clanged. And a light came on inside the kitchen, and then another beside the back door that illuminated the patio. His heart pounding, he ducked into the shadows again. He had to do this, had to be ready. So he reached into his back pocket, where he'd tucked another weapon—a long pipe—and he pulled that out. And he waited.

It didn't take the officer long to open the door and

step onto the patio. He came out with his gun drawn, though. A pipe would be no match for a bullet.

So he needed the element of surprise. Too bad he hadn't picked up two damn rocks.

But as fate would have it, something else moved in the darkness. Undoubtedly an animal.

It rustled the brush just beyond the hole in the yard and drew the officer farther from the house. With his gun pointing toward the brush, he walked right past the shadows where his assailant hid.

Once he passed, his assailant struck out, swinging the pipe at the back of his head. It connected hard, knocking him to the ground.

He made no sound.

No movement.

Was he unconscious or dead?

A twinge of regret struck his heart, which most people probably suspected he didn't even possess. But he had one. As always, though, most of his love was for himself. He was a hell of lot more concerned about his own life than anyone else's.

So he left the officer lying on the ground, and he headed toward the house. After he closed his hand around the knob of the back door, he tried to turn it, but it refused to budge. The damn cop had locked it behind himself.

Maybe he'd suspected the noise had been a ruse to draw him out of the house. Maybe he'd already called for backup in case he didn't return.

But what if he had locked it, he must have had a key on him—some way to get back inside the house. The key was no longer under the pot on the front porch.

If only that had been Colton's skull he'd struck with the pipe...

If the officer had called for backup, it probably would have been Colton. So maybe there would be a chance to strike him yet.

To get rid of him for good.

If the officer hadn't called him, Rae would when she heard him coming. So he swung his pipe again, this time at the window in the locked door. The sound of glass breaking shattered the quiet of the night.

THE OFFICER HAD already warned Rae that he was heading outside to investigate a noise he'd heard. He'd locked the door behind himself and had advised her to open it only for him. He'd only been gone moments when someone had tried to turn the knob. He'd known it was locked; he'd locked it himself.

So he wouldn't have done that, not without alerting her first. He wasn't the one trying to open that door. Fear coursing through her, she'd headed toward the nursery, where Connor was sleeping. Or had been sleeping.

The tinkling explosion of shattered glass awakened him with a scream on his lips. Rae didn't go right to his crib, though. Instead she closed and locked his door behind her.

But was the lock enough?

It was one of those that could be picked with a paperclip. So she pushed her shoulder against his dresser, sliding it across the floor—the legs of it scraping the wood—until it blocked the door. But she'd been able to move it, and she wasn't very big. Someone else would surely be able to move it aside to get to them.

Heart pounding with panic, she rushed around the room, grabbing things to pile on or push against the dresser. She had to make it impossible to move. She had to keep out the threat against her son and her.

But what about the young officer?

What had happened to him?

Was he okay?

She needed to call for help for him and for them. But her house was so far from town that it would be too late for help to arrive—if she didn't manage to keep the intruder out of the nursery.

Away from Connor.

Guilt tore at her—over the officer, over Connor's crying.

And tears stung her eyes, blurring her vision. She blinked them back. She had to be able to see as she pulled her phone from the pocket of her robe.

She should have called for help the minute the officer had stepped outside. Or she should have insisted that he wait for backup before going out there. But he'd shrugged off her concern, assuring her that it was probably just an animal that had made the noise.

It had been.

The human kind of animal—the kind who kills young women and threatens babies and…

She flinched at the thought of what could have happened to the cop. Her fingers trembling, she could barely work her phone, but she managed to find the emergency call button.

A dispatcher would find a close officer—would send the person who could get to the house the fastest. That person wasn't Forrest.

She had no idea where he was or what he was doing. But even if he'd been close, she wouldn't want him here. She didn't want whatever had happened to that officer to happen to Forrest. He'd already been hurt once because of her; she didn't want him hurt again.

"9-1-1. What's your emergency?" asked a voice emanating from her phone.

She could barely hear it over Connor's crying and now over the sound of someone banging against her door.

"Someone's broken in to my house," Rae said. "And I think they hurt an officer—"

"There was already an officer at the scene?"

"Yes," Rae said. Then, knowing that it wasn't always possible for GPS locating to work in her area, she gave her name and address. "Please hurry!"

But no matter how close other police officers were, they wouldn't get to her and Connor in time to save them from the intruder. Something hacked away at the door, something metallic that clanged against the doorknob. It was only a matter of time before the jamb broke and the intruder pushed his way inside to her and Connor.

She planted herself between the doorway and the crib as she looked for a weapon she could use to defend herself and her son. Because whoever this intruder was, however big he was, he wasn't getting to her child—not without one hell of a fight.

Chapter Eighteen

Not wanting to sneak up on Rae's bodyguard, Forrest had called the young officer to let him know he was driving out to her place. But the call went unanswered.

And so did the next one.

And the one after that.

Why the hell wasn't Officer Baker picking up?

Forrest was already pulling into her driveway when the dispatcher's voice emanated from his police radio. "Break-in in progress…"

He didn't even have to hear the address to know that it was Rae's.

"Possible officer down," the dispatcher continued. "He's not responding to radio calls…"

Forrest cursed. He'd known how dangerous the assignment was; he'd been run off the road and injured himself. Guilt weighed heavily on him for putting the young officer in danger and Rae…

He pushed aside thoughts of what could have happened to Rae and Connor. She'd called for help. She was still alive. She had to be.

The call hadn't come in that long ago, and he was here. He stomped on the brakes, slammed the shifter into Park and threw open the door of the SUV. Drawing his weapon from his holster, he headed toward the house. He hurried up the couple of steps to the porch and crossed it to grasp the doorknob with his free hand. It didn't turn; the front door was locked. The intruder hadn't gotten in this way, or if he had, he'd locked the door behind himself.

In his early days of law enforcement, he would have kicked down the door, but if he tried that now, he would mess up all of the rods and pins holding his leg together. Instead he rammed his shoulder against the door over and over until finally the jamb splintered and the dead bolt broke free. He shoved open the door and rushed inside just as a dark figure ran through the kitchen.

"Stop! Police!" he yelled as he raised his weapon. But the man didn't stop. He shoved open the back door and rushed outside.

Forrest couldn't shoot someone in the back, no matter how much he didn't want him getting away. He wanted, even more, to make sure that Rae and Connor were all right, though. Connor's cries rang out, accompanied by Rae's soft, reassuring murmurs.

They were okay. The pressure of guilt eased only slightly on his chest. He had to check for the officer—and try to stop the intruder from getting away. Forcing his leg to move faster, he rushed across the kitchen. But as he headed out the back door, Rae called after him, "Don't go!"

He turned back to make sure she was all right. She stood in the doorway to the nursery, but furniture blocked most of her from view. She'd barricaded the door.

Of course she had; she would have done anything to protect her son, whom she was cradling in her arms.

"Don't go!" she said. "He must have hurt the officer."

That was why he needed to go. And she knew it.

"Barricade yourself back inside," he told her. "Other officers are on their way."

"Then wait!" she said.

He didn't have time to argue, so he just pulled open the back door and headed off into the night. The officer had to be out here somewhere, but Forrest didn't call out to him. Instead he just listened.

The silence was all-encompassing—eerily so. If the intruder was running away, why couldn't Forrest hear his footsteps against the ground, or the rustle of brush as he ran from the yard?

He hadn't talked to Rae that long, hadn't given the intruder that much time to get away. Of course the guy could move faster than Forrest could. Because of the damage to his leg, anybody could move faster than he could. That was why he'd considered it smarter to have someone else guard Rae and Connor. But he'd put that officer in danger.

And now he had to find him and help him if he could.

If he wasn't already too late.

Grasping his gun tightly, he moved away from the light on the back patio, toward the shadows. The officer had to be out here somewhere. Officer Baker was too loyal a lawman to have skipped out on security duty.

The crime-scene tape fluttered in the light breeze, drawing Forrest to the area where he'd found the body. And sure enough, he found another body—lying face-down beside that hole. It was nearly as lifeless as the first one he had found. The officer didn't move, murmur or groan.

Forrest hunched down and felt for a pulse in the officer's muscular neck. A faint beat fluttered beneath his fingertips. He was alive. But just barely.

Blood pooled beneath his head from a nasty-looking

gash on the back of his skull. Even if he survived, he might never be the same—like Forrest.

Something skittered across the patio stones, something that could have been a shoe scraping across the bricks. Was the intruder hiding somewhere in the shadows, like the shooter had been all of those months ago? Was he waiting to attack when Forrest would least expect it?

CHIEF ARCHER THOMPSON cursed himself as much as he cursed what he'd heard of the dispatcher's call. *Possible officer down...*

Damn it. He should have taken those threats more seriously against Rae Lemmon. Now another officer had probably been hurt protecting her and her baby, just like Forrest Colton had been hurt. Holding his cell phone in his hand, he punched in the contact for Detective Colton. A deep voice answered, but the message was prerecorded, promising a call back when he was available.

Forrest hadn't called in his location, but Archer knew where he was. At Rae Lemmon's.

No matter where he'd been, the detective probably would have made damn certain he was first on the scene.

Archer cursed again. He was good friends with Hays and Josephine Colton. The last thing he ever wanted to do was have to notify them that they'd lost one of their sons—especially on his watch.

His watch?

Hell, he hadn't been watching anything. Consumed with thoughts of how he'd failed his sister, he'd started failing his officers, as well.

As he shoved his phone into his pocket, he pulled

out the keys to his SUV. He wouldn't be the first on the scene; he already knew that. But he was going to damn well show up and do whatever he could to save his officers.

And the woman and her baby.

Rae had been terrified when the intruder had been fighting to get inside the nursery. Even though he was gone, she was no less afraid; she just wasn't worried about her and Connor right now. Sirens, ringing out in the distance, announced the imminent arrival of the officers Forrest had said were coming.

But would they get to the house in time to help Forrest? And to help the young officer? Something must have happened to him; he hadn't come back.

Would the intruder?

She shivered as she considered that he might have pulled the same trick on Forrest that he had on the officer. Lure him outside, disable him and then return for her and Connor.

Forrest had told her to barricade herself and Connor back inside the nursery. But as she tried to pull the door closed, it bounced back open against the splintered jamb. The intruder had been determined to get inside—to get to them.

She shuddered as she relived the terror of those moments when the intruder had been so close to them, to hurting her son like his threats had promised. But then Forrest had rushed to her rescue—again.

At risk of endangering his own life.

He wasn't rushing back inside. Was it because he was busy helping the officer?

Or had something happened to him?

Fear had her heart pounding frantically, and Connor,

clasped in her arms, must have felt that fear, as he continued to scream despite her efforts to comfort him. But she struggled to comfort Connor, because she needed comfort so badly herself.

But only one person could offer her that: Forrest.

She needed him to come back to her. She needed him to be safe and unhurt.

Each minute he stayed outside dragged on and on and increased her fear. If not for Connor, she would have gone outside to look for Forrest—to make certain he was all right. But she couldn't put the baby in danger.

Why was he in danger?

What did the intruder want from her? She couldn't stop the murder investigation. She couldn't stop Forrest from doing his job.

But the intruder could.

And maybe he had.

Where the hell was Forrest?

She heard footsteps against the hardwood as someone came in through the front door. But no voice called out to her. It wasn't him.

He'd gone out the back, so he wouldn't have come in the front. But the intruder might have—if he'd circled around the house to come back for her and Connor.

Using her hip, she shoved the dresser back against the battered door to the nursery. It hadn't kept the intruder out last time, though.

And she doubted it would keep him out any longer this time.

Chapter Nineteen

The ambulance tore out of the driveway, lights flashing and sirens blaring. The chief had climbed into the back with the young officer. Two police vehicles drove in front of it and one behind to escort the fallen officer safely to the hospital.

Officer Baker had regained consciousness while Forrest had been checking his pulse. Baker's first concern had been for Rae and Connor, though, not for himself.

He was a good cop. And since he'd been so lucid, Forrest was fairly confident that he'd be all right. He'd been tempted to climb into the ambulance, along with the chief, and make sure the officer arrived at the hospital. But the cop wasn't the only one in danger.

Rae and Connor were also in danger, since the intruder had tried so hard to get to them again.

What had he intended to do to them?

Hurt them?

Kill them?

Killing them wouldn't get Forrest to back off from finding the killer. It would make him so much more determined to stop the guy so that he wouldn't be able to hurt anyone else. Ever.

So, was it the killer?

Or was it someone else?

Someone who might have cased the situation earlier that day when he'd come to visit her.

After watching the ambulance disappear from sight, Forrest walked back into the house. He wasn't the only member of law enforcement who'd stayed behind. In addition to the officers fixing the locks and the broken window of the kitchen door, there was a whole crew of techs in the backyard, looking for evidence from the officer's attack. A few other officers searched the property for the intruder. If he was here, they would find him.

But Forrest was pretty damn certain he'd gotten away. Again.

If only he'd moved faster—if only he'd been *able* to move faster—he might have caught the son of a bitch before he'd even gotten out of the house. He knew he should appoint one of the other officers to protect Connor and Rae. But an image of burly Officer Baker, bleeding and unconscious, burned in his mind.

Forrest didn't want to put anyone else in danger.

But he sure as hell didn't want Rae and Connor in danger either.

She pulled the nursery door shut behind her and joined him in the living room. "Is Officer Baker going to be all right?" she asked anxiously.

He lifted his shoulders in a slight shrug. "I don't know for certain, but he had regained consciousness and was lucid when I found him."

She expelled a little ragged sigh. "That's a good sign then."

It didn't mean he was out of danger, though.

Neither was she.

Yet.

"You need to pack up some stuff for you and Connor," he said. "We need to get you out of here." He should have made her leave the house when he'd first found that body in her backyard—then she wouldn't have been threatened at all.

But the intruder had left a note at her office, too.

Maybe it wouldn't matter where she went; she would still be in danger.

She shook her head. "No. I just finally got Connor settled down again. I don't want to risk waking him up."

"But you're not safe here," Forrest said. "Surely you realize that now."

"I wasn't safe with one officer," she said. But she gestured at him and at the officers who were finishing up with the locks. "But there are more than one here now."

"Not for much longer," Forrest said.

"We're actually done now," one of the young cops chimed into the conversation.

Forrest nodded his permission. "You can leave now."

While they left, Rae stared at him with narrowed eyes.

"They want to get to the hospital to check on their friend," he told her.

She flinched. "Of course. I'm sorry. You probably want to do that, too."

"I'm not leaving you here," he said. "You need to come with me."

"Where?" she asked, and her fear cracked her voice when she added, "Where will Connor and I be safe?"

"With me," he said.

"Then stay," she said. "Stay with me."

IT WAS SELFISH. Rae knew it the moment the words had left her lips. She was putting him in danger again. But the break-in had scared her so badly that she didn't care how selfish she was being. She just wanted to feel safe again, and she only felt safe with Forrest.

"I'm not leaving," Forrest said, "without you."

"I'm not going anywhere tonight," she said. "Connor has already been through enough."

"And if the intruder returns?" Forrest asked.

She gestured at the backyard, which was aglow with lights from the crime-scene technicians. "He might have been brave enough to take on one police officer—but a whole yard of them?" She shook her head. "He's not that..."

What was he?

Why was he so determined to hurt her or Connor? Or was he trying to hurt Forrest?

The best thing she could do for Forrest was to send him away. But he was the only one who really made her feel safe—when she was in his arms. She didn't want him to leave, but she didn't want him winding up in an ambulance. Again.

"We don't know what he is," Forrest finished for her. "Or do you know now? Did you see him?" He stepped closer to her and wrapped his big hands around her arms.

She could feel the strength in those hands and the heat of his touch through the thin material of her summer robe. Her skin tingled, and awareness and desire coursed through her. She shook her head, as much in denial of those feelings as in response to his question.

"But he'd broken open the nursery door," Forrest said, almost as if he doubted her.

"I didn't see him," she said. "I just saw the nursery door being pushed in—along with the furniture I'd stacked behind it—after he broke the lock on it."

"How do you know it's a man then?" he asked.

She opened her mouth then closed it again, pausing to think before replying. "I don't know. I just assumed since he hurt the officer and broke down the door..." Heat rushed to her face with embarrassment that she would be so sexist. "But that doesn't mean that a woman couldn't have done that, as well."

"She could have," Forrest agreed. "You stacked all that furniture against the nursery door."

"To protect my son," she said.

He nodded. "I've seen the strength a mother can summon when her child is in danger."

She didn't know if he was referring to something he'd witnessed while working in Austin or as a volunteer with the Cowboy Heroes or...

He slid his hands up to her biceps and gently squeezed. And she knew; he was talking about her. "You're amazing."

She shrugged. "I'm not so sure about that. I don't know what I would have done if you hadn't showed up when you did."

"You would have fought him off as long as you could," he said, flinching as if the thought brought him pain.

"Him?" she questioned. "Did you see him when you rushed in?"

"Not his face," he said. "But from his build, I believe the intruder was male."

He sounded like a cop. He also sounded as if he was keeping something from her. He might not have seen the guy's face, but he might have recognized something else about him.

"Do you have some idea who it is?" she asked.

"I am looking into leads," he said.

"Who?" she asked.

"Is it just a coincidence that the intruder breaks in after your boss visited today?"

"Boss?" she asked, struggling to focus. Maybe it was because his hands were still on her arms, almost stroking her muscles now. Maybe it was because she wasn't sure what he was talking about. "What…? Oh, Kenneth. He's not actually my boss." Which was good because she probably would have had to quit now.

As it was, she wasn't sure how to handle that situation. If she reported him, would anyone believe that he'd stepped out of line with her? Had he? Or was he just naturally kind of creepy?

"What is he?" Forrest asked, his voice suddenly very gruff, and his deep-set hazel eyes were intense as he stared down at her.

"A colleague," she said. "Sometimes I work on his cases, but not very often, and he never assigns the work to me."

"Then why was he here today?" Forrest asked as he continued to stare at her with such intensity, it almost made her think that he was jealous.

Over her?

Did she mean more to him than an assignment, than someone to protect?

"Why do you care?" she wondered aloud.

"I'm investigating murders and those threats," he said, "so I need to know everything I can about possible suspects, about someone who might have had access to your backyard."

She pointed out the kitchen window, but the lights had gone out now. The technicians must have finished processing the scene. "I would say anyone, but…"

He glanced out the window, too.

And she shivered. "They're gone now."

"The techs, yeah," he said. "But I have a unit posted at the end of your driveway, and another officer will remain in the backyard." He glanced out the kitchen door, his brow furrowing with concern. Clearly he felt as bad as she did that the officer had been harmed protecting her.

"I hope he'll be all right," she said.

He nodded. "Me, too."

The wounded officer wasn't her only concern, though. She didn't want Forrest getting hurt, as well. "With all that protection, I don't need you to stay here, too," she said. "You can go home."

He shook his head. "No, I can't."

"But you said there are other officers—"

He leaned down and brushed his mouth across hers. "I can't leave you," he said.

Relief and desire rushed through her, and she reached out, winding her arms around his lean waist. She wanted to hang on to him for comfort, for pleasure—forever.

But she knew better than to plan on anyone sticking around forever. So she would just make herself be happy with another night with Forrest. Keeping her arms around him, she walked backward toward her bedroom, tugging him along with her.

He stumbled a bit, and she worried that he'd hurt his leg. But then he reached down and lifted her into his arms and carried her toward her bedroom. So there was nothing wrong with his leg; he was just as impatient to be together again as she was. After shouldering open her bedroom door, he pressed it closed the same way and carried her to the bed across which law books were strewn.

"Always working," he murmured, and he stared

down at her with something like awe on his handsome face.

"So are you," she said.

Dark circles rimmed his beautiful eyes, and she knew he'd given up sleep to work his cases. And now he was giving up more sleep to be with her.

He shook his head. "It isn't work being with you. It's pleasure."

That was what he gave to her...when he peeled off her robe and her T-shirt. He pressed his lips to every inch of her body, kissing and teasing with his tongue until she quivered from the ecstasy gripping her body.

He made love to her thoroughly before he even took off his own clothes. Then she kissed every inch of skin he exposed, every muscle, every scar.

She made love to him with her mouth, and with her entire heart—because it was his. He just didn't know it, and she didn't want him to know. She didn't want to be disappointed.

But physically he didn't disappoint. He teased her nipples into taut peaks and made her throb and squirm with the tension that built inside her. Then finally he sheathed himself in a condom, and he filled her.

He filled that hollow place inside her. He completed her, and she clutched at him, matching his frantic rhythm until finally they came—together. The power of their climax rocked and humbled Rae. She'd never felt so much ever—even with him.

The words burned in her throat, the love she felt for him. But maybe it was just the passion. So she held the words inside even as the feeling overwhelmed her. As he overwhelmed her.

"CAN'T YOU DO anything right?" the voice on the phone asked him.

He flinched at the question—flinched because he already knew the answer. No. He couldn't do anything right. He never had.

Whenever he'd tried, he usually only made a bigger mess of things. Of his life and everyone else's.

That was why it was better when he was gone— for all those left behind, but he couldn't leave yet. He couldn't leave with the debt being held over his head right now.

"I don't know what you mean," he lied.

But the caller—whoever the hell he was—snorted in disbelief. "Yeah, right. You screwed up again and you damn well know it."

How did *he* know? Who was he? Did he have eyes and ears everywhere?

Maybe his wasn't the only debt this guy had bought. Or maybe he had other means to control and manipulate other people.

"How did I screw up?" he asked. "No cop is working the murder cases right now. Everybody's trying to figure out who hurt the cop."

Such a long pause followed his pronouncement that he would have thought the caller had hung up on him if not for his cell screen showing that the unknown number was still connected to his. He hadn't answered it the first time the number had called his, but then the notes had started appearing under the door of his motel room.

The threats.

"If just a cop getting hurt distracted the Whisperwood PD this much, then what will happen when you kill one?" the caller questioned.

"You want me to kill a cop." It wasn't a question. He knew this guy—whoever he was—wasn't playing.

"The cop or your kid—you choose."

There was no choice. He'd already cost his kid too damn much to cost her anything else.

Chapter Twenty

What the hell was wrong with him? Why couldn't he keep his hands off Rae Lemmon? It wasn't just his hands he needed to keep off her, though. It was his lips and his body and his...

Forrest swallowed the groan burning his throat and resisted—just barely—the urge to turn around and go back to Rae's bedroom, back to Rae. He still wanted her so badly. But giving in to that desire—again—had been a mistake.

He was supposed to be protecting her and Connor, and he wasn't doing a very damn good job when he kept letting desire distract him from his duty. He pushed open the broken door to the nursery and crossed the room to the crib.

The baby slept peacefully; his little rosebud lips parted on a soft sigh. His face was flushed, either from the ordeal he'd been through earlier that evening or from the heat in the room.

The air-conditioning unit either wasn't big enough to cool off the ranch house that much, or it was old and needed repairs. It just cut the heat and humidity a little bit, but not enough to really cool off the house, though. The night air might have been cooler than the faint trickle of air emanating from the ducts, but it was too risky to open windows.

Too risky with the intruder determined to get to Connor and Rae.

But why?

What could they have to do with the murder investigation—besides the fact that a body had been found in their backyard? Not that it had been all that accidentally found, like Jonah and Maggie had found the body of the chief's long-missing sister.

Forrest was pretty damn sure the body he'd found had been purposely dug up. Why? And who would know it had been there besides the killer?

"Do you know, Connor?" he asked the baby as he reached into the crib and ran his hand over the infant's soft hair. His blood heated with the memory of someone snipping off a lock of that hair to leave on Rae's pillow with the note.

His gut clenched with anger and guilt that she'd had to go through that, that someone was putting her through a mother's worst nightmare—someone threatening her child.

His hand trembled a little against Connor's head, and another little sigh slipped out of the baby's mouth. Not wanting to frighten him any more than he'd already been that night, Forrest pulled his hand away.

He had to make sure that Connor didn't get scared again. He had to make sure that the baby and the baby's mother stayed safe. As he left the nursery, he pulled the door as closed as it could get in the broken jamb and headed into the kitchen. He took out his cell phone and connected himself with the unit guarding the driveway at the street.

"This is Detective Colton. Is everything all right?"

"Except for the chief picking up his vehicle a while ago, there has been no sign of anyone else on the property, sir," the officer replied.

Heat rushed to Forrest's face. The chief had been here while he'd been distracted with Rae. Had he looked into the house? Had he seen that Forrest hadn't been protecting them like he'd promised?

Then the other reason for the chief leaving the hospital sunk into Forrest, and a twinge of guilt struck his heart. "Is Officer Baker all right?" he asked. The chief wouldn't have left him if he wasn't—unless there'd been nothing more for him to do.

"He has a concussion and skull fracture and will have to stay a couple of days in the hospital, but the doctor told the chief and Officer Baker's family that he should be just fine."

Forrest uttered a heavy sigh of relief. "That's great."

He should have checked on him sooner for himself. But he could barely think when he was close to Rae. And when he was touching her, he couldn't think at all. That was why he needed to stay away from her. "What about the officer posted in the backyard?" he asked as he peered out the door, into the night. "Where's he?"

"Backyard?"

"At the crime scene."

"He left with the technicians," the officer replied. "He thought he was only supposed to guard them while they were working."

Forrest swallowed a curse. He was such a damn fool with Rae's and Connor's safety.

Despite his efforts to muffle his oath, the officer must have heard it. "Really, sir, we haven't seen anyone lurking around the property, and with the exception of the chief, nobody has come and gone."

But what if the intruder had still been somewhere on the property? What if he'd hidden somewhere and the officers at the scene hadn't found him?

Then he could be somewhere close—too close for Forrest's comfort. He reached for his holster and drew his gun from it. "I think I'll walk around the house myself, just to make sure everything's okay."

"Sir, one of us can come up and do that for you," the officer offered.

"No," he said. "I could use the air." The air to clear his head, and the distance from Rae so that he could stop being so damn distracted with how he felt about her.

With how much he felt for her. Too damn much.

"After what happened to Officer Baker, are you sure it's safe?" the officer asked.

"You said nobody's come and gone," Forrest reminded the officer. "So it should be safe."

But despite the warmth in the house, a chill raced down his spine, raising goose bumps on his skin. And he knew…

The threat was still here—still too damn close to Connor and Rae. Forrest needed to find it and remove it.

"Do you want us to check in with you at a certain time and make sure everything's okay at the house?" the officer asked.

"Yes," Forrest agreed. That way, if his suspicion was right, there would be protection for Rae. "And if you don't hear from me, come up right away," he advised. "Or if you hear anything suspicious."

Like his gun firing.

He wouldn't mind shooting the son of a bitch who'd been terrorizing Rae and Connor. He wouldn't mind at all.

"Will do, Detective," the officer replied. "But I'm sure we'll be hearing from you soon."

He hoped. But that chill chased down his spine again. He clicked off the cell and reached for the handle of the back door. Maybe he should have woken up Rae to let her know he was going outside. But he didn't want to worry her if there was no reason for his concern.

After all, the officers at the driveway hadn't seen anyone coming and going but the chief. And the chief must not have seen anyone either. So really, maybe the fear Forrest felt had nothing to do with something outside and everything to do with what was inside the house.

Rae.

Connor.

And his feelings for them.

If he went back into the bedroom, he wouldn't just wake up Rae. He would slide into that bed with her, take her in his arms and make love to her all over again.

His body tensed just thinking about it, about her and how damn much he wanted her. But giving in to that desire he felt for her was a betrayal of the promise he'd made to protect her and Connor. And too many people had already broken their promises to Rae.

He didn't want to be the next man to let her down. So he drew in a breath, unlocked the door and pulled it open. After pulling it closed behind him, he drew the extra key to the new lock from his pocket and turned the dead bolt. Shoving the key back into his pocket, he turned around and peered into the shadows.

The moon hung low in the sky, illuminating much of the dark, but for the shadows near the mounds of dirt around the old grave site. Who was the victim and why had she been buried here, on Rae Lemmon's property?

Forrest had found out easily enough who Patrice Eccleston was, but the identity of this body was so far eluding everyone. She'd been dead for a long time, though—probably as long as the chief's sister had been.

Had this woman's family thought—like the chief's had—that she'd just run away? Was there not even a missing-person report on her?

Maybe that was why he couldn't find her—because nobody had missed her. Drawn by thoughts of the mummified corpse, he crossed the yard to the crime-scene tape that fluttered from the poles stabbed into the ground around the hole. More tape had been strewn around another area near the hole, where the officer had been struck. He would be okay, though.

Forrest breathed a sigh of relief for that. He hadn't wanted to put anyone else in danger, but he sure as hell didn't want Rae and Connor in danger either. Why were they? Who would threaten them?

He glanced back at the house, and from the corner of his eye, he noticed some movement behind him. He slid off the safety as he turned, but before he could squeeze the trigger, something swung out of the shadows at him. Metal struck his head right by his temple, and everything immediately went black.

His legs buckled beneath him and he dropped to the ground. And as he did, his last thought was that he'd failed Rae. He'd broken that promise to her.

SECONDS BEFORE NOW he'd stared down a gun barrel; now he stared down at the man who'd held that gun on him. Detective Colton had good reflexes. He was lucky he hadn't taken a bullet. But fortunately he'd moved faster.

Now Colton wasn't moving at all. He tightened his grasp on the pipe and considered swinging it again.

If he killed him—like the caller wanted—maybe this would end now. Maybe the caller would consider his debt paid in full.

He'd struck the younger cop harder and hadn't killed him, though. So he dropped the pipe and leaned down to pick up the gun instead.

If he wanted to make sure Forrest Colton died, he needed to shoot him. Needed to make sure there was no way he would survive.

But when he tugged on the gun, he couldn't get it loose from Colton's grasp. The man was unconscious, but he still held tightly to his weapon. The only way to stop a guy like Colton was to kill him.

RAE JERKED AWAKE, her body nearly convulsing with the strange feeling that had passed through her. She reached out for Forrest, but her fingers slid across tangled sheets. He was gone.

Again.

Every time they'd made love, he'd left her afterward. Was he trying to make it clear to her that he didn't want to stay? She wouldn't have expected him to; she never expected anyone to stay.

But why had she awakened like she had?

She reached for the baby monitor next to the bed and listened for Connor's cry. Maybe that was what had awakened her. The baby was quiet.

But a strange noise did emanate from the speaker, a strange squeak of the floorboards, as if someone was walking around the floor of the nursery.

A smile curved her lips.

That was where Forrest had gone—to check on Connor. That was where she had found him those other times, leaning over the crib, staring at her beautiful son. She'd even caught him singing that one night.

She waited for him to sing again, but he wouldn't want to wake Connor. He only wanted to protect him.

Like he only wanted to protect her.

She was the one who wanted more—despite knowing better, despite knowing that she was just like her mother. Just like beautiful Georgia, Rae had a habit of picking men who couldn't do permanence.

Only temporary.

Like Forrest was only temporarily working with the Whisperwood Police Department. Once the killer was caught, he would leave. Either return to Austin or continue volunteering with the Cowboy Heroes, going wherever they were sent.

But he was here now.

With her son.

Rae crawled out of bed and pulled on her T-shirt and her robe. She needed to protect herself from Forrest, from her feelings for him. But despite the couple of layers of fabric, she still felt naked, like he could see straight through everything, right to her heart.

She loved him.

And if she found him holding Connor as gently as he had in the past, she knew he would see that love on her face. Maybe she should just stay in bed, pretending to sleep, so that he wouldn't know how much he meant to her.

But now a cry emanated from the speaker. Connor had awakened, but the voice that murmured something to him wasn't Forrest's.

She froze with fear for just a second before she

rushed from her room. Would she get to the nursery in time to save her son?

And what had happened to Forrest?

Chapter Twenty-One

Pain throbbed at his temple, pounding at Forrest to wake up. But it wasn't just the pain hammering at him; his heart pounded with fear. He'd left Rae and Connor unprotected. After dragging his eyes open, he blinked away the blackness. Then he pushed his way up from the ground. The gun was in his hand yet. The intruder hadn't wrested it away from him. But his pocket had been turned inside out, and the key was gone.

Cursing, Forrest ran toward the house. His leg throbbed like his head, but he ignored the pain as he pushed himself. The back door stood open, like the intruder had been in a hurry to get inside. So was Forrest.

He didn't even take time to call out to the unit at the road. They would be checking in soon enough, since he hadn't called them. But he didn't want to waste a moment in getting to Rae and Connor.

Then her scream rang out. And he knew he was already too late. She stood in the doorway to the nursery, with a hand clasped over her mouth as if she wanted to take back her scream.

Connor echoed it as he cried out.

He was alive.

They were both alive.

But they were clearly in danger. Forrest rushed up

behind Rae and then pulled her away from the door. Shielding her with his body, he burst into the nursery.

A man held the screaming baby even more awkwardly than Forrest had held him. But maybe that was because he didn't just hold the baby; he also held a pipe that was smeared with blood. Forrest's blood probably. Some trailed from his temple, down the side of his face.

And Officer Baker's...

Forrest cursed and tightened his grasp on his gun. "Put the baby back in the crib," he said. "Right now." He stared down the barrel at the man's face, which looked vaguely familiar. Where the hell had he seen him before?

It didn't matter now, though. Nothing mattered but saving Connor. Would he be hurt if Forrest shot the man?

Rae must have thought so, because she grabbed Forrest's arm and pleaded, "Don't shoot."

Forrest wanted to protect the baby, too, desperately—almost as if he was Connor's father. "Put him down," he ordered the man. "Put him down or I will shoot you."

"Don't," Rae pleaded again. "He's my dad."

That was why he'd looked vaguely familiar. Years had passed—hard years—since the photographs Forrest had seen in the old album had been taken, but he had the same bone structure beneath the wrinkles and dark circles. He was even leaner than he'd been then, and a hell of a lot more desperate-looking.

So desperate that Forrest still didn't trust him with the baby. Even knowing now that he was Connor's grandfather, Forrest believed he still might hurt the baby. To hurt Rae?

Hadn't he already hurt her enough?

"Put down the baby," Forrest said again as he kept the gun barrel trained on the man.

"I'm not going to hurt him," Beau Lemmon said, as if he'd read Forrest's mind or maybe the fear on his face.

"Just like you didn't hurt me or Officer Baker with that damn pipe you're holding?" he asked.

Rae gasped, and her fingers slipped from Forrest's arm. She must have just realized what her father was, the one who'd been threatening her all this time.

The one who'd already tried once to kill Forrest before trying again tonight.

RAE HADN'T BEEN able to look away from her father since first finding him in the nursery, holding his grandson. But now she looked at Forrest, at the blood running down the side of his face. Her father had done that?

And he'd hurt the young officer, as well?

And had driven Forrest off the road, with Connor in the back seat?

She'd been angry with her father for years for leaving her mother and her. But what rushed through her now was so much more than anger. It was hot and vicious and a rage that nearly blinded her with its intensity. She edged around Forrest and rushed across the nursery.

"Don't you dare touch him!" she yelled at her father as she reached for her son.

He released him into her arms. Not that she would have given him a choice. She didn't want him touching her baby. Ever. But especially not now, with that pipe in his hand.

"What were you going to do to him?" she asked, her heart cracking with fear. "Were you going to kill my child? Your grandchild? What kind of monster are you?"

"A dangerous one," Forrest answered for him as he stepped between them again, using his body—his already battered body—to shield her and her baby.

Her father could have killed him. He'd nearly killed the cop.

Her father...

Her stomach churned with the realization. And she'd been upset when he'd deserted her and her mother.

Obviously they'd been better off—and safer—without him in their lives.

"Get out!" she told him. "Get out of here. Now!"

"He can't leave," Forrest corrected her. "Not on his own. He needs to go to jail." And he began reading him his rights.

But her father didn't take his advice; he didn't remain silent. "No. You don't understand. You're in danger. You're all in danger."

Forrest snorted. "Yeah, from you." And with his free hand, he reached for the bloody pipe. "Your fingerprints are going to be all over this. And if you hadn't burned the van you stole to run me and Connor off the road, your fingerprints would have been all over that, too. You're going to jail."

"Then you won't catch the killer," Beau said. "And nobody will be safe until he's caught."

Forrest, standing between them, tensed.

"You have to get Rae and the baby out of here," Beau continued. "They're not safe here. Once I'm in jail, he'll just send someone else after them. After you..." He glanced around as if he could hear them coming. "Or he'll take care of you himself—just like he did those women."

"Who is it?" Forrest asked, but he sounded skeptical, as if he was just humoring her father.

Beau shook his head. "I don't know."

Forrest snorted and then continued reading him the Miranda rights.

Beau held up his hands. "I'm telling the truth. He bought out my gambling debts. He owns me. That's why I was—"

"Terrifying your own daughter?" Forrest finished for him.

"I was trying to save her," Beau said. "Trying to warn her."

"With threats?" Forrest asked.

"Those weren't for her," Beau said. "They were for me. Whoever this killer is—he sent me the notes, threatening my kid. Threatening Rae."

Anger coursed through her again. "You're the one who threatened me. Who broke in here—"

"Into my own house?" he asked. "That's not breaking and entering."

"It's not your house," she corrected him. "Mom left it to me. Do you even know she's gone? That the cancer came back? Do you even care?" She didn't know why she asked; it was clear that he didn't, or he never would have left. Her mother had deserved better. *She* deserved better. "Get him out of here," she told Forrest.

But the detective hesitated. "How did the person get these notes to you? How do you not know who the killer is?"

Beau pushed a hand through his thin gray hair. "I found the notes under my motel-room door, and the calls came from an unknown number."

"Did you recognize the voice?" Forrest asked.

He shook his head.

"Why are you talking to him?" Rae asked. She just

wanted the man gone, like he'd been for all of these years, when she'd actually needed him.

She didn't need him now.

And she would make sure she never needed anyone else. But Connor...

She rocked the crying baby in her arms. He was all she needed.

"He could have killed me," Forrest said. "After he knocked me out, he could have finished me off. He could have finished off Officer Baker, too."

He didn't think her father was a killer. The pressure on her heart eased slightly. She didn't want to believe he was a killer either. She didn't want to believe that she and Connor had that in their DNA.

But...

"The body that was buried in the backyard..." she murmured. "Who was she?"

Her father shook his head. "I don't know."

"But you dug it up," Forrest guessed.

"I knew it was there," he admitted.

Rae shuddered. She'd grown up in this house, played in that yard, and her father had allowed it all, knowing that a corpse had been buried there.

"We'll talk more once I get you down to lockup," Forrest said. Maybe he wanted to spare her the gory details.

But she didn't need his protection from the truth. Just from danger.

"If you lock me up, I won't be able to help you," Beau said. "And she won't be safe until the killer is caught."

"You don't know who it is," Forrest reminded him. "So you can't help me."

"I can find out," Beau offered. "I can bring him to you."

Forrest shook his head. "You think I'm going to trust you?"

"You want to keep them safe, too," Beau said. "You know that's not possible until the killer is caught."

"Stop using me!" Rae said. "You've never given a damn about me or about my mother. Why are you pretending to care now?"

"I always cared," Beau said. "That's why I left. I was more a hindrance than a help to both of you. Georgia deserved better, and so do you." He looked at Forrest now, as if he was wondering if Forrest was worthy of her. "If you care about her at all, you'd get her the hell out of here. You'd do whatever was necessary to keep her and the baby safe—even trust me."

She reached out and touched Forrest's arm again, but not to pull down the gun he was pointing at her father. "Don't," she advised. "Don't trust him."

And just as she said it, her father pounced. He pulled the pipe from Forrest's hand and swung it at his head. A gun went off, the blast deafening.

Connor, who had been crying, suddenly stopped. Was he just in shock? Or had he been hit?

With the adrenaline coursing through Rae, she might have been hit, too, and just didn't realize it yet. She had no idea what was going on—as wood cracked and glass broke—and the room exploded with people and chaos.

She just held her son closely, using her body to shield his as Forrest had the two of them. If anyone had been hit, it would have been Forrest.

He had already been hurt, bleeding, wounded...

Because of her father.

All of the years she'd spent wishing he would come

back haunted her now. She would have been happier and safer had she never seen him again.

And what about Forrest?

Was he all right?

Chapter Twenty-Two

How the hell had he gotten away?

Forrest's arm ached from where the pipe had struck him, but ignoring the pain, he tightened his grasp on the steering wheel.

If only he hadn't let Rae distract him.

But it hadn't been just Rae. An engine roaring down the driveway had drawn his attention away from Beau Lemmon, as well. All that talk of her still being in danger. Of another killer.

Forrest thought that whoever was coming was a threat, not his backup. But it had been the other officers who'd broken down the front door and burst into the house.

By the time they'd arrived, it had already been too late. Beau Lemmon had gotten away. After striking him with the pipe and making the gun go off, the older man had hurled himself out the nursery window.

Forrest cursed himself for not slapping cuffs immediately on the guy's wrists and taking him off to jail. But what he'd been saying...

It had made sense.

"You really think there's someone else?" Rae asked. "That he's not the killer?"

He glanced across the console to where she sat in the

passenger's seat, with her arms wrapped around herself as if that was all that held her together. She looked at him with a faint flicker of hope in her dark eyes.

She needed to believe this.

Needed to believe in something.

"If he was a killer, I would be dead," Forrest said. His head and arm hurt damn badly, though, but she didn't need to know that.

She needed to know her father wasn't the monster she'd accused him of being.

"But he drove you off the road and hit you over the head," she reminded him. Needlessly.

Forrest wasn't about to forget or forgive what Beau Lemmon had done to him and the young officer. "But I think he was acting on someone else's orders," Forrest admitted. "Just like he said."

"That someone bought out his debt and was using it to control him?" she asked, with skepticism in her soft voice.

She deserved to know the truth. "I checked into your father," Forrest said. "And he's done some desperate things in the past to pay back his debts."

She gasped. "Murder?"

"No," he said. "Petty stuff. Breaking and entering. Stealing."

"That might be petty to you," she said. "But not to me. And his hurting people..." She reached across the console then and brushed her fingertips over the lump on his forearm. "Are you okay?"

He glanced at her again, at her face as she peered up at him, at the wound on his temple. She was so damn beautiful—even with as upset as she was.

"I'm fine," he said, not wanting her to worry about him. He was worried, though. And he kept glancing into the rearview mirror. He had a police escort in front of him and another behind, but he wasn't sure if that was a good idea. He might have been better able to spot and lose a tailing vehicle on his own.

Not that he'd lost Beau Lemmon that day he'd dropped Rae at work. Beau was damn good at following. Was he behind them now? Or was he doing what he'd promised? Was he trying to find out the identity of the killer?

Maybe that was why Forrest hadn't gone out the window after him. Of course he'd had to make sure that the people breaking into the house weren't a threat to Rae and Connor. But once they'd identified themselves, he hadn't chased after Beau as fast as he could have.

Despite all of the years the man had been gone, he knew the property well. So well that he must have had a place on it where he could hide from them.

That was why Forrest had insisted Rae pack up Connor and leave. And this time, staring at the broken window and the splintered doorjamb of her son's room, she had just nodded in agreement. Connor slept in his carrier in the back seat, with a couple bags next to him.

"Are you okay?" he asked Rae.

She jerked her head in a sharp nod. "I told you I didn't get hurt."

After the gun had gone off, she and Connor had seemed to go into shock. The blast had been loud, though.

He flinched, regretting that he hadn't put the safety back on, but he hadn't trusted her father. And with good reason.

Over the course of his career, Forrest had met a lot of desperate people, but Beau Lemmon might have been the most desperate of them all. As desperate as he was, though, he hadn't killed.

Yet.

It was hard to say if he could be driven to it, though. For Rae—to keep her safe—he might have actually done it.

"I'm not talking about physically," Forrest said.

She uttered a ragged-sounding sigh. "It was a shock to see him again."

Especially the way she'd seen him—in the nursery, holding her son and a bloody pipe. Maybe the image had played through her mind again, because she shuddered.

"He's long gone now," she murmured.

"I'll find him," Forrest assured her.

"To put him in jail," she said.

He couldn't tell if that upset her or not. "Don't you want me to arrest him?"

"Jail might be the safest place for him," she admitted. "It might save him from himself."

"Gambling is an addiction," he said.

She sucked in a breath, drawing his attention back to her. She stared at him, her brown eyes wide and warm with...

Something he didn't dare name, something he didn't dare hope he saw. But he found himself asking, "What?"

"I can't believe you're defending him," she said, "after everything he's done to you."

"For you," he reminded her. "He was trying to protect you."

She sighed. "You give him more credit than I do. Beau Lemmon has always been most concerned with himself, more so than anyone else."

He flinched over the pang of guilt striking him. He'd

had no idea how damn lucky he was to have the loving, supportive parents he had. "I'm sorry," he murmured.

"I had my mom," Rae said. "And she more than made up for Beau Lemmon."

But her mom was gone, leaving Rae all alone, but for Connor and her friends. She cared so much for her friends that she'd refused to put them in danger. She hadn't wanted to come here either, but he'd convinced her it would be safe.

And he pulled the SUV through the gates of the Colton ranch. He'd brought her and Connor home with him.

RAE HESITATED BEFORE stepping out of the door he'd opened for her. "Are you sure this is a good idea?" she asked as she glanced over at the big farmhouse. Despite the late hour, lights glowed in several of the windows.

"You'll be safe here," Forrest assured her.

"But what about them?" she asked. "I don't want to put your parents in danger." Like her parent had put her in danger with his damn gambling debts.

If she believed him, that is.

If he wasn't actually the killer...

Where her father was concerned, she had no idea what to believe. The only man she wanted to believe now was Forrest. She wanted to trust that he would keep his promise to keep her and Connor safe.

But she didn't want him putting his own life or the lives of his family at risk to do that.

"My parents are happy to have you both here," Forrest assured her.

And he must have been telling the truth because the front door opened and the older Coltons stepped onto the porch. His father wore a plaid robe over his pajamas, and his mother wore a pale pink one. Her white hair glowed in the light spilling out of the house.

"Thank goodness you're here," his mother called out to them. "We've been so concerned."

About their son—of course. He'd already been hurt once protecting her, and now again.

They must hate her or at least resent her.

But when Forrest led her up the steps to the porch, with the carrier dangling from one of his hands, his mother reached out. She closed her arms around Rae and hugged her. "You poor girl," she said. "You've been through so much."

Warmth flooded Rae. From her years managing the general store, Rae knew the Coltons. They had always been friendly to her. But this—opening their home to her and Connor—was beyond friendly.

"You're sure about this?" Rae asked. "Sure that you want us here?" She peered over Mrs. Colton's shoulder at her husband's serious face.

Hays had a face that was hard to read, as his expression was carefully guarded. He studied her for several long moments before a smile curved his lips. "Of course we do, Rae. Of course we do."

The rancher had a reputation for being an honest man, so she wanted to trust him. But she wasn't sure if they had extended their hospitality for her sake or for their son's. Mrs. Colton pulled back now and turned toward her son. She touched the side of his face where the blood had dried.

"Are you okay?" she asked, her soft voice cracking with concern.

He smiled at his mother. "Of course I am. Think of all the times you and Dad called me hardheaded."

"Too many to count," Hays murmured.

Forrest chuckled.

His mother closed her arms around him, hugging him as tightly as she had Rae. Then she pulled back and peered down at the carrier Forrest had in his hand.

"Oh, my…" She sighed. "He's just beautiful. Beautiful."

Pride swelled Rae's heart. He was the reason she was here—that she had agreed to impose on Forrest's parents. She would do anything for Connor.

Just as it was clear that the Coltons would do anything for their son—even put themselves in danger.

"Let's get you all inside," Josephine Colton said as she pulled open the door to the house. "I've already freshened up the nursery for Bellamy and Donovan's baby, so it's all ready for Connor."

That warmth in Rae's heart spread even more. Her best friend was so lucky to have this woman as her mother-in-law. It would be months before Bellamy's baby was here, but Josephine was already eagerly anticipating and preparing for her grandbaby. And even though Donovan wasn't biologically their child, they had always treated him like he was a Colton. So they would treat his child the same way.

But why would they extend their hospitality to Rae and Connor?

Was it because she was Bellamy's friend? Or did they know that something was going on between her and their son? Had Forrest told them…

What?

That they were sleeping together? Well, she was the only one who slept. He didn't. He made love to her and left. Now that warmth spread to her face as embarrassment overwhelmed her.

What had Forrest told his parents?

"Don't worry," Hays told her as he closed and locked the front door behind them.

Forrest and his mother had already headed toward the stairwell that led up to the second story. But Hays hung back to assure her. "You're safe here—you and your boy." He reached out and touched her cheek. "And you're also very welcome to be here."

Tears stung her eyes.

Why couldn't Beau Lemmon have been half the man that Hays Colton was?

Choked with emotion, she couldn't verbally express her gratitude. So she hugged him.

He froze for a moment before gently patting her back. "You've been on your own entirely too long, young lady."

She blinked away the tears and pulled back. "I'm fine. I have my friends and now my son." When she looked for him, being carried up the stairs by Forrest, her gaze focused on the man instead of the baby, though.

She wanted more. She wanted Forrest.

She wanted a love like his parents had—a marriage that lasted. But she wasn't a Colton or Bellamy or Maggie. She wasn't lucky or blessed.

But that was fine.

She didn't feel sorry for herself. She would just be happy that she had Forrest's protection. She wouldn't let herself hope for more—for his love.

As if he'd read her mind, Hays Colton told her, "Don't be afraid."

But was he talking about her hopes for his son? Or her fear for her life?

THIS WAS THE first time he welcomed the unknown caller showing up on his cell phone screen. The first time he actually wanted to talk to the person who'd tried manipulating him into murder.

The murder of a man his daughter obviously loved.

The way she'd looked at Forrest Colton, with such concern, and at him, with such disgust, haunted Beau. He'd let her down. He knew that.

He'd let her down years ago.

But now…

Now he'd done more than disappoint her; he'd devastated her.

Guilt weighed heavily on him. A guilt that he knew he wouldn't be able to shake this time—not with the thrill of a bet or a drink or anything.

He'd screwed up too badly this time. He'd eluded arrest, assaulted not one but two police officers and he'd threatened his own daughter.

At least that was how she saw it. And now he saw himself through her eyes—as a pathetic excuse for a human being. He had to make this right.

Somehow.

So he clicked the accept button and before the man could berate him, he said, "I know I screwed up."

He wasn't sure how the hell this guy always knew, though. Did he have a police scanner? Some way of always knowing what was going on?

"What are you going to do about it?"

"I need to leave town," he said.

The guy chortled. "How the hell are you going to do that?"

"I've got some money stashed at my old house."

The guy snorted. "Yeah, right. If you had that, you would have paid me off right away."

"I didn't want you to know," he said. "I thought I

could get rid of the detective, like you wanted, and save the money for myself."

"You're going to pay me off first," the guy replied, "before you go anywhere."

Beau smiled over what he heard in the guy's voice: greed. Beau understood it well. It was why—even when he was up—that he kept gambling. Because he wanted more.

This guy had to have money somehow—enough that he'd bought up Beau's debt. Yet he wanted more. Beau had been counting on it.

"My girl left the house," he said. "All the cops should be gone soon, too. I'm going to go back and get it. Then I'll bring it to you. Where can I meet you?"

And who the hell are you?

"I'll meet you," the man replied and clicked off the phone.

Beau uttered a shaky sigh. It was what he wanted. But he knew this was the most dangerous gamble he'd ever taken. This one could cost him his life.

Chapter Twenty-Three

Forrest wanted to come inside the bedroom with her and take her into his arms—just to hold her, to comfort her. But he didn't trust himself to leave it at that, to leave her alone. And he hadn't told his parents how he felt about her, that he was doing more than protecting her. He was falling in love with her. Hell, he'd already fallen…hard.

"Do you have everything you need?" he asked from the doorway of the guest room next to the nursery. It would have been used for a nanny if his mother had ever had one to help with the boys. But she hadn't.

Rae grasped the baby monitor in her hand and nodded. "This was how I knew he was in there with Connor." She shuddered.

"I'm sorry," he said, guilt pressing heavily on him that he'd allowed the man to get into the house.

"It wasn't your fault," she said. "None of it was your fault. It was his. What would he have done to Connor if I hadn't heard him?"

Forrest had to reach out now, had to pull her trembling body against his chest to comfort her. "He wouldn't have hurt him."

She gently skimmed her fingertips along his swollen temple. "He hurt you." She shuddered. "And Officer Baker. He might have killed him."

Forrest shook his head. "No, he's going to be all right. Beau hasn't killed anyone."

But she pursed her lips as if she wasn't sure. "He admitted knowing that body had been buried in the backyard. How would he have known that?"

"The killer's been in contact with him," Forrest reminded her. So how did Beau not know his identity? Maybe the old gambler was better at bluffing than his debts would suggest. Maybe he did know.

Rae's brow furrowed with skepticism. "Yeah, right."

"You don't believe him?"

"I don't believe anything he says," she replied, and her voice cracked. "When Mom got sick, he said he would come back and that he would be a much better husband and father when he did. But he never came back, not even for her funeral."

Forrest's heart ached with her pain. He wanted to take it all away from her and give her nothing but love. He didn't know if she wanted that, though, or just the protection he'd promised her. He hadn't done the greatest job at keeping his promise, though. Her father had gotten inside the nursery, had gotten his hands on Connor.

But Forrest couldn't believe that he would have hurt his own grandson.

Rae sighed. "I'm sorry. All of that happened a long time ago. I should be over it now."

"His return brought all of those feelings back for you," Forrest surmised. "It must have been a shock to see him there." And he hadn't been there for her, hadn't protected her from that.

"It shouldn't have been," she said. "You were asking about him. You suspected it could have been him."

"I didn't really think he was the one threatening you and Connor," he admitted. Having been blessed with awesome parents himself, he couldn't imagine one of them threatening him or his child.

"You thought he was the killer," she said. "So why don't you think that anymore?"

He touched the bump on his head that still tingled from her fingertips sliding gently over it moments before. "He could have killed me."

"Maybe he thought he had," she suggested. "Maybe he didn't realize you weren't dead." Tears pooled in her eyes, revealing how hard it was for her to confront what her father could be: a killer.

"Stop," he told her. "Stop worrying about it, about him. Just get some rest."

Dark circles rimmed her big brown eyes as she stared up at him. There was something in her gaze besides worry and concern, something like what he was feeling. But was it real? Or was it only his wishful thinking putting it there?

He started leaning down, to look closer, to be closer.

He wanted to kiss her—needed to kiss her.

But the ringing of a phone drew him back to his senses. It wasn't his cell; it didn't even sound like a cell phone. His parents still had a landline, though, since the reception wasn't the greatest at the ranch.

Who would be calling at this time, though?

It was closer to dawn than midnight now. "Go to sleep," he urged her. "And maybe Connor will sleep in after tonight."

"I should stay in the nursery with him," she said with a worried glance at the closed door.

He wrapped his fingers around hers, which were wrapped around the baby monitor. "You have this. You'll hear him if he wakes up."

Just like she'd heard her father on the monitor.

She flinched, as if remembering that, and he wanted to hold her again, wanted to stay with her instead of going to his own room. As he opened his mouth to suggest it, he heard a creak on the stairs.

His hand went to his holster, and he whirled around to his father. "Just me," Hays Colton said as he held out a cordless phone toward him. "And I'm not sure who this is, but they want to speak with you."

Everybody with Whisperwood PD had his cell number. Who would be calling him here? And especially at this hour.

"Sorry, Dad," he said as he took the cordless from him.

His father offered a weary smile to him and to Rae. "It's never boring when you and your brothers are home," he said. He patted his son's broad shoulder. "And that's a good thing."

After all of the months he'd spent volunteering for desk duty with the Cowboy Heroes, Forrest would have agreed with him. He would have agreed if not for the danger Rae and Connor had been put in.

He turned back toward her. "Get some rest," he urged her. "I'll take this in my room." He forced himself to walk across the hall, to leave her alone.

She murmured a good-night to his father before stepping into the guest room and closing the door. Forrest did the same, stepping into his room and closing the door.

Then he raised the cordless phone to his face and asked, "Who is this?"

"It's Beau."

Despite his assurances to Rae that her father wasn't a killer, his blood chilled. The man must have been hiding in the shadows somewhere, must have overheard that Forrest was bringing the man's daughter and grandson back to the Colton ranch. Had he followed them?

VOICES EMANATED FROM the baby monitor. But Rae knew the men who talked weren't in the nursery. She'd watched Forrest go to his bedroom. And the other man she could hear…

Forrest had assured her that he wouldn't get close to her again. Her father.

The baby monitor must have been on the same frequency as the cordless phone Forrest was using, because the reception was as clear as if they were on a conference call with Rae.

"Where are you?" Forrest asked her father.

"It doesn't matter where I am now," he replied. "It's where I'm going to be and who I'm meeting. You're going to want to be there, too."

"The killer?" Forrest asked, but there was skepticism in his voice now. He wasn't as convinced as he'd tried to sound to her that her father wasn't the murderer.

"Yes," Beau replied. "I tricked him into meeting me."

Was the killer whom he'd tricked, or was he trying now to trick Forrest?

Fear had her heart pounding furiously hard.

"Where?" Forrest asked.

"At my house," Beau replied.

And Rae bristled that he kept calling it that. He'd given it up years ago, when he'd left and never returned. It was hers now—her home and Connor's.

"You can't call in a bunch of police units, though,"

Beau warned him. "Or he'll get away before we get a chance to see who he is. You need to come alone."

And Rae's blood chilled. Was her father setting up the man she loved? Was he trying yet again to kill him?

She wanted to shout into the baby monitor. But she had the receiver, not the transmitter. They wouldn't hear her through it.

"When?" Forrest asked.

"Right away," Beau replied. "He should be here any minute now."

Forrest cursed. "You didn't give me enough damn time to get—"

"Just you," Beau warned. "Or you'll blow it."

And that was why he hadn't called sooner. He hadn't wanted to give Forrest time to call for backup.

"You can't call this in," Beau continued. "He might have someone within the department or be someone within the department. He knows too much."

Rae tossed the monitor down on the bed and rushed toward the door. When she pulled it open, Forrest was already in the hallway. She ran to him. "Don't go!"

He tensed. "What?"

"I heard the call—on the monitor," she said. "It's a trick."

He shook his head. "I don't think so."

"The killer—whoever he is—wants you not to work the murder cases," she reminded him. "This is how they're going to get rid of you." And her father was either going to help or do it himself. "Please don't go!"

She threw her arms around him, clinging to him, like she'd clung to her father when he'd headed out the door all those years ago. "Please…" Sobs cracked her voice.

As if he was in pain, Forrest grimaced. "I'm sorry, Rae. I have to."

She shook her head. "No, you don't. You can send someone else."

He shook his head now. "No. I won't put anyone else in danger."

"Then you know it's a trap," she said.

"I know it's my best chance of catching your father and finding the killer," he said. "I have to take it."

Her father had said something similar—whatever game he'd been leaving to play had been his best chance at changing their fortunes, at helping them.

"I'm doing it for you," Forrest said. "And for Connor."

She shuddered. "I didn't think you were anything like him," she said. "But you are. If you really cared about me and Connor, you wouldn't go. You wouldn't leave us."

"You're safe here," Forrest assured her.

"But you're not," she said. "You're rushing right into danger."

"That's my job," he reminded her. "It's what I do."

She pointed toward his bad leg. "It's what nearly got you killed. Is it worth it?"

"To stop killers and protect innocent people?" he asked. "Of course it's worth it." He pulled away from her then and headed toward the stairs, his limp even more pronounced than it usually was.

She couldn't help but think it would be the last time that she saw him. That he wouldn't come back to her.

Words burned in the back of her throat.

I love you.

She wanted to tell him. But would he stop? Would he believe her?

Would he care?

Despite his limp, he was already down the stairs.

Then the door opened and closed as he left, taking her opportunity with him. She'd missed her chance to tell him how she felt about him. Would she have another opportunity?

Would she ever see him again?

His cell phone vibrated across his bedside table, and beside him in bed, Bellamy murmured in protest of the interruption of her sleep. She needed her rest.

So Donovan grabbed the phone and rushed out of the room. But when he stared down at the screen, he saw that he had two calls coming in at the same time.

Forrest and Rae.

Weren't they together?

What the hell was going on?

He hit a button and connected first with Forrest. "What—"

"Get out to the Lemmon house," Forrest ordered him.

"Is that why Rae's calling me, too?" Donovan asked. "Is she in danger?"

"No, she's at the ranch."

"Ranch?"

"Our ranch," Forrest said. "With Mom and Dad. She's safe."

Donovan's blood chilled. "But you're not."

And that was why Rae was calling him.

"I'm meeting her father there," Forrest said. "He's the one who ran me off the road and assaulted Officer Baker."

Donovan cursed. "That son of a bitch—"

"He's working for the real killer," Forrest said.

"Who—"

"He doesn't know," Forrest said. "That's why he's lured him back to Rae's—to find out."

It sounded more like he was luring Forrest there. "It's not safe," Donovan said.

He'd left his clothes and gun in the bedroom. But as much as he didn't want to wake Bellamy, he didn't want to lose his brother either. He had almost lost him once already. He rushed back in to grab his jeans and his holstered weapon.

"Wait for me," he said.

"I'm already here," Forrest said.

Before Donovan could say anything else, his brother disconnected the call. He'd gone in alone—without backup—just like the day he'd nearly died.

And Donovan couldn't help but think that this time Forrest might not make it.

Chapter Twenty-Four

Forrest had a flashback to that day he'd walked into a warehouse to meet a potential witness and gunfire had erupted. He had nearly died that day.

The witness's call to meet had been a trap. This probably was, too. Just like Rae and Donovan had warned him.

But it was a risk he had to take if he wanted to make sure the nightmare for Rae and Connor ended, if he wanted to make sure they were safe. And they meant more to him than his own life.

He had to do this, had to take this risk.

He shut off the headlights as he approached her driveway. Even with the lights off, he didn't turn into the drive. Instead he parked his car on the side of the rural road. Before opening the driver's door, he pulled the fuse for the dome light. From that other trap, he'd learned not to announce his arrival.

And to be prepared. He drew his weapon. He'd been meant to die that day, but his shooter had been the one to die instead. He'd thought his life had ended then, too. But now he knew differently. He knew there was so much more to living than work. There was family.

He had a wonderful one.

But he wanted another one.

He wanted a family with Rae and Connor. The only

way he'd have a chance of that, though, was to make sure they were no longer in danger.

To do that, he had to put himself in danger first. But would Rae forgive him for leaving after she had begged him to stay?

The only way he'd find out was if he survived this meeting. So he clasped his gun tightly in his hand as he headed toward the house. It was dark—all of the lights were off and the nursery window was boarded up.

Instead of walking down the driveway to the front porch, Forrest slipped around the back. The ground was uneven, causing him to stumble and nearly fall.

He swallowed a curse, not over the pain shooting up his bad leg but over the noise he might have made. He didn't want to alert anyone to his presence. Yet.

Was it just Beau here?

Or was the killer here, too?

Or were they one and the same?

He hoped not, because Beau knew this property too damn well. He'd already hidden on it too many times, with the police being unable to find him.

How would Forrest?

He knew one place where Beau kept turning up—at the grave he'd admitted to digging up. He'd turned up there to attack the young officer and to attack Forrest.

Forrest's head still pounded from the blow Beau had dealt him. If he returned to the site, he risked getting hurt worse. But it was a risk he had to take—for Rae and Connor.

Keeping to the shadows at the side of the house, Forrest headed around it, to the back. He flinched with every rustle of grass beneath his feet and every twig snapping under the heels of his boots. But then something drowned out the faint noises of his walking: an engine.

One revved in the driveway before tires squealed, and the noise grew fainter as the vehicle drove away. Had he been too late?

Had they already left?

Maybe Donovan had put in a call for backup, and like Beau had warned him, the killer had access to police dispatch. He cursed.

Another curse echoed his. But faintly.

Someone hadn't left. Someone else was hiding somewhere in the darkness.

Then a groan followed that curse, and Forrest pinpointed the direction of the sound. Just as he'd suspected, it came from the crime scene.

He rushed forward and noticed that the yellow tape no longer fluttered between two of those poles. It had snapped and now lay on the ground in two pieces. He stepped closer, his foot sinking into the loose soil. Then he peered into the hole.

And like he had twice before, he found another body. The first light of dawn illuminated the swollen face of the older man.

"Beau," Forrest called out.

"He's gone," the older man murmured. "You were too late."

Forrest scrambled down into the hole with him. As he did, he holstered his weapon and reached for his phone. "I'll get help…"

But Beau reached out and clasped his hand around the phone. "No."

"You're hurt."

"I'm dying," he said, his voice just a husky rasp.

As the light grew, Forrest could see the marks around his neck, too. He'd been strangled like the other victims.

"You can survive this," Forrest assured him.

Beau used his other hand to gesture toward his chest and to the end of the pipe sticking out between his ribs.

Forrest flinched and cursed. The pain had to be intolerable. And the strength of the killer...

"Who is he?" Forrest asked. "Who did this to you?"

Beau shook his head. "No."

"You saw him," Forrest said. "You had to see him."

"I did," Beau acknowledged. "But I made a deal."

"A deal with a killer?" His killer—because Beau was right. He was dying. There was no way he could survive with the blood gurgling out around the pipe shoved deep within his body. Not even if Forrest called for help.

"He won't hurt Rae and the baby if I don't say who he is."

"And you trust him?" Forrest asked.

Beau just stared up at him.

"You trust him?" Forrest repeated.

Then he realized that Beau couldn't see him or hear him anymore. He was gone.

But Forrest wasn't alone. Dirt sifted down into the hole as someone approached it, and a dark shadow fell across him and the dead man.

He'd thought the killer had left, but maybe when he'd seen Forrest's SUV parked on the road, he'd circled back to finish off him like he'd done Beau.

He reached for his holster to draw his weapon. But another gun already cocked. And he had no doubt it was aimed at his head. He wouldn't be able to shoot his way out of this trap, like he had his last one.

AFTER FORREST HAD left, Rae hadn't even tried to sleep. She'd known it would be no use—not with Forrest out there, alone. No. He wasn't alone.

When Donovan had returned her missed call, he'd

been on his way to her house to meet Forrest. But Forrest had left long before he had. He would have already been there. He would have already walked into whatever trap her father had set for him.

Tears stung her eyes, and she stared down at Connor with blurred vision. She cradled the sleeping baby as she rocked in the chair she'd found in the nursery. Probably the same chair in which Josephine Colton had rocked all of her children.

How could her father be such a monster? How could he have threatened her and Connor and tried to kill officers of the law? And the man she loved.

Of course he didn't know she'd fallen for Forrest Colton. Forrest didn't know either. She should have told him when the words had been burning the back of her throat.

She should have told him then, because now she might never get the chance to tell him that she loved him. She blinked and focused on Connor.

Forrest was so good with him, so gentle, like he was with her. He was a good man.

That was why he'd insisted on leaving, on putting his life in danger. Because he was a good man, intent on taking care of everyone else before himself.

The one person he'd thought would take care of him had taken off when he'd needed her most. Rae couldn't understand how the woman he'd loved could have abandoned him. She couldn't understand how anyone could abandon him.

She should have chased him down the stairs, should have insisted on going along with him. Maybe her father wouldn't have hurt him if she'd been present. But knowing how protective Forrest was, she knew he wouldn't have allowed it. He would never willingly put her in danger.

Just himself.

It was his job.

Could she live with that, if he lived? Could she live with his putting himself in danger over and over again? Because every time he left the house for his job, he might wind up leaving her forever.

That was why she'd chosen not to wait for a man to start her family. Her dating history had proved to her that she had her mother's luck with choosing men; she picked ones who couldn't commit for life.

Forrest Colton had no problem with committing. His problem was that he was committed most to his job. His dangerous job. And that commitment might have gotten him killed.

He'd been gone so long. He'd left when it was dark, and now the sun had risen, pouring light and warmth into the already-sunny yellow nursery.

She'd heard footsteps earlier. People moving around the house—probably Forrest's parents. How worried were they? How did they handle all of their children being in dangerous professions?

How would she handle it if Connor someday chose a high-risk career?

She gazed down at him with such awe, wondering what kind of man he would become. He had her father's genes in him. Would that make him a gambler? And selfish?

But he had her mother's and hers as well, so maybe he would be kind and generous and hardworking. What he needed, she realized now, was a strong male role model.

A man like Forrest.

Who put other people's safety before his own. It was noble. For him.

But so damn hard on those who loved him, like she did.

The doorbell pealed, the bell a faint tinkle this far from the front door. The nursery faced the front of the house, where the driveway was.

Lifting Connor, she carried him to the window and peered out. An SUV was parked on the driveway, with lights fastened to the roof of it. An officer stood beside the driver's door, while the passenger's door was already open.

Forrest wouldn't have rung the bell for his own house. The visitor had to be someone else—the chief, no doubt.

Wouldn't he be the one who made the notification when one of his officers was killed in the line of duty?

Was that what he'd come here to do—notify Forrest's parents that he was gone?

THIS WAS THE worst damn part of his job. The chief hated making notifications. Hell, he shouldn't even be doing this one. He'd been asked not to, but he figured she had a right to know as soon as possible…in case she wanted to see his body before they took him away.

When the door opened, it was Hays who stood in front of him. Dark circles rimmed his eyes, and he looked tense with worry. "Archer, it's early for a visit."

Hays was a rancher; he'd probably been up for a while. It wasn't the hour he was questioning, but it was the purpose.

"I'm here to see Ms. Lemmon," he told his old friend.

Hays sucked in a breath. Then, his jaw taut, he asked, "About my son?"

Archer furrowed his brow with confusion. "Forrest wanted to do this himself." And now he understood why; the single mom was more than someone the detective was protecting. She was important to him.

When she rushed down the steps to greet him, it was clear from the fear on her face that Forrest was important to her, too.

"Is he all right?" she asked. Tears already streamed down her face with the emotion overwhelming her. "Is he?"

Were her tears for her father, though, or for Forrest? Archer wasn't sure now who she was upset about.

But he began his notification as he always did, "I'm sorry for your loss."

And a small scream slipped through her lips as she slipped to the floor. Hays was there, with his arm around her, lifting her back up, letting her lean against him. The Coltons were good people, important people in Whisperwood.

But that wasn't why the chief felt so damn bad about being here. He felt bad for Rae Lemmon. The young woman had already lost so much.

"Your father, Beau Lemmon, died earlier this morning," Archer continued.

Rae gasped again. "My father?"

"Yes, you were aware that he'd returned to town." At least that was what Forrest had told him.

She jerked her chin in a sharp nod. "Yes, he was the one threatening me and my son."

Hays tightened his arm around her. "I'm sorry, honey," he murmured.

"And Forrest," she continued. "He tried to kill Forrest." Her voice cracked. "How is he?"

She was obviously afraid that she'd lost him, too. She wasn't the only one who was afraid of that. Archer wondered himself.

Chapter Twenty-Five

Forrest had been gone too long. He knew it. But he'd wanted to make sure he—and the crime-scene techs—didn't miss a single clue that might lead them to the killer of the women and of Beau Lemmon.

He hoped like hell they would find some DNA, something that would lead them to the real monster. Beau Lemmon hadn't been a monster. He'd just been—as Rae had once said—flawed.

How was she?

She hadn't returned to her house with the chief like he'd thought she might. But then, after what had happened at her house, would she ever want to come home to it?

He didn't want her to—he didn't want her here, where so many terrible things had happened. Hell, he could have died here himself when Beau had struck him over the head, and just a few hours ago when that gun had cocked.

Fortunately it had been his brother holding the weapon, and not the murderer. Donovan hadn't recognized him right away, crouched in the shadows of the old grave. And the new one.

It had become Beau Lemmon's grave. His body was gone now, though. And that was why Forrest had finally left to return to the ranch. When he drove up, he found his parents on the porch. His mother held Connor in her lap as she rocked in the swing, while his father leaned against the railing beside them, making faces at the baby.

Warmth spread through Forrest's chest. He loved the two of them so much. "Babysitting?" he teased.

"Heard you've been doing some of this yourself," his father mused with a curious glance at him.

They knew. They knew he'd fallen for the baby and his sweet single mother. He didn't bother denying it; he just grinned at them.

"Your services might no longer be required," his father said.

And Forrest furrowed his brow. "You threatening to take over my job?"

"We're only watching him while Rae gathers up his stuff," his mother said, with disappointment heavy in her voice. "She's leaving."

Forrest cursed and then shook his head. He had to remember not to swear in front of the baby. Eventually Connor would be repeating words. But Forrest might not be around anymore when he did—if Rae had her way, apparently. She'd been mad when he'd left last night. She was probably furious that the chief—not he—had done the notification.

"Is she okay?" he asked.

"You would know better than we would," Hays remarked with a curious glance.

They had their suspicions about his relationship with Rae, but apparently they didn't know if it was going to last. Neither did he.

He'd been such an idiot by fighting his feelings like

he had, thinking that she was anything like Shannon. Rae wasn't the kind who took off.

Or she hadn't been.

When he rushed up the steps, he found her in the nursery, packing, just as his parents had warned him. "So you're the one leaving now," he mused.

She didn't look up, but she tensed. "There's no reason to stay."

"No reason?" he asked. Didn't she feel the same way about him that he did about her?

"My father is dead," she said, her voice curiously flat and emotionless. But when she lifted her face to meet his gaze, her eyes were red and swollen. She'd been crying.

And he hadn't been here to hold her, to comfort her. Guilt squeezed his heart in a tight grip. "I'm sorry," he murmured. "I was too late to save him."

"You shouldn't have gone at all," she said, her voice cracking now as her emotions rushed back. "You could have died with him."

He shook his head. "I've been doing this a long time," he reminded her. "I'm a good cop." Even with his disability. The chief was giving him a chance to prove it. Now he just had to find the killer.

With so many of his family members working the case now, it was just a matter of time before the killer was caught and brought to justice for all of his crimes.

"He was tricking you," she said.

Forrest shook his head. "No. He was trying to help me."

She snorted. "Yeah, right. Did he tell you who the killer was?"

He shook his head again. "No. But he kept that secret

for you," he told her. "He made a deal with the killer that he'd keep quiet if the guy left you and Connor alone."

"So then Connor and I absolutely can go home," she said. "Alone." She drew in a deep breath. "We don't need you anymore."

He sucked in a breath of his own, but just to brace himself for the rejection that was probably to come. She was furious with him, and for good reason. He'd left just like her father had—when she'd begged him not to go.

And he hated himself for it. Not nearly as much as she apparently hated him, though.

"I need you," he said. "I need you and I need Connor."

She narrowed her eyes with suspicion. "Why?"

"Because I love you," he said. "I love you both. You're the reasons I left last night—you and Connor. I wanted to make sure you'd be safe. You two mean *everything* to me. And if you give me the chance, I will prove that to you. I will never, ever leave you again."

Rae didn't say anything. She just turned and ran from the room. Ran away just like Shannon had.

Maybe he was just that unlovable.

RAE WAS TOO overwhelmed to speak. Emotions rushed through her—relief, fear and a love so powerful that she wasn't sure how to handle it. If she could handle it.

And that was why she was so afraid.

But she could trust Forrest. He was nothing like her father. But if she believed what Forrest had told her, her father had come through in the end. His very last act in life had finally been a selfless one.

Tears stung her eyes, so when she turned back toward the room in which Forrest stood, she could barely see him. But his shoulders were slumped with exhaustion and maybe disappointment.

She hadn't handled his proposal well—if that was what that had been. "Aren't you coming?" she asked him.

He turned toward her now, his brow furrowed with confusion. And she held out her hand to him. He moved slowly, his limp more pronounced than she'd seen it since he'd been in the car accident.

But that hadn't been an accident.

"Were you hurt last night?" she asked with concern.

"Not last night," he replied as he joined her in the hallway.

She'd hurt him just now. "I'm sorry," she said. "It's just so hard for me to believe."

"What is?" he asked.

"That you love me."

He moved faster now, across the hall. He pushed open his bedroom door, then reached back and pulled her inside with him. "Why is that hard to believe? Don't you know how amazing you are?"

A smile tugged at her lips.

"You're beautiful and smart and so damn loyal and generous and—"

She rose on tiptoe and pressed her mouth to his, shutting off his words. She kissed him with all of the desperation she'd felt the night before, with all of the fear and the love she hadn't let herself express.

He pulled back, panting for breath, and murmured, "Do you believe me? Do you believe that I love you?"

She could see it in his face now, in his warm gaze and in the tentative smile that curved his lips. "Yes," she said. "And I love you, too. So much." The emotion overwhelmed her. "I wanted to tell you last night.

I should have told you. If something had happened to you…" Tears stung her eyes, making her nose wrinkle.

He leaned down and kissed it. "Nothing happened to me. And I don't think anything will happen to you or Connor now either. But I still want us to be careful. To stay here."

"Will your parents be okay with that?" she asked. "We're not imposing?" She'd felt guilty for having them watch Connor while she'd packed up his stuff.

He chuckled. "Are you kidding? They're both doting on their new grandson right now."

"New grandson?"

"That's how they see Connor already," Forrest said. "That's how I see him, too—as my son. I hope you'll let me adopt him and make it official."

Her heart felt as if it would burst, it swelled with so much love. She'd wanted Connor to have a father someday—a father like Forrest, whom he could count on. But grandparents…?

She hadn't even thought about everything her son hadn't had—until he had it now. "Thank you," she said. "Thank you for being the most amazing man."

He shook his head. "I'm not the best bet, you know," he warned her. And she could see the seriousness in his eyes now, the doubt and fear. "I may not be able to get another job because of my disability. I may not be able to play with Connor like I'd want—"

She pressed her lips to his again to stop his words and to show her love. But then she pulled back and assured him, "You're a hero, Forrest Colton. You've saved us so many times, and not just physically. You've saved me emotionally. I was scared to open up my heart, to trust anyone. I'm not a gambler like my father. But you're not a bet. You're a sure thing."

He smiled again. "We're a sure thing."

"Yes, we are."

He lifted her then and carried her the few steps to his bed. It might have been his old room, but thankfully it wasn't a twin-size bed but a four-poster king-size one. The mattress dipped beneath their weight as he joined her. Clothes were tugged off or pushed aside until they were together again, their bodies joined like their hearts and souls.

Rae had never felt anything as right—as perfect—as making love with Forrest Colton. They knew instinctively how to move, where to touch, where to kiss…

He drove her crazy with his lips and his fingertips. And she returned the favor with hers. They moved faster and faster, with perspiration wetting their skin and tension building inside them. Then finally it broke within Rae—pleasure shuddering through her. She cried out his name before burying her face in his neck. His body tensed beneath hers. He gripped her hips and drove a little deeper into her before his pleasure filled her. He groaned and released a cry of his own. Her name.

"I love you," he said. "So damn much."

She smiled. "You don't sound too thrilled about it."

"I'm kicking myself for the weeks I wasted," he said. "I should have said yes when you asked me to dance at the wedding."

"Why didn't you?" she wondered.

"I thought you were just feeling sorry for me."

And his pride wouldn't have been able to handle that.

"Not at all," she assured him. "I thought you were handsome and so alone…" And she'd been so alone then, too, despite having just given birth to Connor the month before.

"We're not going to be alone ever again," he promised her. "We will always have each other."

She hadn't believed she'd ever find a love like that for herself. A love like the Coltons had. But now she knew it was possible—because she'd fallen for a Colton, and soon she and Connor would become Coltons, too.

A PROMISE WAS a promise.

Usually he wouldn't have worried about keeping one. But Beau Lemmon had died without revealing his identity. So maybe laying off the guy's kid and grandkid was the right thing to do—to hold up his side of that promise.

And hell, they were the best distraction to keep the Austin detective from working his cases. He'd fallen so hard for them that he was going to stick close, even if they were no longer in danger.

But that didn't mean they'd stay safe. Promise be damned, nobody was safe...if they got too close to figuring out who he was...

* * * * *

COMING SOON!

We really hope you enjoyed reading this book. If you're looking for more romance, be sure to head to the shops when new books are available on

Thursday 8th August

To see which titles are coming soon, please visit

millsandboon.co.uk/nextmonth

LET'S TALK
Romance

For exclusive extracts, competitions
and special offers, find us online:

facebook.com/millsandboon

@MillsandBoon

@MillsandBoonUK

Get in touch on 01413 063232

For all the latest titles coming soon, visit
millsandboon.co.uk/nextmonth

MILLS & BOON

THE HEART OF ROMANCE

A ROMANCE FOR EVERY KIND OF READER

MODERN

Prepare to be swept off your feet by sophisticated, sexy and seductive heroes, in some of the world's most glamourous and romantic locations, where power and passion collide.
8 stories per month.

HISTORICAL

Escape with historical heroes from time gone by. Whether your passion is for wicked Regency Rakes, muscled Vikings or rugged Highlanders, awaken the romance of the past.
6 stories per month.

MEDICAL

Set your pulse racing with dedicated, delectable doctors in the high-pressure world of medicine, where emotions run high and passion, comfort and love are the best medicine.
6 stories per month.

True Love

Celebrate true love with tender stories of heartfelt romance, from the rush of falling in love to the joy a new baby can bring, and a focus on the emotional heart of a relationship.
8 stories per month.

Desire

Indulge in secrets and scandal, intense drama and plenty of sizzling hot action with powerful and passionate heroes who have it all: wealth, status, good looks…everything but the right woman.
6 stories per month.

HEROES

Experience all the excitement of a gripping thriller, with an intense romance at its heart. Resourceful, true-to-life women and strong, fearless men face danger and desire - a killer combination!
8 stories per month.

DARE

Sensual love stories featuring smart, sassy heroines you'd want as a best friend, and compelling intense heroes who are worthy of the
4 stories per month.

To see which titles are coming soon, please visit

millsandboon.co.uk/nextmonth